Joe turned up the radio. Sunday afternoon – and the all important Top Forty. It was somewhere in the top five. They knew that much.

It wasn't at five.

It wasn't at four…

"If we're not at number one this week…" said Franco Rosetti.

"Got to be!" interrupted his son. "Got to be! If it's not mine … it's *his*!"

He paced the room, like a caged animal. "I couldn't bear it if it were *his*!"

His hands were running with sweat. He wiped them down his jeans. "Please … let me be number one. I'll do anything!"

Denis Bond

SCHOLASTIC

Scholastic Children's Books
7–9 Pratt Street, London NW1 0AE, UK
a division of Scholastic Publications Ltd
London ~ New York ~ Toronto ~ Sydney ~ Auckland

Published in the UK by Scholastic Publications Ltd, 1995

Copyright © Denis Bond, 1995

ISBN 0 590 55693 2

All rights reserved
Typeset by TW Typesetting, Midsomer Norton, Avon
Printed by Cox & Wyman Ltd, Reading, Berks.

10 9 8 7 6 5 4 3 2

*For
Ken Oxtoby*

*With thanks to
Jim Beaney for Romany research,
Sedgehill School,
Sue Farrington and Maurice Gloster
and
the BBC's production team of* Top of the Pops

Who's Who

In Alphabetical Order

Abi	A gypsy
Chas Atkins	A successful record producer; owner of KANSIT studios
Sherry Barbin	America's Queen of Pop
Belcher	A gypsy; friend to Terry Smith's mother
Keith Bell	A recording engineer/producer at Triumphant Studios
BJ	Managing director of record company, Blunt Edge
Bif	Ex-drummer with the Thunderdomes
Gary Brenn	Member of the pop duo, Hym
Jim Buckley	A school teacher
Bury The Rabbit	A pop group headed by Ray Rosetti

Nick Cox	The landlord of the Regent Tavern
Andy Davis	An engineer/record producer at Denson Sound Studios
Christine Dilks	Wayne Fielding's girlfriend
Sandy Dukes	A television chat-show host
Elaine	A make-up supervisor
Wayne Fielding	A member of the pop duo, Hym
Joe Fisher	The manager of pop superstar Pete Shannon
Ruby Gold	An American blues singer; long-time friend of Sherry Barbin
Santiago Gomez	A publicity agent
Gran	Maureen's grandmother
Helen	An assistant at the Regent Tavern
Huw	A resident singer at the Regent Tavern
Hym	British pop duo: Wayne Fielding and Gary Brenn
Bob Jamieson	A PE teacher
Jimmy	(Big Jimmy) A gypsy. Son of Abi and Sylvie
Joline	Sherry Barbin's personal assistant
Robbie Jones	A DJ working for Viscount Radio
Phil Lemont	Manager of pop duo, Hym
The Leroys	Twins: Mark and John; members of Bury The Rabbit
Levi	A gypsy
Mick Mahoney	A tinker
Conrad Matius	A manager for pop singers
Maureen	A schoolgirl; an original member of Bury The Rabbit

Maurice	An artiste at the Regent Tavern
Max	A pop video producer/director
Patcha	A British girl pop singer; produced and managed by Kendrick Simpson
Pepperrazzi	An all-girl British pop group, produced and managed by Kendrick Simpson
Lady Perdita	Daughter of Princess Catherine and thirty-ninth in line to the British throne
Piru	Children's nanny and general assistant to Imogen Shannon
Franco Rosetti	Businessman father of Ray Rosetti and manager of Bury The Rabbit
Ray Rosetti	Lead singer with Bury The Rabbit
Scotty	(Phillip Scott) Drummer with Bury The Rabbit
Pete Shannon	Internationally successful pop superstar
Imogen Shannon	A top model; Pete Shannon's wife
Kendrick Simpson	Record producer, songwriter and pop manager
Terry Smith	A young gypsy and struggling pop star
Billy Smith	Terry's younger brother
Joshua Smith	(Josh) Terry and Billy's father
Stan	A theatrical costume-supervisor
John Stellar	A cameraman
Del Stuart	A record producer
Rica Stubbs	A pop music journalist

Suki	A young model
Sylvie	A gypsy; Abi's wife
Thunderdomes	A heavy metal group
Stavros Vardakis	Head of Sherry Barbin's record company
Buck West	A very wealthy ex-male-stripper; now deals in real estate
Zena	A models' agent

What's What

In Alphabetical Order

Basic Beat	Record company run by Chas Atkins, Bif and Scotty
Blunt Edge	Hym's record company
Denson	Recording studios
Fat Tracks	Joe Fisher's "indie" label
Flicks	Local disco for Terry and Maureen
GO!	A teen magazine
KANSIT	Chas Atkins' recording and rehearsal studio complex
Sloop	Record label for Pete Shannon and Bury The Rabbit
Triumphant	Recording studios
Zena's	A top model agency
Zodiac	A promotions company

Book One

She's number one! When I've knocked her off the top of the charts, let's talk *then*, eh, honey?

SHERRY BARBIN

I hate being a nobody. I want people to know my name. I want 'em to buy my records and put pictures of me on their bedroom walls.

TERRY SMITH

It's a number one. Without a doubt. And if *you* don't record it, *someone* will … and it'll sit at the top of the charts for weeks.

PHIL LEMONT

Got no intention o' waitin' for the giro
Or windin' up servin' in a burger bar.
I'd bust a gut before I give up losin'
My faith in me to make it as a star!
  And it's easy!
  You know what I mean?
  Easy!

ROSETTI/SCOTT

Chapter 1

The spotlight fell on the handsome profile of the lone figure in the tight white vest and 501s, leaning nonchalantly against the proscenium arch. The audience gasped as one.

"Gary!" they screamed.

"Gary!

"Gary!

"Gary!"

His tanned and tattooed biceps flexed as he slowly lifted one arm, running the palm of his hand across his number-one cropped, blond hair.

"Gary!"

One leg moved to the beat of the intro – the intro to Hym's latest top-twenty entry – as he turned to smile at his thousands of adoring fans.

The screams reverberated around the theatre, sending a shivering thrill along his spine.

"Gary!"

"Gary!

Another spot hit the back of the stage, lighting the second member of the dynamite duo; his legs apart, his head hung low. He was similarly dressed, his jet-black hair also cropped, his muscles identically tattooed and tanned and glistening with oil.

"Wayne!" they screamed.

"Wayne!

"Wayne!

"Wayne!"

He lifted his head and grinned.

> *"Come on!"* he began to sing.
> *"Come on! Come on!*
> *Slide into yer new blue jeans."*

Gary raced across the stage and joined his partner, belting out the second line to Hym's latest hit,

> *"Come on! Come on!*
> *Tonight you're gonna top the scene..."*

Several fans rushed the stage.

"Gary!"

"Wayne!"

> *"Slow down, Sugar,*
> *Stuck on you, tho' I don't know why.*
> *You're sweeter than apple pie-yie!"*

"Wayne!"

"Gary!"

"You got me movin'
Temperature's goin' way up high.
High! High! High!"

Hym's ecstatic manager, Phil Lemont, watched his boys from the lighting-gallery. The beautiful woman at his side, dressed down in faded jeans and baseball-cap in an attempt to avoid recognition, watched enthusiastically.

He turned to her. "Well?"

Unsmiling, she drawled in a famous New York accent, "Fine, so far, honey."

"Garyeeeeee!"

"Waaaaaayne!"

A gigantic mechanical hand was slowly lowered and came to rest downstage. Its vast fingers uncurled, allowing both boys to climb aboard before it was lifted up ... and out into the auditorium above the heads of the fans, now screaming more wildly as they reached up, desperately trying to touch their idols.

"Waaaaayne!"

Many of them burst into tears.

"Garyeeeee!"

The music continued:

"Now I've seen yer top the bill
O' the floorshow,
There ain't no doubt
What you're about:
Just hear 'em yell for more, oh
I've gotten to believe
You're Queen o' the UV."

The American superstar grinned. "Yeah! Right on!"

Phil Lemont knew he'd cracked it. She was interested.

"Expensive robotics, honey!" she sighed. "They ain't gettin' that on my tour. No way."

Phil laughed. "I wouldn't have expected it, Sherry."

"They're support. That's all."

"Of course."

"But they're good."

"Thanks," he replied, proudly.

"How many hits they had here?"

"Five."

Her eyes widened. "In two years?"

"Less than."

"You're puttin' them out a bit fast, ain't yer, honey?"

He shrugged. "That's how Blunt Edge wants to do it. And who wants to argue with their record company?"

She threw her head back and laughed.

"Well … in your position…" he stammered, looking embarrassed at having delivered such a crass comment to America's Queen of Pop.

"Yeah … I'll take 'em!" she said. "*If* the deal's right. I'll talk it over with my manager and get the ball rollin'."

He was greatly relieved. "Thanks, Sherry."

She smiled. "Don't thank me. Thank your boys. They're good."

"Yeah."

"Not sure how they'll go down in America, but…"

"I just want to give them a chance."

She nodded in agreement, asking again, "*How* many hits?"

"Five."

"But no number one."

"We're working on it! The Christmas one should've done it … but there was some novelty disc in the way."

"Yeah, so I hear. What about the album?"

"It's ready to go. Nearly."

She laughed again. "After five hit singles, I should think so!"

"The record company want a number one first."

She was amazed. "Really?"

"It's not my choice."

"If *I'd've* waited for *my* first number one, honey, they'd've gotten an album from a very old lady."

The song came to an end as the robotic hand slowly lowered Hym back on to the forestage.

Gary strode perilously close to the grabbing hands stretching out from the darkness of the pit.

"Garyeeeee!"

"Hello, London!" he called.

The screams reached fever-pitch.

Wayne joined him.

"How' ya doin'?" he yelled.

"Waaaaaayne!"

"That was our latest single!" he shouted, trying, impossibly, to top the screams. "So buy it!"

"We're off to Tokyo next week!" Gary informed them.

"No!" they wailed.

"Garyeeeee!"

"And this one," added Wayne, "is shooting up the Japanese charts!"

The intro to their previous single, the number two hit "Show Me", sent the already frenzied fans into near hysteria.

"I've seen enough, Phil," said Sherry Barbin. "I've got a flight from Heathrow at ten. Leave it with me, eh?"

Chapter 2

Terry Smith leapt out of bed and reached across to his brother, gently shaking him awake.

"Billy. It's the gavvers."

He slipped his jeans over his pyjama trousers and grabbed for his tattered plimsolls.

The light from the police car flashed on and off, lighting up the trailer's smaller bedroom: blue, black, blue, black…

Billy moaned. "What d'they want now?"

Terry crossed into the passageway which separated their room from their parents' bedroom and saw his mother sitting on the edge of her large double bed, staring into space.

"Where's Dad?"

"Out there, i'n't he! I tried to stop him, but you know what 'e's like. He has to get involved."

Billy joined them. "What do they want?"

Mother shrugged. "I think they're at Mick Mahoney's waggon."

Terry returned to his room to put on a sweater.

"Don't *you* get mixed up in it, Terry."

"If Dad's out there, we should *all* be!" he replied.

He leapt down the trailer steps just as the shouting began.

Mick Mahoney was shouting from his trailer window.

"What d'yer want from me this time?"

One police officer called out to him, "Just a word, Mick. Get dressed and come and have a chat, eh?"

Mick Mahoney responded aggressively, "I remember the last chat we 'ad, when yer bruised me ribs, yer little 'itlers."

The police officer neared the trailer. "If you don't come out, we'll come and get you."

Terry's father approached the officer. "What's he supposed to have done?"

Another officer, younger, covered in acne, took his arm. "Why don't you go back to your caravan, Joshua? This one's got nothing to do with you. For a change."

Joshua Smith pulled his arm away. "If you're arrestin' one of ours, then it's got everything to do with all of us, yer gorgio pig."

Levi yelled as he crossed the mud from his own trailer. "He's been with us all night, in the pub. So he can't 'ave done nuffin'!"

A second police car, light flashing, entered the camp.

"What the…?" shouted Abi.

Joshua began to rage. "*Two* paddy-waggons? What you expectin'? A riot or suvink?"

Four police officers leapt from the second car.

Terry came to his father's side. "Leave it, Dad. Please. You know what Mick Mahoney's like."

8

Joshua turned on his son. "Go back to bed! This ain't nuffink to do with yous."

Billy joined them. "He's probably been nicking lead from the estate."

"He's been with us, all night!" snapped Joshua. "He ain't nicked nuffin'. But that don't stop 'em lockin' 'im up, do it? Look what they done to me."

"It ain't nickin' lead we're worried about this time, Joshua," said the acned policeman. "It's a bit more serious than that."

"He's been with us all night," argued Levi. "In the Three Stars. Then a take-away."

"What sort of take-away?" asked the policeman, with a sneer.

Mick Mahoney left the trailer window.

The police officer called back over his shoulder, "He's coming out!"

The trailer door burst open and a scrawny, snarling Alsatian, lips curled back, leapt down the steps and sank his teeth into the police officer's thigh.

Mick Mahoney screamed out, "Get him!"

Two officers rushed to their colleague's aid and tried to pull the dog off. The dog turned, snapping at both of them, before taking a second bite at the bloodied leg.

One officer took out his truncheon and beat the dog about the head until it fell unconscious into the mud.

"My dog!" screamed Mick Mahoney.

Joshua grabbed the young acne-covered officer around the neck and dragged him to the ground.

"Dad! Don't!" yelled Terry. He and Billy backed away to their trailer steps where their mother stood, eyeing the scene, pathetically.

"I knew it," she said softly. "He'll be sent down again. I knew it."

As one officer radioed for help, "Assistance urgently required at the Berryfield gypsy camp – over…" travellers and police lashed out at each other, rolling over in the mud, punching, beating each other with sticks and truncheons. All the dogs were unleashed, adding to the mayhem, barking, growling and snapping at all, whether gorgio or gypsy.

"Inside, you two," said Terry's mother.

Billy yelled. "Dad! Come away!"

"Please!" Terry added.

Joshua had given the young gavver a good belting and left him groaning. He turned to look back at his trailer, yelling, "Get to bed, will yous? Leave it to us!"

As the blue light, still flashing on and off, lit up Joshua's face, Terry thought he looked strange. Pained. He'd seen his father in fights before. Many times. But tonight was different. Joshua enjoyed a good fight and always emerged, even with bruised cheek or split lip, like the conquering hero, grinning and bright-eyed. Tonight he looked sickly.

Mother knew there was something seriously wrong and rushed down the trailer steps towards him.

"Josh?"

He was wheezing, trying to catch his breath.

"Get me indoors."

She took his arm and led him towards the trailer. Billy rushed to help, taking the other arm.

Terry stood at the foot of the trailer steps, staring, unable to move.

Joshua, supported by his wife and younger son,

10

managed to climb slowly to the top trailer step where he clutched the door frame, gasping, one fist pressed against his chest.

"You're all right, Dad," said Billy, trying desperately to reassure his father and himself. "You're OK."

Joshua lost his grip on the door frame and was too weak to grab for it again. He tumbled backwards down the steps, landing at Terry's feet.

"Sweet Jesus!" cried his wife. She screamed out, "Call an ambulance!"

No one heard her cries above the shouting and beating and barking.

She turned to Terry. "Quick! Ask Jane to use the phone!"

Terry didn't move.

"Terry!"

Billy saw that his brother *couldn't* move.

"I'll go, Mum!" he shouted as he sped across the campsite.

Terry watched him disappearing, until the stiffness left his limbs … and then he ran, overtaking Billy and heading for the main house.

Chapter 3

The excited fans packed the narrow street at the back of the theatre, gazing up at the dressing-room windows, hoping for a glimpse of either of their heroes. Gary and Wayne, exhausted, were slumped in front of the make-up mirror, panting and sweating profusely, each trying to catch their breath.

"You were fantastic," said Wayne, at last. He reached over and patted the back of Gary's sweat-sodden vest.

Gary glanced sideways at him and grinned. "You too. Brilliant. What a show, eh?"

"The best."

The chanting voices rose from the street:

>   *"We love you Gary … oh yes we do!*
>   *We love you Wayne. We love you too!"*

Wayne laughed. "Go on," he suggested to Gary. "Give them a thrill."

Gary crossed to the dressing-room window, making

a two-second appearance, just to tease, raising screams of, "He's there! Garyeeee! Garyeeee!"

Gary laughed and strode back to the mirror. "Your turn."

Wayne rose from his seat and moved to the window.

"Waaaaaayne!"

He waved to them, sending them frantic with desire, their screams deafening the police who were trying unsuccessfully to confine them to the pavement.

Gary smiled. "I think they like us."

"They love us. *Love* us!" Wayne enthused.

"This only happens in dreams."

Wayne suddenly looked serious. "The thought of all this coming to an end…"

"Hey! Come on!" said Gary. "This isn't going to end. Not for years and years."

Wayne reminded him. "Three years, Gary. That's the average life of a pop group, isn't it?"

Gary rushed across to his partner and wrapped his arm playfully around his neck. "Aah, but we ain't no average pop group, are we?" he said. "We're Hym. And we're going on and on."

"No solo deals?"

"No solo deals!"

"United we stand…"

"…divided we fall."

"Let's tease 'em some more," Wayne grinned. "Let's give 'em something to scream about."

He crossed to the window and gazed down at the open-mouthed, yelling fans.

Firstly he waved.

They waved back, screeching, "Waaaaaayne!"

Slowly he peeled off his damp, white vest: up … revealing his glistening and powerful pectorals … and then over his head.

The fans gasped. One felt as though she would faint as the window was opened and the vest was flung down towards her. Clawing hands tore at the material as each fan desperately strove for just a small piece of their idol's clothing.

Their manager entered the room and tutted. "Leave them alone," he said to Wayne. "And shut that window. I can't hear myself think."

Wayne did as he was told and returned to his seat.

"Well … you were great," said Phil. "Very impressive."

"Thanks," they both replied.

"Now, Tokyo…"

"I hope we're not staying at some cheap hotel," joked Gary. "Oh, but then we wouldn't be, would we, Phil? Seeing as you're coming with us."

"You can take your tent, Phil," laughed Wayne. "It'll keep our expenses down."

Phil took no notice of the jibes. "So, it's four o'clock on Friday at the airport, OK?"

"OK."

"And don't be late, Wayne!"

Wayne sighed. "I'm never late. It's Baby Blue Eyes there you should be telling."

Phil turned to Gary. "OK, Gary?"

"Yeah."

"Now, here's the best news I've had since we started," smiled Phil Lemont. "You had a VIP in tonight."

They were curious.

"Who?" asked Wayne.

"Don't tell me, let me guess," said Gary, quickly, as he winked at Wayne. "It was Prince Charles. He wants us to take part in the next Prince's Trust concert."

"Better than that," replied Phil, confidently. "It was Sherry Barbin."

Both lads were stunned into silence.

Phil laughed. "Cat got yer tongues?"

"You're joking!" gasped Wayne. "Sherry Barbin?"

"No joke," said Phil, seriously. "She was out front and she thought you were great."

"And?" Gary's heart started thumping. He knew what Phil had in mind for Hym.

"Gerrich Sister have just pulled out of her show ... and she wants you as support, on her US of A tour."

Wayne leapt from his seat, punching the air. "Yeah!"

"I know it's short notice," continued Phil, "but –"

"When do we go?" Gary asked, excitedly.

"Hold on! Hold on!" said Phil, his tone of voice threatening to dampen their enthusiasm. "We haven't signed anything yet. We haven't talked money. But if it all goes smoothly, you're gonna have to fly to the States straight after Tokyo."

"Fantastic!"

"Brilliant."

"I can't come with you," explained Phil. "I've got to get back to London as soon as the Tokyo gig's over, so we must settle all the details within the next few days. Costumes. Lighting. Press-calls. Everything."

"What about the robotics?" asked Gary. "Are we transporting those?"

"No," said Phil. "No robotics."

Gary looked disappointed.

"We don't need them, Gary," Wayne assured him. "It's only extra pressure. We're not using them in Tokyo. If we just concentrate on the music and polish some of our old routines…"

"Yeah, you're right," concluded Gary. "We'll knock 'em dead."

"She wants to use the session musicians you're using here," went on Phil, "but that'll depend on the unions. You'll have to leave me with that one to sort."

"I can't believe it," whispered Wayne. He affectionately ran his hand over Gary's spiky blond hair. "We're gonna crack America, Gary."

Gary grinned at him. "Sure are."

"Right!" said Phil. "I'll let you get changed. Car's coming in half an hour. Let's hope some of those fans have got fed up with waiting by then."

"We're going for dinner at my mother's," said Gary. "Do you want to come with us, Phil?"

"Thanks for the offer," Phil replied. "But too much to do, Gary. Enjoy yourselves."

He left.

"Your turn!" Wayne said, winking at Gary. "Go and thrill them."

Gary crossed to the window and opened it.

"Garyeeee! Garyeeee!" they screamed.

Wayne called to him. "Don't just stand there, you great poser! Throw 'em your vest!"

Chapter 4

Terry was pleased with the first verse. He sang it to himself over and over again. The hook was good, too. Very catchy. He just hoped that it was original, that he wasn't inadvertently repeating something he'd heard on the radio. He sang it again, louder this time, as there was no one to hear him. The rest of 'em would've reached the river by now. Terry was always last. Who cared? He hated cross-country running; he hated Jamieson even more! And what good did cross-country running do anyway?

"Improves the cardio-vascular system, lads! Gets those lungs working!"

Terry's lungs were all right as they were. The voice proved it!

> *"Call on me*
> *When you are lonely,*
> *Though I know I can only*
> *Be a friend…"*

He was gonna be a star. No doubt about it! Though he knew it wouldn't come easy. Not with his gypsy background. Not like it would for some. But if determination to succeed meant anything at all, then he'd make it. All he needed was a step on the ladder, then nothing would stop him going all the way to the top.

Jamieson turned back from the park gates and cut through the wood to the gravel path, along which most of his boys had run. Three were missing. He knew who they were and was irritated that his least favourite was among them.

Terry shuffled along the gravel path, running in short spurts, walking, running again. His feet hurt. His bright red vest only served to show just how pale his arms were. Pale and thin. His shorts, supposedly white, but leaning towards grey, were too long. Hand-me-down vest and hand-me-down shorts.

> *"If you knew*
> *How much it hurts me*
> *To be left on the outside,*
> *Looking in…"*

Bob Jamieson stepped out from the wood on to the path. He could see the boy approaching in the distance, the sun glinting off his spectacles. Terry stopped, placing a hand over his forehead and squinting.

"Oh, no!" he said. "Why can't he leave me alone?"

Jamieson bellowed, "Get a move on, Smith! You're not out for a Sunday stroll!"

Terry quickened his pace, despite the pain in his heels.

"Move it, lad! You're puffin' like my old granny!"

He limped the last few yards and stopped in the PE master's shadow.

"What's the matter with you?" sneered Jamieson.

"It's my feet."

"*Sir!*"

"It's my feet … *sir!*"

Jamieson looked at the boy's tattered plimsolls.

"It's no wonder, is it? Look at the state of those! How do you expect to run in shoes like that?"

"They're my brother's … sir!"

"Your brother's?"

"Yes, sir."

"He's in year nine!"

Terry looked away, avoiding the icy-blue stare. He was afraid of the powerfully built teacher. He feared him and he envied him. He coveted his body and the long, blond hair which flopped over his ruggedly handsome face. He envied him and he hated him.

"Where're *yours*?"

"I haven't got any. Sir!"

He hadn't had a new pair since his fourteenth birthday. He was sixteen now.

"Then how's about asking your father for some?"

Terry began to feel hot. "I have. I'm getting a new pair as soon as he comes home."

Jamieson knew the answer to his next question. Terry stared at him, almost daring him to ask it. Jamieson stared back.

Should he? Should he ask, "Home from *where*, Smith?"

Behind the glasses, Terry's eyes began to well up.

"My dad's in hospital!" he said.

"Is he? I'm sorry to hear that, Smith."

"He is!" Terry suddenly shouted. "I know you don't believe me!"

Jamieson was shocked at the aggression. "Who said I didn't believe you?"

"He's in hospital with his heart!" Terry's whole body was beginning to shake. He whipped off his glasses, which were steaming up. "He's not in prison. He's in hospital, you bastard!"

He turned and sped back along the gravel path, forgetting the pain in his heels.

Jamieson was furious. "Come here!" he bawled.

Terry didn't hear him. He could hear nothing but the pounding of his heart and his heavy breathing as he ran faster and faster towards the disused drinking fountain. He leapt a low fence, crossed the putting green and ran on into the rhododendrons, where he collapsed to the ground and sobbed.

"What's that noise?" whispered Scotty.

He placed a hand on Rosetti's arm. "Listen."

Ray Rosetti took the cigarette from his lips and cocked his head on one side.

Scotty whispered again, "This way."

They trod lightly through the rhododendrons, following the sound, which changed from a sob to a low whimper. Terry heard them approach. He hurriedly wiped his eyes on the back of a muddy hand and replaced his glasses.

"Well, if it isn't old Smithy," grinned Phillip Scott. "What are *you* doin' here?"

Terry scrambled to his feet. "I'm sorry," he said. "I didn't know anyone was here."

"Well, you do now," snarled Rosetti.

"He's all right," said Scotty. "He won't say nothing." He produced a cigarette packet from his shorts pocket, opened it and offered it to Terry. "Here. D'you wanna fag, Smith?"

"I don't smoke," replied Terry.

Ray Rosetti mimicked the boy's words. "I don't smoke." He took a long drag on his cigarette and held the smoke for a few seconds before letting it out in a series of rings.

Scotty watched, admiringly.

"What *do* you do, eh, Smith?" asked Rosetti. "Apart from stink?"

Terry turned and began to walk away.

Rosetti called after him. "Oi! Pikie! Where d'you think you're going?"

Terry stopped in his tracks, then turned back and glared.

Rosetti slowly approached him.

"I don't think we said he could go, did we, Scotty?"

Scotty followed his friend.

"Come here, Smith!" added Rosetti.

Terry didn't move.

Rosetti held out his half-smoked cigarette towards the boy.

"Here. Have a drag."

"No."

"You're not going to report us, are you, Smith?" asked Scotty.

"*I* don't care what you do," replied Terry.

Ray Rosetti took a final drag on his cigarette, threw the stub down at his feet and worked it into the ground with the toe of his plimsoll.

"D'you think we can trust him, Scotty?" he asked as he calmly removed Terry's glasses with one hand and held them in the air. "I suppose you could always say you didn't see us, couldn't you, Smith?"

"Give me them. Please," pleaded Terry.

"Oh, come on, Ray," added Scotty. "Give 'em to him."

Scotty had begun to feel sorry for the boy, as he often did. He knew there was always the choice, of course: either run with the hounds or be chased by them. From day one Scotty had decided to join Rosetti's pack.

"Cor, these ain't half strong, Smithy," smirked Rosetti, as he put the glasses on the end of his nose. "You must be nearly blind."

"Give them to me, please," said Terry. "I can't see."

Rosetti retreated further into the rhododendrons.

"Aah, can't you see, Smithy?" he called. "Then you won't be able to see where I'm burying them, will you?"

He fell to his knees and covered the glasses with a pile of twigs.

Scotty decided he'd had enough. "I'm going back, Ray," he said. "Give us me matches!"

Rosetti took the matches from his shorts pocket and handed them to Scotty, who hurried off towards the putting green.

"I'll see yer later!" he yelled.

"Hold on!" Rosetti called after him. "I'm coming!"

He placed his hands on Terry's shoulders and began to spin him round. "Bit like blind man's buff, isn't it?"

Terry punched out at Rosetti, but missed. Rosetti was surprised. He was angry, yet amused. People didn't hit him. Ever!

"Here! What's this?" he said, threateningly. "You didn't try to punch me, did you, Smith?"

"Give me my glasses."

"Because people who punch me, especially filthy gyppos, get punched back!" He held his clenched fist in front of Terry's face, as a warning. Then he decided that he might as well use it. After all, he hadn't hit anyone for weeks.

He punched Terry in the mouth. Terry yelped and put a hand to his cut lip.

"Don't be late for the shower, will you, Smith?" laughed Rosetti. And he strolled after Scotty across the putting green.

Chapter 5

"I thought we'd eat in the conservatory, darlings," said Gary's mother. Her cut-glass English accent put Wayne on edge, as always. "That'll be nice, won't it, Wayne?" she asked, rhetorically. "I've lit it with candles."

"Yes. Very nice, Mrs Brenn," he replied.

They passed through the chandelier-bedecked hallway, on through the large dining-room and out into the plant-filled conservatory.

"Make yourselves at home," she said, "and I'll go and get some ice for the drinks."

"She means *you*, Wayne," joked Gary. "I *am* at home."

She raised an eyebrow. "You most certainly are not, darling," she scolded. "Not since you decided to settle yourself into that grubby little London flat." She winked at Wayne, just to let him know that this was *not* a family argument, and headed for the kitchen.

Gary sighed. "She'll never let me grow up. She hates me living in London."

"It's because she can't keep her beady eye on you any

more," tutted Wayne. "Perhaps you should've stayed here in Henley. At least you'd have had your washing done."

Gary laughed. "I prefer freedom to clean shirts, thank you."

Mother returned within minutes, pushing the drinks trolley.

"Now, you're not driving, are you, Wayne?" she asked.

"No. I'll get a cab."

"Fine. So … scotch? Gin? Or what?"

"Scotch'd be great, thanks."

"I take it Dad isn't going to be here?" asked Gary.

"No, darling," she replied as she lifted the whisky decanter. "Sends his love, but he can't make it back until Friday night." She smiled at Wayne, informing him, "Business in Ireland."

"Oh. Right," he said.

"Then I won't see him before I go to Tokyo," said Gary.

"No, darling. But you're only away for a wee while, aren't you?" She poured whisky into three crystal tumblers.

Gary looked at Wayne and grinned. "Well, actually, no," he replied. "We're not away for just a wee while."

Wayne noted how Gary's voice always changed when he was in his mother's company. His fans had never heard him speak like this, his street accent momentarily pushed aside and replaced with perfectly rounded vowels.

"We're not coming straight back to London," he continued. "We're off to the States."

She was pleasantly surprised. "America?"

"Yes."

"Well, I never."

"It could be our big break," said Wayne. "We're the support band on Sherry Barbin's tour."

"Who?" asked Mother.

Gary looked at Wayne and shook his head. "Forget it. She won't have heard of her."

Wayne could hardly believe that there was someone who hadn't heard of Sherry Barbin.

"So are you going to have hit records out there, do you think?" she asked.

They both laughed. "That's the aim, Mother," said Gary.

"Maybe that's where you'll get the number one you've been after for so long," she enthused. "Your dad was saying you really ought to do one of those big records from the sixties. A reprise ... or whatever you call it. Something that the Beatles did. *They* had number ones."

"We write our own material, Mrs Brenn," Wayne patiently tried to explain. "We don't do other people's songs. Old *or* new."

She playfully wagged a finger at Wayne. "Then perhaps it's time you did!"

Having seen Wayne to his cab, Gary returned to the kitchen and helped his mother load the dishwasher.

"Nice meal, Mum. Thanks."

"It's a pleasure, darling." She kissed him on the cheek. "Did *he* like it?"

"Wayne? Yes, I think so."

"He's a strange lad," she said.

Gary tutted. "There's nothing strange about him at all."

"He's a bit…" She wondered if she should say it.

"A bit what?"

"A bit vulgar."

Gary laughed. "Vulgar? Wayne? Where did you get that idea from?"

She sighed. "Well, he certainly hasn't had your breeding, has he?"

Gary was irritated by her comments. "He didn't go to a fee-paying school, if that's what you mean."

"Well…"

"But he's not dim."

"I didn't say he was dim, darling."

"He's a great singer."

"But not a scholar and a gentleman." She smiled.

"Maybe not."

"I hope he's not into drugs or anything, is he?"

"Mother!" he pleaded. "How many more times? No. He doesn't take anything."

"Except extremely large whiskies."

He laughed. "You poured them!"

She laughed. "So I did."

"So what are you writing at the moment?" he asked her.

"A third novel in my Sleuth series," she replied. "Not that that would interest *you*, of course. You haven't read the first two."

"I'm too busy," he replied, guiltily. "I *will* read them. I promise. I'll take them to Tokyo with me."

"I wish *you'd* taken it up," she sighed.

"Writing?"

"You showed such promise at school."

"I *do* write," he argued.

She sneered. "Lyrics. To pop songs. Anyone can turn out that sort of rubbish."

He laughed again. "*You* couldn't."

She playfully pulled his ear. "Listen here, my boy, it'd shock you if I suddenly wrote a number one hit song, wouldn't it?"

He pulled away from her, and rubbed his ear lobe.

"Anyway, I don't just write lyrics," he informed her. "I keep notes all the time. I've got a diary. When this is all over, I'm going to write a novel about the pop business."

She looked at him with a serious expression on her face. "Are you really, darling?"

"Really."

She flung her arms around him. "That's my boy!" she laughed.

He held her tightly. "I won't allow you to read it though," he whispered, mischievously. "I wouldn't want you to know what I get up to on the road."

"I can guess," she replied.

She let go of him, turned back to the dishwasher and continued to load the dirty dishes.

"So, any more thoughts of going solo?" she asked.

"I'm working on it."

"Good!" she said. "I'd much rather see Gary Brenn up there as a solo performer. You don't need Hym, darling. And you certainly don't need Wayne Fielding."

Chapter 6

"D'you think Rosetti'll lend her to me for one night?" whispered Bob Jamieson. The PE master lounged back on one of the two tubular-framed chairs placed in the centre of the school hall and watched as Maureen helped her boyfriend to set up the equipment on the stage. He placed his arms behind his head and stretched out his legs.

"Behave yourself," Jim Buckley hissed. "You'll end up before judge and jury if you're not careful."

Jamieson grinned at the warning from his teaching colleague and long-time friend before he sat upright, with his eyes still fixed on the girl. "She's not under-age," he laughed. "And she knows what she's doing. Look at her."

Maureen loosened her school tie and undid the top button of her blouse. She ran her fingers through her cropped blonde hair and then turned to Rosetti.

"Is that *it*?" she asked him. "I'm so hot."

"You sure are, honey-chile," he replied, mocking the deep-south accent of his rhythm'n'blues heroes.

He put his arm around her waist and kissed her cheek. "Yep. We're ready," he replied. "Let's get this show on the road."

"She may *look* as though she knows what it's all about," said Jim Buckley, "but she's just a little girl at heart."

The other members of the band, having set everything up, joined the lead singer and his girlfriend on stage and began to tune their instruments.

"The Trollenberg Terrors!" grimaced Jamieson. "I didn't know they were in this group."

The Leroy twins, John and Mark, similarly gauche in appearance, toothpick-thin and with blond (almost white) hair atop their pimpled faces, picked up their guitars as one, and strummed.

"From what I hear," said Jim Buckley, "*they're* the talent."

Scotty started pounding away on the drums.

Bob Jamieson jumped. "I'm really looking forward to this," he said sarcastically. "All my favourite people in one group."

"And talking of your favourites," said Jim Buckley, raising his voice above the tuning guitars, "what happened to Terry Smith today?"

"I've no idea."

Jamieson couldn't take his eyes off Maureen as she leapt up and down to Scotty's drum-beats.

"He came in from the run fifteen minutes late. With a cut lip."

"Yeah." Jamieson sighed deeply.

"Didn't you ask him what happened?"

"What's the point?" He turned to face Jim. "Every

word that kid utters is a lie. Anyway, you're his form master. You're in charge of his welfare."

Jim Buckley defended the boy as usual. "He doesn't lie."

Bob raised his eyebrows. "Like his dad being in hospital, d'you mean?"

"Is that what he said?" Jim was surprised.

"That's not *all* he said. I could've killed him!"

"Perhaps it's true. Perhaps he *is* in hospital."

Bob laughed. "Oh, I'm sure! The last time his dad was in prison he told you he was in Australia, didn't he?"

"Yes."

"Visiting relatives."

"That's what he said."

Bob sneered. "I'm sure Adelaide's full of pikies."

"It's a shame," said Jim. "He's very bright, you know. The only one of mine who'll leave here with any decent qualifications."

"That *is* a shame! He's the only one who won't *need* qualifications! He'll get by the same way as his father does!"

"We're nearly ready, sir!" Maureen called.

"I'm sorry, Jim," said Jamieson. "I know he's one of your favourites."

Jim Buckley stared ahead at the stage. "I just feel sorry for him, that's all. Don't forget I've got those two good-for-nothing yobbos in the same form," he added, nodding towards Rosetti and Scotty. "Totally useless and yet spoilt to death. They make Terry Smith seem like an angel."

"At least you've got the Immaculate Maureen to

brighten your day," replied Jamieson. "You haven't got to put up with the Pimply Pair! Messrs Personality Plus! The Languishing Leroys!" He laughed. "Perhaps that's what they should call their group!"

Jim sniggered. "How about The Zits!"

Both teachers guffawed loudly, catching Rosetti's attention.

"We're ready, sir!" he called.

"OK, Ray!" Jim called back. "Let's be hearing you!"

"What *do* they call themselves?" whispered Jamieson.

"Bury The Rabbit!" smiled Jim.

Jamieson's jaw dropped. "Bury The *what*?"

The Immaculate Maureen had been going out with Rosetti for six months, since she'd joined his pop group. He was the first real boyfriend she'd had, though she'd never been short of offers. She'd always been popular with the boys and not just because of her good looks. She also had a great sense of humour. Those girls who weren't jealous of her often remarked what a good-looking couple she and Ray Rosetti made, her delicate features and short, blonde hair helping him to appear darker, tougher and more handsome than he already was.

Occasionally one of the older boys, unaware of her steady relationship, would ask her out. But she would always refuse, though she was always careful not to offend. She was content to be with Rosetti. He could afford a lifestyle she liked. He had two rooms to himself at the top of his parents' house, his own video and CD player, the best-cut clothes of anyone his age and enough money to take her out every Saturday night.

"This one's called, 'Easy!'," Rosetti announced into the mike. He turned to his group: "A-one, a-two, a-one, two, three, four…!"

Scotty and the Leroys blasted a deafening sound from the stage.

"Here we go," grinned Jamieson.

Rosetti sang:

> *"Didn't take to schoolin'; got no int'rest,*
> *Couldn't take to doin' what I had to do.*
> *I'm rebellin', to prove I'm something*
> *I aim to get me somewhere … tellin' you!*
> *And it's easy!*
> *You know what I mean?*
> *Easy!"*

Jamieson turned to Jim Buckley. "They're a bit loud, wouldn't you say? Well, *Rosetti* is!"

"You're not kidding!" yelled Jim. "Axl Rose meets Cilla Black!"

Rosetti's voice was harsh, and the less-amplified Maureen could hardly be heard. Jim wondered how he would tell them, in the nicest possible way, that their voices didn't really blend. They'd approached him earlier in the week, asking if they could play at the after-school disco and Jim had said that he'd have to listen to them first.

"My dad'll bring everything here in the van," said Rosetti. "He reckons we're really good and he's going to manage us."

"Really?"

Franco Rosetti had given his son everything that

money could buy and Jim wasn't surprised to hear that he was also prepared to put cash into Ray Rosetti's dream of becoming a pop star.

"What does Franco Rosetti know about pop music?" Bob Jamieson had sneered. "He sells ice-cream, doesn't he?"

"He owns a frozen-food company," corrected Jim. "A bit different."

"So he's going to freeze and package his darling boy, is he?"

"I don't know about *freeze* him," replied Jim. "But he'll certainly package him and sell him."

Jamieson rose from his seat. "D'you mind if I creep away? I'll leave you to tell them how talented they are."

"Oh, *thanks*!" said Jim.

"I'll see you about eight in the Woodman," Jamieson added. "And don't forget to bring the new lyrics."

"By the way…" Jim grabbed Jamieson's arm. "She *is* under age," he smiled. "She's only fifteen!"

Bury The Rabbit went on. And on. And on.

> *"Shoot your promos on Antigua's beaches
> And take me there with you, to feel the sun…"*

Rosetti didn't seem unduly concerned when Jim suggested that his group needed a little more practice. He was still confident in its ability and he could just see that music-press headline: *NUMBER ONE BAND NOT GOOD ENOUGH FOR THEIR SCHOOL DANCE!*

And as Jim gave his pep-talk, Franco Rosetti lurked

in the background, saying nothing and jangling the keys to his van.

Jim eventually left the hall and found Terry Smith scuttling up the corridor towards the school's main exit.

"What are you doing here?" he asked, firmly.

"I was watchin' them play," said Terry.

"And?" Jim was curious.

"They're useless!"

"You think so?"

"Rosetti can't sing."

"You could do better, could you?" laughed Jim.

"Much!"

The two walked on, to where Billy was waiting for his elder brother.

"Come on!" he yelled, raucously. "Where've you been?"

"They just need a bit more practice, that's all," said Jim.

"And they'll get it, won't they?" replied Terry. "With Rosetti's dad's money, they can't fail!"

"Bit o' jealousy there, lad, don't you think?" Jim winked at the lad, trying to make light of it.

But for Terry, this was far too important. "Yeah, I'm jealous! All that dough. All that stuff his daddy's bought him … and he's no idea how to use it." He began to walk off with an arm around his brother's neck. Then he turned.

" 'Course I'm jealous!" he said. "Ain't *you*?"

Chapter 7

The Los Angeles smog had cleared earlier than hoped for, allowing the track-suited Sherry Barbin, surrounded by her half-dozen similarly clad minders, to jog along Acacia Boulevard, followed by sweating journalists and photographers all vying for the best pictures and the "exclusive" quote.

Her body had never looked so good, the daily workouts and her specially prepared macrobiotic diet keeping her lean and fit for the gruelling tour which was only half-way through. She'd always hated California, even though she'd made two major movies here. The sunshine and the supposedly laid-back people did nothing for her. She needed that buzz she got from New York, and was looking forward to the last dates of the tour, when she could perform to the audiences she understood, go jogging through Central Park and maybe – if she could find the time – visit her newly widowed father, still living in the Bronx.

"Hey, Sherry!" one of the journalists puffed, as sweat trickled from his hair and dripped off the end of his nose. "Have you seen the reviews for Patcha's New York concert?"

She said nothing. She wasn't going to give him the bitchy headline he was after. Everyone knew she had no respect for the diminutive English star, now topping the Billboard charts with a remake of that old Smokey Robinson classic. Patcha had, thought Sherry, a Minnie Mouse voice, but had been cleverly packaged by Kendrick Simpson, one of the most successful ever producers of the British music industry. Sherry loathed his music. "Computer pop with no heart," she called it. "All lip-gloss and no soul." But she was aware of its potency. And she secretly admired how the multi-millionaire Kendrick Simpson continued to churn out hit after hit after hit.

The journalist went on, "They said that Patcha should never have undertaken a live tour; that they can't wait for you to follow her into the city to show how it should be done."

Sherry decided to reply. "She's number one! When I've knocked her off the top of the charts, let's talk *then*, eh, honey?"

"D'you think *Paraiso*'ll do it?"

"You betcha!" She knew the new single couldn't fail.

Another reporter called after her: "Sherry, what do you think of Kendrick Simpson?"

She fought from screaming out, "British wallpaper music, honey." Instead, she just laughed. She recalled those unsubstantiated tales about Pepperrazzi: four trashy-looking, pouting young women in knee-length leather boots, who'd had more hit records in the British charts than any other female group before them. Produced, of course, by Kendrick Simpson. She'd heard how Sandy, the lead vocalist and spokesperson for the group, had felt a bit cheesed off with the latest Kendrick Simpson composition and before recording the track, had decided to go to the studio's kitchen to make herself a cup of tea. Here she bumped into an old friend who led her into a long discussion about the Simpson Hit Machine phenomenon. When she returned to the studio, she found to her horror that the track was finished and was in the first stages of being mixed. She wasn't on it … but this hadn't stopped her miming to the record on *Chartbusters*.

The minders had had enough and hoped the run was almost over. One of them eyed the pick-up which followed them, ready to take them all in when Sherry decided to quit. He shrugged at the driver. It looked as though this was going to be a long one.

"Sherry! Do you get on well with Hym?"

She wished the journalist hadn't asked that.

"Fine, honey."

"The *LA Times* says this morning that they were booed off stage in Detroit."

She grinned. "You're a reporter, honey. You know not to believe anything you read in the papers."

"So you're saying it's not true?"

"It's not true. Hym are doin' just fine."

Sherry liked their music and felt they had a good chance of cracking the American charts. They'd certainly proved to be the perfect support band for her thirty-date tour of the States.

Even after seventeen of the dates, Sherry hadn't

tired of their music … but she *had* tired of *them*. They were no fun; were never part of the entourage. When the other guys had a few drinks or played cards on the long trips between cities, Gary and Wayne sat alone. Sleeping. Or reading. Or whispering to each other. What *was* it with them? She was sure it wasn't Gary who was the killjoy. It was the other one: Wayne, the serious looking one who was a little older than his cherub-faced partner. Or was it simply that Sherry had taken a fancy to Gary? He was only eighteen, which made him very desirable. She wondered if he liked older women. She was nearly thirty, but had the body of a twenty-year-old. She'd like to get closer to him but she could never get him on his own. Wayne was always lurking somewhere nearby. She'd have to get her personal assistant, Joline, to sort it out for her. Maybe Joline could arrange it in time for the post-concert Hollywood party they were attending tonight.

"Right! That's it!" called Sherry to her minders.

They all seemed greatly relieved.

The pick-up stopped and they climbed inside, wiping off the sweat with the white, freshly laundered towels which had been set out for them.

"Home James," said Sherry with a smile to the driver. "And don't spare the gas."

The pick-up sped away towards the tour hotel, pursued by cars and vans packed with journalists.

Wayne Fielding checked that the hotel corridor was empty. At this time of the morning, when Sherry and her minders were out jogging and the musicians and sound crew were still dead to the world, a deathly hush hung over the fifteenth and sixteenth floors; floors which had been reserved especially for the Sherry Barbin Road Show. Security staff were guarding the stairs and elevators, but none were conspicuous. Wayne tapped lightly on Gary's door and waited.

"Who is it?" Gary mumbled, drowsily.

Wayne pressed his mouth against the door and whispered, "It's me. Let me in."

There was no reply from Gary.

"Gary! Let me in!"

"It's only nine o'clock. I'm not up."

"Please," Wayne pleaded, child-like.

Gary sighed deeply. He didn't want this. Not again.

"I need to talk to you. I'm frightened. Please, Gary. Let me in."

Gary Brenn reached for his dressing gown and then opened the door. His scalp was glistening greasily through his number-one cut. His eyelids were still half closed.

Wayne entered, looking immaculate. Dressed in purple sweat-pants and white vest, he'd obviously been up for hours.

"What d'you want?"

"I need to talk."

" 'Bout what?"

"I'm sorry about last night."

"Forget it." Gary switched on the kettle.

"I came on a bit strong, didn't I?"

"You're not joking!"

He sighed deeply. "I'm sorry, Gary."

"Couldn't you have told me all this later?"

"I couldn't sleep."

"You've got to stop all this, Wayne," Gary warned him. "What happened … happened. We've got to forget it."

"I can't!"

"You must. It's getting to be like it's no fun any more, Wayne. We used to have a laugh."

Wayne sighed again. "I know."

"And I can't see the point of doing all this, if we can't enjoy it."

"Look, I've got to say something." Wayne perched on the edge of Gary's unmade bed. "I know I've said it before, but you've got to believe me…"

"You're not trying to run my life."

"That's right. I'm not."

"You could've fooled me. I was only chatting to that sound guy last night and you went mad. He wondered what the hell was going on."

"I thought he handed you something. A packet."

"I told you. He didn't hand me anything. But even if he did, Wayne, it's got nothing to do with you."

"I told you why," replied Wayne. "Hym is all I've got, Gary. I've given up everything for it. I don't want to see it blown out of the water. I just couldn't bear it."

"Look, Wayne … it was your decision to give up your girlfriend … and everything else for this duo. I didn't even know you then. It had nothing to do with me."

"But I've sacrificed everything for us…"

"For *you*!"

"For *us*! For Hym! If we're going to be really big … worldwide … it'll take every waking moment. There's no room for anything else –"

"Aw c'mon, Wayne!"

"– and there's definitely no room for bad publicity! We've got to give it all we've got!"

Gary crossed to the cups and put coffee in two of them. "I *do* give it everything I've got!" he said, sulkily. "I can't give it any more! I helped to build our success just as much as you did."

"And you nearly destroyed it, if you remember! If you hadn't done what you did…"

"Don't go on and on about it! Please, Wayne. What's done is done!"

"I know! I know!" he shouted. He sighed and lowered his voice. "Look … I'm sorry about last night," he went on. "I really am. I don't mean to lose my temper like that. It's just…"

"You've got to stop it, Wayne," Gary half-whispered. "I can't go on with you threatening me all the time. It's my life!"

"But it's not just *your* life, Gary!" Wayne argued. "Don't you see that? If you destroy it for Hym, we both go down the pan."

Gary indicated the coffee. "I suppose you want one?"

"Please."

There was silence.

Finally, Gary handed a cup of coffee to Wayne. "Wayne," he said, convincingly. "Listen to me. For once and for all … I'm not *on* anything. No one's handing me little packages of drugs. I'm not planning a solo career. I'm not having secret little meetings with the record company. I'm not doing any of the things you've suddenly got so paranoid about. And I'm just as determined as you to see Hym go on to worldwide success."

Wayne stared at Gary with tears in his eyes. "Why can't I believe you?" he asked plaintively.

Gary shrugged. "I don't know, Wayne. I really don't know. But I do know I can't go on like this. I'm only eighteen, Wayne. I want some joy. I want a bit of life. You used to be such fun to work with. What went wrong?"

"You know what went wrong," whispered Wayne. A tear dropped into his coffee cup.

"Can't we forget the past? Please, Wayne?" He crossed to him and put his arm around his partner's neck. "We don't have to fight like this. Let's put Tokyo behind us, eh? No one knows. And no one *needs* to know. You've got to trust me, Wayne."

"I *want* to trust you," Wayne cried.

"You must! And if you don't calm down, Wayne … if you don't control your temper … then something awful's gonna happen. I just know it!"

Chapter 8

Phil Lemont jetted into Los Angeles in time for what he'd called the Hollywood Supergig. He could hardly believe his boys had come so far, so quickly, and was pleased with the meeting he'd just had with Hym's record company, Blunt Edge. The future of his manufactured pop group looked bright... "Just so long," as BJ (Blunt Edge's managing director) had put it, "as that older one keeps his mouth shut."

Wayne had had several warnings about his extra-ordinary behaviour since the Tokyo gig and he was beginning to get up the noses of not a few important people in the business. In Boston he'd had an outburst with a top TV chat-show director, who he'd felt had favoured Gary in his camera shots; he'd halted a press-call in Utah, simply because he felt that a young dewy-eyed journalist was getting too personal with her questions. Then, to top it all, he'd stormed out of a studio in New York, where their photo-session was taking place, after an argument about the lighting.

Phil Lemont had promised BJ that he'd tell Wayne

Fielding to keep his temper in check.

"He's not a bad lad, BJ," he'd tried to explain. "He's a very talented boy, and he used to be great fun. The pressure of work ... or something ... I dunno ... *something* must have got to him. He's very highly strung."

"He'll be highly strung by his gonads," threatened BJ, "if he doesn't get himself sorted out. Tell him I'll do it personally."

"Three minor incidents, that's all, BJ," said Phil. "I told you I'd sort Wayne out. He only needs a gentle talking to."

"Then do it!" snapped BJ. "If we lose the American record deal, Blunt Edge goes under, taking Hym and all our smaller acts with it! You *know* we're hardly breaking even ... what with those damned expensive robotics. And that was your idea, remember!"

"I'll see to it, BJ, I promise."

"Tell him one more wrong move and we'll replace him," BJ went on. "There are a thousand good-looking, muscle-bound youths out there who'd jump at the chance he's been given."

"All right. All right. I'll tell him." Phil hung up the receiver. He was trembling with rage. He'd worked so hard in this business and his only really big success had been with Hym. He was nearing forty but looked older, having gained too much weight through excess alcohol and having lost a great deal of hair due, he insisted, to the stress factor of being a pop manager. His break had come late. He'd managed two all-female bands, three solo male singers and a string of groups; everything from heavy metal to rap.

Having had the idea for Hym, two young, good-looking well-built lads whose voices blended well in a recording studio, Phil advertised in the music press and then set about auditioning hundreds of young hopefuls. Gary Brenn had a deep, bluesy voice and sounded like the best of the black soul singers. Wayne's voice was high, but powerful. Together they were magic. The hype before the release of their first single painted a romantic, though false, picture of how the boys had met whilst working out in the gym. They soon discovered that they shared many interests, including making music, so, the story went, they hired a demo-studio to record some numbers they'd written together. They'd sent a tape to Phil, who'd signed them up and within two months had got them a recording deal with Blunt Edge.

Phil didn't want to lose Wayne, but he knew that BJ was right. If Wayne Fielding continued along this path he'd recently started to tread, he would jeopardize the future of Hym, Blunt Edge and last, but by no means least, Phil Lemont himself. So he'd determined to warn Wayne tonight. After the show.

Phil arrived at his boys' dressing-room just as they left the stage, dripping with sweat, to screams from the excited fans.

"You were good," understated Phil, as he handed them their towels.

"Thanks a lot, Phil," grinned Gary. "Couldn't you have said we were *very* good?"

"All right. You were brilliant!" he said. "Here. I've brought you some beers."

"Duty free?" laughed Wayne. "How generous!"

"Where's the champagne and roses?" added Gary.

Phil opened one of the cans and took a swig.

"How much did you see of it?" asked Wayne.

"All of it … except the last number," replied Phil. "The kids were going spare. Not bad, eh, for a support band?"

Wayne wiped the towel across his cropped hair, checking in the dressing-room mirror continually, to make sure he looked rugged but not unattractive. "When did you get in from London?" he asked. "We were expecting you last night."

"About two hours ago."

"And how was BJ?"

"He was OK, actually. He thinks the new single'll be a smash here in the States, but he's got different ideas for back home. He wants to flip it over."

"I've always preferred the B side, anyway," said Gary.

"Me too." This from Wayne. "But BJ's right. They're not into that sort of thing here."

"Have you brought the remix with you?" asked Gary.

Phil took a cassette from his briefcase.

"Here. Nothing to play it on, though."

Wayne grabbed for his personal stereo and put in the cassette.

Phil looked down at his feet, occasionally swigging his beer, awaiting Wayne's reaction, which he hoped would be favourable. Gary began removing his make-up with a tissue. He, too, was hoping that Wayne wouldn't be too critical. He'd caused such a fuss over the previous mix. The horns were too upfront. Or so *he* thought.

Wayne listened, his face growing thunderous.

He whisked off the headphones after the first verse.

"No! I'm not having that!" he said.

Phil looked up at Gary through the mirror and raised his eyebrows.

"What's the matter with it?"

"It'll have to be done again!" snapped Wayne. "I can't hear my voice on it at all!"

"Of course you can!" said Phil. "Don't be stupid."

Gary snatched the cassette player, rewound the tape and listened to it from the beginning.

Wayne glowered at Phil. "Whose name's gonna be on this single, then? Hym? Or Gary Brenn?"

"Please, Wayne," pleaded Phil. "Listen to it again. It's the best thing you've done. It'll be huge."

"I don't care if it's the most mega record since 'Thriller' – I'm not on it! And if that goes out as our next single, I'm not promoting it. So you call that creep BJ in London and tell him, OK? I'm fifty percent of Hym and it's *me* that made this group. It's me that does all the talking on the chat-shows. It's me that has to sort out the hotel rooms when you've mucked up the bookings. It's me that has to supply Gary with his make-up and hold his hand when we get the call to go on stage, 'cause he's nearly wetting his pants in terror. Without me, Hym couldn't carry on! And if you think it could, then why don't you replace me with some bimbo who'll kow-tow to you and Mr Know-It-All BJ?"

"Don't push me, Wayne!" whispered Phil. "Don't push me!"

"Oh, *I* see!" hissed Wayne. "So that's what you've

been discussing with BJ, is it? You *are* thinking about replacing me? That's exactly what I thought you were up to!"

Gary removed his headphones. He was pale. He'd tried to listen to the song, but couldn't concentrate. He was terrified that Wayne would become violent.

"Actually, Phil," he said, "Wayne's right. You can't hear him on the track. It'll have to be done again."

Wayne stabbed an accusing finger at Phil. "There! See? So just you get on the phone to BJ and tell him. Wayne *and Gary* want another remix!" He stood and headed for the door. "I'm going to watch Sherry's act from the side. Are you coming, Gary?"

"In a minute," Gary replied.

Wayne left.

Phil gasped. "What the hell is he on?"

Gary gulped. "What d'you mean?"

"Is he taking anything?"

"No. No, of course not."

"Then he needs his head looking at! It's like talking to Jekyll and Hyde."

"*Tell* me about it!"

"Is it the touring he can't stand … or what? Something's very wrong in that head of his, that's for sure."

"I know."

"What is it, Gary? Has he said anything?"

"No. Not really," he lied. "Only about the duo splitting up. He's very frightened about that."

"But that's what he's pushing for, by the looks of it."

"Did you mean what you said, Phil?" asked Gary. "Is BJ going to replace him?"

"It's been talked about, yes. Would it bother you?"

"He'd go totally mad! Off his tiny rocker!"

"But would it bother *you*?" he repeated. "If he left? I mean, you've got to think of your future, son."

Gary thought about that night in Tokyo when, totally spaced-out, he'd done what he'd done. And he was sure that Wayne, if he were pushed from the duo, would tell all.

"No. I don't want him to leave," he said, quickly. "Not yet, Phil. I'm sure he'll be all right. Tell BJ I'll calm him down. He'll be OK, Phil."

Chapter 9

Terry leapt to the trailer window, wiped off the condensation with the back of his hand and gazed out across the campsite. He'd wondered if the wheels he'd heard, churning up the mud outside, belonged to the car bringing his mother home from the hospital. He saw only Levi's van, arriving with the scrap. It was getting dark and car headlamps were beginning to light up the nearby M25. Terry watched these commuters flash by, leaving the busy metropolis for the comfort and respectability of the Kent Weald.

On the far side of the site, Sylvie struggled to her trailer with a bucket of water. Hers was the only authentic Romany waggon remaining here. She and Abi nightly built their fire and ate in the open, and whilst there were some on the site who found this idea nostalgic or romantic, Terry had no such thoughts. He wanted so much to lead the life of his peers. One day he would have a proper house, with running water and a bathroom. And he'd do his best to persuade Mum and Dad to move in with him, although he knew they'd refuse.

They didn't like houses. Mum hated them. Hadn't she said, many times, that she'd never live like the gorgios? She was happier in a trailer. So he'd make sure that her trailer was the best that money could buy, with windows that fitted properly in the winter. And Dad would never again have to go on the "social". And Terry would show how much he loved him by buying him a horse. He'd loved his horses. Terry had seen the photo of him riding the black and white mare. He'd looked so happy in those days. He'd be happy again. And he'd love Terry right back, so grateful he'd be for the horse. And Mum and Dad wouldn't shout at each other any more. There'd be no need for rows. Not if they had enough money. It was only the lack of money that caused the rows. And without the rows and without the worries over money and with the windows that fitted properly, Dad would be well again. And Terry wouldn't be forced to go to the hospital to see the man he loved so much withering before his eyes.

"D'you wanna cuppa tea?" Billy slowly approached with a mug filled to the brim. The tea dribbled down the side of it and plopped on to the carpet.

"Oi, careful!" said Terry. "Mum'll kill you!"

"D'you think he'll be all right?" Billy was concerned not only at the possibility of his father's death, but at what that would do to his mother. "She won't have to sell dollies at the bingo again, will she?"

Terry shuddered at the idea. The last time they were short of money and Mum had been out with the pegs, she hadn't come home all night. A police cell, followed by a fine in the courts, had left them even shorter.

"Don't want no gavvers round 'ere again," said Billy.

Terry put his arm round the boy's shoulders. "He'll be all right," he said. "Dad's as strong as an ox."

Belcher pumped on the horn as the car pulled up outside. Terry saw his mother climb out and approach the trailer.

"*He's* not comin' in with 'er, is he?" asked Billy.

"Looks like it," replied his brother. "Why doesn't he go to his own trailer and leave us alone?"

Belcher had been good to them, ferrying Mum to and from the hospital every day and making sure that they always had enough to eat. But Terry and Billy felt uncomfortable whenever he was around. He seemed to be taking over. Controlling their lives. Doing Dad's job!

Her face was pale, her headscarf pulled tightly back. "How is he?" asked Terry.

" 'Bout the same," she replied. She turned to Billy. "Make us a cuppa tea, boy."

"Yous ought to go and see him, you know," said Belcher. His huge frame filled the door between the kitchen and the "room". He moved slightly to one side, allowing Billy to squeeze through to the stove.

"I *will* see him." Terry almost whispered the words, afraid that anything more audible would constitute a promise. "I'll see him when he's better."

Mother began to remove her coat. "You've got to face it, Terry love," she said. "He may not get…" Her words trailed away. She draped her coat on the back of a chair and covered her eyes with one hand.

Billy lit a gas-ring and placed the kettle on top of it. He silently watched the flames, turning through red to a watery blue.

Chapter 10

Sherry Barbin's motorcade wound its way up to the Beverly Hills home of ex-stripper and one-time Mr Universe, Buck West. The mansion with its tennis courts, stables and Olympic-sized swimming pool was proof that Buck West's business acumen was as big as his more famous asset. While he'd been posing his way to stardom as a member of the male-stripper revue *Heaven's Angels*, his earnings, wisely invested in Hollywood real estate and armament sales to the Middle East, had made him almost as wealthy as the rapidly diminishing Texas oil barons. He was happy to have retired when he did, at the grand old age of thirty-two.

On the way to the mansion, Sherry had her chauffeur stop at the Beverly Hills Hotel to pick up her friend, Ruby Gold, who'd just arrived from Las Vegas, where for the past six months she'd been the support act to some of the biggest stars in town.

"More like the biggest *jerks* in town, sugar!" she

54

grinned, her smile dazzling through her luscious, shiny lips. She climbed into the back of the limo, and kissed Sherry on the cheek. "Good to see yer, hon! I've missed you like crazy." Her voice sounded hoarse.

"How's Vegas?" asked Sherry.

"I hate Vegas and you know it. Listen to the voice, sugar. The air out there is killing it. I ain't goin' back. No way. Not even if they offer me ten times what I'm getting now."

"You should've come on the road with me, like I said."

Ruby laughed. "So's I end up calling *you* a jerk, too? No fear, honey. I'd prefer to keep our relationship cool. I like it just the way it is. No business connections. All fun!"

"You'll be top-lining soon, you'll see," encouraged Sherry. "The new album'll chart and the offers'll flood in."

Maybe, she thought. She looked out at the movie-star homes, vowing that some day she'd be living in one of them.

"I've been hearing wonderful things about your tour, Sherry," she said.

"Yep. It sure is goin' just how I meant it to."

"An' they've ripped poor old Patcha to shreds!" She laughed, loudly. "Her New York concert was, by all accounts, a total disaster."

"Are you surprised?" asked Sherry. "When Miss Minnie Mouse decided to change her image from sugar-candy queen to sex-kitten, I *said* she'd bomb. She can't be *me*, no matter how hard she tries! She can't sing, for starters. And somebody shoulda told her that you don't change into a sex-siren overnight just by donning some slinky, leather cat-suit."

Wayne Fielding hadn't wanted to attend the party and, had it not been for Phil Lemont's intervention, he felt he may have persuaded Gary to have stayed behind at the hotel, too.

"We're *going*!" insisted Phil. "If we're going to break America, you've got to be seen at these functions."

"But Buck West's a stripper, Phil!" snarled Wayne. "Is that really the sort of publicity we're after?"

"*Was* a stripper!" contradicted Phil. "He's now one of the richest businessmen in California. And that means that his past is conveniently forgotten. You're in the US of A now, Wayne! Not Bromley-By-Bow! He could even have been to dinner at the White House, for all we know."

A hired, very English, major-domo had announced Hym's arrival as they entered through the main doors and walked the length of the chandelier-bedecked, palatial hall, to be greeted by Buck West, who was in full evening dress. Wayne and Gary, in their jeans, sneakers and open-necked shirts felt totally out of place. Phil, in his naff M&S suit, felt likewise.

"Good to see you guys," said Buck, shaking each of them warmly by the hand. "Champagne is being served on the patio and food is in the dining hall. If you want anything else – and I mean *anything* – just ask one of the waiters."

"Thanks," said Phil.

"Have a nice time, eh?" added Buck and he turned to greet more just-announced guests.

Gary, Wayne and Phil wandered towards the floodlit patio – a vast area, filled with miniature orange trees, palms and loud, expensively dressed revellers. A waiter immediately pushed a silver tray towards them and each took a glass of champagne.

"Well, that's really diplomatic, isn't it?" laughed Phil as he listened to the background music drifting gently from the bougainvillaea-camouflaged speakers.

Wayne and Gary listened.

"I don't believe it!" exclaimed Wayne.

It was Patcha's number one single.

"Sherry Barbin's biggest rival," frowned Gary, "and they've got the nerve to play it at a party where she's the guest of honour."

Phil couldn't stop laughing. "If La Barbin hears it, somebody'll be for the chop, you can bet yer life on it."

"I haven't seen her, yet," mused Gary. "D'you think she's changed her mind about coming?"

"She's picking her girlfriend up on the way, so I hear," said Phil. "Some black soul singer called Ruby Gold who's doing quite well for herself out here." He grinned. "Got to admit it though, haven't you?" he added as he moved his body in rhythm with Patcha's record. "It's a good sound."

Wayne and Gary looked at each other. Something was afoot. Phil had always hated Kendrick Simpson's productions.

"You *are* joking, I hope?" said Wayne.

Phil dropped his smile. "No. No, I'm not joking. I've been listening to her album, actually. It's good."

Gary sneered. "Do me a favour, Phil. I've heard it. It stinks."

Wayne backed his partner. "She's terrible, Phil! She comes out with all this 'I want to be taken seriously' business in the music press and then, when she gets up on stage, she can't do it. She can't sing! At all! She doesn't even move well!"

"I'm sorry," interrupted Phil, seriously, "but I don't agree."

"All right! Out with it, Phil!" snapped Gary. "We weren't born yesterday. You've been talking to Kendrick Simpson, haven't you?"

"Well…" Phil hesitated.

Wayne paled. "Not about us, I hope. You *know* I hate his kind of music.

"Me too!" added Gary.

Phil's mouth went dry. He stopped a passing waiter and grabbed for another glass of champagne. Wayne did the same.

"So?" demanded Gary.

"He sent us a demo," explained Phil. "And he asked if Hym would be interested in recording it."

"And you told him where to get off, I hope!" replied Gary.

"All I ask," went on Phil, "is that you listen to it."

"No!" from Gary.

"No! No! No!" from Wayne.

"It's a number one. Without a doubt. And if *you* don't record it, *someone* will … and it'll sit at the top of the charts for weeks."

"No!" This from both of them.

"You need a number one! If the new album is going to do what we want it to do, you *need* a number one single!"

"So we'll write one!" said Gary. "Anything Kendrick Simpson can do, we can do!"

"Better!" agreed Wayne.

Phil drained his champagne. "Look, lads," he explained, "*I* know you don't need the likes of Kendrick Simpson to write and produce your material, but you try explaining that to the record company. I've had BJ on my back for a fortnight talking about this potential number one from Kendrick Simpson which'll boost Blunt Edge's future profits. I mean … give me a break, lads! What can I do?"

"You simply say, '*NO!*'" hissed Wayne.

"If we go with Kendrick Simpson," argued Gary, "we'll have two or three smash singles. Then what? He's only kept Patcha and Pepperrazzi supplied with hit material because he *manages* them too. All the other Kendrick Simpson hit acts have been chewed up and spat out. Look what happened to The Minders."

"Oh, come on!" laughed Phil. "The Minders blew it when their fans realized what they were up to."

"No! That's not true!" argued Wayne. "Kendrick Simpson just dumped them!"

"Yes! Because of the expected scandal!"

"Give over! The fans had no idea what was going on!" argued Gary. "Kendrick Simpson killed them."

"Well, he wouldn't kill you two for that reason, would he?" said Phil. He paused, then added, in hushed tones, "Or would he?"

"I need the toilet," said Gary, hurriedly.

He stopped a passing waiter, who was on his way to replenish his empty silver tray with more glasses of champagne.

"Where's the loo, please?"

The waiter stared at him, blankly.

Phil translated the request into American. "He means the bathroom."

The waiter grinned. "I'll show you the way, sir."

Chapter 11

Bury The Rabbit's unsuccessful audition did nothing to reduce the numbers who'd arrived at the after-school disco on Friday afternoon. Rosetti himself, his pride firmly intact, danced unpartnered in the centre of the hall, arrogantly presuming that most of the girls had their eyes on him. Maureen stood some distance away, half watching him, half listening to Tracey, Scotty's red-headed girlfriend.

Terry could feel the music vibrating through every muscle. He tried for a while to forget the problems at home. He needed to drown in sound. He *had* to dance. He crossed the hall, interrupting Tracey in mid-sentence.

"There's a lot 'ere, in't there?" he said to Maureen.

Scotty let go of Tracey's hand and turned on Terry, aggressively. "What do *you* want, Smith?"

Tracey giggled.

Maureen stared at him. He'd rarely spoken to her. Terry had always been there, on the far side of the hall, on the other side of the classroom, watching, never

61

partaking. He was just Smithy the gyppo. Now he was here, within their circle, talking to them. Just like any of the other boys.

"Yes. More here than usual," she replied, kindly. "I think they wanted to see Bury The Rabbit play, but Mr Buckley reckons we're not good enough."

Rosetti had stopped dancing. He stared across at them, hardly able to believe what he was seeing.

Scotty caught his friend's eye. "I think you'd better disappear, Smith," he said, not threatening, just warning.

"He's OK where he is," said Maureen.

Terry summoned the courage to ask her. "D'you wanna dance?"

Tracey giggled again.

"Why not?" smiled Maureen. She led the way on to the floor, not looking back, expecting him to follow.

Rosetti tore across the hall and grabbed her arm. "Where are you goin'?" he asked.

"Just dancing." Her feelings for Rosetti had never included fear.

"Not with him, you're not!"

Maureen pulled her arm free. "You don't own me. I'll dance with whoever I want."

Rosetti's face flushed. He approached Terry and placed both hands on the boy's shoulders.

"I don't know what you're trying to do, Pikie, but I'm warning you…!"

Jim Buckley had seen the trouble brewing from the beginning but, being the only teacher on duty, he'd hoped it would subside without intervention. He tried calmly to mix from one disc to another as he kept an

62

eye on the small group gathering around Rosetti.

"Hit him, Ray!" said one of them.

Maureen glared at Rosetti. "You dare!"

"You don't 'alf think you're good, don't you, Rosetti?" said Terry.

"Let him go, Ray!" Maureen tried to push between them.

Rosetti released the boy from his grip. "Go on," he said. "Back to your caravan where you belong, Pikie."

Terry walked slowly away, mumbling to himself.

Rosetti couldn't hear what he was saying, but warned him nevertheless, "Watch it!"

Terry turned. "Yeah, you *think* you're good. But you're rubbish!"

Maureen's eyes pleaded with Terry to stop. She could see the pulse beating in Rosetti's neck.

"Bury The Rabbit!" sneered Terry. "Crap! You can't play and you can't sing."

Rosetti gave one last warning. "I'll do you, Smith!"

But Terry refused to be quietened. "You've only got a group 'cause of yer daddy's money! All that dough ... all that stuff ... and you've no idea how to play it. You're rubbish!"

Satisfied that he'd had his say, Terry turned and began to walk towards the staircase.

Scotty called after him. "At least Ray's dad *earns* his money!"

Terry stopped in his tracks. He was waiting for the next line.

Rosetti delivered it. "He didn't *nick* it!"

Terry looked back over his shoulder, his voice quaking. "What d'you mean?"

Rosetti turned his back on him, dismissively. "You heard! Thievin' pikies!"

Scotty laughed.

Maureen looked away, embarrassed to be part of the group.

Jim was the first to see Terry hurtle across the hall towards Rosetti. He leapt from his chair, sending the stylus skidding across the record. Those dancing, stopped, moaned in unison and then fell silent.

One shouted, "Fight!"

Terry had the back of Rosetti's shirt collar in his grip and was pulling him down towards the floor. Rosetti couldn't breathe. He tore frantically at the shirt, trying to get some air, his eyes bulging with terror. Maureen screamed. Scotty tried to pull the boy off. Jim grabbed Terry's hair and pulled at it until he'd let go of Rosetti. Rosetti gasped for air as he rubbed his reddened neck.

"He's mad!" he croaked.

"What the hell do you think you're doing?" yelled Jim.

"Smith started it, sir!" said Scotty.

Jim turned on him. "Shut it! I'm not talking to you."

Rosetti pulled himself up to his full height, aware of his gathering audience. "He said we were rubbish," he panted.

"We?" asked Jim, angrily. "Who's *we*?"

"Bury The Rabbit," said Rosetti.

Terry was still shaking. "He called me a pikie. He said my dad was a thief!"

Jim glared at Rosetti. "Did you?"

Rosetti feigned incredulity. "No, sir!"

"He didn't, sir!" said Scotty.

"Go home!" yelled Jim. He turned his anger on everyone gathered, including the innocents. "Go home! All of you! I'm not spending my free time running clubs for thugs!"

The comment was unfair and he knew it as he watched them all amble away, murmuring their disappointment.

"Sorry, sir," said Maureen as she left the hall arm in arm with Tracey.

Jim crossed to the turntables and began to disconnect the equipment. Terry followed him. He wanted to apologize for his behaviour; to explain how it had happened. It didn't matter what Rosetti and Scotty or any of the others thought about him. They'd always hated him anyway, just because of what he was. But Terry didn't want to lose Jim Buckley's respect.

"Sir..." he mumbled.

Jim turned. "You going to help me clear up, or what?"

Terry silently gathered up the records and packed them into their wooden boxes.

Chapter 12

Joline grabbed Gary by the hand as soon as he'd left the bathroom.

"Hello there. I've been looking for you everywhere."

He looked startled. As far as he was aware, Sherry Barbin's personal assistant had never given so much as a glance in his direction. And he certainly hadn't gone out of his way to make contact with this dumpy little creature with the furrowed brow and horn-rimmed specs who was always rushing around, notepad in hand.

"Where's the other half tonight?" she asked.

He sighed. "If you mean Wayne, he's talking to our manager."

"You mean you've been let off his lead for two minutes?" She laughed. "I don't believe it!"

Gary was irritated by the statement, although he knew exactly what she meant. He was trapped every single minute of every day and couldn't recall having many conversations on the tour without Wayne standing by his side, listening to every word, often answering for him.

"Shall we go for a little walk?" asked Joline, adding quickly, when she saw the hunted look in his eyes, "Don't worry. I'm not trying to seduce you. I just wanna show you something."

Wayne grabbed the lapels of Phil Lemont's suit and dragged him from the sofa, shaking him awake.

"I want to go back to the hotel, Phil. If you're not coming, arrange a car for me!" he demanded. "I've had enough."

Phil's words were slurred, almost inaudible. "All right. I'm coming." He tried to stand upright, but as Wayne let go of him, he slumped back on to the sofa.

"Phil!"

"I'm a bit slewed," mumbled Phil.

"A *bit*? You're out of your head!"

"Is Gary ready to go?"

"I've no idea!" snapped Wayne. "I haven't seen him for hours."

"Well, why don't you go and find him while I sort out the car?"

"It'd serve him right if we left him!"

Phil pulled himself to his feet again. "Leave him? Don't be ridiculous. *I'll* find him."

Staggering from one side of the room to the other, he made his way out towards the pool, oblivious to the stares of those around him as he yelled, "Gary! Gary!"

Buck West, grinning, watched him go. Then he approached Wayne.

"He won't find your friend out there," he said. "Come on, I'll show you where he is."

He led him along the red-carpeted hall, past several closed doors and through the library, where several of the guests sat engrossed in Hollywood gossip and intrigue, and on into what Buck laughingly referred to as the Royal Dining Room.

Finally they came to a dead end: a solid wall of books ... shelf upon shelf of leather-bound, immaculate and obviously unread volumes.

Buck removed one large encyclopaedia and groped towards the back of the shelf, pressing a button.

The shelves – and the whole wall – began to open inwards: a vast door into a hidden chamber.

Buck grinned, "Welcome to the Pleasure Dome."

Wayne entered cautiously, hoping he wasn't going to discover what he suddenly realized was a probability.

He eyed several of the guests, including Sherry Barbin and a beautiful black girl seated at her side, snorting and smoking and pill-popping; indulging in a fiesta of drug-taking which was orgiastic, even by Hollywood's standards. And there too was Gary! And though most were oblivious to the new-arrivals, each lost in their own private heaven, it was Gary who noted Wayne's presence and stared across at him, wide-eyed and grinning inanely.

"No!" wailed Wayne, a desperate, pathetic cry from the heart. "No! No! Gary!"

Sherry Barbin rose from her seat.

Her face was thunderous. "What the...!"

Wayne cried out hysterically, "I'll kill him! I'll kill him!"

Chapter 13

The class fell silent, listening in awe, amazed at the power behind the voice. He strummed his guitar as he sang:

> *"You call on me*
> *When you are lonely,*
> *And I know I can only*
> *Be a friend…"*

None here had ever dreamed Terry Smith had such talent, least of all Jim Buckley.

> *"If you knew*
> *How much it hurts me*
> *To be here on the outside*
> *Lookin' in…"*

The cabaret during the last double period before the Easter break was a regular end-of-term occurrence for Jim's form. Some presented short sketches, others told jokes, but rarely did anyone sing. Not even Rosetti could be persuaded to perform without amplification.

Terry finished his song and bobbed his head in a modest attempt at a bow. Most watched him open-mouthed as he returned to his desk, where he began polishing his glasses. Some giggled. Rosetti stared out of the window. No one applauded. The pips sounded, signalling the start of the holiday, and they all cheered.

Terry was asked to stay behind as everyone else was dismissed.

"Great voice," said Jim.

"Thanks." Terry smiled.

"D'you fancy doing a little job for me during the school break?"

"What's that, then?"

"I've written a couple of songs. Well ... to be precise, Mr Jamieson and I have written a couple of songs."

Terry wondered where this was leading.

"We're going to make some demos."

"Yeah?"

"You'd sing them much better than us."

Terry shrugged. Jim took this to mean that he wasn't interested.

"So you won't do it?"

"I'll do it for *you*," replied Terry.

Jim knew what he meant. "Mr Jamieson's all right, you know. His bark's worse than his bite."

Terry lifted his guitar and laid it across his shoulder.

"I'll do it for *you*!" he repeated.

* * *

70

Maureen took a short-cut through the back of the metalwork block on her way home. Terry was collecting his bike from the sheds as she passed.

"Give us a ride, superstar!" she called.

Terry almost broke the padlock trying to release the bike quickly, in order to catch up with her.

"If you carry my guitar, you can sit on my cross-bar."

She laughed. "I was only joking." She walked to the bus stop and searched her pockets. "Oh, no!" she said. "I've left my bus pass in Ray's bag and he's gone swimming with Scotty."

Terry grinned. "You'll have to walk." He was grateful for the missing pass. It meant he could spend a few more minutes with her.

"It's not too far," she said.

Terry felt unusually confident. "Can I walk with you?"

"If you like."

They passed through the block of flats on the Belling Estate and into a tidy street of well-kept council houses.

"I was supposed to be going swimming with them," said Maureen, "but my gran's got the nurse coming."

She stopped at the crumbling, green gate to her house.

"D'you want to come in for a cup of tea?"

"Won't your gran mind?"

Maureen smiled. "Why should she?"

She waited for Terry to padlock his bike to the fence and then led him into the house.

"Is that you, Maureen?" Gran called from the kitchen.

Maureen whispered to Terry, "She always says that." She called back, "'Course it's me. Who did you think it was?"

Gran appeared in the hall in her wheelchair and peered over the top of her glasses at the visitor.

"This is Terry," said Maureen. "He wants a cup of tea."

"You and me both, love," replied Gran. "Put the kettle on, Mo."

She wheeled herself towards the front room. "Let's have it in the parlour. Then I can keep an eye out for the nurse."

Maureen grinned at Terry, who followed her into the kitchen.

"She seems nice," said Terry.

"She's great." Maureen filled the kettle at the sink, plugged it in and pressed the switch. "She's in a lot of pain, but she never complains."

Gran called from the parlour, "Bloody nurse is always late!"

Maureen giggled. "Well, she doesn't complain very often, put it that way."

She placed three teabags into the pot and reached up to the shelf for two mugs and Gran's cup and saucer, which she placed on a tray.

"Why d'you live with your gran?" asked Terry. He immediately began to worry that she might think he was too inquisitive.

"My mum's dead."

"Oh!" Terry wasn't sure how to react. "Sorry."

"'S all right. It was a long time ago. She had an accident."

Maureen took a bottle of milk from the fridge. "You don't want it in a jug, do you?" she asked.

"Er … no," Terry stammered.

She placed the milk bottle on the tray beside the mugs.

"She slipped. Or so they say. She was coming home from work and there was a lot of people at the station. And she slipped."

"That's terrible." Terry was embarrassed.

"Gran nearly went mad. She was her only daughter."

"Where's that tea?" Gran called. Perhaps she'd heard. Perhaps she was trying to shut Maureen up.

"Give us a chance," Maureen laughed. "Kettle's not boiling yet." And as an afterthought, she called, "Do you want anything to eat?"

"There's some swiss roll in the blue tin," Gran replied. "That horrible one … with the violets on."

"So what about your dad?" asked Terry. "Where's he?"

"I've no idea," shrugged Maureen. "I don't know and I don't care."

Terry was shocked. "Of course you care. He's your dad!"

"I hate him," said Maureen. "And so did my mum."

Terry had never heard anyone speak about their parents like that. Not even Belcher. And *he* had good reason to. His parents had deserted him when he was only eight and if it hadn't been for Terry's uncle Render, taking him in and bringing him up like one of his own, Belcher would've gone into Care.

Maureen put the sugar bowl and a teaspoon on to the tray and decided to change the subject. "You've got a great voice. I couldn't believe it. And it was a brilliant song."

"Thanks. Mr Buckley said so too. I'm going to help him make a demo. One of his songs."

"Really?" Maureen was surprised. "I didn't know he wrote songs."

"But don't say anything, will you?" Terry added quickly. "I don't want anyone to know."

" 'Course I won't," she said. "You sing much better than Ray, you know."

Terry began to panic. "Don't tell Rosetti, will you? Especially not him."

Maureen laughed. "Don't be daft. I don't tell Ray everything, you know. I don't tell him anything important!"

Terry had assumed that Rosetti and Maureen would know everything about each other. They'd been together for ages.

"We talk about records and the group and clothes and that." She giggled. "And we talk ever such a lot about Ray Rosetti." She laughed, loudly.

Terry didn't. If Ray Rosetti knew that Terry Smith had been laughing about him...! He daren't think about it.

Maureen saw the look on his face.

"We have a good time together," she volunteered. "He's nice. He takes me to places I've never been before. I like him. I like him a lot, but ... well ... you know. There's nothing in it!"

Terry didn't mean to say it. The words slipped out. "He's not nice. He's a yob. I don't know what you see in him."

She poured boiling water on to the teabags. "His dad's loaded, you know."

"I know!"

Maureen noted the bitterness. "It's not everything, you know, Terry. I mean … it's nice, I admit. *Very* nice. But being well-off brings its own problems, you know." She shrugged. "Or so Mr Rosetti keeps telling me."

"It's everything to *me*!" replied Terry. "*I'd* like a few of the problems that go with being rich!"

Maureen smiled at him, mischievously. "You *wouldn't* like it."

Terry grinned at her. "Wouldn't I just? I wanna be stinking rich. And unbelievably famous!"

"A superstar, right?" she laughed.

"Too right!" Terry began to sound very serious. "I hate being a nobody. I want people to know my name. I want 'em to buy my records and put pictures of me on their bedroom walls."

Maureen laughed. "I wouldn't want to put a picture of you on *my* bedroom wall. I'd have nightmares."

"You would. You wait 'til I'm famous!"

Maureen reached up for the blue cake tin.

"I'll *wait*," she said.

"She'll go mad!" laughed Rosetti as he pushed his wet towel into his bag. He held up Maureen's bus pass for Scotty to see. "Look!"

"She'll do you," grinned Scotty. "She'll have had to walk."

They decided to take it to her before going home, knowing that she'd need it the following morning.

Besides, they both fancied a cup of tea with Gran, who always made them welcome.

As soon as they'd entered the street, Scotty recognized the bike. He stared at Rosetti, wondering why he hadn't reacted.

"Nurse is still there," said Rosetti. "The old girl won't be pleased to see us if she's having her legs done."

The nurse left the house, passed the bike and got into her car.

Rosetti looked at Scotty.

"I *thought* you hadn't realized," said Scotty. "That's Terry Smith's bike!"

Rosetti stared at the bike, then at Scotty.

"Right!" he fumed. "He's 'ad it! And so's she!"

Chapter 14

According to newspaper reports, Hym had returned to England to prepare for a series of TV specials, Sherry Barbin's press officer having stated that it was an offer that the boys couldn't refuse. The star had magnanimously agreed to their departure, replacing them with the top rock band, Crack.

Wayne had slept badly, worried that the meeting with BJ at Blunt Edge's offices would mean the end of his short pop career. He knew that he would have to bite his tongue and he also knew that he'd find that an impossible task.

"We've no intention of dropping you," said BJ, coldly. "Well…" he added, "we've no intention of dropping you *yet!*" He stared across his desk at Wayne, almost ignoring Gary, silent, sitting at his partner's side. "Perhaps that's what you *want*," he added. "Perhaps you're hoping that Blunt Edge will terminate your contract immediately so that you can go ahead with the solo projects you're preparing."

Wayne tried to interrupt him.

"But we've got contractual obligations to fulfil," BJ went on. "And until we've raked in the money from *them*, Hym is with Blunt Edge. Right? There's the new single to be released here and in the States and the album deal with Japan."

"We're not preparing solo projects," argued Wayne. "And we don't want you to drop us. We just want more say in how Hym is managed."

"Then talk to your manager!" snapped BJ.

"But he does everything you *tell* him to do," protested Wayne. "He's even suggesting we record a Kendrick Simpson number. And that's not what we're about. We hate the Kendrick Simpson stuff. And so did Phil until you told him what you had in mind."

"The Kendrick Simpson material we listened to was fine," said BJ. He smiled at them. "It's great. There's a number one single there, without a doubt."

Gary spoke. "We don't want to do it."

BJ shrugged. "Then don't do it."

Wayne glared at him. "What?"

"If you don't like it, don't do it. It's as simple as that. If you can come up with a number one single, then we'll forget Kendrick Simpson."

"And if we don't make number one?" This from Gary.

"You've *got* to have a number one!" He sighed. "Look, lads, you're doin' great. Fanbloodytastic if you ask me ... but a number one will make an *incredible* difference to the sales of the new album."

"If we ever get it mixed," grumbled Gary.

"We're almost there with it," BJ assured him.

"And," he went on, "it'll be much easier to sell Hym to the world if we can honestly say that you're the number one British band. So … if that next single doesn't make it to the top, then I'll persuade Phil that the only sensible thing to do is to go with a Kendrick Simpson song, right?"

"And if we refuse?" asked Wayne.

"*Then* we'll dump you." He laughed. "Only joking, lads." He stood and crossed to his drinks cabinet. "Beer?"

"So why did you want to see us?" asked Wayne, wondering why the LA incident hadn't, as yet, been mentioned. "It wasn't just to tell us that you're *thinking* about dumping us if we don't hit number one."

"No, of course it wasn't," agreed BJ. He brought three cans of beer to the desk. "It was to tell you that I've been auditioning."

Wayne felt his heart racing. He *knew* it!

"I've got a potential replacement. Built like the proverbial … and very handsome. Great voice. And ready to step into your shoes at a moment's notice."

Wayne took a can of beer with a trembling hand.

BJ reached across the desk, grabbed the boy's shirt-front, menacingly, and, without raising his voice, stated, "We – Blunt Edge – are struggling for survival. And you, sunshine, are not making it easy for us."

He let go of the shirt. "So watch it, eh?"

He grinned at Gary and Wayne. "Drink your beers."

"Have another half," pleaded Wayne. "There's no need to rush home, surely?"

Gary looked around the pub and saw that it was

beginning to fill. "I don't think I can cope with the hassle tonight." He checked his watch. Six-thirty. The pre-West End theatre crowds were arriving. "I don't fancy getting into some conversation with a group of fans."

"Our fans wouldn't use this pub," sighed Wayne. "You know they wouldn't. Go on. Have another half."

"No. Honest. I've gotta go." Gary slipped on his jacket.

Wayne half-whispered, "I suppose you've got some assignation, have you? You're not meeting Phil on the quiet, are you? Without me?"

Gary froze. "No. I'm not meeting *anyone*. I just want to go home. All right?"

"Hoping to score, are you?" he sneered. "Why don't you linger around Soho? There're plenty of pushers around here."

"I'm not *on* anything, Wayne. I don't *need* anything. And I'm not meeting Phil. I just fancy an early night."

Wayne stood and grabbed for his mac.

"There's no need for *you* to leave," Gary said, thinking, For God's sake stop following me everywhere I go. "*You* have another half."

"I'll walk to the car park with you."

"There's no need Wayne. I'm a big boy, now."

"I *want* to."

They passed through Soho Square, towards Berwick Street Market and on to Old Compton Street.

"So what about that bit about us preparing our solo careers, then?" said Wayne. "Where did he get that from?"

"I've no idea."

They walked on in silence.

At the entrance to the car park Wayne put the question to him. "The truth, Gary, eh?"

"What?"

"It's *you* he was talking about, wasn't it?"

"*Who?* What are you trying to say?"

"It's you that's planning a solo career, isn't it?"

"Don't be ridiculous."

"Does Phil know? Have you and he worked this all out together? Ride to success on the back of Hym and *my* hard work? Get our first number one ... and then out on your own? Is that it?"

"Wayne, please!"

"I bet that's what you've planned, isn't it?"

"No!"

Two girls, passing through Old Compton Street on their way to a cinema, stopped and stared. They couldn't believe it. Gary and Wayne. Hym. Their pin-ups. Their idols. There. Across the road ... outside the car park. One screamed. A *little* scream; more a high-pitched squeak. The other gasped.

"It's them, isn't it?"

"Yeah!"

They ran across the road.

"Gary! Wayne!" they shrieked.

"Can I have your autograph?" one said, so excited she could hardly breathe.

Wayne turned on them. "We're having a row!" he shouted. "Go away!"

Chapter 15

Jim had arranged to meet Terry on the path which led to the campsite and the boy, who seemed excited about recording the demo, chatted incessantly as they approached the trailers. Jim was nervous. His preconceived ideas about gypsy camps were, in part, valid. There was plenty of mud, piles of twisted metal and rusty car chassis. Dogs barked and growled at him as he passed each trailer and one old mongrel leapt at his heels. Terry kicked out at it, sending the overweight dog sprawling on its side.

"He's great, that one," laughed Terry. "He don't like gorgios."

Controlled aggression sat on the faces of the men and women they passed and they glared at the intruder, wondering who he was and what he wanted. This was gypsy territory, the world of travellers, where outsiders were rarely welcomed.

Inside, Terry's trailer seemed surprisingly spacious: four separate rooms, all spotlessly clean and adorned with ornaments of china, of glass, of silver, but mostly of brass. On every available surface were framed photographs: grandparents, uncles, nephews, cousins and babies. Jim's eye caught a painting on the wall. A magnificently decorated Romany waggon, horse drawn.

"D'you like it?" asked Terry's mother. "*I* painted that. Only by numbers ... but *I* did it."

She welcomed him immediately and, although reticent about her own life and her husband's ill-health, she made Jim feel at ease and able to ask what he'd come to ask.

Of course she didn't mind Terry making a demonstration record. "It'll keep him out o' trouble, won't it?" and "Couldn't you take Billy wiv yer too?" and "Where is this place, then? Over the water?" and "Can he really sing, my Terry?"

Jim left the site, liking the woman considerably more than he'd hoped. She was gentle and obviously cared greatly for her kids. Moreover, she'd welcomed a stranger into her home without a second thought, which was more than Jim's own mother would have done. And this was the woman he might have dismissed many a time, with a flick of the hand, not noticing the eyes, as she tried to sell him lucky heather at the tube.

Chapter 16

Maureen was expected at eight. "Don't be late," Ray had said, and she wasn't. She knew he'd take her somewhere special and she'd eaten little, hoping it would be to the Chinese.

"Enjoy yourself, darling," her gran had told her. "You're not sixteen every day."

She pressed the bell and waited. Rosetti's father opened the door and was, she felt, peculiarly cold. He wasn't smiling, nor did he greet her with the usual kiss on the cheek.

"Happy birthday, Maureen," he said, flatly.

"Shall I go up?" she was about to ask him. She always went straight up to Ray's sitting-room. But Franco indicated that she should wait in the lounge.

"In here, love. He shouldn't be long."

She wondered if Ray had planned some big surprise. Maybe he'd gathered all their friends together upstairs, for a surprise birthday party.

Mrs Rosetti decided to leave the room as soon as Maureen entered. "Well, what have *you* been up to?" she asked, not waiting for a reply.

Ray entered, wearing his scruffiest jeans and an un-ironed shirt.

So we're not going out tonight, thought Maureen. And there was obviously no party. Ray would rather be seen dead than appear like this in front of his friends. She was disappointed. He carried no flowers, no present, no card. Surely, he couldn't have forgotten her sixteenth? He'd been making a fuss about it for weeks; embarrassing her with lines about her being legal now ... and how the law couldn't touch 'em for it.

"Hi!" she smiled. She eyed him up and down. "Well, *you've* made an effort tonight, haven't you?" she giggled, trying not to show her disappointment.

"I really can't believe you've had the nerve to turn up," he hissed.

At first she thought it must be some kind of joke, but when she saw the look in his eyes, her face paled. She wanted to say, "What d'you mean?" but the words refused to come out.

"Been saving it all this time for the pikies, 'ave yer?" he said.

Suddenly she knew.

He mimicked her. " 'Oh, no, Ray. I don't want to do anything like that, Ray.' " He sneered at her. "I bet you didn't! How long's it been goin' on then?"

"Oh, for God's sake," she said. "Don't be so stupid."

"I saw him," he mumbled. The words were choking in his throat. "I saw his bike outside yer house."

"He came in for a cup of tea."

His delivery became even more venomous. "And what else did you offer him?"

She couldn't believe what she was hearing. "Oh, *please*! He walked me home. You had my bus pass, Ray!"

"Well, did you?" He was trembling.

"Did I what?"

"You know!"

"What are you talking about?" She was furious at the accusation.

"How many others have you been with, then?"

"Nobody." Her eyes filled with tears.

"Give over. Little Miss Innocent!"

She burst into tears. "I've never. Ever. With *anyone*."

"How could you go off with a pikie?" he yelled.

He raised his hand and she flinched. And he knew he'd gone too far.

"Right!" she said, coldly. "That's it! I'm not having *that*!"

She brushed past him and stormed into the hall. He followed her.

"Maureen! You get back here!" he demanded.

Franco Rosetti appeared at the top of the stairs and tried to calm his son. "Now come on, Ray. Leave it, boy."

Ray Rosetti sneered, glaring at Maureen. "Yeah. He's right. You're not worth it."

"I think it'd be better if you left, don't you, Maureen?" Franco called down, sheepishly.

Maureen glared, first at the father, then at the son.

Then she left, slamming the street door behind her.

Passing the blue Mercedes in the drive, she slumped at the side of the Rosetti van and sobbed. How could he? How could anyone be so cruel? The tears were short-lived: her distress was quickly replaced by a cold determination not to repeat history. She remembered her father's cruelty, her mother's tears. There would be no replay.

Chapter 17

"Don't think I'm kinky or anything," laughed the photographer, "but…" He grinned.

"I trust you," replied the good-looking lad.

The photographer placed a fried egg, not long out of the pan, but just long enough to be lukewarm, on to the lad's face.

"Ugh!"

He stood astride him, looking down on to the egg. "Sorry about this," he said. "It won't take me long."

He shot one roll of film.

"Great," he said. "Well done." He deftly scooped up the egg without breaking it and threw it into a bin. Then he handed the male model a towel to remove the grease from his face.

"What are the shots for?" asked the model.

"An insurance company," the photographer replied. "An internal brochure for their staff."

"Strange pictures." He removed the grease and began changing from the suit he was wearing into his jeans and sweatshirt.

"*Aren't* they? Clever, though. 'Don't be left with egg on your face'."

The model grinned, then asked, "Shall I invoice you or the client?"

"Me. Two hours at double time, right?"

"Right."

The photographer adjusted his lamps and started to re-set for his afternoon shoot. "Have you been keeping busy?" he asked.

"Not bad, I suppose. Well, you know how it is at the moment."

"Don't I just."

"I think our agency's doing a lot better than others. I've got mates with Walkers' Models who haven't worked for two months."

The photographer nodded. "Yup. Zena's still got it made. I don't go anywhere else for models now, unless I'm pushed. She's not greedy. Some of the fees these agencies are asking now are just OTT. Especially Top-Zeds."

"Mind you," smiled the model, "if you insist on shooting on Sundays, what can you expect?"

"It's very rare. It's only if I'm asked to do a rush-job. And do you know ... male models from Top-Zeds won't do anything but stand there looking pretty. Get them to do what you've just done and they'd freak."

The model laughed. "I don't care *what* I do so long as I get paid."

"I hear Zena's just taken back Imogen Shannon on to her books," said the photographer.

"Just 'Imogen'. She doesn't use the 'Shannon'."

He fastened his belt, looked into the mirror and brushed back his jet-black hair with his finger-tips.

"What's she coming back into the business for?" asked the photographer. "She must be loaded." He grinned. "She's got it made, hasn't she, married to one of the world's rock superstars? So, why work?"

"Bored, probably. Pete Shannon's always off on tour and she's left looking after the kids."

"Have you seen her?"

"Yeah. She was in the agency last week, when I went in with some new photos."

"And?"

"How d'you mean?"

"How's she looking?"

"Great. Same as she ever did. She's incredible." He began writing out his invoice. "Why? Are you thinking of using her?"

"*Me?*" He laughed. "I couldn't afford Imogen. Unless *the client* was prepared to pay her sort of money."

"You might be surprised," the model informed him. "I think I know what she's asking. Try her." He paused. "But not on a Sunday. You certainly couldn't afford to pay her double time."

"I'll think about it."

"Have you got another shoot today?" he asked, tearing out the invoice from his book and handing it to the photographer.

The photographer grimaced. " 'Fraid so. Some pop group."

"Really? Who?"

"Hym."

The model made a gagging sound as he placed two fingers in his mouth.

"I take it you don't like them."

"Do *you*?"

"I wouldn't know. I've *heard* of them, of course…"

"You could hardly have avoided hearing about them, with all that publicity."

"I don't think I've ever heard them sing, though. I've not even seen any pics." He laughed. "I haven't taken much interest in pop music since Elvis died!"

"You haven't missed much. Well … let's just say Hym isn't my type of music. Pete Shannon, yes! Hym definitely not!"

"What do they look like?" The photographer was curious.

"They're very good-looking … in a manufactured sort of way."

"Pleasant?"

"On the TV chat-shows, yeah." He picked up his bag which contained his suit, invoice book, powder-puff, hair-lacquer and blue eye-dew, and flung it over his shoulder. "Thanks for the work," he added. "See you again, I hope."

"Sure. Thanks."

The model left.

Hym arrived thirty minutes later, accompanied by their driver/chaperon, a burly, bearded, six-foot Scot known as Big Mac.

Wayne gave a cursory glace towards the photographer, then turned on the Scotsman. "You don't have to follow us about like a lap-dog, you know. Why don't you go for a ride? Pick us up in a couple of hours."

"I've been told to stay with you," replied Big Mac.

"*Who* told you?" snapped Wayne.

Gary grinned, sheepishly. He knew why they were being chaperoned. These were orders from Phil Lemont. Wayne was to be watched at all times.

"*Who* told you?" repeated Wayne, angrily.

"Phil Lemont. Wherever *you* go, *I* go."

Wayne sighed and raised his eyebrows at Gary. "Can you believe that? What does he think we are? Two little kids?"

Gary continued to grin.

The photographer called out to them, "I take it you two are Hym."

"Well, we're not the London Philharmonic, are we?" tutted Wayne, irritated that they hadn't been recognized.

The photographer had been in their company for thirty seconds and already he hated them.

"Dressing-room's over there," he said curtly, pointing to a small room next to the studio kitchen. "If you'd like to get changed, I'll finish setting up the lights."

Wayne and Gary headed for the room.

Big Mac followed them.

"You're not coming into the dressing-room too!" said Wayne. "I don't care what Phil told you. You can wait outside." He dragged a chair from the dressing-room and placed it near the door. "Here! Sit *here*! If we need you, we'll call you. Until then, sit quietly and read your paper."

Big Mac sat silently, fantasizing what he'd do to this kid if he didn't have a mortgage, a wife and three children to worry about.

The photographer shot two rolls of the lads in their denim and then suggested that before they changed into their Paul Smith jackets, he'd do a couple of rolls without shirts.

"No!" said Wayne.

"It'll look good," the photographer assured him. "You've got great physiques. It'll look really good."

"No!" Wayne was adamant.

"Why not?" asked Gary. "He's right. It'll look great."

"I'm not showing my body," replied Wayne. "Not beside yours."

"Why not?" from Gary.

"Because I haven't had a chance to get to the gym in weeks. That's why."

"Neither have I."

"No, but you're younger than me! And your body's looking better than mine, lately. I don't mind having shirtless photos done on my own. But not when I'm standing beside you."

The photographer felt that the boy just needed a little persuasion. "I'm sure you're just being modest," he said.

"Listen!" Wayne snapped. "I know what I'm being! Do as you're told and take the shots that the record company asked you to take! Right?"

Big Mac looked up from his newspaper, wondering what he was going to have to report back to Phil Lemont.

"Right!" the photographer snapped back. "So get changed, eh?"

They did.

They were ready before the photographer had finished altering the back-drop and adjusting the lighting.

"Won't keep you a moment, lads," he said, trying to sound unfazed by Wayne Fielding's unnecessary outburst. "Why don't you wait in the dressing-room. I'll yell when I'm ready."

"Is there a phone I can use?" asked Gary.

"In the front office," replied the photographer. "Press three to get an outside line."

"Who are you calling?" asked Wayne.

"My mother," replied Gary.

"What for?"

"Because I'm going there for dinner tonight. I want to tell her what time I'll be there."

"Aren't you coming for a drink afterwards?"

"No."

"Why not?"

"Because I'm going to my mother's, that's why!" He began to head for the office.

"Don't forget to ask for her advice as to what shots we should have done next," Wayne called after him, sarcastically.

Gary took no notice of the jibe.

Wayne returned to the dressing-room and stared into the mirror, checking his appearance. He removed Gary's bag which had been placed on the make-up surface in front of them, so that he could get closer to the reflection, inspecting his eyes and nose for any

94

unwanted particles. He noticed the tiniest of spots beginning to redden on his chin and sighed. He hadn't brought any powder with him. Gary nearly always carried some, being more prone to pimples. He searched his partner's bag ... and found nothing with which to hide the blemish. He dived deeper into the bag and eventually discovered the tiny make-up box, buried beneath Gary's diary.

And he was immediately curious!

He crossed the dressing-room and checked that the door was shut ... then he returned to the diary and opened it, flicking through page after page until he came across:

Saturday 9th February.
Phil picked me up at two and drove me to some studio in Knightsbridge. Brilliant place. Layed down two tracks: "Gone On You" *and* "Save It". *Rough mixes were brilliant.*

The colour drained from Wayne's cheeks. He closed the diary and pushed it back into the bag, just as Gary entered.

"She's not in," he said.

Wayne, still in shock, mumbled, "Who isn't?"

"My mother. I've left a message on the answer-phone."

"Brilliant," said Wayne under his breath. "Brilliant."

"Ready, lads!" called the photographer.

Wayne turned to Gary. "He's ready!" he said. "He's ready to take photos for absolutely no reason whatso-ever."

Gary stared at him, wondering what was coming next.

"Because," continued Wayne, "by the time these photos are in the mags, Hym won't exist, will they?"

Gary tried to smile. "What are you talking about?"

"Hey, Gary!" said Wayne, trying to make his voice sound light: trying to sound as though he'd been suddenly inspired. "I've got a great idea for a song."

"Really?" Gary responded flatly. He knew Wayne was up to something.

Wayne, still sounding excited, added, "Yeah. It's called, 'Gone On You'. Brilliant title, don't you think?"

Gary reacted quickly, surprised at his own inventiveness. "So, you fell for it, did you?"

"What?"

"My diary. I *knew* you'd been reading it! That's why I left it there for you! That's why I wrote about making the demos. Just to catch you out! And that's exactly what's happened."

"Don't give me that! I've never touched your diary before!"

"And you shouldn't be touching it now!" yelled Gary. "It serves you right for sticking your nose in!"

"BJ was right! *I* was right! You and Phil have been planning your solo career."

"Give over!"

Wayne grabbed the boy by his shirt collar and dragged him across the dressing-room. He began screaming out, hysterically, half-crying, half-groaning, "You evil back-stabbing…" With a forceful upper-cut he punched into Gary's eye. A second blow smashed into the boy's mouth.

Big Mac rushed into the room and tore the two apart.

Gary slumped against the wall and slid to the floor, blood running from his mouth, his eye already swelling. Wayne collapsed to his knees, taking the boy's head in his hands, whispering, "Oh, Gary. What have I done? Oh, no! I'm sorry." His breathing was heavy. "I'm sorry! I'm sorry!"

The photographer stood at the door, staring at them in disbelief.

"Well ... what a pretty sight," he said. "The next shots'll be a real turn-on for the fans, won't they?" He turned to Big Mac. "Get these idiots out of here," he ordered. "And tell Blunt Edge that if they want to keep this quiet, they'd better settle my invoice pronto!"

Chapter 18

At first, Bob Jamieson disapproved of Terry Smith's presence in the recording studio, but on hearing the boy's voice he flashed a smile of acceptance at Jim.

"Bit better than you, isn't he?" he said.

"Just a bit," laughed Jim.

The studio was small, a private business venture for a professional sound engineer, on contract to Triumphant Records. Terry recognized the name of Keith Bell immediately as the co-producer of Billy Druid's album, *Blue By Blue*.

"Best LP I've ever heard," he said.

Keith naturally took to the lad straight away and was determined to get the best result he could from the song.

He spoke to Terry through the talk-back system. "We're just winding back."

Terry adjusted the cans and cleared his throat. He made a thumbs-up sign through the glass partition to the control room, where Jamieson and Buckley smiled back, encouragingly.

"OK. Standing by. Let's go for a take," said Keith.

There was a pause.

"Tape running."

Terry listened to the intro, then sang:

> *"He's circlin' way up in the sky*
> *Reachin' out for the sun.*
> *Ten thousand eyes pursuing him*
> *Since the fall has begun.*
>
> *Who let the sparrow die,*
> *Now that he's learned to fly?"*

His lone voice, high and haunting, filled the control room. Terry was the only one able to hear the backing as he sang into the microphone. He knew it was only a demo. He knew it didn't matter if the end result wasn't perfect, but it was important to give it everything he'd got. Terry Smith was, for just the one afternoon, standing out from the crowd in the way he wanted to stand out. Not as an inferior being, but because he was talented. He'd become the focal point for three adults, two of whom he respected. And even the third had smiled at him. Jamieson had actually smiled at him! And all because he could sing!

> *"Falconers, black, with birds of prey,*
> *Mean to bring him back down.*
> *No small bird has the right to fly*
> *Far away from the ground.*
>
> *Who let the sparrow die,*
> *Now that he's learned to fly?"*

Keith Bell brought up the guitar track a little. Then the drums.

"Not bad," said Jamieson. "Not bad at all."

"Not bad?" grinned the engineer. "He's brilliant!"

> *"Thinking he can take it,*
> *Hearing crowds upon the ground jeering.*
> *Though he thinks that he can make it …*
> *He never will!"*

Chapter 19

Two years previously

Wayne took the tube from St John's Wood back to his council flat in London's East End. The session at the Abbey Road studios had been shorter than he'd expected as the engineer had known exactly what he'd wanted. He and two girl session-singers had sung the lines:

> *"...And I lit another cigarette*
> *Though I haven't smoked in years.*
>
> *All alone on the freeway...*
> *Yeah, alone on the freeway..."*

And that was it. Rock superstar Pete Shannon's latest masterpiece was recorded in Los Angeles. Mixed in New York. With new backing vocals added (before the remix) in London. No wonder he goes on from success to success, thought Wayne. All that time and money spent on one single, the title track from the new album.

Joe Fisher, Pete's famous, overweight, cigar-smoking manager had supervised the session and, when satisfied that the singers had done a good job, handed them the money – in cash, as always.

During the short tea break Wayne had thought about telling the girls (and letting Joe Fisher overhear) that he'd been short-listed for a new duo being formed by Phil Lemont, with the possibility of a recording deal with Blunt Edge. The pair would be called Hym. Two young, very well-built lads. Great idea. One had already been chosen, Gary Brenn. Fantastic voice. Wayne would find out today if he'd been lucky enough to pip Ashley Gibb, another session-singer, well known in the industry, at the post. He finally decided not to say anything, not wanting to be left with egg on his face if he failed to secure the deal.

There were no messages on his answerphone and it was almost eight o'clock. Surely Phil Lemont must have come to a decision by now? He made some tea and half-watched *The Avenue*, his mind on far more important issues.

Christine wouldn't be home from the studio until midnight, though he'd expected her to have rung, just to see if he'd heard anything. He wondered if she were jealous.

Stuck in that children's programme, spending every day talking to a pig and a rabbit, well aware that had she been in the right place at the right time *she* might have been in Wayne's position, on the edge of stardom.

They'd met at Beat 2, one Saturday night, a year

earlier. And Wayne had to admit that it was only because he'd recognized Christine Dilks as the presenter of the pre-school puppet show, *Pigsty and Hutch*, that he'd approached her, offering to buy her a drink. And they'd climbed the steps to the gantry overlooking the dance floor and watched, through the flickering strobe, as five hundred ravers, glistening with sweat, gyrated to the latest sounds from Manachic. And as the go-go dancers took their positions on the rostra in the centre of the dance-floor, teasing the punters by bumping and grinding in their ripped T-shirts and jeans, Wayne reached out and gently stroked Christine's arm.

The phone rang.
  "Yes?"
  "How yer doin'?"
  "Who is it?"
  "It's Phil Lemont."
  "God! Tell me!"
  "It's on!"
  "D'you mean you want me?"
  "Welcome to Hym."
  "I can't believe it."
  "*Believe* it!"
  "When do we start?"
  "Come and see me tomorrow. At eleven. Meet Gary."
  "Brilliant!"
  "'Bye."
  "'Bye."

That was the *good* news. The *easy* part really. Now came the hard part. Now he had to explain to Christine how

103

it had to be. For the sake of his future, for the sake of the fans for whom Hym was being marketed, Wayne Fielding couldn't be seen to be anything but single and available! He couldn't risk it. Christine had to move out. Back to her own flat. They could still be friends. Communicate by telephone. See each other from time to time in a mutually convenient place. A secret place. Where nobody would recognize them. Where nobody would recognize *him*, Wayne Fielding ... pop star!

Christine sat on the edge of the bed and sobbed.

"I don't believe what I'm hearing. For God's sake Wayne ... have you gone mad? You can't just throw me out. What have I done?"

Wayne stood at the opened wardrobe, taking out blouses and skirts, folding them and putting them into Christine's suitcase. He looked at his watch. It was nearly one o'clock in the morning. He thought he'd explained it all very carefully. He didn't want a fuss. He just wanted her to leave. Couldn't she see how important this was? After six years of auditions, countless demo-tapes, meetings with prospective managers, he'd now cracked it. Not only a personal manager, but probably a recording contract into the bargain. It was all he'd ever wanted.

"But you said you loved me."

"I did. I *do* love you, Chris. But I can't just throw away the chance of becoming a pop star. Can't you see that?"

Christine rushed across the room and slammed the wardrobe door. She dragged the half-folded blouse from Wayne's hand and screamed out, "Stop *doing* that!

I'm not going, Wayne! I'm not going! I love you!"

Wayne lowered his voice to a whisper, "Keep it down, will you! Do you want the whole block to know?"

Christine fell on to the floor and curled up into a ball, sobbing, "I don't believe it. Tell me it's not true, Wayne."

Wayne walked to the kitchen. "I'll make you some coffee."

They sat on either side of the kitchen table, sipping coffee, not looking at each other. Christine's eyes were bright red, the tears still rolling.

"I'm sorry, Chris. Really I am," sighed Wayne. "Although it might all seem so new to *you* – like I've decided all this on the spur of the moment – I promise you that I've been thinking about this from the day we met. I knew that if the big one ever came along … it would have to be different between us."

"Then why didn't you *tell* me on the day we met?" shrieked Christine. "I'd never have moved in with you if I'd known."

The doorbell sounded.

"That's the cab," said Wayne.

Christine stared at him, in horror. "Oh, no," she whispered. "You've even called me a cab. You *are* serious. You really mean me to go … in the middle of the night. Without any warning."

She stood and walked, zombie-like, to the door.

"Your things," Wayne reminded her.

"*You* want them out … you *throw* them out!" replied Christine. "Just like you've thrown me out." She opened the door.

"Car for Miss Dilks," announced the cabbie.

"Yes. Thank you. Will you wait downstairs? I'm just coming."

The cabbie left.

"I'll never forget this as long as I live," said Christine. "It's killed me. And this whole thing will kill you too, Wayne."

Wayne's face hardened. "Don't blackmail me, Chris. If you try anything then I'm sure the press would just love to hear about the private life of the best-loved children's presenter on television."

Christine stared at him, unable to take in all she was hearing. "I didn't mean that, Wayne," she said calmly. "I wouldn't dream of doing anything like that. *I* wouldn't hurt *you*. Not for the world. I *love* you. That's not what I meant at all."

Chapter 20

Jim had slept soundly, content in the knowledge that Terry Smith had given "Sparrow" everything he'd got. It'd been a great day in the studio and Keith Bell had delighted them all by saying that it was one of the best demos he'd ever produced.

The phone rang early.

"Hi! It's Keith," the voice announced. "I've been on to somebody about your boy."

Jim was hardly awake, particles of sleep still holding his eyelashes together. "My boy? Terry Smith, d'you mean?"

"The A&R man from Sloop Records'll see you. When can you get there?"

"How about two minutes ago?" Jim laughed.

"Tomorrow morning," said Keith. "About ten, with one of those cassettes I ran off for you."

They tried not to get too excited as they waited in Sloop's palm-filled reception, sipping slot-machine coffee from polystyrene cups. An overweight, greytempled businessman in a pin-striped suit sat opposite. The smell of his cigar-smoke hung heavily in the air.

"It'll all come to nothing," said Bob Jamieson. "He won't like it."

Jim Buckley understood the playing down. It was the best way to avoid disappointment. After all, success in the pop industry couldn't be this easy. Their first song. Their first demo. Their first visit to a record company.

But just *supposing*, he thought. Already he could hear his record on the radio; see it entering the charts. He was giving up teaching, moving from bedsit to detached house, from Mini to Merc.

"Anything's possible in this business," said the fat man as he tapped ash from his cigar on to the soil of an ailing yucca. He leaned forward and offered a plump, ring-covered hand to Jim. "Joe Fisher," he said.

Jim and Bob introduced themselves. "We're here to see the A&R man," explained Bob.

"Oh yeah? Nice guy," said fat Joe.

Jim told him why they were there. "We're teachers." They told him all about their song-writing, their demo and their sixteen-year-old pupil with the incredible voice.

Joe listened, seemingly interested. He'd heard it all before, but he listened, nonetheless. Then it was his turn.

"I manage Pete Shannon," he said.

"Really?" replied Bob Jamieson, trying to appear unimpressed, sounding as though he met managers of pop superstars every day of his life.

Jim recalled that Pete Shannon was on the Sloop

label. He'd even bought a couple of his singles when he was at college.

"I think they're a bit worried here," Joe went on. "I'm starting my own independent label and Pete's contract with Sloop is up for grabs next year. So they can't do enough for me here at the moment."

"You aim to take him away from Sloop, then, do you?" asked Jamieson.

Joe shrugged. "Probably. Depends on what they've got to offer in the way of up-front readies."

The phone at the reception desk buzzed and the secretary picked it up.

"Second floor, room seven," she called to Jim and Bob.

Joe Fisher, aware that he'd impressed them sufficiently, pulled a business card from his top pocket. "If you get no joy, give us a call," he said. "I can't promise anything, but if your boy's as good as you say he is, I'm prepared to listen."

They knocked at room seven.

"Yeah?" shouted the A&R man. He was talking to someone on the phone in a cod Mid-Atlantic drawl, his feet up on the desk, leaning back in his swivel-chair. There wasn't a glance towards Jim and Bob as they entered.

The room was plushly furnished: grey, thick-piled carpets, more palms. Spotlights on the ceiling carefully picked out framed gold discs on every wall and most, they noted, were Pete Shannon's. For minutes they stood, feeling uncomfortable, waiting for the phone call to end.

"Don't give me that, pal!" he suddenly shouted into the phone. "D'you really think I'm that green?" He slammed down the receiver, slid his legs from the desk and stared at the two men opposite him.

"Yup?"

He was younger than both of them.

"Keith Bell said you'd see us," Jim almost stammered, feeling like a schoolboy in the Head's study.

"Oh, right," he said. "What you got? Cassette?"

Jim handed him the demo.

They expected to be offered a seat, but he obviously intended to keep this meeting as brief as possible. He swivelled round in his chair and put the cassette on to play.

Jim's mouth was dry. Please let him like it, he thought. But in his heart of hearts, he knew. His dreams of instant fame and fortune were already beginning to drift away.

The intro started. The man's face was expressionless. As Terry Smith sang, a shiver of excitement shot along Jim's spine, but still the A&R man's face gave away nothing. He switched off the machine and swivelled back with the cassette in his hand.

"Nope," he said.

"But you haven't listened to it," protested Bob Jamieson.

"I've heard enough," he said. "It's not right for us. Try one of the indies."

The phone rang and he picked it up. "Yup?"

Jim and Bob left the office.

Chapter 21

To the accompaniment of a Latin-American beat, the snake wound its way through the long grass towards her. It slithered across her bare foot and out of vision. A naked man appeared from behind the tree and faced the woman. She moved forward, her voluptuous body, tanned and oiled, touching *his*. She reached up into the tree and picked an apple, shiny and green, and handed it to the man who smiled at her and took a bite. She sang,

> *"Before the myrrh and frankincense*
> *Before we lost our innocence,*
> *Before the storm; before we changed.*
> *I wonder, could it be the same?*
> *Woh woh, yeah yeah,*
> *In Paraíso."*

The video had outraged guardians of morality across the USA and, in many of the cities throughout the mid-west Bible-belt, copies of the new Sherry

Barbin album had been publicly burnt on bonfires, in a religious protest that almost equalled the one which had been spearheaded against the Beatles when John Lennon had declared that his group was more popular than Jesus.

MTV had transmitted the offending video just once, removing it immediately from their play-list as the howls of protest swept like wildfire across America. Pirated copies sped right across Europe and within seven days of the release of the single, "Paraíso" had shot to the top of the American charts. Sherry Barbin was ecstatic, not least because she'd removed Patcha from that coveted number one position.

Wayne ejected the video. He and all the other guests who'd attended Buck West's party the previous week had been handed complimentary copies, along with the CD single. Just seeing her again had made his blood boil and he could hardly believe it was only a week ago: so much had happened since then. Firstly there was the removal of Hym from the Sherry Barbin Roadshow and then the threat of his being replaced by some unknown singer. And now, after the fight with Gary, there was this obligatory appointment with BJ at Blunt Edge. "Ten o'clock Monday morning. Don't be late! Or else!"

Wayne ate a piece of toast with marmalade and drank a cup of tea. He didn't have much of an appetite, knowing for sure what would happen today. They wouldn't remove him. They couldn't do that. Not with the Japanese deal in hand. But there'd be more warnings and threats and he really felt that if BJ pushed him too far he'd have to tell him everything. He'd have to tell him what Gary and Phil were up to: that BJ's suspicions were well founded. That it was *Gary* who was planning a solo career and that if Blunt Edge's contract wasn't watertight with Phil Lemont then Hym was yesterday's news and all that money spent by Blunt Edge to promote Hym as "The Band for the Future" would just disappear down the drain. Yes! If it came to it, Wayne had no doubt that he'd let BJ know exactly what had been going on behind all their backs! That'd be one in the eye for Phil Lemont. And for Gary Brenn.

He arrived, by cab, dead on ten o'clock and made his way straight to BJ's office where, without knocking, he entered and sat.

"Well, you've really blown it this time, haven't you?" said BJ calmly. "I can hardly believe that you've deliberately made yourself unemployable in the business you're supposed to love so much."

"Oh, come on!" replied Wayne. "It was a disagreement which led to a scrap, that's all. We're in each other's pockets almost twenty-four hours a day. It's no wonder we get on each other's nerves."

"A scrap?" gasped BJ, incredulously. "Have you seen Gary's face this morning?"

"No."

"If you ask me, you've got the makings of a psychopath."

"It can't be that bad," sneered Wayne. "Two little punches. That's all I gave him. Anyway, I apologized to him. It won't happen again."

BJ stared wide-eyed at the boy. "I don't think you

know what I'm saying, Wayne. Of course it won't happen again."

"It *won't*."

"No. I *know* it won't. It won't happen again because you won't be seeing Gary again."

The realization hit him. "What do you mean?"

"I mean you're sacked. Dumped!"

Wayne's mouth dropped open.

"And it's a wonder Gary isn't suing you for assault into the bargain."

"You can't dump me!" There was a tremor in his voice.

"I've already done it, son!"

"But what about the Japanese deal? What about the book?"

"It's worth cutting our losses *now*! We can't have you taking Blunt Edge to the brink of disaster. We've got to rethink our strategy and see if we can salvage the company without Hym."

"You can't," said Wayne. "You know we're the only act making you money."

"Yeah, but we happen to think that Gary might just be a bit more popular than you. We're launching him as a solo act."

"Who's *we*?" asked Wayne, already sure of the answer.

"Phil Lemont and Blunt Edge. Gary's been making some demos; laying down a few tracks. He's good. He's *very* good!"

So he *knew*! Gary and Phil had come clean.

Wayne began to shake. "*I'm* good! He's no better than me."

"But *he's* not a maniac, is he?"

"You *can't* dump me!" He was becoming desperate. "What about my contract?"

"We haven't got a contract with *you*, Wayne. Blunt Edge have a contract with Phil Lemont for a group called Hym."

"But if you deliberately stop Hym from existing…?"

"Look, son, if you insist that we honour our contract with Hym, we *will*. We'll replace Gary with another singer. A new partner for you. I'm not saying that he won't have a voice like a fox on heat. I'm not saying that the songs *we* choose for you to record will be hit material and I'm not saying that the distribution will be all that it might be, but if you insist that Blunt Edge honour their contract with Hym, then that's what we'll do!"

"You creeps!" exclaimed Wayne.

"Not *us*, Wayne. *You!* You've had so many warnings. And you've taken no notice whatsoever."

"Couldn't you give *me* a solo deal too? I could make it on the strength of Hym. And I can write my own material. I don't need Gary Brenn."

BJ was astounded. "A solo deal? You? Get outta here!"

"Please, BJ," begged Wayne. "I know I can do it on my own. I never wanted to be part of a duo anyway. I'm a solo performer."

"There's no room in the charts at the moment for *two* young, male … body-builders!" stated BJ. "There's only room for *one*. And that's Gary. He's younger than you. He's better-looking than you. And he can sing better than you. Gary Brenn is going to be *the* number one pop singer in Britain within the next few months. No doubt about it. And you, son, are washed up!"

Wayne stood. "That's what you think!" he said. "I'll show you! I'll make you eat your words. You and that creep Phil Lemont. And Gary Mr Nice Guy Brenn! I'll show the lot of you!"

"Get out," hissed BJ. "Get out of my sight!"

Wayne returned to his flat, panic-stricken. What was he going to do now? He had to find another manager. And quick. He had to get a solo recording deal while Hym's latest record still lingered at the bottom of the charts. He had to write a smash hit. And he had to get to number one before Gary Brenn. He had to!

And he had to have someone to talk to. Hym had taken up all of his time over the past two years and he'd lost touch with all his old friends. He suddenly realized there was nobody to turn to. He'd been so obsessive about his work that everything else in his life had taken a back seat. But it wasn't too late to get it all back. Those friends whom he'd ignored while Hym's career was on the up, those who'd rung and found him unresponsive and often downright offensive, would surely understand the pressure he'd been under. Most of them had been Christine's friends too and they'd surely kept in touch with her. Wayne looked up the number and dialled Christine's flat.

She would be delighted to hear from him. Probably come over straight away with a bottle of wine. And they'd probably cuddle up as Wayne told her everything. And he'd ask her advice.

There was no reply. Not even an answerphone. Then he remembered. It was Monday. She'd be rehearsing. He dialled the BBC.

"BBC. Good morning."

"Can I have the *Pigsty and Hutch* production office, please."

He waited to be put through.

The PA picked up the phone. "*Pigsty and Hutch.*"

"I'm sorry to bother you," said Wayne. "Could you tell me if the cast are rehearsing at the Centre today, or at the rehearsal block?"

"The rehearsal block," she replied. "Do you want me to connect you?"

"No thanks," said Wayne. "I'll call back later."

He looked at his watch. Twelve o'clock. He grabbed his coat and made a dash for the Underground.

As he crossed the road from North Acton station towards the rehearsal block, it seemed to Wayne as though he'd never been away. He'd visited here with Christine at least once a week, watched the rehearsals, chatted with other members of the cast, lunched in the canteen. So much had happened in the past two years as he'd gone from obscurity to stardom. And he wondered just what Christine's reaction would be as they came face to face.

The Underground had been pretty well empty. Just a few old people who'd obviously never heard of Hym and one young man, mid-twenties, who'd flashed a smile of recognition and then passed along the carriage without bothering him. But now, that was about to change. A group of young schoolgirls, in their lunch-break, were outside the rehearsal block, autograph books in hand, waiting for any famous faces that might appear.

"Wayne!" screamed one of them as he entered the forecourt.

They all rushed towards him, pushing their books and pens into his hands. And he grinned as he signed each autograph while exchanging words of affection with the excited fans, thinking, if only they knew that from today, Hym no longer exists.

He entered the lobby and approached the desk, but the security guard had seen him surrounded by the clamouring girls and, half-recognizing him as "one of those pop singers" waved him on with a smile.

Wayne eyed the board and noted that *Pigsty and Hutch* was rehearsing in room four. He decided to take the lift to the top floor and wait for Christine in the canteen. They'd be breaking at one-thirty. They always did!

He paid for a ham salad and a glass of white wine and sat on a central table where he could see and be seen. He remembered that the last time he was here he was thrilled to see Dickie Clews on the next table and Cyndy Beckworth queueing for a cheese omelette and he remembered stammering, "Hi!" to Meg Dowel on the stairs as she and he and Christine left the canteen together. But that was when he was a nobody. Now he knew that less famous artists than himself would be nudging their lunch-companions and whispering, "Isn't that ... whatsisname ... from Hym?"

He saw Gail enter the canteen with a script under her arm. His eyes followed her as she paid for a few lettuce leaves and some grated carrot and searched for a corner table, where she wouldn't be noticed. That was the difference between actors and puppeteers, he thought. Actors love to be the centre of attention. Puppeteers only come to life once they've got their hands up their alter-ego. Once she was seated, Wayne picked up his plate and his glass of wine and crossed the canteen to join her.

She stared at him for a few seconds.

"Wayne!" she suddenly gasped. "How lovely to see you. How *are* you?"

"I'm fine," he said. He'd forgotten how much Gail resembled the rabbit which she operated. The long, unblinking lashes perched above those lazy, expressionless eyes and the two front teeth which, when resting, overlapped her bottom lip. "And how are *you*?"

"Very well," she replied, adding quickly, "My goodness, haven't you made a wonderful success of your career. I think Hym are fantastic."

"Thank you," he smiled. He kept his eye on the door, waiting for Christine to enter. "It's been great fun."

"I bought your first single," she said.

"Thank you," he grinned.

He was sure he saw her nose twitch.

She picked up a piece of lettuce and nibbled it between her front teeth. "So what are you doing here?" she asked. "A television special?"

"No, nothing so grand, I'm afraid," he replied.

"Oh!" She sounded surprised. "The papers said that you'd come home from the Sherry Barbin tour to do a special."

"Well, you know what the press are like."

He kept eyeing the door.

"What's she like? Sherry Barbin? I think she's *wonderful*! What's she like?"

"Wonderful."

He saw Albert, who played the pig, pop his head round the canteen door, grimace at the length of the queue and disappear again.

"Wasn't that Albert?" asked Wayne.

"Yes." She twitched her nose again and lifted a forkful of grated carrot to her mouth. "Gone off to the pub, I expect. He doesn't need much of an excuse." She leaned forward and whispered, confidentially, "Actually I'm a bit sick of working with a pissed pig."

Wayne tried not to laugh.

"Have you seen Christine recently?" she asked. Then added, "Of course you haven't. You've been in America."

"No. No, I haven't seen her," he responded. "That's why I'm here. I thought I'd buy her some lunch."

Gail put down her fork and stared at him. "Wayne! You don't mean you've come here to meet Christine?"

"Yes."

"But she's not with us any more. She left ages ago."

Wayne was taken aback. "Left?"

"Yes. Didn't you know?"

"No."

"Ooh, yes. It was about … well, almost two years ago. I'm really surprised you don't know."

"But why?"

"I'm not really sure," explained Gail. "Nobody is. She just came in one day looking absolutely ghastly.

It was the day of the producer's run. Anyway, she couldn't carry on. She was really strange. They sent her home and we had to cancel the recording and were told we'd have to do all that week's episodes the following week. At first we all cursed her, but then when a new presenter suddenly arrived on the following Monday morning and we were told that Christine had left, having had some sort of breakdown, we all forgave her, of course. Nobody's seen her since. I've rung her loads of times but there's been no reply, so whether she's moved or not, no one knows." She took another mouthful of carrot. "So, now tell me," she said, "what's Gary Brenn like to work with? I do find him dishy."

Chapter 22

Joe Fisher had expected the call. Only one demo in a thousand ever caught the attention of Sloop's A&R man. Joe also knew that unless there was something really special about the boy, there was little chance of him taking Terry Smith under his own management wing. But he *was* looking for virgin talent for his new indie label and he'd promised to listen to the demo.

At first sight of the boy, flanked by his teachers, Joe stifled a laugh. He was fairly good-looking behind those appallingly unfashionable glasses, but with the mousy, badly cut hair, the scruffy jeans and the dirty, scuffed trainers, Terry Smith looked no inch a pop star. But Joe spoke kindly to the boy, directing questions in such a way as to extract some information about his background. For the most part Terry was monosyllabic, frightened that in saying too much he would reveal that he was a gypsy. That had to be hidden at all costs. It had nothing to do with his singing; nothing to do with this probing gorgio. If

Terry Smith were to make it to the top, it would be *in spite* of his background, not *because* of it.

Joe ran the cassette three times in a row, not saying a word between plays. But Jim noticed the excitement in the fat man's eyes. His smile broadened to a wide grin as the song reached its third conclusion.

He looked at Terry. "You're no Pete Shannon, lad," he said. "But you'll do. Let's give it a go."

Longing for a celebratory drink, yet aware that he'd promised to deliver Terry back to the campsite, Jim arranged to meet Bob Jamieson later that evening. He drove the boy along the M25, unable to contain his bubbling excitement. Terry seemed amazingly cool.

"Aren't you pleased?" asked Jim.

" 'Course I am. It's what I've always wanted."

There was a long silence.

"Do you want me to come in and tell your mother?"

"*I'll* tell her," said Terry.

"Don't you go getting any ideas about leaving school yet though, Terry," warned Jim. "Exams *first*, me ol' matey!"

"What do I need exams for?" asked Terry.

Jim was unsure if he were being serious.

"To fall back on, of course," he said. "It's not secure you know, this recording business. If it all goes wrong you'll need those qualifications to get a proper job."

"A proper job?" Terry turned up his nose at the prospect.

Jim pulled up outside the campsite and Terry climbed out.

Jim wound down the window. "Think about it, Terry," he said seriously.

"I've been thinking about it for years," replied Terry. "And *nothing's* going to stand in my way!" He was about to walk off but stopped, then turned and popped his head through the open window. "Mr Buckley ... thanks!"

As Jim turned the corner he saw Maureen walking in the direction of the campsite. She recognized the car and waved.

He waved back.

What's she doing around here? he wondered.

Wayne poured himself another large gin and tonic, hoping to anaesthetize himself before the programme started. He'd wondered at first if it would be better to go out to a pub rather than to stay at home and watch Gary on the Sandy Dukes Show, but then he realized that sooner or later he'd have to face the fact that Gary Brenn wasn't just going to fade into obscurity. Blunt Edge and Phil Lemont were determined to make him into a huge star and Wayne knew that he'd have to face up to that fact and to fight the good fight, competing for the number one slot with a record of his own.

He sipped on his gin.

It was all easier said than done. The material that Wayne was writing now was far superior to the songs he'd co-written as a member of Hym, and a substantial amount of his savings from the royalties from Hym's early hit records had been spent on the hire of a recording studio, session-musicians and a producer. But still he hadn't found a decent manager to take him on. Two whole months and not a bite. He couldn't understand it. Surely any pop manager worth his weight could see that Wayne Fielding had the potential of being Britain's number one pop idol?

Feeling very much alone, Wayne had tried to contact Christine several times but there was never any reply to his telephone calls. Eventually he went to Christine's flat and having knocked and waited for ten minutes, he was informed by a neighbour that Miss Dilks had gone to Spain.

"To Spain? Are you sure?"

"Yes. I'm watering her plants for her," replied the old woman. She coughed on the cigarette hanging from the corner of her mouth. "She's paying me," she added proudly. "I'm not doing it for a favour. It's a proper job."

"But how long has she been away?" asked Wayne. "I've been trying to get her for ages."

"Months," she explained. "And she said she didn't know when she'd be back. But I know she was thinking about looking for a place to buy out there." Then she added, taking Wayne into her confidence, "I hope she doesn't come back yet awhile. I need the money."

"Where in Spain?" he enquired.

"She's doing it by standing order. Straight into my bank." She grinned. "It's a *proper* job," she repeated.

"Do you know whereabouts in Spain she's gone to?" he asked again.

"Majorca," she said. "Hold on. I've got the address somewhere."

She disappeared into her flat for a few minutes before

returning with a piece of paper. "Here. I've copied it down for you."

Wayne looked at it.

"Menorca," he mumbled. He wasn't surprised.

"Yes. Majorca. It's very hot there, isn't it?"

Menorca. That's where they'd taken their two holidays together. And Christine had said *then* how great it would be to live there. To run a little bar. Away from all the pressures of show-biz.

"*I* wouldn't like it," coughed the woman, the ash on her cigarette about to drop on to the landing. "All that heat. Can't be good for you."

"Thanks," said Wayne. And he left, clutching Christine's new address.

"First there were two of them..." announced Sandy Dukes.

The girls in the audience screamed.

"...Well-built ... good-looking ... talented..."

They screamed again.

Dukes grinned. "A bit like me, really."

The audience laughed.

"And now there's only one!"

"Gary!" screamed one, lone girl. The rest laughed.

"Gary Brenn!" shouted Dukes.

Hysterical screams.

Gary entered and sat in the questionee's chair. He smiled at Dukes, then grinned and waved at the excited fans who screamed even louder.

Wayne wondered if Gary had taken all the Hym fans with him. The mail had certainly dropped off: from thousands of letters each week to the odd twenty sent on by the record company.

"You've gone solo," said Dukes, a slight surprise in the voice.

"Yes."

"Why *is* that … when Hym were doing so well?"

"I just needed to be on my own. I don't think Hym were heading in the direction that I wanted. I want to do more ballads and serious stuff and Hym was a bit too lightweight."

"But aren't you worried about losing these faithful fans?" Dukes gestured towards the audience.

The fans screamed again. Gary smiled at them.

"No. I'm still doing *some* up-tempo stuff, but … well, it won't be quite so commercial as before. We're doing … I mean *I'm* doing…" he laughed. So did the fans. "…An album with all sorts of stuff on it."

"So what about the fights then, between you and Wayne Fielding?"

"What fights?"

"Isn't that what most of the papers have been telling us? That's why the split took place, isn't it?"

"No. Not at all."

"No fights?"

"None."

Dukes teased him. "Not even an itsy-bitsy argument?"

Gary laughed. "No."

"So you and Wayne are still great mates."

"Yes."

"You go out and have a pint together, do you?"

"We're both so busy."

"But you would, if you weren't so busy?"

"Sure."

"How was the Sherry Barbin tour?"

"Great."

"You enjoyed touring the States?"

"Loved it."

"And you built up a huge following there, we've been told."

"Yup."

"So why suddenly return to London before the tour was finished?"

Gary grinned.

"Bit silly, wasn't it?"

"I wasn't feeling too good," replied Gary. "I was very tired. And my manager suggested I came home … to rest."

"Which you didn't."

"I came home."

"And launched yourself as a solo performer within a couple of months."

"As soon as I got home I realized that it was the pressure of touring I couldn't stand. I was OK as soon as I got back home."

"You were homesick."

"You *could* say that."

"And Wayne?"

"He was fine. He wanted to carry on with the tour, I think. He's got a lot more energy than me."

"What's *he* doing now?"

"I believe he's getting a new single together."

"So … there's a possibility you'll both be battling for the number one slot in the charts?"

"Possibly."

"But you'll be there first, because your new single's out today."

The smoke began to rise from the adjoining set.

"That's right. I'll have to keep the number one slot warm for him."

"So let's hear it."

"OK."

Gary crossed to the set, climbed on to the rostrum and picked up his guitar.

Dukes talked to camera.

"A number written and produced by star hit-maker, Kendrick Simpson…"

Wayne gasped.

"…called 'Take It All' … this is Gary Brenn!"

Sounding even more commercial than any Hym record had ever sounded, "Take It All", the sure-fire number one hit which BJ and Phil Lemont had asked Hym to record was, without doubt, destined to make Gary Brenn the hottest pop act in Europe … *and*, possibly, on the other side of the Atlantic.

"No!" screamed Wayne at the TV screen. "No! You've sold out!"

The phone rang and Wayne picked it up, shouting into the receiver above Gary's smash-hit.

"Yes?"

"I see you've got it on too," said the voice.

Wayne reached for the TV's automatic control and switched off the sound.

"Who is this?" he asked.

"It's Rica Stubbs." The voice was husky with a strong East London accent.

Wayne was surprised. He hadn't seen the pop journalist for months, long before Hym had set off on the Sherry Barbin tour. She was the only journalist he liked. Apart from being very street-wise, unlike most of the upmarket journalists he'd spoken to, she was also very young. Not yet twenty, she was still on the same wavelength as the pop fans for whom she wrote her columns. And she really got down to the basics: she socialized with the pop stars and found out what really made them tick. She'd also given Hym some good press and particularly favoured Wayne.

"Hello Rica," he said, surprised. "I haven't seen you for months."

"So ... what do you think about the record, then? Our little Gary's debut?"

"What do *you* think?" He put the ball back into her court.

"Number one."

"Do you think so?"

"Don't you?"

" 'Fraid so."

Rica laughed. "I thought you'd be happy for him. He was very nice about you, wasn't he?"

"Yeah. The two-faced…"

"Now look, Wayne," she said, sounding serious. "We all know what happened, of course, but some of us are keeping mum."

"I appreciate that," replied Wayne. "I've noted which ones have done the dirty on me."

She laughed again. "I knew you would. Anyway, I've got something to tell you, Wayne. But keep my name out of it, OK?"

"OK."

"You've been trying to get a manager, right?"

"It's impossible."

"And do you know why?"

"Tell me."

"The three managers who've shown an interest in you … Dick Shanty … Saul Baker and…"

"…Conrad Matius," concluded Wayne.

"Right."

"Well?"

"They all contacted Phil Lemont before giving you a final 'yes'. They loved your music. All three of them. But they wanted to know from Phil exactly why you left Hym."

"And?"

"Phil told all of them that you were poison. That if they took you on, they were in for all sorts of trouble."

"Did he now?" Wayne began to shake with fury.

Rica sounded sympathetic. "Look, Wayne … if you don't want to die altogether in this business, you'd better get Phil to shut his mouth."

"Thanks, Rica," he said.

"*I* know it's all bull," she added. "It's obvious that Phil Lemont is trying to kill you so that Gary Brenn has no competition. So I'd get someone on to it if I were you. Get a lawyer. Threaten to sue for libel. You've got to do something. And PDQ."

"You're an angel, Rica," said Wayne. "Bless you. I won't forget this." He hung up.

He knocked back the last of his gin before picking up the receiver again and dialling Phil Lemont's home number. Phil picked up the phone. Wayne hung up. Then he called for a taxi.

"Wayne?" said Phil. His face paled. "What are you doing here? Come in, mate. Have a drink."

"Thanks, but no thanks!" hissed Wayne. "What I've got to say can be said on the doorstep. I'm warning you now, Phil," he went on, "if you keep blackening my name, I'll make sure I kill Gary's chances of ever becoming the idol you've set out to make him."

"I don't know what you're talking about," stammered Phil. He was afraid that Wayne would become hysterical. He'd heard everything from Gary. *Almost*.

"You've told three managers who were thinking of taking me on that I'm poison. I *know*, Phil. I'm sure you'll be surprised to hear that I've got a few friends left in this business. And they've told me. So I'm warning you that when the next prospective manager rings you, you tell him I'm a good boy, right? I don't want any of this poison bit or I shall go straight to the press and tell them the truth. I shall tell them exactly what Gary and I got up to in Tokyo!"

"What are you talking about?" sneered Phil.

"Just mention Tokyo to Gary ... and watch his face," snarled Wayne.

"This is all a wind-up!" snapped Phil. "I'm not stupid. Gary hasn't got any secrets from me..."

"Really?"

"Really! If anything happened in Tokyo, I'd've known. I was there! I'm warning you, Wayne ... you start any nonsense and we'll sue you for every penny you've got."

"So you do that!" said Wayne. "That would be great publicity for Gary, wouldn't it? I'd stand up in court and swear what happened is true. I'd even tell the same story under a lie-detector."

"Any scandal would ruin *you* too!" said Phil, who was now beginning to wonder if there was any truth in what the lad was saying.

"If you carry on doing what you're doing, Phil, I'm ruined anyway! But if I go down because of what you're telling people, I promise you I'll drag Gary Brenn, Blunt Edge, Kendrick Simpson and *you* down with me. And I can do it! Believe me! Just you ask Gary to fill you in on the details."

Phil was shaking. He now knew that Wayne wasn't lying.

"Right?" said Wayne.

"Right."

Wayne turned to leave.

Phil called after him.

"If I keep my mouth shut…?"

"Then so will *I*!" replied Wayne.

He left.

Chapter 23

Terry's life seemed to change within the space of a few days. It was easier to dream, now that the dream appeared tangible. And the more that he dreamed, the less he felt trapped, which made the site seem less muddy, the trailer not quite so claustrophobic.

Between visits to Joe's London office, he played his guitar with renewed fervour, creating new songs, jotting down ideas. And Maureen was always there to encourage him.

Jim was disappointed, but not surprised, to find that Terry hadn't returned to school after the Easter break. There was a note in the register, coldly informing him that Terry Smith had found employment and wouldn't be taking his exams.

"Do you blame him?" grinned Bob Jamieson when Jim showed him the note. "I wish I were in his shoes."

Jim called Joe Fisher on the school secretary's phone.

"It's got nothing to do with me, Jim," protested Joe. "That's entirely up to Terry. And quite honestly," he added, "I don't think it's got anything to do with you, either. He's not a kid. He's a young man with a bright career ahead of him … just so long as he plays his cards properly."

Jamieson whispered in Jim's ear, "Ask him what's happening about the record."

Jim waved the comment aside. Terry's decision to quit school seemed, at that moment, of greater importance.

"Ask him about the record!" insisted Jamieson.

"All right. We'll see you on Saturday," said Jim. " 'Bye." He hung up the receiver.

Jamieson was irritated. "So?"

"He said it was all Terry's idea."

"Jim!" hissed Jamieson. "If you think I'm gonna lose any sleep over some pikie quitting school, you've got another think coming! It's our song I'm concerned with."

"We've got to chew over the details on Saturday," said Jim.

Maureen was just leaving the campsite as Jim arrived. He'd noticed the girl's odd behaviour at school. She was usually the centre of attention; always surrounded by friends. Today she'd not spoken to anyone. Her split with Rosetti was obvious to all. He looked unwell, his eyes sunken and dark. Not once had they glanced at each other during registration, and at break Jim had seen him in the library, seemingly engrossed in a text book. His cronies had temporarily abandoned him – even Scotty, who now spent every minute of his free time with Tracey.

"Hello, sir," said Maureen. "Come to see Terry?"

Jim realized the girl knew everything.

"He's about to have tea," she said. "That's why I'm leaving."

Jim forced a smile and headed for the Smiths' trailer.

Mrs Smith welcomed him like an old friend. She'd been delighted with Terry's news and couldn't thank Jim enough for his help.

"Is he gonna be famous, sir?" asked Billy.

Jim realized how difficult it would be to break through the euphoria, but he tried, nevertheless, to put the facts, pure and simple, to a sullen Terry and his attentive family.

"That's daft," said Mrs Smith, finally. "If my Terry stays on at school and this record comes out and he's too busy with his exams to push it, what happens?"

"He needs those qualifications," sighed Jim. "Can't you see? There are thousands of lads out there, all in the same position as Terry, all trying to get record deals…"

"I've got one!" snapped Terry. "That's the difference!"

"He may have success with this record," Jim continued, "but then again he may not. *Then* what?"

"He can make another one," countered Billy.

"I know thousands of unemployed people with qualifications," exaggerated Terry. And as an after-thought, "I hate school!"

Mrs Smith decided, politely, to bring the conversation to a close. "I've got to get tea ready, Mr Buckley," she said. "I'm going to the hospital tonight."

136

Belcher thumped loudly on the trailer door and entered.

"Ain't yous finished tea yet?" he asked, ignoring the presence of the stranger.

"This is Mr Buckley," explained Terry's mother. "Him who got Terry into the singing."

"Is it now?" said Belcher. There was no handshake. No smile. He turned and spoke gruffly to Terry. "Come on. You're old enough to get your own tea. Your mother'll be late."

"I'm sorry," said Jim. "I was just leaving."

He felt intimidated, afraid – and he wondered what role this bear-like man played in Terry's life.

"Will you think about what I've said, Mrs Smith?" he added as he headed for the trailer door.

"I'll think about it, Mr Buckley," she replied, softly. "But it's Terry's life, ain't it?"

Terry followed Jim from the trailer.

"I'll see you off, sir."

The two walked in silence, threading their way through the mud and clothes lines, towards the main gate. Jim had said all that he'd needed to say.

"I know you're only thinking about what would be for the best, sir," said Terry. The sullen expression had been replaced by one of frustration. "But you're wrong. It's not what's best for *me*! You … you don't understand." He was trying to teach the teacher. "You could *never* understand!"

"Try me," replied Jim, kindly.

There was so much Terry wanted to say. If only he could explain. If only he could speak to Jim in the same way that he spoke to Maureen. He wanted to tell him how grateful he was for the introduction to Joe. How grateful he was for not being treated any differently from the other kids, just because he was a gypsy. How grateful he was to the teacher for always standing up for him when the likes of Rosetti started the name-calling.

Grateful! Grateful! Always grateful!

Gorgios would never understand!

How could they?

"I can't," he said, and he turned and walked back to the trailer.

Chapter 24

Joe Fisher pushed the contracts across the desk to Terry. "Get your father to sign there," he said. "And here. And this one. Both copies."

"Can't my mum do it?" asked Terry.

"It doesn't matter to me who signs 'em, just so long as they're signed."

Terry flicked through the papers, noting the hereinafters, the hithertos and a host of indecipherable phrases.

"It's standard," said Joe. "Don't worry. I won't bleed you."

Terry's new manager opened his cocktail cabinet. "A drink, eh? What d'you want?"

"Nothing, thanks," replied Terry. "Unless you've got some Coke."

Joe smiled and reached for a bottle of Perrier.

Terry was keen to get straight down to business. "What about the song, then? You said you wasn't sure."

"Oh, I'm sure, all right," said Joe. He poured

himself a large scotch on the rocks. The ice cracked as he brought the glass to his desk. "I'm sure it's not right for *you*. It's a good song, but it's too folksy."

"I don't know what you mean," said Terry.

"Sounds like a cast-off from The Byrds." He laughed. "But then you've never heard of The Byrds, have you?"

"No."

"If we were doing that song now, I'd go for a strong, solo female. It's definitely not for you, sunshine. You wouldn't stand a chance with it." He took a sip from his drink. "I'll have to look around. Got to be a ballad, though. I've no doubts about that."

"What about one of *my* numbers?' asked Terry.

Joe was mildly surprised. "I didn't know you wrote."

"I can't write it down," said Terry. "But I've got some good ideas."

"Well ... make a cassette for me and I'll see if there's anything we can use."

Terry's thoughts immediately turned to Jim. How would he take the news that his song wasn't going to be used? He wondered if he should go and see him and break it to him gently. Tell him that it wasn't his fault and that it was Joe's idea. Say that he was sorry and how grateful he was for everything.

He decided he couldn't do it. He wondered why he should! Anyway, that was Joe's problem. He'd leave it to him. It was time to stop worrying about Jim Buckley. It was time to stop being continually grateful. There was his career to concentrate on. And from now on ... that was all that mattered!

140

Chapter 25

"Mum?"

"Yes. Why aren't you here, darling?" she asked. "Have you forgotten you were supposed to be coming for Sunday dinner? You said you'd be here by six."

He carried his phone across to the window, making sure there were no chinks of light peeking through the drawn curtains. "No, of course not. I've been trying to call you for the past hour."

"Oh, sorry, Gary," she said. "Your father called from Dublin. Then Auntie Liz, and you know how she never stops talking."

"Family trait," he said.

She laughed, warning, "Now, watch it!"

"I'm not there for dinner," he explained, "because I can't get out of the flat."

"What do you mean? You've locked yourself in?"

"Don't be ridiculous, Mum," he grinned. "The place is besieged by fans. That's why. Hundreds of them. They've been here for ages."

She laughed. "I hope they're not trampling all over that tasteless communal lawn."

"They were," he said, "when I last looked."

He heard the chant begin again:

"We love you Gary, oh yes we do!"

"You'll be asked to pay for it," said his mother. "It's a good job you're rich."

"I wish!" he grinned. "Still maybe after today…"

"Why? What's happening today?" she asked.

He sighed. "It's Sunday, Mother!"

"Yes, dear," she replied. "I know it's Sunday. You were coming for Sunday dinner, remember?"

"But now I'm not."

"Now you're not."

"We were going to listen to the Top Forty on the radio, together," he reminded her, "before we sat down to eat."

"So we were," she said. "To see where your single has got to."

He crossed the room and walked into the den, which now housed his mini-recording studio.

"Are you moving about?" his mother asked. "Your voice has gone a bit distant."

"Yes," he replied. "I'm putting the radio on."

"Had I better go and do the same thing?"

"If you want to see if 'Take It All' has reached number one, yes," he said. "Phil thinks it's very likely."

Then he heard the chant from the street,

"Number three,

"Number three,

"Number three…"

More than one fan had brought along a radio.

Then followed the chorus of "Take It All" … sung by a choir of hundreds.

"Don't bother, Mum," he said. "It hasn't made it."

"Oh," she whispered, sounding extremely disappointed. "Never mind, darling. Perhaps it'll get there next week."

"Perhaps," he said.

Chapter 26

Joe's call came as a bombshell. Jim had arranged to meet Bob at the Woodman for a lunch-time pint, before they set off for London. The phone dragged him from the shower.

"It's Joe. Got a bit o' bad news, I'm afraid."

Jim didn't know what to expect. "There's nothing wrong with Terry, is there?"

"No. He's fine. Like a kid with a new toy."

Then Jim knew. It had to be the song.

"It's 'Sparrow', I'm afraid."

"You want a re-write on it?"

" 'Fraid not," replied Joe. He sounded genuinely upset about giving the news. "It's just not right for Terry."

"We've got plenty more material we can work on." Jim was clutching at straws.

"I think I've got something else lined up," explained Joe."

"Another writer?"

"Yes."

"What about using ours on the B side?"

"Got that too," said Joe. "I really am sorry."

Jim couldn't speak.

"You see, Terry's decided to write his own stuff."

"I see."

He *didn't* see. He didn't understand how the boy could do this to him. He hung up. How was he going to tell Jamieson?

Chapter 27

Bury The Rabbit had gathered at the Rosetti home not, as they thought, to rehearse – but because Franco wanted to talk to them. The Leroy twins, in their usual self-contained manner, sat as one, flicking through magazines from the coffee table, occasionally whispering to each other. Scotty had brought along Tracey and had been dropping hints since their arrival about the girl's talent.

"She can really sing, you know, Ray. Better than Maureen."

Ray Rosetti hadn't shown much interest in the idea and Franco was totally against it.

"No more girls, Scotty," he stated firmly. "They only cause problems. Now that Maureen's gone, it's just the four of you."

He sent the sulking Tracey into the kitchen to chat with his wife, whilst he talked business.

"I've booked a studio for the seventeenth," he informed them. "No demos this time. We're going for the real McCoy."

Scotty looked at Rosetti and smiled.

"But you keep it quiet! Right?" Franco went on. "Not a word at school. I'll call your parents and tell them the same. I don't want any more irate phone calls from the Head, telling me that the group's interfering with your studies. We'll cross that bridge when we come to it. Right?"

"Right!" said Rosetti Junior.

The Leroys nodded.

"So keep it hush-hush! And that includes you, Scotty!"

Scotty looked at him wide-eyed and innocently.

"I don't want Tracey to know."

"She won't tell anyone, Mr Rosetti," protested Scotty.

"The school-boy game-playing's over, Scotty," threatened Franco. "I'm putting one hell of a lot o' readies into this venture and I promise you faithfully, one word from you to Tracey and you're dropped! I've already got another drummer lined up. Right?"

Scotty fell silent.

"Right?" repeated Franco.

"I won't say a word, Mr Rosetti," said Scotty.

"I think you should record that song you did in class," said Maureen as they carried the cassette recorder into the back room.

Terry had arrived at Gran's house with a carrier bag filled with scraps of paper and a dog-eared notepad. His head buzzed with tunes and he couldn't wait to start.

" 'Call On Me'?"

"Yes. It's a good song."

He pushed the door to, so Gran couldn't hear them.

"First things first," he grinned, as he removed his glasses and put them into his shirt pocket.

He placed the cassette recorder and his guitar on the sofa-bed and then put his arms around Maureen's waist, pulling her gently towards him.

"Come here," he said, softly, leading her further into the room.

He gently brushed his lips against hers.

She responded, lifting her hands and running her fingers through his hair, sighing. How different this was from Rosetti's forceful kisses. Naively she'd believed that that was the way it had to be. Terry had shown her it wasn't. This was ... beautiful. His kisses made knots in her stomach; made her tingle.

He leaned back, looking deep into her eyes. They seemed cloudy; her pupils dilated. He wondered if his looked the same to her.

"I know I shouldn't say it," he said. "I know it's too early and all that ... but ... I think I love you."

"Oh, Terry," she moaned, softly. "Terry, *I* love *you*. I'm sure I do."

> "*Call ... call on me,*
> *You'll find a stranger.*
> *Gotta change,*
> *It's not the same any more.*
> *I've been down, I've been a loner.*
> *Don't intend staying one any more.*"

Terry switched off the cassette. He had all he needed for Joe.

148

"I'll go and make us some cocoa," said Maureen.

"Don't forget me," smiled Gran, as she wheeled herself into the room.

The cushion behind her shoulders was beginning to slip and Terry crossed to her and straightened it.

"Thank you, love." She grabbed his hand. "How's your dad, Terry? Any better?"

"Just the same," he replied. "I've got this awful feeling…"

"He'll be all right," said Gran.

That's what people had said to her, when her Ralph was ill, all those years ago. But they were wrong.

"You'll see," she repeated. "He'll be all right."

There was a brief silence as Terry's mind wandered to the hospital and back.

"Does this record man … Joe … know anything about it?" asked Gran. "I mean, if anything *should* go wrong and you have to go off somewhere for a few days. Not that it will, I'm sure, but…"

Terry knew what she meant.

"No. I haven't told him. I haven't told him anything about my family. Well, not much anyway."

"He knows you're a gypsy, though?"

Terry looked down at his feet. "No," he mumbled.

"Oh!" said Gran. She was surprised. Surely he wasn't trying to keep *that* secret?"

"I don't want him to know. I don't think it's got anything to do with him, do you?"

She smiled at him. "No, Terry. You're right. What's it got to do with anybody?"

Maureen eventually entered with a tray of mugs. "I've put two sugars in yours, Terry," she said.

"He doesn't want any sugar," chuckled Gran. "He's sweet enough."

The cocoa was comforting, reminding Terry of days long past, when he and Billy, dressed in their pyjamas, cheeks burning and smelling of soap, had sat on Dad's knees and had been bounced up and down as he sang to them. Travellers' songs. Songs that Terry couldn't remember now. And they'd giggled and saved their last drop of cocoa until it had gone thickly cold, not wanting to finish it; not wanting to be told it was time for bed. And Terry had asked if he could play "barbers" and had raked forward Dad's Brylcreem-covered hair with his fingers until it covered his eyes completely, which had made them all laugh, including Mum.

And he realized that he'd probably never hear Dad sing again. And he knew that he was expected to go and see him; that it was his duty. But how could he make Belcher understand that he just couldn't bear it? The kidney bowls and the white-capped women in cloaks, squelching along the polished corridors in their flat-bottomed shoes. And the smell of antiseptic, trying to cover but only highlighting the smell of sickness, including that of his father. And he felt guilty. And bad. Deep down bad. Not at all sweet. Not sweet, Gran. No. Not at all sweet!

Chapter 28

The studio, booked for the day, was Triumphant; the producer, Keith Bell. Rosetti sang the lyric and meant it:

> *"Got no intention o' waitin' for the giro*
> *Or windin' up servin' in a burger bar.*
> *I'd bust a gut before I give up losin'*
> *My faith in me to make it as a star…"*

The Leroy twins joined him,

> *"And it's easy,*
> *You know what I mean?*
> *Easy!"*

Scotty looked on with pride, his drum-track already laid down and approved by all.

Keith mixed and re-mixed until he and Rosetti were satisfied with the result. It was the first time he'd taken the reins as a producer in his own right. No co-production deal on this one, therefore this single was as important to him as it was to Bury The Rabbit. And Keith Bell had connections at Sloop Records. He rang the A&R man and arranged an appointment.

Chapter 29

Wayne had decided to leave on Wednesday, not wanting to be around for Thursday's television transmission of *Chartbusters*, knowing that Gary Brenn had reached number three with his first solo single, "Take It All".

He'd taken an indirect flight to Menorca, deciding to stop off at Barcelona, where he'd avoided La Sagrada Familia and other great tourist attractions and headed straight for a bar on La Avenida Diagonal. Here he felt he could eye up the girls without the fear of being recognized, Hym having failed to make any impression on the Spanish charts. He'd returned alone to his hotel at five o'clock the following morning, feeling even more of a loser. His confidence had gone ... and with it, he felt, his ability to pull.

On the short flight to Menorca his spirits lifted a little, remembering the great times he'd spent here with Christine; and he couldn't wait to see his ex-lover again and to tell her that he wanted her back.

From Mahon airport he took a taxi to Christine's address in Sol Del Este, but on finding the house boarded up with a "for sale" notice outside, he returned in the same cab to Mahon Port, searching for familiar faces among the few bars that were open on this mild, sunny lunch-time.

He found Enrique in the empty Ka De We croissanterie, sitting on a bar stool, chatting to the barman.

"Wayne!" yelled Enrique. He leapt up from his stool and rushed forward to greet him. "*Cómo estás?*"

Mixing Spanish and English customs, he kissed Wayne on both cheeks and then shook his hand vigorously.

"Have you seen Christine?" asked Wayne.

Enrique stared at him, blankly.

"*Mi novia*, Chris."

"Chris! Ah, *sí*! Chris."

"Yes. Chris. Have you seen her?" Wayne repeated.

"*Ahora vive aquí.*"

Wayne looked across at the barman. "*Habla inglés?*" he asked.

"A little," he grinned.

"Would you ask him if he knows where I can find my girlfriend, Chris?"

The barman spoke to Enrique. "*Quiere saber dónde está su novia … Chris.*"

Enrique explained and the barman translated that Christine had opened a tapas bar in the small town of Alayor.

"Does she open at lunch-time?" asked Wayne.

"I don' thin' so," replied the barman. "There are no' too many tourists yet, but ees possible she making prepared the bar."

"*Gracias*," smiled Wayne. He picked up his bag, preparing to leave. "See you soon, Enrique. *Hasta pronto.*"

Enrique smiled warmly at Wayne. "*Sí*," he replied. "*Hasta luego*, Wayne."

The door was open.

Wayne entered and walked straight up to the bar counter. Christine had her back to him, loading a shelf with bottles of cola.

"Hi, Chris!"

She turned. And stared in disbelief. "Wayne!"

Wayne looked her up and down. She was more beautiful than he'd remembered.

"You're looking great," he said.

"You too." Christine could hardly speak. She felt her heart fluttering. "What … what are you doing here?"

"I've come to see you."

"Oh!" She began to tremble. "Why?"

"Do you mind?" asked Wayne.

"No. No, of course not," replied Christine. "I'm … I'm delighted." She crossed the bar, closed the door and locked it. "Let's go upstairs to the flat," she beamed. "It's fantastic to see you. I want to hear *everything*. I'll make some coffee and you can tell me all." She wrapped her arms around him. "I can't believe it. You look … wonderful!"

They climbed the stairs to the apartment.

"You sound as though you're not very keen on England any more," grinned Wayne.

"England?" She laughed. "There's nothing wrong with dear old England. But I wouldn't want to go back."

"Not even for me?" teased Wayne.

Christine reached over and affectionately touched his cheek. "Not even for you, Wayne … much as I love you."

"Do you?" asked Wayne. "Really?"

"Love you? Yes … of course. I loved you from the day we met and I still feel exactly the same way."

"I still love you too," said Wayne. "I haven't stopped thinking about you since the day you left."

Christine grinned. "Since the day I was thrown out, you mean." She quickly changed the subject. "So how's Hym?"

Wayne was surprised. "Don't you know?"

"I don't know *anything* … except this little island," laughed Christine. "I only ring home occasionally to talk to my mother and she's hardly likely to know anything about Hym, is she? I don't think she ever knew that *I* was on the telly."

"Well … we've split," Wayne informed her. "Hym finished months back."

"Really?" Christine sounded shocked. "Why? I thought you were going great guns."

"It's a long story," explained Wayne. "But basically it was Gary Brenn's doing. And I was ripped off by the record company." He paused, reflecting on the horror stories he could, but wouldn't, tell Christine. "So I've been looking for a solo deal."

"Any luck?"

"Not yet," said Wayne. "But there's plenty of time.

I'm getting a tape together."

"So where do you live now?"

"Same place."

"The same?" Christine gasped. "I thought you'd be living in a mansion by now."

"I'm still waiting for royalties," Wayne explained. "I've had *some*, but I've spent it on making demos."

"*Vámonos*, eh?" suggested Christine suddenly. She wanted to change the subject. "Let's go to the beach."

The mile-long Son Bou was almost deserted, the summer beach bars still in the early stages of construction.

"This brings back memories," sighed Wayne. "We were really happy here, weren't we?"

"On top of the world," agreed Christine. "That's why I had to return. And as soon as I got here I knew that this is where I want to stay."

They strolled among the dunes, enjoying the first rays of summer, knowing that within two weeks the Brits would be pouring on to this beach from the nearby hotels.

"But a tapas bar?" smiled Wayne. "It's hardly you, is it?"

"We'll see," replied Christine. "If I can't make a living at that, I'll try something else."

"Here?"

"Of course, here. This is my home now. The only reason I've got for going back to England is to pack up the flat."

"But won't you miss being in the business?"

"Show business?" She laughed. "No way, José! I

was never as ambitious as you, Wayne. I didn't have to be the number one. Except in love."

"I'm so sorry for what I did to you," said Wayne. "It's been one of the greatest regrets of my life."

"Never regret what you've done in life," preached Christine. "Only regret what you *haven't* done." She put her arm around Wayne's neck. "Life's so short, Wayne. You have to grab what you feel is right. Grab the opportunity when it comes your way, 'cause it may never come your way again. And that's what you *did*! You wanted to be a pop star. You had the chance. You took it. And you succeeded. Good luck to you."

Wayne stopped walking. He put both his arms around Christine's waist and looked into her eyes. "I didn't realize how much I missed you," he sighed. "I love you, Chris."

Christine smiled. "And me, you."

After a restaurant supper of red mullet and salad, they returned to the flat above Christine's new bar and drank *anís con hielo* and continued to talk about old times. Wayne hadn't felt so happy since those early days, when after a few glasses of wine they'd excitedly discuss their dreams for the future. And he suddenly realized that he could, after what he'd been through, give it all up and settle down here … with Christine. They could run the bar *together*. Possibly put on some entertainment nights, with Wayne singing to the punters. It could, if they worked hard at it, become the number one bar on the island. The "in" place where tourists and Spaniards alike would gather to be entertained by British ex-pop star … Wayne Fielding.

158

Christine yawned and stretched. "Well," she said, "sorry to be a bore but I'm whacked. Bedtime, I think."

Wayne couldn't wait to hold his lover in his arms once again. Why had he thrown all this away? It was so, so stupid.

"Where are you staying?" asked Christine. "Are you in a hotel?"

Wayne laughed, sure that this was a joke.

He playfully ruffled her hair. "I'm staying here, of course."

"No," said Christine, gently. "No, Wayne. You're not staying here."

"But…"

Her voice hardened. "I'm sorry, Wayne. I love you very much. Still. But – it's over."

Wayne began to feel faint. "What?"

"It's over, Wayne," she repeated. "I've got a new life here. And I like it. I like it a lot."

"I'm going to join you here," said Wayne. "I've decided to pack in the pop career. I'd rather be with you. I love you."

"I love you too, Wayne," smiled Christine, tears welling in her eyes. "But I've had to cope without you."

There was a knock on the door.

Wayne knew immediately. "No," he whispered.

"Yes," affirmed Christine. "A taxi. I ordered it while you were preening yourself in the bathroom. Getting yourself ready for a night of passion with your ex-lover. The one you almost destroyed. Remember?"

"Oh, no … please, Christine," Wayne begged,

wrapping his arms around her and squeezing her tightly.

Christine felt she would choke on the tears she was fighting to hold back. Her throat was tight. She could only just speak.

"Go, Wayne. Now!"

"But I love you!" He began to sob.

"So?" replied Christine. "What's that got to do with anything?"

"But it's one o'clock in the morning!" screamed Wayne. "You can't just throw me out! I've got nowhere to go."

"How about the airport?" suggested Christine, coldly. "There's a flight back to London in the morning."

She picked up Wayne's bag and pushed it into his hand.

"*Go!*" she said.

Chapter 30

Maureen was, to say the least, impressed by the luxury of Joe's office-cum-home. She'd never visited this part of London's West End before; never seen the opulent houses which stretched from the bustle of Oxford Street northwards to the Planetarium. Terry led her through a cobbled mews past neat rows of newly painted cottages to a three-storeyed semi, the detached side of which overlooked a narrow alley.

Terry pointed upwards to a tiny window, where the wisteria ceased its climb. "That's his office," he said. "The rest of it is his house."

Maureen sighed. How different it was from the Belling Estate. She and Gran had always considered themselves fortunate not having to live in the flats with their graffiti-daubed lifts. So often in the past, when she could still walk with the stick, Gran had laughed about her "lucky legs".

"Without these we'd've been put up there," she'd say, pointing to the eighth floor of Toronto House.

Terry pressed a bell and waited.

"Yes?" a voice asked on the intercom.

"It's me, Joe," said Terry.

There was a buzz as the door opened, automatically. How posh, Maureen had wanted to say, but she bit her tongue, determined not to be a disappointment to Terry as they entered Joe's portrait-lined hallway.

Joe was pleased, if somewhat surprised, to meet Maureen. Her name had never been mentioned, and the possibility of a girlfriend in Terry's life hadn't occurred to him.

Joe realized he knew very little about Terry Smith's private life. He knew there was a younger brother and that both parents were living, but from the address he'd been given, he couldn't picture what sort of home the boy came from. Letters were addressed to him "c/o Jane at Berryfield".

Jane owned the land, collected the rents and allowed the use, occasionally, of the telephone. From here the electricity was generated and, for a few pence, a shower arranged. "Berryfield" looked good on paper, but Terry's appearance, in his well-worn clothes, belied the suggestion that his lifestyle was in any way grand. The more Joe had questioned, the less information Terry had offered. But now there was Maureen. And with a little coaxing, Maureen would tell him all he wanted to know.

From the Persian rug on which she stood, she gazed at the pictures, the curtains, the lamps, the chester-field with its leather upholstery. Her eyes darted from one luxurious item to another, her mouth slightly agape, looking for all the world, thought Joe, like a modern day Eliza Doolittle on her first visit to Higgins' place.

162

Maureen was suddenly aware of her awkwardness, her desire not to seem too impressed and her feeling of not belonging. Most of all, she was aware of her shoes. Had she wiped them thoroughly before she'd entered? Or had she brought dirt, or mud or, please no, anything worse from the street on to the Persian?

"Make yourselves at home," said Joe. "I'll go and get us some coffee."

Make yourselves at home. Maureen grinned within, but sat, saying, "Thank you."

Joe seemed pleased with the songs and chose two, having no doubts whatsoever that they were single material, and Terry was delighted that the A side was to be Maureen's favourite, "Call On Me". His mind dashed back, fleetingly, to the cross-country run: to Jamieson, to Scotty, Rosetti and the cut lip. And he glanced at Rosetti's ex-girlfriend now sitting beside him on the settee, and he laughed at the irony of it all.

"I'll get them arranged and book a studio," said Joe. "Just leave it with me."

The doorbell rang and he picked up the entry-phone.

"Yes?"

"It's Pete."

"Come on up, Pete," said Joe as he pressed the door-release button.

Terry knew, though Maureen didn't, that "Pete" was Pete Shannon.

"We'll go," said Terry.

Maureen couldn't understand the hurry.

As they left, Pete Shannon was just climbing the stairs. Terry shook, excited to be so close to a superstar.

Maureen's knuckles whitened as she gripped the banister on seeing the world-famous face.

"Hi!" said Pete Shannon, and he was gone.

Maureen, eyes widening, mouthed to Terry, "That's Pete Shannon."

"Yes," said Terry, trying to sound cool, "I know. I thought I told you – Joe manages him too." He grinned. "I'm gonna end up like him one day. You watch!"

Chapter 31

A list of appointments had kept Terry busy all week. There were visits to Chelsea, Fulham and Knightsbridge for his everyday wear: shirts, 501s and shoes. The hair was cut and slightly streaked.

"Just enough," said Joe, "to catch the studio lights," adding, with a wink, "it's got to look good on *Chartbusters*."

Terry's heart beat faster. This was his dream of dreams. *Chartbusters*: Horizon TV's music show where so many of today's pop superstars had begun their climb to fame and fortune.

"Do you think I'll get on it?" he asked.

"I don't see why not, do you?" replied Joe.

Terry smiled at him. The teeth were noted: they had to be polished (one was in need of a crown). The spectacles were replaced by contact lenses; Permawear in piercing blue. Fairy-Godfather Joe was preparing his male Cinders for the ball.

Terry stared in Gran's mirror at the handsome

stranger who faced him and was aware for the first time in his life of the true power of money. Maureen stood behind him, gazing at the reflection. She'd never realized he was quite so good-looking.

She laughed, "Well, if you don't make it, at least you've got the clothes."

He grinned. "I *will* make it. No doubt about it!"

Maureen left him, still staring at himself, while she went to the kitchen to prepare Gran's tea.

Terry posed, miming the guitar and noting the newly whitened teeth as he smiled at the imaginary camera. The country was tuned in to *Chartbusters* to hear the number one record. Terry sang:

> *"Gotta get myself in line,*
> *Find the words to say to you,*
> *Tell you how I feel 'cos I'm*
> *Hung up waitin' on you.*
> *You call on me*
> *When you are lonely…"*

Maureen called from the kitchen, "Terry! Come and help me butter some bread."

Chapter 32

Rica Stubbs had been offered the Rosetti interview only twenty-four hours earlier and had leapt at the opportunity. A white-label promo had been sent from Sloop Records in advance to *GO!* teen magazine's pop page and Rica had no doubt about the potential of "Easy". Sloop had obviously signed up a dead certainty in Bury The Rabbit and this debut single was a sure-fire top-twenty hit, given adequate exposure, of course. Rica couldn't wait to meet the man behind the voice. She'd seen the photo of the group, sent with the promo, and she'd liked what she'd seen.

She wasn't disappointed. Rosetti arrived at five-thirty, as arranged, just as most of the staff were leaving. He wore his scrubbed denims and sneakers, and his mother's sunbed had heightened his dark-skinned good-looks.

He contrived, convincingly, to peer smoulderingly at the interviewer through the quiff of his gelled black hair, which fell down over his dark brown eyes. He answered softly and with mock humility, taking care to use the smile on the occasions when he felt he needed to score points.

Rica Stubbs rose from her chair and perched on the corner of her desk. Rosetti, seated, looked up into her eyes. He'd heard she was young, but he was surprised to see that she was only a few years older than himself.

"So, you're still at school?" she asked.

"That's right." He laughed. "Aren't you?"

She laughed too. "Not quite," she replied.

"Yeah, I'm still at school. Year eleven. Scotty, the drummer, and I are in the same form."

"And the Leroy twins?"

"The year above. I was elected to do the interview," he added, with a smile.

"Elected?" She raised an eyebrow. "Very democratic."

"We're a team," said Rosetti. "No one person in the band is more important than the other."

"So what happens if the record's a hit?"

"How d'you mean?" He smiled again, adding, "I *hope* it's a hit."

"What happens about school?"

"I'll probably leave," he replied. "I *am* sixteen."

"And the others?"

"That depends on them. And their parents, of course."

"And if their parents want them to stay on?"

"We'll survive," said Rosetti. "We'll have to do as much promo work as possible during the holidays."

"What sort of school do you go to?" asked Rica.

"Just an ordinary, rather large comprehensive," he

replied. He seized the chance to volunteer information he felt was important to the interview. "We're all
working-class boys, you know; council houses and all
that. It's pretty rough where we live."

"And you want to get away from all that?" She was
trying to lead him to a pre-conceived byline.

"Wouldn't *you*?" said Rosetti. He smiled at her.

She smiled back. "*I did!*"

They both laughed.

"No, I wouldn't leave my roots," continued Rosetti,
still smiling, aware that she was aware of the untruthful
hype. "I'm not saying I enjoy poverty, but I couldn't
join the jet-set. I could never be part of all that. And
d'you know, Rica," he went on, "there's a lot to be said
for people like us. We've got our heads screwed on the
right way. I'm sure you know what I mean!"

She refused to acknowledge the remark.

"We know what's important in life," he said.
"Money isn't really that important."

"And what *is* important to you?" she asked.

He grinned, musing, "What *is* important to me?"

"Yes."

He stared at her. "You're really beautiful, you
know," he said.

She held his stare ... and then shrieked with
laughter.

He was surprised by her reaction.

"Give over!" she cackled. "Where do you think I'm
coming from?"

"No. I mean it," he said.

"You want good press, more like," she replied, still
laughing.

"And will I get it?" His eyes were twinkling.

"You may do," she replied, twinkling back. "You'll have to wait and see, won't you, Mr Rosetti?"

Chapter 33

Terry lay awake, against his will. He knew it was very late; probably the early hours of the morning, as he could hear few cars passing on the M25. He didn't want to reach for his watch for fear of waking Billy, who was breathing deeply and had been asleep for hours. Through the partition which separated them from Mother's bedroom, the sound of her clock ticked in rhythm with his heart. It was hours earlier when he'd heard her crying, softly; when he'd wanted to go to her and say, "It's all right, Mum. Don't worry," but didn't, because he knew, deep down, that it probably wasn't.

And besides, it wasn't like the face on the trailer door, when *he'd* cried all night, fearing that the gavvers had come to get him; when Mother had scooped him from his bed and lifted him up, forcing him to touch the shape which moved only when the wind blew, proving it was just the shadow of the elm outside, diseased and crumbling. No, it wasn't like that at all. But he wished it were. He wished he could point to the shadow of the bogeyman and say, "It'll be gone by morning, Mum, then everything will be the same as it was. With you and Dad and Billy and me, all together like before. But a bit different this time, because I'm going to be rich. And you won't have to cry again."

Tomorrow was the beginning of how it was going to be. Tomorrow he was going to cut his first disc. It would be such an important day and his desire for rest was paramount. He had to sleep! And sleep, as sleep does, kidnapped the conscious state when it was least aware, and in so doing, presented the subconscious as reality.

The coffin was open, his father's eyes staring at him. Romanies he'd never seen, but whose names he'd heard mentioned, passed by, placing small bags of coins at his father's head. Outside the tent in which the coffin lay, dozens sat cross-legged on the damp grass, some crying, a few wailing. Huge bunches of flowers, yellow and red, hung at each corner of the tent, while small, copper vases, also filled with flowers, decorated its entrance.

Terry put his hand into the coffin and touched his father's forehead. It was cold and felt not at all like flesh. His father winked an eye and tried to smile.

"Come to see me at last, eh, Terry?"

"Almost too late, Dad," the boy replied.

"Almost."

The corpse closed its eyes as Belcher covered it with the lid and began hammering in nails.

He turned to Terry. "He's gone, son. I'm your father now."

172

Then they were all outside a Romany waggon, carrying burning torches. The mourners watched silently as Levi threw his torch inside. Flames licked their way along the curtains until, with a thunderous roar, the whole waggon was burning. Sparks shot ten feet in the air as Terry watched the waggon crumble and spit.

His father rose up through the flames, shrouded in smoke, and hovered above the mourners. Terry had never seen him look so peaceful, so young. Attired in his best, with the new boots he'd bought for this special day, he smiled down at those watching.

"It's all true," he said. "I promise yous." And he drifted upwards and disappeared.

The heat grew more intense and Terry gasped for breath. He woke, sweat popping from his hair and running down his face. His pillow was soaked, his sheets no better. He sat up in bed and leaned his head on the wall, taking deep breaths and trying to reason with himself that it was only a dream. Just a dream!

I'll go and see him tomorrow, he thought. After the studio.

Chapter 34

"Come in, Mr Fielding," he said flatly. "Take a seat."

Wayne entered the bank manager's office and sat facing the bare, high-tech desk, behind which sat the glum-faced, grey-haired man.

"I'm surprised you've even seen me," said Wayne. "I usually only communicate with computers in this place."

The manager attempted a smile and failed. "I always deal personally with those who express a desire for me to do so," he replied.

Wayne took the letter from the inside pocket of his jacket and pushed it across the desk.

"It's this," he said.

The manager studied the contents of the letter and placed it down in front of him. "And how can I help?" he asked.

"That letter says I can't have any money!" said Wayne. "How am I supposed to exist if I can't draw out any more cash?"

The manager sat back in his chair. "Mr Fielding, you are already five hundred pounds overdrawn."

"Four hundred and eighty," Wayne corrected him.

"You haven't paid any funds into your account for two months…"

Wayne sneered. "Five hundred is nothing. This time last year I had thousands in there."

"And you have no overdraft facility. Of course we had to send you that letter. We only want to know when you can expect to receive more funds."

"Soon," replied Wayne. "You know what I do for a living, don't you?"

"You're a pop singer."

"Yes. And our lives don't fit into your normal little boxes. I can't tell you, month by month, what I'm going to earn. Some months it's thousands of pounds and some months it's nothing at all."

"You're not the only self-employed person who banks with us, Mr Fielding," stated the bank manager, coldly.

"All I want," requested Wayne, "is another five hundred. My royalty statement will be arriving within the next few weeks, but I must have the cash today. It's urgent."

"And how much do you expect to receive in royalty payments, may I ask?"

Wayne stood and thumped on the desk with his fist.

"*I* don't know!"

This time the bank manager managed to raise a smile.

"Well, if *you* don't know, Mr Fielding, how am *I* supposed to know?"

Wayne glared at him. "If I don't have five hundred quid today, my whole career could be in jeopardy. Please!"

The bank manager stood and out-stared Wayne. "No, Mr Fielding. I'm sorry. If you bring me a royalty statement from your record company and it looks healthy, then we'll discuss this matter further, but until then, I'm sorry. There's nothing I can do."

"I'll take my account somewhere else," threatened Wayne.

"*Do*, by all means, Mr Fielding," the manager smirked. "If anyone else will accept your overdraft, we can arrange to transfer the account forthwith."

"I'll show you!" hissed Wayne. "I'm not being written off by some two-bit pen-pusher like you." He strode furiously towards the door, opened it and turned, stabbing a finger at the manager. "You're not going to treat me like you treat all your suburban Mr Averages who borrow from this bank. I'm a star!"

Wayne left, slamming the door behind him.

The bank manager sat. "Shine on!" he mumbled.

Wayne listened to the playback of his latest demo.

"What do you think?" he asked the engineer.

"It's good," the engineer replied. "But then they've all been good, Wayne. I can't understand why you can't get a manager."

"Me neither," lied Wayne, who knew the reason. "Ten great tracks. I've got enough for a brilliant album there."

"Most of the tracks would be hit singles too," the engineer enthused.

"Do you think so?"

"No doubt about it."

"I've got to see two more managers next week," Wayne informed him, "and I've persuaded Conrad Matius to listen to my stuff again."

The track ended and the engineer stopped the tape. He was silent for a while. Wayne knew what he was about to say.

"This is a bit delicate, Wayne," he began.

"You want paying."

"It's not *me*," he rushed on. "It's the boss. He asked me not to let any more masters leave the studio until we're paid. It's not just you. We're owned money by all sorts of artists."

"But it's only this track that I haven't paid you for, isn't it?"

"No. Your cheque bounced for the last session," he stated, looking embarrassed. "The ballad."

"Oh!"

"Sorry, Wayne."

"Not your fault. It's just that I was hoping to take everything to Conrad Matius."

"We'll keep both tracks safe, of course," he went on. "They'll be locked up securely. And as soon as your cheque clears, we'll let you have the masters."

"Couldn't run off a cassette of them for me, could you?"

"Sorry."

"OK, OK," sighed Wayne. "I understand."

"So when should we re-present your bounced cheque?" he asked.

Wayne shrugged. "You'd better leave it for a few

weeks, until my royalties are in. I'll give you a call."

"Rica? It's Wayne," he said.

"Wayne?"

"Wayne Fielding."

"Oh! Hi. How ya doin'?"

Wayne detected the unusual coolness in her voice. Whenever he'd called Rica Stubbs in the past, she was always so friendly. Over-the-top friendly. He knew she fancied him. Everyone in the business knew how Rica Stubbs took a fancy to good-looking, well-built lads. And Wayne Fielding fitted that description perfectly.

"Are you all right?" he quizzed her.

"Sure."

"You sound a bit down."

"Far from it. A bit tired, but not down."

"I was wondering if you could do me a favour, Rica?" he asked.

"Go on."

"I've got another meeting with Conrad Matius next week and I'd really like him to take me on … and I was wondering if you could have a word in his ear."

She was silent.

"You still there?" he asked.

"Well, it's a bit difficult, Wayne," she said.

He was taken aback. "Difficult? I thought you knew him well?"

"That's the problem," she replied. "We're a bit too close, really. And he's just taken on some West Indian guy I recommended to him. It'd be pushing it a bit if I asked him for another favour so soon. Sorry, Wayne."

He was deeply disappointed. "S'OK. I under-stand."

"But if there's anything else I can do…"

"Not at the moment, Rica. But thanks anyway."

"As soon as you get a deal, let me know," she went on. "And we'll work on something for the press, eh?"

"Yeah. Great. Speak to you soon." He hung up.

Rosetti, wrapped in a towel, emerged from her bathroom.

"Who was that, at this time of night?" he grinned. "Another lover?"

She looked up, unsmiling, at the olive-skinned hunk before her.

"No. Not a lover," she said, somewhat sadly. She tutted and shook her head. "Although I hate to say it … I think it was just yesterday's news."

"Eh?"

She took his hand and squeezed it, comfortingly. "Not *your* problem, Ray. Not yet."

Chapter 35

Despite the lack of sleep, Terry arrived thirty minutes earlier than arranged at Denson Sound Studios, where he found Maureen already waiting for him.

"You got here all right, then?" he asked, taking her hand.

"Easier than I thought," she replied. "I've even been for a coffee."

None of the big stores had yet opened, but the sandwich bars were already dispensing freshly filled rolls to queues of people picking up their lunches before going into work. Terry pushed at the studio door, expecting it to be locked, which it wasn't. He was about to introduce himself at the reception desk when Joe appeared, looking, thought Terry, ridiculously casual for a man of his weight, in blue jeans and pink sweater, the sleeves of which were pushed up to just above the elbows.

"You look…" Terry struggled for the word, "…comfortable."

"No point in dressing up on studio days," replied Joe, as he puffed on his cigar. "It's going to be a long, stuffy day in here."

"You don't mind me here, do you?" asked Maureen.

"Delighted, Maureen," the fat man replied. "Just so long as you don't have any ideas on production."

Having shown them the studio, which was far larger than Terry had expected, Joe led them up an iron staircase to the control-room where, sitting at the multi-track machine, pushing buttons, was the producer.

"Hi!" He rose from his seat and shook Terry's hand. "Great song!" he said.

Joe introduced him as Andy Davis. "Andy was the engineer on Pete Shannon's last album, and he knows as much about production as anyone in the business."

"Should do, after all these years," smiled Andy.

There was a crackle on the huge speakers set on either side of the control-room and Andy's recorded voice boomed through them.

"Take four!"

Music followed. A mid-tempo drum beat. A piano rose in volume to equal the drums, then sank again to be swamped, almost replaced, by the sound of a wailing saxophone.

"Well?" shouted Andy, above the music. "What d'you think?"

"Love it," said Terry. "What is it?"

Joe clipped his ear and laughed. "It's the backing track to your song, you berk," he said. "What do you think it is? 'Hickory, Dickory, Dock'?"

Terry's mouth dropped open. "I don't recognize it at all," he said.

"You wouldn't," replied Andy. "Not after that awful cassette I was given."

Terry listened until the tape had finished.

"It's brilliant!" he said.

Joe grinned. "You wait till you hear the B side. They weren't easy to arrange, but Andy's worked miracles."

"We recorded them yesterday," said Andy. "A hot bunch of session musicians, including, would you believe, Rick Wain." He ran the track back to the beginning and placed the lyric sheet, neatly typed, in front of him on the control-desk. "I'll sing it to you. Show you where to come in."

After a couple of dummy-runs, Terry went down into the studio to start work, and although Joe was both surprised and delighted that Terry seemed to have "Call On Me" in the can after the third take, Andy went on and on recording until he was completely satisfied with the result.

"OK, Terry," he said finally. "Come up and listen."

Terry, his heart thumping excitedly, returned to the control-room and, having received a glowing smile from Maureen and a pat on the back from Joe, sat before the control-desk and waited to hear the rough mix of his very first single.

As the intro started, he reached out for Maureen's hand. His palm was sweaty and he clutched her just a little too tightly.

Let it be good, he said to himself. Let it be a hit.

The first verse began:

"You call on me
When you are lonely..."

Terry was surprised at just how good his voice sounded. He knew he could sing, but...

Joe winked at him. "Think you've cracked it lad!" he said. "It's got HIT! stamped right through it!"

"D'you think so?" asked Terry. "Really?"

Joe smiled. "We'll have you on *Chartbusters* within the month."

Rosetti read the review aloud,

BURY THE RABBIT. 'Easy' (Sloop)

Pop rap from four schoolboys with their eyes on the charts. Back to the classroom, lads. There's a lot to learn!

The Leroy twins grinned nervously.

"They know nothing!" snapped Scotty. "I hate that paper anyway. They never get it right!"

Franco smiled and reached into his briefcase for the second pop weekly.

"Isn't this the one you usually read?" he asked.

Scotty took the paper and flicked through it, looking for the singles review page.

"Well?" asked Rosetti, his voice trembling.

Scotty scanned the page. "No. Nothing here." He was nervous, his eyes hardly focusing. Then he saw it! He read it silently.

"Come on!" shrieked Rosetti. "What's it say?"

"I don't believe it," Scotty mumbled.

Rosetti grabbed the paper and read:

A flawless, squeaky-clean production on this debut single from Hym soundalikes, Bury The Rabbit. A trite up-tempo dance ditty about wanting to be a star. Innocuous, unoriginal and boring. In short, the perfect chart record.

"What?! Hym soundalikes?" he screamed, throwing the paper across the room.

Scotty grinned. "I thought you loved Hym, Ray."

Rosetti glowered. "If I had to pick the crappiest, most untalented couple of idiots on vinyl, Hym'd top the list!"

"It's the 'boring' bit that gets me," added Scotty. "I mean … how can he possibly say that 'Easy' is boring?"

"He also says it's the perfect chart record," laughed Franco, as he picked up the paper and began re-assembling the pages. "The perfect chart record! And that's what it's all about, lads!"

Terry was beginning to tire. His voice had cracked twice in exactly the same place, but Andy continued to direct him patiently, encouraging him to play with the song; to give it more light and shade. The producer preferred this number to the A side and wondered if Joe had made the right decision about "Call On Me".

"Let's do the third line again," he said. "I'll drop you in."

Terry listened through his cans, breathing heavily all the time, swallowing, trying to clear the clogged-up feeling from the back of his throat. The red light was on. This time the voice mustn't crack! He sang:

> *"Since then love's gone bad*
> *Losin' all we once had,*
> *Now I've no one to turn to…"*

"White?" asked Joe, his plump fingers hovering over the buttons on the coffee machine.

"Yes, please," replied Maureen.

Pretending to tire of listening to the same three lines being repeated over and over again, Joe had used this as an excuse to fetch coffee.

"Coming with me, Maureen?" he'd asked. "I can't carry four."

Now he was alone with the girl who knew everything about the boy in whom Joe was about to invest a great deal of money, the truth was out.

"A gypsy?" said Joe. "Really?"

"Oh, dear," sighed Maureen. "I'm not sure if I should've told you that." She looked worried. "Perhaps you ought not to say anything, Joe."

"Don't worry, my dear," he replied. "Our little secret. I won't say anything."

He smiled. Maureen thought the smile was genuine. But had she looked into the fat man's eyes at that very moment, she might have read a different story.

They sipped coffee and relaxed as best they could as Andy started the tape.

"You understand it's only a very rough mix?" he said.

They listened excitedly, first to "That's The Way" then to the A side.

"I'm sure it'll make it," said Andy. "It's a good song and he sounds great."

"Production is superb, of course," laughed Joe.

"Of course," grinned Andy. "That goes without saying."

Terry was silent.

Maureen lightly punched his arm. "Well, super-star? What do you think?"

"I think it's brilliant," said Terry. "I can't believe it."

The phone rang and Andy picked it up.

"Phone call for you, Terry," he said. "In reception."

Terry was surprised. "Nobody knows where I am," he said, "except…"

Maureen began to pale.

Terry's mouth felt dry.

He calmly and very slowly walked to the reception area.

Maureen followed him.

He could hardly make out the gabbled words.

"It's Billy," was all he heard. Then a choking, muffled sound. A long pause. Then again, "Hello Terry? It's me. Billy. I'm at the hospital."

Terry began to feel faint. His chest tightened. One leg trembled. He couldn't keep it still. He held the receiver away from him at arm's length, trying to hold back the news. He didn't want to hear it. Not yet. He was about to leave for the hospital anyway. As soon as he'd finished at the studio. A train from Charing Cross and then … and then that green bus … he couldn't remember the number … what *was* that number? That *green* bus … *that* would take him straight there. Right to the door. He'd worked it all out. And he'd go into the ward, past all the coughing, hollow-faced men, and up to his father's bed. And he'd see his father sitting up, looking healthy and smiling. And he'd say, "Sorry I didn't come earlier, Dad. I really am sorry. I *meant* to. *Kept* meaning to, but … it's not that I don't love you. I *do*. But…" and still he held the phone away from him, the muscles in his arm stiffening as, in the distance, he could hear Billy's voice, sobbing now and saying, "Terry? You there? Can you hear me?"

I don't want to hear you, thought Terry. Don't tell me. Don't tell me. Not now. Not yet. Please not yet!

Maureen took the phone from his curled fingers.

"Hello, Billy. It's Maureen," she said.

"Not yet. Please not yet. Not yet," said Terry. "Not today."

Maureen half-whispered into the receiver, "Oh, Billy. I'm so sorry. I really am. Yes. Yes, of course. Yes, I'll tell him."

Chapter 36

Maureen felt strangely irreverent about even *wanting* to go to the after-school disco, but Terry was obviously going to be preoccupied with his family for at least three or four days and she felt lost without him. He'd advised her not to come to the campsite for a while, as outsiders weren't welcomed at gypsy wakes.

She was sure that Rosetti wouldn't be at the disco as he hadn't been at school all week. She'd wanted to ask Scotty if Ray had got himself a job, or if anything was happening for Bury The Rabbit, but she'd figured that her curiosity could only be construed as showing interest in her ex-boyfriend. So she kept herself to herself and worked hard, spending all her free periods in the library, revising.

The toilets were, as always on Friday afternoons, bursting with girls applying make-up, brushing hair and changing clothes. Maureen decided to use the toilet on the second floor, next to 3S. Hardly anyone ever used this tiny loo, not only because it had just one mirror which was badly cracked, but also because it was next door to Mrs Sheldon's science lab, and most of the girls, even those in 6A, were terrified of her.

Maureen ran the brush idly through her hair, her thoughts on Terry and Billy, wondering how they were coping, not only with their own tragedy, but with that of their mother. Maureen, unlike most of her school friends, knew what it was like to have to come to terms with the death of a parent. She harked back to the prayers she used to say in those last few minutes just before sleep, and to the times when the chicken bone broke in her favour, allowing her a wish. And those prayers and those wishes had always been the same. "Don't let her die." She remembered the panic that used to cramp her stomach when she'd thought, what would happen if…? But it *had* happened. And it had happened to the person she'd loved most in the world. But she'd got over it. She'd never forget her mother. Never. But the pain had gone. And so would Terry's. In time.

Through the mirror, just above the NKOTB sticker which had been placed there some years before, Maureen saw the door open. Tracey entered, carrying her bag in one hand and a newspaper under one arm.

"Hello, Mo," she said. "You've decided to use the quiet one too, have you?"

Maureen cursed inwardly. She'd wanted to be alone. The last person she felt she could talk to now was Tracey. But here she was, tossing her red hair and obviously having no intention of leaving Maureen's side for the rest of the afternoon.

"Scotty's not coming," she said. "He's gone home."

"Oh," was all Maureen could muster.

"So we'll have to dance together, won't we?" added Tracey as she began putting on her eye-liner.

For minutes neither of the two girls spoke as they painted their faces, staring into the mirror, each on either side of the crack.

"Have you two had a row?" Maureen eventually asked, fearing that if she didn't make the effort to communicate, there'd be an embarrassing silence.

"Of course not," smiled Tracey. "He's got to talk business with Ray, hasn't he?"

"Has he?" Maureen tried not to sound interested.

"Yeah. It's tomorrow morning. And they haven't sorted out what they're gonna say yet."

Maureen was irritated. "Sorted *what* out?"

Tracey stared at her through the mirror. "You don't know, do you?"

Maureen turned to face her. "Know what?" she snapped.

"They're on the radio tomorrow morning. Radio Viscount. Doing an interview with Robbie Jones."

Maureen turned back to the mirror. "Really? I never listen to Viscount."

"Oh, you should!" enthused Tracey. "He's ever so good, is Robbie Jones. And he's already played their record a couple of times. He reckons it'll be a hit. Well, it will, won't it?"

"Their record?" At last Maureen understood.

"Yeah," replied Tracey. "They wanted to keep it all quiet. Mr Rosetti told them to. I was the only one who knew," she added, smugly. "But now it's all out in the open, with the reviews, isn't it?" She picked up the paper which she'd placed on top of her bag. "Have you seen them by the way?"

"Er … yes," said Maureen, not wanting to see Rosetti's name in print, realizing that she'd have to react favourably, and knowing that she couldn't.

"Weren't they good? Well *one* of them was. *Quite*."

"Yes," said Maureen.

"You all right, Mo?" Tracey looked at her through the mirror. "You look a bit funny. You all right?"

"Yes," replied Maureen. Then, "No, not really. I've got a bit of a headache. Look, I don't think I'll bother going to the disco," she said. "I don't really feel like it."

"Oh," said Tracey. "That's a shame. I won't have anyone to dance with."

Maureen headed for the door. "Sorry, Trace. I'll see you Monday, OK?"

"Yeah. See you," replied Tracey.

Maureen left.

Tracey had the mirror to herself. She ran the brush through her long, red hair and grinned at her reflection.

Maureen got up early and frantically searched for Viscount on the radio dial. What she'd said to Tracey was true. She never listened to Radio Viscount. She had no idea who Robbie Jones was, but she knew that she'd have to face up to the fact that Bury The Rabbit had released a single and that it was being given air-time.

Gran joined her, wheeling herself into the parlour,

with buttered toast for both of them sitting on her lap. She seemed excited. She'd always liked Ray and Scotty and she missed their visits. Oh, she liked Terry too. Terry was a nice boy. But Terry didn't listen to her stories in the same way as Ray and Scotty used to. Terry only smiled when she talked about the blackout and the American GIs and their gifts of chewing-gum and stockings. Ray and Scotty always laughed. Sometimes they'd laughed until they'd cried; all of them, including Gran herself. And Ray had brought her chocolates, or flowers, or a Barbara Cartland at least once a week. Yes, she liked Ray and Scotty and she was pleased they were on the verge of success.

"What's the record like, Mo?" she asked. "Is it good?"

"I don't know, Gran," Maureen replied. "I haven't heard it yet."

Chapter 37

Robbie Jones was twenty-two and ambitious. In just a few months he'd moved from hospital radio to a small pirate station on the East Coast. Now the prestigious *Saturday Morning Live* on Viscount Radio had given him the opportunity to present in-depth interviews. At first he was reluctant to lose needle time in order to talk to local dignitaries, or to discuss the whys and wherefores of the Neighbourhood Watch scheme, but on proving he was much better than he'd first anticipated, he'd now begun to enjoy the programme and already had his sights set on a future BBC TV contract.

The station itself was growing in popularity. It was the first commercial station in the area and people were already beginning to switch over from the major London independents. The *Saturday Morning Live* show had boosted the listening figures through two controversial interviews which had hit the national dailies. Robbie Jones wasn't one to mince his words. His questions were forthright and he expected forthright answers.

This morning, the hospitality room at Viscount was full. Bury The Rabbit were the least important of Robbie Jones's guests, but he always liked to have somebody connected with the pop scene in the thirty-minute slot leading to the eleven o'clock news. The board in Reception read, *"RADIO VISCOUNT WELCOMES..."* This was followed by a list of names, none of which Rosetti recognized. Bury The Rabbit was fourth on the list.

Through the glass panel which separated the reception area from the studio, Robbie could be seen, mixing from one record to another as he chatted to a young actress who was appearing in a pre-West End play at the nearby theatre. The interview, interspersed with commercials, jingles and music from Viscount's play-list, could be heard throughout the reception area, including the hospitality room. A reel-to-reel tape, set behind a locked glass cabinet, recorded the programme as it was transmitted live.

Rosetti was nervous, Scotty not quite so, as he'd realized that most of the questions would be directed at Bury The Rabbit's frontman. The Leroys had stayed away as Franco had told them their presence was unnecessary. In truth, he feared that their reticence at an interview of this kind would only be a hindrance to the group. So the Leroys sat at home, listening excitedly to the programme.

Maureen, too, was excited, but at the same time she felt, deep down inside, a sickening sense of envy. She would, had she not walked out on Rosetti, still be part of Bury The Rabbit. The feeling shamed her. She'd hoped to be noncommittal this morning, to listen as an outsider, not pre-judging. But she couldn't. She tried, but she couldn't! And there was Terry, of course. What would he be feeling as he listened to Rosetti's voice on the air-waves? Her shame grew. Terry wouldn't be listening. Ray Rosetti's interview on the radio and the fact that Bury The Rabbit had released a record before *him*, would, had Terry known about it, have been just an irritation. The death of his father was devastating.

"In just a few minutes," said Robbie Jones, "I'll be chatting to Ray Rosetti."

Rosetti gulped.

"He's the vocalist of a band calling themselves, 'Bury The Rabbit'. And this is their first single…"

Rosetti's voice sang out,

"Didn't take to schoolin'; got no int'rest…"

Robbie's production assistant led Scotty and the trembling Rosetti from the hospitality room into the studio, where the music continued to play. Robbie Jones looked up and smiled. "Hi, lads!" he said as he set up the next commercial carts.

Scotty whispered to Rosetti, "It's *live*, don't forget! So watch yer mouth."

At home, the Leroy twins looked at each other and grinned. Tracey bounced up and down on her sofa, giggling. Maureen smiled at Gran and turned up the volume.

And Terry stared into the coffin, with clouded eyes, at the man with the smart suit and new boots.

Chapter 38

Levi didn't like the look of the stranger who'd entered the public bar. Sunday lunch-time at the Three Stars had been the same for as long as the travellers could remember, and everyone who used the pub knew that the saloon was for gorgios and the public bar was for gypsies. Naturally, somebody just passing through and wanting a quick pint couldn't possibly have known, but this one *wasn't* just passing through. Levi was sure of that. The questions were there, in his eyes! He wasn't a gavver, but he had the look of one. He could have been a reporter from the local press, but Levi thought he knew all those by sight. All the local gavvers and reporters were well known since that trouble at the campsite, when Mick Mahoney had set his dog on the gavvers come to arrest him. (The day that Joshua Smith had had his heart attack.) For weeks afterwards the campsite was teeming with gavvers and reporters, leading to even more trouble; and then the RSPCA had been called in for some reason.

"Must've thought Mick's dog 'ad been starved and fancied a gavver for 'is dinner," Abi had joked. But the joke began to wear thin when stories started to appear in the press about the squalor of the gypsy camp.

"All lies!" Abi had yelled when someone had read the story to him. "All lies!"

Anyway, Mick Mahoney wasn't even a gypsy. He was a tinker. And unlike the rest of them, he'd spent most of his adult life slammed up in the starry. Though that was no reason for slamming him up this time, for something he definitely hadn't done.

"I'm sorry to bother you," said the stranger.

A few of the gypsies looked up from their beers and stared at him.

"What d'you want?" asked Levi, aggressively.

"I don't know if you can help me…" continued the stranger. He tried to avoid the eyes, by gazing at the wood panelling behind Levi's head. "But I'm a writer and…"

"What d'you mean, writer?" asked Levi. "You mean you're a reporter?"

Abi's youngest son leapt to his feet, sending a wash of beer across the table. Big Jimmy, as they called him, was the tallest of them all, unshaven and looking much older than his seventeen years. His trade as an asphalter had given him huge biceps which he always displayed and was continually flexing. The stranger was terrified.

"I hope you ain't writin' nuffink about us, mate!" he said.

"Hold on!" interrupted Abi. "How much you gonna pay us?"

The stranger began to shake.

"Look, I'm sorry," he said. "I didn't want to cause a fuss."

"You won't!" snapped Levi. "Not if yer disappear, you won't!"

Big Jimmy sat down and returned to his beer-drinking.

The others stared at the stranger, who decided it was time to leave.

Travelling through the High Street which led to the M25, the stranger passed a florist who was taking in his last tray of bedding-plants.

"You've only just caught me," said the florist. "Forgotten the wife's birthday, have you?"

"How did you guess?" He pointed to a bunch of cellophane-covered red roses in a plastic bucket. "I'll have those."

As the florist wrapped the dripping stems, the stranger made what appeared to be polite conversation.

"Do you open every Sunday?"

"Only mornings," replied the florist. "Unless we've got a lot to get ready for Monday. Then we don't open at all."

"Weddings and things?"

The florist laughed. "Not many weddings on a Monday. Plenty going to the church, but not to get married!"

The conversation was heading in the direction the stranger had hoped it would.

"You not busy tomorrow, then?"

"Only *one* tomorrow. A big 'un, mind you. Me and

the missus were up with the sparrow's fart."

"Do you mind if I ask you something?" said the stranger.

"Ask me what you want, mate." The florist handed him his flowers. "So long as it's not how much mark-up there is on red roses." He laughed.

"Is it a gypsy funeral?"

The florist looked at him. You couldn't really tell nowadays. Lots of gypsies had gone away, got good jobs, prospered. They only returned for the funerals.

"That's right," was all he said. He took the stranger's money and gave him his change.

"I'd love to see it," said the stranger. "They're usually quite spectacular, aren't they?"

So he *wasn't* a gypsy.

"This one will be," replied the florist. He pointed across the road to a closed café. "Sit in the Greasy Spoon with the OAPs if you want to see it. It passes about half past two. Should be a good 'un."

"Where's it heading?"

"Saint Barnabas', for three, right over at Sancton Heath. But I wouldn't go there," he warned. "They won't take kindly to you gawping."

The stranger thanked him and left with the roses. He threw them on to the back seat of his car and drove to the nearest telephone box.

"Well?" asked Joe Fisher.

"Saint Barnabas', Sancton Heath, tomorrow at three o'clock," he replied.

"Well done," said Joe. "You know what to do."

Apart from the old man in the white peaked cap,

searching for riches with his metal-detector, Bournemouth beach was empty. It had rained through-out Saturday night and had continued into this unusually cold June Sunday morning. Bury The Rabbit arrived in the hired bus followed by the transit, bringing the film crew and its equipment. Rosetti hadn't checked the story-board in detail, but Franco had discussed his ideas with Max, the director, who'd made a few, improving suggestions. All realized that the promo video was almost as important as the single itself, and although this coastal location was to illustrate only the final verse of "Easy", it would take the whole day to shoot.

Max looked up at the black clouds and sighed. "Flaming June!" he said. "Look at it! We'll be lucky if we get any sunshine at all today!"

"We'd better!" shivered Rosetti. "This is supposed to be Antigua!"

Before noon, although the clouds had cleared completely and on parts of the beach the sand had dried to a powdery gold, it was still very cold.

"Right!" said Max. "Let's move it!"

Still wearing their overcoats, scarves and gloves as a protection against the bitterly cold wind which was blowing in from the sea, the crew began setting up in the sand – school desks and chairs, a large blackboard and easel and three authentic-looking prop palm trees.

Bury The Rabbit returned to the bus with Elaine, the make-up supervisor.

Rosetti was pleased he wasn't going to have to be costumed like Scotty and the Leroys, who in their short trousers, school caps and ties, looked like overgrown infants.

"What a load of prats!" he laughed.

Scotty was annoyed. "It's your father's idea! We'll end up looking like a bunch of idiots while you stand there like Joe Cool!"

"I'm the sex-symbol of this group, Scotty," said Rosetti, without a trace of humour. "If I dressed up like you lot, we'd *all* lose street-cred."

"But it's all right for *me* to lose street-cred though, isn't it?" snapped Scotty.

Rosetti was firm. "Yes!"

Stan, in charge of wardrobe, tucked and pinned, before passing each of his artistes to Elaine, who only needed to cover a few pimples with powder.

Rosetti's make-up was to take much longer and was less pleasant. Dressed only in Bermuda shorts, he shivered and cursed as Elaine applied deep-tan body lotion with a cold, wet sponge.

"This is disgusting," grimaced Rosetti.

"I'm sure," replied Elaine, sympathetically. "But it'll look great."

When the make-up had dried, Stan carefully helped Rosetti into a dressing-gown in an attempt to keep him warm, whilst Elaine used a handful of coconut oil to sweep back the hair from his forehead.

"Your audience wants to see that beautiful face," she joked.

Rosetti grinned up at her. "Yeah. Handsome, ain't I?"

"Very," replied Elaine and she meant it.

Max knocked and entered the unit bus, checking to see if Bury The Rabbit was almost ready.

"I don't want you out there until it's absolutely

necessary, lads," he informed them. "It's brass monkey weather, I'm afraid."

"Just give me a couple more minutes, Max," said Elaine. "I'm nearly done."

Max was about to leave, when Rosetti called to him.

"Max?" He was leaning back in the make-up chair, looking up at the director, as Elaine dabbed at the only remaining white blob under his ears with her sponge.

"Yes, Ray?" asked Max.

"That cameraman…" said Rosetti.

"John Stellar?"

"Yeah." Rosetti had taken an instant dislike to him from the moment they'd met. On introduction he'd hardly looked up from his *Guardian* crossword as he'd mumbled, "Hi!" to the group's lead singer. "Did you choose him?"

"I won't work with anyone else on promos," replied Max. "I prefer using film to video and he's one of the best. Why? Is there anything wrong?"

"I don't like him," said Rosetti.

Max was taken aback.

"He's very nice, Ray," interrupted Elaine. "I've worked with him lots of times." She turned to Stan, who was hanging up Scotty's jeans. "*Isn't* he, Stan?"

Rosetti flared. "Excuse me! I'm talking to the director, not the make-up girl!"

Elaine felt her cheeks going red. As a freelance make-up artist, she'd worked for many production companies and with hundreds of famous film and television names and she couldn't remember ever having been spoken to in such a way.

The Leroys looked at each other and grinned and

Scotty gazed out of the window, looking at nothing in particular.

"Doesn't he realize how important this promo is to us?" Rosetti went on.

"Of course he does," replied Max. "Promos are important to every group."

Rosetti sneered. "He couldn't even be bothered to put down his newspaper when we were introduced. Does he realize who I am? Does he realize that it's my father that's paying his wages?"

"It's just his way," smiled Max. He couldn't understand why Rosetti was getting so worked up. "He's always like that. Even with the big stars. He gives the impression that he doesn't care, but…"

"And does he?" snapped Rosetti. "Or is it just a case of 'this is just some unknown little pop group, so I'll take the money and run'?"

"He cares!" replied Max, firmly.

"I hope so! My dad's worked hard for his money. I don't want it wasted!"

The first assistant poked his head round the door.

"Ready when you are, Max."

"Thanks," said Max. He turned to Elaine. "Send them out as soon as you've finished with them, darling."

He left the bus and walked across the beach to the desks, chairs and palm trees.

Rosetti leapt up from the make-up chair and followed him.

"Max!"

The director stopped and turned, waiting for the lad to catch up with him.

"Sorry, Max," said Rosetti. "It's just…"

"I know," interrupted Max. He put an arm around Rosetti's shoulder. "It's only nerves."

"Yes."

"You'll be all right."

"It's so important, Max," continued Rosetti. "I know that 'Easy' can be a hit. But its success depends on this really, doesn't it?"

"I've had more promos shown on *Chartbusters* this year than you've had birthdays," smiled Max. "Stop worrying."

Rosetti smiled back.

"And they've all had the same cameraman," added Max. "John Stellar. OK?"

"OK," said Rosetti.

Max walked on as Rosetti returned to the bus to apologize, half-heartedly, to Elaine.

The members of the crew were, at first, excited by "Easy", but with replay after replay on the tape machine, they became bored, then irritated, then finally sick to death of the number. This wasn't, however, unusual on their pop-promo shoots.

The first shot had Rosetti lying on the sand, sun-bathing ... and singing into the camera, while Scotty and The Leroys tore up their school books and threw them into the air:

> *"Shoot yer promos on Antigua's beaches*
> *And take me there with you to feel the sun..."*

"Cut!" called Max. Then, "Check the gate!"

John Stellar checked his camera to make sure

everything was OK. It was.

Rosetti was dreading the next shot, gritting his teeth as he walked into the sea. The water was freezing; the wind even worse. He closed his eyes and took a deep breath as he courageously allowed the water to rise above his shorts. Then he turned to face the shore, where the lens of the camera was staring out at him.

"Cue music!" shouted Max, his voice battling with the wind, now howling through the sand-dunes behind the beach. The tape of "Easy" started again.

"And action!" he yelled.

Rosetti tried to relax his muscles which had become knotted with the cold. He consciously stopped his teeth from chattering and strode to the shore, miming,

"Plug me with confidence the way you know how
Till I'm on my way to be the number one!"

He stepped on to the beach, placed his hands behind his head and held his face to the sun. Through the camera lens anyone could have mistaken Bournemouth for Antigua. Rosetti looked warm and comfortable in the make-believe tropical sunshine.

"Cut!" yelled Max. Then, "Check the gate!"

Elaine hurried across to Rosetti and wrapped the dressing gown around his shoulders. His body shook, his teeth chattered and the tip of his nose was beginning to turn blue.

"I'm fffreezing!" he stammered.

"Well done, Ray," said Max. "It looked very good."

"Sorry," called John Stellar from over his camera. "Hair in the gate!"

"Oh, dear!" said Stan, who tried hard not to smile.

"What does that mean?" asked Rosetti.

"Sorry, Ray," replied Max. "No good. We'll have to go again."

Rosetti threw the dressing gown at Elaine, glared at the cameraman and walked back into the sea.

By the time Max was happy with the shot, Rosetti had emerged from and returned to the sea no less than four times. It had taken just over an hour to complete and tempers were flaring; Rosetti's in particular. The crew sighed with relief when Max finally called, "Cut! That's a wrap!"

Rosetti, now fully clothed and trying to lift a hot cup of coffee to his lips with trembling hands, didn't attempt to speak to anyone as the bus set off for the town centre, looking for the fish restaurant which had been pre-booked by Max. Scotty tried to humour him, disappointed that the day, which should have been one of great excitement for Bury The Rabbit, had turned out to be so tense.

"You looked really good, Ray," he said. "No one who sees it will realize you were freezing to death."

In his naïveté Rosetti had assumed that the cameraman hadn't been fully concentrating on what he was doing. He didn't realize that it wasn't unusual to take an hour or more to shoot what appeared to be one very simple scene.

In truth, John Stellar was one of the most respected cameramen in the business, having worked on several major British movies and numerous TV commercials.

"It shouldn't have been like that," said Rosetti. "Amateur!"

The back room of the restaurant, reserved for party bookings, was large enough to seat crew and cast on six separate white-clothed tables and Rosetti made sure that he sat as far away as possible from John Stellar.

Stellar looked up from his menu and called across the room to him, kindly, "Feeling a bit better now, Ray?"

Rosetti snapped. "No thanks to you, mate!"

The cameraman put down his menu and crossed to Rosetti's table.

"Come on, lad," he said. "Don't be like that. You wanted it to look right, didn't you?"

"It would've looked right on the first take if you'd've been competent at your job," replied Rosetti.

John Stellar decided there was no point in trying to communicate with him. He thought of the "thank you" party that Status Quo had thrown for him and he looked at the watch given to him by Sting, and he smiled at this idiot's accusation as he strolled back to his table.

But Rosetti wasn't going to let it rest.

"You couldn't give a monkey's, could you? It's just another pop promo. Just another group trying to make the charts and just another fast buck for you!"

Stellar tried to stay calm. He looked at his menu, though he wasn't seeing the words.

Max called across to Rosetti, "That's enough, Ray!"

Stellar mumbled, "I don't have to take this from some jumped-up school kid!"

Rosetti leapt from his seat and hammered his fist on the table. Scotty's empty wine glass tumbled over.

"I'm the star of this group, Stellar!" he screamed. "And my father's paying your wages, so just you watch it, or I'll make sure you never work again!"

One of the burlier prop-men calmly crossed the room, grabbed Rosetti around the throat and punched him, not hard, but enough to quieten him.

"Shut your mouth, punk!" he said as he pushed Rosetti back into his chair.

The meal was ordered and eaten in embarrassed silence.

Chapter 39

The cars and lorries stretched from Saint Barnabas',
right along Heath Drive and into Sancton High
Street. The priest had conducted many gypsy funerals
but had rarely seen quite so many flowers. The late
Joshua Smith was obviously well known and well loved.
Heath Drive split the cemetery in two. The old part
surrounding the church was, except for a few reserved
plots, full. Close to the church itself, a circle of elabor-
ately carved headstones commemorated the lives and
deaths of the Kings, the Moores and the Lees. The
graves were well kept, though some of them were over
fifty years old, and freshly cut flowers had been placed
at the foot of each one.

Terry and Billy tried to comfort their mother as
they walked behind the coffin, which was carried from
the church, through the old part of the cemetery,
across Heath Drive (where a policeman had to stop
the traffic) and on into the new part. The flowers
represented items that had been part of Joshua
Smith's life; his tankard, over-flowing with beer, his

shovel, a pack of cards, the horse he once owned and the truck which had replaced it. The wreath from Terry and Billy, in two-feet-high letters, spelt DAD.

Terry didn't hear the words; he was conscious only of his mum's stifled sobs and the white, drawn face of young Billy. But he knew it was something about ashes and dust. And as the coffin was lowered, he thought of Epsom Downs and the sunshine and the waggons and the gypsies in their rolled sleeves and the horses, so *many* horses, and the two fortune-tellers both claiming to be the real Gypsy Rose Lee. And he knew it was gone for ever. And he wasn't sure which of the tears that rolled down his cheeks were for the loss of his childhood, and which had been caused by the cold wind blowing up from the river to the heath beyond.

And neither was he conscious of the stranger in the old part of the cemetery, who was capturing his tears with a telephoto lens.

Chapter 40

Ruby Gold was relieved to have finished the three-week gig at the Saraha Club Casino in Lake Tahoe. As a support act to the extraordinary soul singer Mel Janus she'd felt, during her thirty-minute contribution to the show, as though she were invisible to the majority of Janus' fans. They didn't want to sit through this comparatively unknown singer's set. They'd come all this way to see *him*.

On the bus to LA she reflected on her flagging career. Neither of the past two albums had succeeded in charting and the next single, her manager had suggested cruelly, was a last-ditch attempt to elevate her to star status. It was to be written and produced by Kendrick Simpson. Who else? And Ruby, who hadn't even heard a demo of the song, wondered if it might be called "The Sword of Damocles".

From LA she flew to New York, spending three fun days with Sherry Barbin. Sherry needed this well-earned break. She hadn't stopped work in nine months, having had yet another number one single since the enormously successful "Paraíso". The album from which both singles had been lifted had gone platinum, leaving Patcha struggling for survival. Kendrick Simpson was worried. A top-ten entry had eluded Patcha since March and he'd decided it was time to prepare the way for a *new* female singer; someone who could give that American, Sherry Barbin, a run for her money. He'd listened to hundreds of tapes, sent to his office by desperate pop managers, all wanting that golden key to the charts, a Kendrick Simpson composition. And he'd chosen just three of them. Ruby Gold was the one he'd pinned his hopes on, not least because of the publicity that would come her way when the press discovered the identity of her best friend. He'd decided that from the three hopefuls, Ruby would get the sure-fire hit number and the production on it would be his best ever. She certainly had a great voice and if she looked as good as she did in her pictures … she couldn't fail.

"To London?" asked Sherry, surprised. "Why do you want to spend the rest of the summer there? It rains."

Ruby laughed. "I don't need the sun, sugar. My skin has all the tan it needs."

"You could come on the Canadian trip with me."

"No thanks. I need to rest. I can't keep up with your partying night after night. I'm going to see the Tower of London and Hyde Park and…"

Sherry yawned. "How boring!"

"I need time to think, too," explained Ruby. "I need to evaluate my career. And my whole goddam life."

She didn't mention her appointment with Kendrick Simpson.

From New York she took the flight to London Heathrow and booked in at the Savoy. She needed two days in which to sleep, to recover from jet-lag.

And then she was ready!

She took a cab to the North London address she'd been given and introduced herself with a wide grin.

"Hi! I'm Ruby Gold. And I'm here to make a hit record."

Kendrick Simpson loved her.

Wayne Fielding checked the sheets of A4 sent from Phil Lemont's accountant.

"I don't believe it!" he said aloud.

The royalties from Hym's third and fourth singles hadn't even, it appeared, covered the costs of cars and minders, let alone air fares, hotels and telephone expenses. He was being ripped off and he knew it. But without a lawyer, which he certainly couldn't afford, how was he to prove it? The dues on their last single, the biggest hit of all, weren't accountable until the following spring. And in the meantime, how was he going to live? He had to find a job. And quick!

Gary Brenn, the other half of the dynamite duo, had no such problems. "Take It All" had spent the whole of June in the top ten; two weeks at number three ... and even now it was lingering around the lower thirties. He realized that the follow-up to such a massive hit was going to be difficult, though he'd heard a rough mix of the backing track to "Only Me And You" and had been knocked out. He'd arrived at three in the afternoon to record the vocals, aware that

Kendrick Simpson was using the morning session to record a new girl singer, though he had no idea that that girl was Ruby Gold.

"Honey!" she screamed when she saw him enter the control room. She was sitting beside Kendrick Simpson listening to a playback of her just-recorded single.

Gary remembered. And paled.

Kendrick stopped the tape. He leapt up from his chair and shook Gary's hand. "Hi, Gary," he said. "We'll be about an hour, so if you want to go and make some coffee..." He added, "...I would have introduced you to Ruby, but you two obviously know each other."

Gary began to sweat. "Hello, Ruby," he stammered. "Nice to see you. I'll ... erm ... I'll just go and make some coffee then."

Ruby followed him to the kitchen, leaving Kendrick Simpson to play around with the mix.

"Well, you've done just fine since you ditched that partner of yours, haven't you?" she laughed. "Top five, eh?"

"It only reached number three," he mumbled, shyly. "And only in Britain."

"*Only?*" she shrieked. "What *I'd* give for a top-forty single in *Iceland*!"

Gary laughed.

"So what's your new track like?" she asked him.

"I think it'll be great, but I'm not sure about another top five." He took two mugs from the draining board and began to rinse them under the tap. "Do you want one?"

"Please," she replied.

"And what's *yours* like?" he asked her.

"It's a smasheroo, I hope."

"Perhaps we'll be battling with each other to get to the top," he suggested.

"Maybe. Now wouldn't that be just dandy?"

"So, how long are you staying in London?" he enquired.

She gripped his arm, playfully, "Long enough for us to get to know each other a bit better, honey."

He grinned nervously at her. He wasn't sure if she were coming on to him, or if this was just a game.

"Where are you staying?" he asked.

"The Savoy. Why?"

"Just curious."

"Oh," she said, mock-disappointedly. "And there I was thinking it was because you wanted to visit me." She laughed.

"Do you want me to?" He was surprised. And excited.

"Yeah," she said. "I'm short of company in this city."

"When?" he asked, eagerly.

She shrugged. "Whenever."

"Tonight?"

"Yeah," she said, softly. "Tonight. Why not?"

Wayne gulped back another whisky as he watched the video for the third time in succession; Hym performing their first hit on *Chartbusters*. He looked good. He sounded good. And that cherub-faced, blue-eyed number gyrating beside him couldn't touch him for talent. And yet he'd succeeded in getting a number three solo single! The envy was eating him up inside. He had to get out for some air. Walk the streets for a while … just to get his head together.

He allowed the first taxi to pass, arguing with himself: "Don't be stupid, Wayne. You can't be seen there."

He hailed the second one. "The Regent Tavern," he said.

"The Savoy," said Gary. The taxi headed for the West End.

Gary Brenn had been delighted with the session. And Kendrick Simpson had been delighted with Gary Brenn, having no doubts that "Only Me And You" would be a smash hit. A number one? Nobody could be sure about that. But he certainly wasn't *ashamed* of the follow-up.

It was one of the Regent Tavern's busiest nights and Wayne stood in a dark alcove by the door, terrified that someone would suddenly recognize him and yell out to their friends, "Hey! Look! There's that boy from Hym."

He was greatly relieved, if not a little jealous, to see Rab Sleightholme, the lead singer with True Grit, who was also here to watch the cabaret but who'd been star-spotted and was busy signing autographs.

"Well, well, well! We're full o' pop singers tonight," said the barman as he placed Wayne's drink in front of him. He smiled broadly. "Nice to have your custom."

"Thanks," replied Wayne.

"Ice?"

"Please."

He placed some ice cubes into the scotch and pushed Wayne's money back across the bar. "This one's on the house," he said.

"Really? Thanks."

The lights began to dim as the speakers blasted out the sound of Jimmy Somerville. The stage curtain parted and to cheers from the audience, a bikini-clad blonde handed two batons of fire to a large, balding man dressed in a tight, leopard-skin leotard.

"Good novelty act, this one!" the barman shouted above the music to Wayne. "But then I suppose *you're* here to listen to our singer."

"Erm … yes. That's right," replied Wayne.

The barman leaned across the bar with outstretched hand. "I'm the landlord by the way," he said. "Nick Cox."

"How do you do, Nick," yelled Wayne, shaking the proffered hand, while at the same time glancing at the fire-eater, who was slowly running the flames across his bare arms.

"We've had some great acts over the past two or three months," said Nick. "The best."

"So I've heard," replied Wayne.

"Pity about you and that other one splitting up."

"Yes."

"Still, he's doing brilliantly, isn't he?"

"You *could* say that."

"Four weeks on high with his first record."

"Yes."

There were screams of approval from the audience

as the fire-eater began to juggle with the burning batons.

"Four weeks, eh?" laughed Nick. "I bet you could spit razor-blades, couldn't you?"

"Well…"

"So when's *your* first single coming out then?"

The cheering grew louder.

"I'm not sure." Wayne shouted. "I've got a few legal problems to sort out first."

"Well … if you need something to do while you're waiting," grinned Nick, "you know where to come!"

"Well, I don't think…"

"Our resident singer's leaving on the fourth of September," he went on. "Got a cruise."

"Oh?"

"So … if you're at a loose end and want to try out your new material here –" he laughed. "To a very discerning audience … then give me a buzz."

"Thanks," said Wayne. "I'll think about it."

His face dropped. Had it really come to this?

He knocked back the last of the scotch, ordered another and watched as the novelty act appeared to swallow not only the fire before him, but the entire flaming baton.

"Well!" giggled Ruby Gold. "I'm glad you came."

He kissed her. "Me too. It's been a fun night. Thanks."

"You're good company, hon. It's a pity we didn't get time to get to know each other a bit better in LA."

He wrapped his arms around her. "Certainly is."

She smiled at him. "You do know that Sherry had the hots for you, don't you?"

He was shocked. "No." He laughed. "Give over."

"Seriously."

"She's not my type," he grinned.

She suddenly sounded serious. "Am *I*?"

"Very much so."

"I'm older than you."

"Only a bit."

"Not *too* old, then?"

"Far too old." He winked at her. "I can see you again, I hope?"

"Yeah. I'd like that," she said, wistfully. "I'd like that very much."

They held each other tightly. She hadn't felt this way for years. He'd *never* felt this way. His heart was thumping, his legs shaking.

"We missed out on so much in LA," he sighed.

"You can say that again! It was your partner's fault. If he hadn't gotten crazy like that, you wouldn't have been whisked back to London!"

"Yes…"

"What *is* it with him? What planet's he on?"

"He used to be OK." Gary was momentarily lost in thought. "Yeah. Everything was fine. Then it all changed. I got very frightened of him, you know."

"Frightened?"

"Terrified. It got worse and worse until I thought he'd drive me crazy. I got to hate him in the end."

"He was the crazy one," she said.

Gary began to protect him. "He wasn't always like that. We used to have great times together. But I did something very stupid when we were in Tokyo … and it freaked him out. It changed him totally."

"What did you do?" she asked.

"I can't tell you. It was really, really terrible. I haven't told anyone."

She squeezed him more tightly. "Then perhaps it's time you did, honey. Perhaps you should get it off your chest."

He wanted to. He wanted to tell *someone*. The great weight lay so heavily on his mind.

"If you knew some of the things that Sherry and I have gotten up to," she went on, "it'd blow your mind. What you did can't be so bad."

He was quiet.

"I tell you what…" she tried to coax him. "If you tell me what terrible thing you did in Tokyo, I'll tell you what Sherry did in Dallas."

He smiled at her. It would be a relief to tell someone. The whole thing had been gnawing away at him since Wayne had gone. He'd felt so alone with his guilty secret and he was sure he could trust Ruby.

"Well?"

"I'm not sure."

She gently persuaded him. "Oh, come on."

"If you tell anyone else," he whispered, "I'll…"

It took him ten minutes to describe, in detail, what he'd done. It was ten minutes he was to regret for the rest of his life.

Book Two

How easy it is to pull, when you're riding high in the charts.

PETE SHANNON

I don't need Terry Smith. He needs me! I could make him into something. I could make that boy a rock 'n' roll star!

JOE FISHER

Brilliant! Number one, here we come!

RAY ROSETTI

Shoot your promos on Antigua's beaches
And take me there with you, to feel the sun.
Plug me with confidence, the way you know how
Till I'm on my way to be the number one!
And it's easy!
    You know what I mean?
    Easy!

ROSETTI/SCOTT

Chapter 41

Joe was playing a cassette of "Call On Me" when Terry arrived at the office. There was no discussion about the funeral which was a relief, as Terry had found the tragedy almost too much to bear. He needed to escape, albeit briefly, from the darkness of the trailer.

"I'm not unhappy with the song," said Joe. "It's got great potential, but it needs to be remixed."

Terry didn't agree. He liked it just the way it was. But Joe was adamant. It was going to be the first release on his new indie and he couldn't risk failure.

"I'm thinking of using Del Stuart to remix it," said Joe. "Do you know his work?"

Terry had heard of him, but couldn't recall anything he'd done.

"Three top-five singles this year, so he knows what he's doing. Doesn't come cheap, mind you." Joe reached for his wallet. "That reminds me. Here." He handed Terry a fifty-pound note.

"What's this for?" asked Terry. "You've given me my fares this week."

"Why don't you take young Maureen somewhere nice?" smiled Joe. "How is she, by the way?"

"All right, I think. I haven't seen her since the studio."

He began to feel guilty. He'd told her he'd see her after the funeral, but with things as they were, it was too difficult to leave the campsite. It had been bad enough trying to communicate with all those people he hardly knew (distant cousins and aunts, telling him how much he'd changed and what a pity it was that his father had never seen him looking so smart) without Belcher having to drop his bombshell. And there were the insults from Uncle Render, once he'd got drunk, with references to Terry's earring and why didn't he wear it "no more?" and "What d'you think you are? A gorgio?" And the laughter. And the talk of chavvies and vardas and some words that Terry knew and many that he didn't. And the more they drank, the obscurer the language became and Terry couldn't understand what they were saying … and neither did he wish to.

Then the talk of Darenth Wood and the memories of the hop-fields. And they laughed when they should've been crying and they spoke of early days when they should've been thinking of his father, buried six feet down and unable to join the party.

And he and Billy had gone to sit by Abi's fire and had stared into the flames, dreaming of how it was. But Belcher interrupted, sitting between them cross-legged on the ground and they didn't want to hear what they'd guessed he was going to say.

"It was your dad's last wish that we moved on. He asked me to take the trailer north. All of us. Up Leicester way."

Billy poked the fire with a stick and watched the sparks fly upwards. "I don't wanna go to Leicester!"

"There's more up there," said Belcher. "There's nothin' left down 'ere for your mother and not a lot for me!"

So instead of going to see Maureen, Terry had stayed to comfort Billy.

"She's a nice girl," said Joe.

"Yes."

"And she's very fond of you."

"I know."

Joe decided the time was right. "She was telling me about your background. Very interesting, Terry." He spoke kindly, trying not to make a big thing of it.

Terry was horrified. "She *what*?"

"She didn't realize I didn't know. Not that it matters, of course."

"She had no right!" said Terry. "It's got nothing to do with you!"

Joe put his hand on the boy's shoulder. "Don't be daft, Terry. It's got everything to do with me. I've got to know all about you, even if it's just to protect you from the press. I mean, suppose you make it really big…?"

Terry fell silent. He knew it would have had to come out eventually, and he didn't blame Maureen. She wouldn't have done it on purpose.

"And I've been thinking, Terry," said Joe. "It could be good publicity."

"No!" said Terry, firmly.

Joe tried to reason with him. "Terry, there's nothing wrong with being a gypsy."

"No! Definitely not!"

Joe crossed to the window and opened it. He stared at the wisteria, just creeping its way along the windowsill.

Terry approached him. "Look, Joe, if you use my family background for publicity, I'm off, do you understand? You can stick your record and everything that goes with it! It's not *that* important to me."

Joe turned to face him. "I thought it was everything to you, Terry?"

"I'm warning you, Joe. I mean it."

"All right. If that's what you want," grinned Joe. "If you don't want me to mention your family … then I won't. It's no big deal, son."

He opened his cocktail cabinet.

"What d'you want?" he asked. "Perrier?"

Chapter 42

Wayne sifted through the pile of final demands, wondering how he would manage to pay the gas bill before they came to cut him off. How different it was from this time last year when he'd spend hours reading through the mountain of letters sent from his army of fans. Still, the odd love-letter managed to find its way to the record company and was forwarded without comment from BJ, but as time moved on, these became fewer and fewer. How easily the fans forgot. One minute they'd promised undying devotion, the next ... they'd moved on to a new pop idol.

Among the bills was a square, well-sealed, white envelope and Wayne hurriedly ripped it open to discover an official RSVP invitation to a charity gig. He was surprised that he'd been invited and wondered who'd drawn up the celebrity list. For weeks, the AIDS benefit concert in Hyde Park had been promoted on London's Capital Radio and Wayne had even thought that he might attend ... just as a punter, of course. He'd never expected to be on the official guest list, among all those luminaries of the British pop scene. The list of performers for the concert seemed endless: Pepperrazzi, Katrina and the Boy, Tubular Funk.

Patcha, despite her recent descent in the popularity polls, was to open the first half of the show; and the great Pete Shannon, prior to his latest American tour, was to top the bill: "The Superstar Attraction."

Wayne took the tube, crushed among scores of excited ticket-holders, head hung low, alternating between fear and hope that he'd be recognized. Some stared and pointed, but nobody spoke to him. At Marble Arch he left the Underground and walked to the park where he flashed his invitation and was shown in the direction of the VIP tent, an enormous marquee erected behind the performers' podium.

With a glass of white wine in hand, he threaded his way through the throng of famous faces: Susan Shand, Backup, 3-Kyd Live.

On the far side of the marquee, he saw the rotund manager puffing on a large cigar and his mind raced back to the time when he, Wayne Fielding, was paid, cash in hand, to do some backing vocals on Pete Shannon's album, "Alone On The Freeway". Pete's manager, Joe Fisher, had since then grown into an even fatter cat, his prosperity reaching greater heights with the worldwide success of that album.

Wayne struggled on through the crowds, determined to be near Joe Fisher and to ask him, if there were an opportunity, for an appointment. Conrad Matius would be a great manager to be with. Joe Fisher would be even better.

"Wayne!" said a voice from behind him.

He turned and gulped nervously when he saw one of the sound crew from the Sherry Barbin Roadshow.

"How ya doin', Wayne?"

Wayne couldn't remember the boy's name. And he didn't want to be chatting to a minion when he should be circulating among those who could aid his career.

"I'm fine," Wayne smiled politely.

And he didn't want to be reminded of that dreadful tour ... and Sherry Barbin and Ruby Gold ... and Gary.

"Couldn't believe you'd left the tour so suddenly," said the boy.

"We had to get back to do a TV special," lied Wayne.

The boy grinned. "Not what *I* heard. The American half of the crew were telling all sorts of wild stories about you and Sherry."

"Whatever you heard was a pack of lies." Wayne continued to smile. "You know how these rumours spread."

The boy looked disappointed. "Oh! What a shame!" he said. "And there was I, thinking you were Jack the Lad."

Wayne marvelled at the way the story must have grown. He winked at him. "Well, there you go!" he said.

"Are you performing today?"

"No," replied Wayne. "I'm a VIP guest, just like you." He shook the boy's hand. "Look, I'll see you later, right? I'd better do a bit of mingling with the mighty."

"I thought you might have been doing a Hym number with Gary," said the boy, innocently. "For old times' sake."

Wayne felt a buzz shoot through his head.

"He's not here, is he?"

"Gary?"

"Yes."

"Yeah. I thought you must've come together."

"No. No, I didn't know he was invited." Of course he's here, thought Wayne. How stupid. He's just had a massive hit single! He's flavour of the month! Of course he was invited.

"Of course he was invited," echoed the boy. "The show's being promoted by Kendrick Simpson, isn't it?"

"Well," said Wayne, trying to appear nonchalant, though he could hardly hold his glass of wine still. "Well, it'll be nice to see him again. Thanks for telling me."

He left, moving on towards Joe Fisher, his eyes darting around him for a cropped head, atop a confident smile.

Gary stood in the Remembrance Tent, his arm wrapped around Ruby Gold. The enormous patchwork quilt before them stretched across the tops of more than fifty tables before rising up the sides of the tent, where it was eventually suspended from the ceiling.

"Amazing, eh, honey?" gasped Ruby.

Dozens of people milled around, looking at the needlework: the pictures, the captions, the names of the dead.

"Sad, though," said Gary. "There but for the grace…"

"Go any of us," concluded Ruby. "A grim reminder, sugar. A warning." She kissed him on the cheek.

One young man in his early twenties crouched, looking closely at one of the names on the quilt. He reached out and touched it tenderly as a tear rolled down his cheek.

"D'you think it's a boyfriend or a girlfriend he's lost?" whispered Gary.

Ruby shrugged. "Does it matter? It was obviously someone he loved."

They stared at the young man and as Gary prayed for him, Ruby thought about the funerals of many friends in LA that she'd recently attended.

The amplified voice of the famous Sandy Dukes broke the silence.

"Ladies and Gentlemen – Welcome!"

The crowd of thousands cheered.

"We can't promise you sunshine today," continued Sandy Dukes. "We can't promise you that there'll be enough hot dogs and burgers and beer to go round…"

The crowd began to whistle and jeer, good-spiritedly.

"But we *can* promise you the best concert you've seen in years! The *great* are here!"

The crowd cheered.

"The *almighty* are here!"

The crowd cheered.

"And *I'm* here!"

The crowd, laughingly, booed him.

"So what more could you want?" he yelled. "Apart from … *Patcha!*"

The music blasted from the speakers as the diminutive Patcha leapt from the wings to the stage, grabbed the microphone and squeaked out a medley of Kendrick Simpson hits.

Gary and Ruby hurried back into the VIP tent and made their way to one of the dressing-room areas. Gary, as an unadvertised surprise guest, was on next. Kendrick Simpson had told him that as soon as Patcha had finished her third number, she'd hand the microphone to him and he was to launch straight into "Take It All".

He was happy to follow her. He had no respect for Patcha, and her squeaky little voice could only make *his* sound more powerful. He had two numbers to perform: the big hit, "Take It All" and the about-to-be-released single, "Only Me And You". Then he and Ruby could relax and enjoy the rest of the show. Gary, like the majority of the audience, could hardly wait to see the great Pete Shannon.

"I don't believe it, sugar!" gasped Ruby, as she grabbed Gary's arm. "Look!"

Just feet away, nervously sipping his wine as he eyed the fat man with the cigar, stood Wayne Fielding.

Gary began to sweat. "What do we do?" he whispered. "Ignore him?"

Ruby looked at Gary, disapprovingly.

"You've seen that list of names in the Remembrance Tent, honey. Life's too short. Go and say, 'Hi'."

Gary nodded. "You're right."

He crossed to Wayne and gently tapped him on the shoulder, fearing the reaction he might get.

Wayne turned, took a sharp intake of breath … and then smiled.

"Gary!" he said. His cheeks began to flush.

They stood, staring at each other, each one waiting for the other to make the next move.

"Hi!" said Gary. "How ya doin'?"

"Fine. How are…?" He suddenly flung his arms around Gary, and the boy responded warmly. "Good to see you, Gary."

"And you."

"Great to see you being so successful."

"I couldn't've done it without you, Wayne," replied Gary, seriously. "I learnt so much from you."

"Thanks. That's nice."

"Look, I'm on stage in a minute," rushed on Gary. "But why don't we get together afterwards and watch the rest of the show together? Me, you and Ruby."

Wayne wasn't surprised to hear Ruby's name. He'd read the tabloids. He'd seen the pictures of Ruby and Gary, hand in hand, at the Royal Film Gala. He looked over Gary's shoulder and saw Ruby waiting outside the changing area. She waved to him. He waved back.

"Yeah, that'll be great," replied Wayne.

"And you can tell me all about your new record deal!" shouted Gary above Patcha's sudden over-amplification.

Wayne smiled. "I see old Minnie Mouse is still squeaking out the hits," he said.

Gary laughed. "I'd better go, Wayne. I'll meet you back here in about half an hour, eh?"

As the cheers died down, Gary approached the front of the stage, microphone in hand.

"Thanks," he said. "Thanks for putting that one in the top five. Greatly appreciated."

The crowd cheered again.

"I'd just like to say, that no matter what stories you've read about Hym, we had a great time together."

The crowd yelled.

"It was fantastic for me. I loved every minute of it. And whatever anyone tells you … Wayne and I are still good mates … and there's no doubt that he'll be back with you before the end of the year."

There were a few cat-calls and whistles.

"Anyway, enough of that!" continued Gary. "This is my latest single, 'Only Me And You'."

Had Wayne heard the comments, he might have thrilled to them. But as soon as Gary had left to get changed, he'd turned his back on Joe Fisher and all the gathered stars and left the marquee, walking right across the park until he came to Lancaster Gate, his head brimming with thoughts of Hollywood and Tokyo and gas bills.

Chapter 43

Terry waited at the school gates and watched as everyone left. There was no sign of Maureen. As he noticed Jim Buckley crossing the playground towards his car, he hastily looked around for somewhere to hide. But it was too late. The teacher had seen him and was approaching.

"Hello, stranger!" called Jim. "I can hardly believe it! You look so different!"

"Hello, Mr Buckley." Terry couldn't look him in the eye. "I'm waiting for Maureen."

"How's it all going, then?" Jim seemed genuinely interested.

"OK."

"I was sorry to hear about your dad."

"Yeah. We were expecting it, though."

"So ... how's the record?"

Terry began to feel hot. "I'm sorry about what happened," he said. "It wasn't my fault. Honest. Joe didn't think the song was strong enough. I didn't have any choice."

Jim smiled. "It doesn't matter, Terry. I'd have liked it to have happened of course, but, well ... *c'est la vie*!"

"I'll get you a copy of the single as soon as it comes out," said Terry, adding quickly, "if you're interested, that is?"

"Of course I'm interested, Terry," replied Jim. "And thanks. That'd be great."

Bob Jamieson placed his sports bag on top of Jim's car and yelled across the playground, "Are you going to give me this lift or not, Mr Buckley?"

He'd seen Jim talking to a pupil and hadn't, at first, realized it was Terry Smith. When he recognized the boy, he strode over to them.

"Well, if it isn't the little pop star," he sneered.

Jim knew there could be trouble and tried to calm the situation.

"He looks good, doesn't he, Bob?" he said.

"Joe Fisher bought you all this lot, did he?" asked Bob Jamieson, eyeing the clothes.

"Yes." Terry was nervous. His old fear of Jamieson returned. Memories of cross-country runs and wall bars, showers and towel-flicking surged back. And the name-calling. Most importantly, the name-calling. And he was happy that school was behind him and that he'd never again have to face the changing-room. But he couldn't understand why he was still afraid of this teacher who was no longer part of his life.

"How's your dad?" asked Bob. "Still in hospital, is he? Or has he gone to see your relatives in Australia?"

Jim was horrified. He knew that Bob couldn't have heard about it. Bob wasn't cruel, despite what Terry Smith thought.

"He's dead!" said Terry.

Bob was speechless. He looked to Jim for confirmation.

"Yes. Terrible, isn't it?"

"I'm so sorry," stammered Bob. "I didn't mean —"

"It's all right, Mr Jamieson," replied Terry. "Don't be embarrassed. It'll happen to all of us one day. Including you."

He began to walk towards the main staircase.

"I'll bring you that single, Mr Buckley," he said. "I won't forget!"

Maureen was sitting in the cloakroom with her arm wrapped around Tracey, who was sobbing. Neither of them heard Terry approach.

"Oh, Tracey, don't," whispered Maureen. "It'll be all right. You'll forget him, you'll see."

Terry coughed.

When Maureen looked up and saw him standing there, she smiled and mouthed, "Won't be a minute."

She returned to comforting the almost hysterical Tracey with the clichés, "There's plenty more fish in the sea, Trace," and "You're too good for him," while all the time she was thinking that she'd much rather be comforting Terry. They had so much to talk about. So much to catch up on. And here she was, giving solace to the red-head whom she didn't really like.

Tracey eventually dried her eyes, which were beginning to match her pink cardigan, and slipped on her coat. She saw Terry and was startled.

"Don't worry about me," said Terry. "I'm just waiting for Maureen."

"It's Scotty," explained Maureen. "He's left school and he's told Tracey that he'll probably be too busy to see her for a while."

Tracey's face crumpled. "He's a rat," she whined. "I hate him." And the tears started to flow again.

"Has Scotty got a job then?" asked Terry as he and Maureen walked home to Gran's house.

Maureen realized that so much had happened in such a short space of time. She knew she had to tell Terry about Bury The Rabbit and their single and the interview on *Saturday Morning Live*.

"Yes," she said. "Ray Rosetti's left too."

She decided she'd explain everything over a cup of tea at Gran's.

Mother understood, though Belcher didn't, why Terry wanted to go out for the night. She'd not have done the same when *she* was young; when *her* father had died. But times were different. She knew it wasn't for lack of feeling. She knew that Terry had cared deeply for his father.

"It's not been two weeks," said Belcher. "Ain't you got no respect?"

Terry didn't respond.

"You're still in mourning, you know," Belcher went on. "Anyways, where d'yous get the money from?"

"From Joe," replied Terry, guiltily, knowing that Belcher had paid for everything since his father had been taken ill.

"That's good, innit?" said Belcher, sarcastically. "I spend my money making sure yous get fed, while yous go and spend yours on nights out with your gorgio girlfriend."

Terry pulled the fifty pounds from his pocket and held it out towards Belcher. "Here," he said. "Take it. It doesn't bother me. I'll stay in."

He meant it. It wasn't right. Why should Belcher have to pay for everything? Anyway, it only gave him more control over the family. More power.

Belcher looked at the money, then stared into Terry's eyes.

"Put it away!" he growled. "I don't need yer money. Your *mother* might, but—"

"No," Mother quickly interrupted. "No. I don't want it."

Terry slipped the money back into his pocket.

"You've got to sort yourself out, boy," went on Belcher. Terry detected the repressed anger in his voice. "And pretty quick too! All this singing bit might be all right for some. Those that can afford to hang about doing nothing. But it ain't all right for the likes of yous!"

Terry stared at his feet. The lecture was just like the ones that Dad used to give. The "I'm a man of the world, son," type of lectures. "I'm older than you, therefore I *know*." Sweeping statements about life, encompassing everything from European Unity to the after-life, when in truth, God bless him, he knew nothing. Except this site, the price of a ton of lead and the licensing hours of the Three Stars.

And the voice of the man who used to take two hours to read the front page of the *Sun*, trailing his index finger along each word as he mouthed the letters, trying to link them together, would get louder and angrier. Full of sound and fury, signifying nothing. Nothing that was of any value to Terry.

But still Terry loved him. And now he missed him. He missed him badly. And Belcher wasn't his father, nor could he ever hope to be.

"We'll be off soon," said Belcher. "I've told yous. We're going north. And you've got to decide if you're coming with us."

"I'm not," Terry replied firmly.

"I can't support yous if I'm not here." Belcher's voice was getting louder, sounding just like Dad's.

"I'll support myself," replied Terry. "If the record thing fails, there's lots of things I can do."

"You could always come with us, Terry." His mother's voice was low and plaintive.

Terry went to her. "Oh, Mum. You know I can't," he said. "I'll come and visit. Often. But–"

"I know," she replied. "You're better off down here."

He wasn't sure, but he thought the tears were beginning anew in Mother's eyes. She'd cried so much since Dad had died and the rims of her eyes looked sore. So red. He knelt by her chair. He wanted to be alone with her. He wished that Belcher would go to his own trailer for a while. Just for a few minutes. But Belcher was practically living here now. And soon he'd sell his trailer and move in completely, taking over Terry's bed. Or his father's. He'd wondered about that before, but had dismissed the thought because he *had* to. He didn't want to believe *that*.

"D'you think Dad would've minded if I went out

tonight, Mum?" asked Terry. "Really? D'you think he would've cared?"

Terry's mother smiled at him. "He'd probably have told you to go and have a good time, son."

Belcher sneered and mumbled the words, just loud enough for Terry to hear. "You never went to see him when he was alive, so I shouldn't let him bother you now."

Terry kissed his mother on the cheek for the first time in years. He'd often wanted to, but something had held him back. She didn't respond physically. She didn't put an arm round him or stroke his hair as she used to when he was a toddler.

"You're a good boy," was all she said.

For many years after, Terry would recall that one line: "You're a good boy."

To outsiders it might have sounded strange. To those families who touch and say what they feel, it could have been construed as cold. But Terry knew what she was trying to tell him. She loved him very much but, "You're a good boy," was the only way she could express it.

So with his mother's approval and with fifty pounds in his pocket, he and Maureen went "over the water" to the bright lights of London's West End, where McDonald's fed them and gave them plenty of change. And with enough put by for a late cab home, they headed for the Dome, that most famous of famous London clubs.

It was here that the light-show, reputed to be Europe's most extravagant, teased and thrilled, excited and chilled as it circled the dome before (accompanied by Tchaikovsky's 1812) it descended to the dance floor, like some great alien spacecraft.

Famous faces from the world of television and film arrived nightly, but it was the glamorous models on the arms of their pop star boyfriends who set the cameras flashing.

Terry and Maureen arrived to find the crowd spilling off the pavement and into the road.

"Look at this lot," said Maureen, disappointedly. "We'll never get in."

" 'Course we will," said Terry. "It's supposed to hold thousands."

The huge, flat-nosed bouncer in the dinner jacket put his arm across the door, stopping Terry and Maureen from entering the foyer.

"How old are you?" he asked.

"Eighteen," lied Terry.

"Give over," replied the bouncer.

Another dinner-jacketed man approached them. He was leaner and gentler.

"I'm sorry, sir," he smiled. "The licensing laws are very strict. I'm sure you understand."

Maureen and Terry returned to the railway station, amused by their inability to join the jet-set.

"Who needs it anyway?" said Maureen.

"*I* do!" laughed Terry. "And when I'm famous, I'll show 'em."

They knew there was still time to return home to their local disco. *Flicks* was open to the under-eighteens twice a week. There was no alcohol on sale, but that bothered neither Terry nor Maureen.

Maureen was surprised at Terry's good humour,

considering everything he'd been through in the past few days. She'd thought that the news of the Rosetti single would have added to his misery, but he'd reacted calmly, sighing, "Oh well, that's show-biz."

In truth, it hadn't come as a shock to Terry. He knew that with the backing of the Rosettis' money, there would definitely be a single for Bury The Rabbit, even if Franco Rosetti had had to launch his own indie to release it. But Terry was also sure that it would flop.

"Rosetti can't sing," he said. "And all the promotion in the world won't get him a hit single."

Maureen wasn't so sure. She'd heard the record and she'd liked it.

Flicks was practically empty, its popularity having waned since the entrance fee had been doubled. The half-dozen dancers on the floor were all girls and Maureen knew each one of them by sight and some of them to speak to. A dozen or so boys hung around the bar, sipping Cokes and gyrating to the music which the DJ, disappointed at entertaining such a small crowd, played over-loudly by way of compensation.

One of the girls picked up her bag and left the floor, heading for the toilets. She saw Maureen and stopped.

"Hello, Mo," she said.

Maureen recognized her as the girl who worked on Sunday mornings in the paper shop. They'd met several times through a mutual friend, but Maureen couldn't remember her name.

"On your own, are you?" asked the girl.

"This is Terry," Maureen said quickly, hoping that

the girl wouldn't mention Rosetti.

"Finished with Ray, have you then?" added the girl, insensitively.

Terry answered for her. "That's right."

"Bit stupid, wasn't it?" cackled the girl, not even casting a glance towards Terry. "Fancy leaving him just as he's about to become a pop star." She continued on her way.

Maureen turned to Terry. "Sorry."

"Let's dance," said Terry.

They danced on and on, record after record. Maureen wanted to stop; to sit, to break for a drink and to talk. But Terry was using the music to empty his mind. He had to erase, if only momentarily, the pictures of the coffin, of the camp fire and of Belcher.

Maureen recognized the intro immediately. She wanted to grab Terry's hand, to lead him to the bar and to shout at him so that he wasn't aware of what the DJ was playing. The boys at the bar placed down their Cokes as one, and joined the dancers on the floor. Everyone knew this sound. Everyone loved it. Terry loved it too. He loved its raw energy. The production was great. And the lead singer's voice sent a shiver along his spine.

Terry had no idea that he was dancing to "Easy" by Bury The Rabbit!

Franco Rosetti had decided it was time to stop playing games and to get down to the real nitty-gritty. He'd invited Scotty and the Leroys, along with their parents, to discuss the future for Bury The Rabbit.

"Things are looking good," he declared, "but we've

really got to decide where we're going. We've either got a group of school kids who play part-time in a band, or we've got a group of professional musicians with the ability to make a great deal of money."

He directed his comments at Mr and Mrs Leroy. "Ray and Phillip have left school, as you know," he said. "They want to concentrate totally on the future of the group. So I'm asking you to make a decision. We'd like the twins with us, of course, but if you feel they should stay on at school, then we'll have to replace them. I'm sorry, but that's the way it is."

Mr and Mrs Leroy weren't surprised. They'd been expecting this since the release of the single and had discussed its implications between themselves and the twins. Finally, they'd decided it had to be the boys' decision.

The phone rang and Franco reached for his mobile. A few minutes later he placed it down on the coffee table, grinning at the expectant faces before him.

"There's been a development that'll help you to make up your minds," he stated. "That was Robbie Jones from Radio Viscount."

"Really?" said Scotty.

They were all surprised. Franco hadn't mentioned Robbie Jones since the *Saturday Morning Live* broadcast.

"Anyway, he's made some calls to a few people and it looks like 'Easy' will be going on to the BBC playlist next week."

"Hey!" yelled Rosetti. "Fantastic!" He grinned at Scotty. "Top Twenty here we come!" He turned to his father. "Well done, Dad!"

"Cheers!" added Scotty.
"A glass of champagne, anyone?" asked Franco.

Chapter 44

Mark and John Leroy lounged on Mark's bed, their backs resting against the wall covered with posters from pop's rich past: Hendrix, Clapton, Fleetwood Mac. John idly strummed his guitar.

"I know that one," said Mark, as he looked up from his latest read, *Rock Through the Seventies*.

John continued to play the well-known intro as Mark threw down his book, picked up his own guitar, and joined his brother in song.

"*Everyone* knows this one," grinned John.

"'You Really Got Me Going'," sang Mark.

John stopped playing. "Who's it by then? The original, I mean?"

"The Kinks."

"Right. What year?"

Mark replied without hesitation, "Nineteen sixty-four." He laughed, adding. "Number one."

"For how many weeks?" asked John. "Bet you don't know that."

"No idea. Bet you don't know either."

"One. One week."

"Yeah? Is that all?"

"Knocked off the top by Herman's Hermits."

"Who?" shrieked Mark, adding, "Give me another one!"

John strummed the intro to "All Along The Watchtower".

"Hendrix!" they both yelled. "The Master."

There was a light tap on their bedroom door and the twins' father opened it. "Can we come in?" he asked. "We've got to talk, boys."

Mark and John put down their guitars. "Of course."

Their parents sat opposite them on the edge of John's bed.

"We've talked about it," said Mark, seriously. "And we'd both like to take a chance. Isn't that right, John?"

John nodded.

"And the A Levels?" asked their mother. "You're half-way through the course. And you know you're going to get good grades."

"We know," said Mark. "But music's the only thing we want to do."

Father looked at them stern-faced. "And suppose it all fails? Suppose Bury The Rabbit doesn't do what you think it's going to do? What then?"

"If you went to university," added their mother, "and got your degrees ... then you could start on the music again."

"Not with Bury The Rabbit," said John.

"There'll be other groups," argued their father. "You're both very talented musicians, boys. You don't need Ray Rosetti or Phillip Scott. You could do it on your own."

Mark didn't agree. "We couldn't."

"But you write really good songs, Mark," said Mother. "Does Ray know you write songs? Does Franco know?"

"No," replied John. "Scotty does. We've played some of our stuff to him."

"And?"

"He says it stinks," grinned Mark.

Father frowned. "What does *he* know? He's not the brains behind Bury The Rabbit."

John and Mark looked at each other and smiled.

"Oh, *is* he?" asked Father, surprised.

"He's much more talented than Ray," Mark informed them. "John and I really trust his judgement."

"He's good," added John. "And he thinks we can sing. He thinks we're really good. Better than Ray."

"Well there you are, then," said their mother. "You can sing and no one's in doubt about how well you play those guitars…"

"But we couldn't do it on our own," shrugged John. "Ray can stand up there and do all the chat."

"Gift of the gab," agreed Mark.

"Gift of the *gob*, more like," John corrected him.

Both twins laughed.

"We couldn't do all that stuff – all the interviews and things."

"And talk to the audience and all that."

"We just play."

"We play well," confirmed John. "But that's *all* we do."

"You'd find another band where you could do just that, surely?" said their father.

John shook his head.

"Ray Rosetti has got everything," explained Mark. "He sounds good and he looks great…"

"And he's got the chat," added John.

"And with Scotty's help, he's written some really good songs."

"He's gonna make it really big," said John. "And we want to be with him when he does."

Their parents looked at each other in despair. Their father sighed.

"We've got to take the risk, Dad," said Mark. "We really want to do it."

"Please don't stand in our way," added John. "We'll make it. We promise you."

Mark smiled at them. "And we'll make you really proud of us."

"Well…" said their father, "if you're absolutely stuck on the idea?"

"Stuck like glue!" grinned John.

"Then, we wish you all the luck in the world," smiled their mother. "And if you ever need any help…"

"We're here for you," concluded their father.

"Thanks, Dad," they both said together. "Thanks, Mum."

Chapter 45

Ruby sat opposite Gary in the bar at Gatwick Village, awaiting the departure of her LA flight.

A woman approached and thrust a pen and a scrap of paper in front of Gary. "Here," she said. "Sign this."

Gary automatically signed the autograph without looking up.

"It's not for me," said the woman. "Sign it to Claire, will you? She's my daughter. She thinks you're wonderful."

"Thanks," smiled Gary. He wrote, *To Claire*.

"No need to thank *me*," she said. "I can't stand pop music myself."

She left, clutching the autograph.

Ruby laughed. "The price of fame, eh?"

Gary forced a smile. "That's the bit I could do without."

Ruby reached across the table and grabbed Gary's hand. "I'd accept all of it," she said. "Even *that*. Just let me have the chance."

"You will," Gary assured her. "Your single's gonna be a biggie. I know it."

She pulled away from him and peered down into her brandy glass, sighing, "Oh, yeah, yeah, yeah. So why'd they hold up the release, eh? They can't be as sure as you about it."

"You've got it all wrong, Ruby," he lectured. "Kendrick Simpson knows what he's doing. He's got inside info on what's being released this month. If the competition is too high, he'll wait."

"Blunt Edge is releasing *yours* next week!" exclaimed Ruby. "And BJ must have inside knowledge too."

"That's different," explained Gary. "I'm a fellah. It's probably going to be a hot month for the top female singers. You've got to trust Kendrick, Ruby."

She swigged back the last of her brandy. "I do."

"So why don't you stay, eh?" he asked, plaintively. "Stay for the promo of 'Only Me And You'. I can take you to all the gigs. You'll be seen by everyone in the business. It could only be good for you."

She laughed. "Gary, my little innocent, I've been to every gig possible with Sherry Barbin Superstar, and not once have I gained a single dime from it. Why should *you* be any different?"

Gary looked away, hurt by the put-down.

"Sorry, honey," said Ruby. She squeezed his hand again. "That wasn't a snipe at *you*. As far as I'm concerned I'd rather be with you any day than with Sherry."

"So stay!" begged Gary.

"I've got work to do."

"You can work in London."

"I can work more in Vegas."

"You *hate* Vegas."

"I hate *London* when I'm not working."

She leaned forward and kissed his forehead. "I need to work, Gary," she whispered, gently. "I'll be back as soon as they set a date for the release. You understand that, don't you? I can't hang around here, living in your shadow. It'd drive me crazy, hon!"

"I understand," he replied, softly. "I love you, Ruby."

"I love you too, sugar," she said. "But a girl's gotta do what a girl's gotta do!"

She reached into her bag for a pencil and wrote a number on a beer mat.

"This is Sherry's number in Malibu," she said. "For God's sake don't let anyone get hold of it. I'm with her till the sixteenth ... then I'm off to Vegas. I'll call you from there, OK?"

"OK."

"And stay safe while I'm away, eh?" she pleaded. "Remember the quilt."

Chapter 46

The production meeting to discuss the promo of "Call On Me" was held in Joe's office. Over tea and biscuits the video's director gave his ideas for location, costume and theme, which he illustrated by holding up the storyboard for Joe and Terry to see.

Terry felt as excited as that day in the studio when he'd first heard his arranged music. Now he was looking at his lyric in picture form although, as with the music, he couldn't quite see where everything fitted.

"It's a song about unrequited love," explained the director. "A boy who's in love with a girl who's totally oblivious to the way he feels. Right?"

"Right," replied Terry. He ran his eyes over the storyboard, noting the big country house, the girl with the long, blonde hair and the boy in the ragged clothes.

"You sing about being on the outside, looking in," continued the director.

"Why is the boy dressed in rags?" asked Terry.

"It's up to you to say if you don't like the idea, of course," said Joe, "but we thought we could base it on the Dickens story, *Great Expectations*." He winked at Terry. "Which is what we have for *you!*"

Terry looked blankly at the two men. The only Dickens he'd ever read was an excerpt from *Oliver Twist* and that was only because it had cropped up in an English exam paper.

"In *Great Expectations* you've got this character called Pip," explained the director, "and he's in love with this classy bit of stuff called Estella. He's very poor and she's very rich, you see, so he doesn't stand a chance of getting off with her. That's why we've gone for the ragamuffin idea."

"I see," said Terry enthusiastically. "So we're in period costumes, are we? From Dickens' time?"

"*You* are," smiled Joe. "That's where we're changing it. In the new treatment, Estella's a modern day, rich girl. A sort of Sloane." He laughed.

Terry liked the idea. "Who's going to play the girl?" he asked.

The director aimed his question at Joe. "Did you manage to book Suki?"

"Yes," replied Joe. He smiled at Terry. "You'll like her, Terry. She's a stunner."

Maureen took the day off school to accompany Terry to the location: a large rambling house with extensive grounds near Surbiton. Vans, cars and cables were spilling all over the lawns as Terry and Maureen arrived, half an hour late, with an apologetic taxi driver whose knowledge didn't include the wilds of Surrey.

Joe introduced Terry to the owner of the house; a tall, elegant woman in her mid-fifties who offered, with a smile, one hand, while the other held on to the collar of her over-zealous red setter.

Terry's co-star had already arrived. Suki, from Zena's Model Agency, was young, slim, blonde and, thought Terry, extraordinarily beautiful. Maureen thought so too. But she also felt a pang of jealousy when she noted that Terry couldn't take his eyes off her.

Coffee and bacon rolls were served in the unit bus where Terry found his costume, labelled with his name and draped across a wire coat hanger.

"So, you're Terry," said Suki, sweetly. "Nice to meet you."

"You too," replied Terry. "This is Maureen."

Suki flashed a smile at Maureen. "Hi!" She shook Maureen's hand. "Are you in this epic, too?"

"No," smiled Maureen. "I'm just along for the ride."

"And the bacon rolls, I bet?" giggled Suki.

Maureen laughed. "Yes, and the bacon rolls."

"Have you seen the storyboard?" asked Terry.

"No," replied Suki. "But the director explained the idea on the phone. It sounds good, doesn't it?"

"*I* think so," said Terry.

"I love the idea of playing Estella from *Great Expectations*. She's quite a hard little character, isn't she?"

"I don't know," confessed Terry. "I haven't read it."

"Oh, she's wonderful," went on Suki. "Wonderful *to play*, I mean," she giggled. "Not a wonderful person."

258

She looked into the mirror and began to brush her hair gently. "She's cold and arrogant and so cruel to Pip."

Terry smiled at her through the mirror. "Don't be too cruel to me, will you? It *is* my first video!"

She laughed, an infectious high pitched giggle ... which set Maureen giggling along with her.

As the director and his crew set up for the first shot, Joe led Terry away from them.

"Would you mind wearing this, Terry?" he asked, quietly. He opened his hand to reveal a new, golden earring. "I thought it'd look good on you."

"I'm not wearing an earring!" replied Terry, instantly.

"But you *used* to wear one!" pleaded Joe. "I can see the hole."

Terry looked down at his feet.

"Look, Terry," Joe whispered, as though it were a secret just between the two of them, "*you* know and *I* know why you don't want to wear an earring. But it's stupid. Everyone's wearing them. You don't look at someone who's got an earring nowadays and assume he's a gypsy."

Terry remembered the last time he wore his. It was games morning, when he was in year nine. Jamieson insisted that all jewellery was handed to him before the run. He took the rings, the gold and silver chains and watches without comment, but when Terry handed him his earring he'd said, "Thank you, Terry."

Jamieson had never called him Terry. He always called all the boys by their surnames. Terry was always

"Smith". But it was that moment after the showers, just as they were getting dressed, that Terry had never forgotten. Jamieson's unblinking eyes hadn't left Terry as he dried himself on his towel. He was smirking at him in a sinister manner, making Terry tremble so much that he could hardly reach for the clothes on his peg. Jamieson had then called out, "Seven watches!" The boys went to retrieve them. "Two chains!" The same. "And," he announced loudly and effeminately, "one earring!" All the boys laughed as Terry took the earring from Jamieson, vowing that he'd never wear it again. Even though it was now fashionable, Terry never went back on his vow. That afternoon he lost it, deliberately, on the way home from school.

And here was Joe, holding out an earring, almost begging Terry to wear it, because, "It'll look good on you." And Terry thought of Jamieson and that song of his which was rejected and replaced with "Call On Me". And with a gesture of defiance he took the earring from Joe and pushed it through the almost grown-over skin of his ear lobe, making it pop and trickle with blood as he crossed to the set to shoot the first scene, wanting more than anything in the world for Jamieson to see the video on television as the pikie's record climbed up the charts.

Terry wandered from room to room of the house, staring open-mouthed at the pictures on the walls and running his fingertips over the antique vases and various objets d'art. Re-take after re-take had him bewildered at his luxurious surroundings and, as he acted, he mimed to his song, played over and over

260

again on the tape machine.

From the garden he stared in at the drawing-room, where Suki sat at a desk, writing.

He mimed:

> *"If you knew*
> *How much it hurts me*
> *To be left on the outside*
> *Looking in."*

Through the window, she smiled coldly at the boy in rags, before approaching and drawing the curtains.

"Symbolically," explained the director, somewhat pretentiously, "shutting him out of her life."

He was delighted at the way Terry responded to his direction. Seldom had he directed a pop singer with any acting ability and Terry's performance was all the more remarkable considering it was his first time before a camera.

As they shot the last scene, Suki returned to the bus and found Maureen aimlessly flicking through a magazine. She was bored and felt that she would have been better off at school. Joe had advised her not to get in the way while they were shooting and, worried that Terry might be inhibited by her presence, he'd asked her to stay on the bus.

"How's it going?" she asked Suki.

"I'm finished for today, I think," she replied. "Unless they want me to do any close-ups."

She poured herself a coffee and went to sit beside Maureen.

"I take it you're still at school?" she asked.

"Yes," said Maureen. "More's the pity."

"When do you leave?"

"I'm not sure," she replied. "I'll take my exams first and see how I get on. Probably next year."

"So you don't know what you'll be doing for a living then?"

"No," said Maureen. "Not really. Depends on my results."

Suki sipped her coffee. "Oh, yes. I suppose it does."

"I wouldn't mind working in a bank," volunteered Maureen. "But that depends on my maths."

"In a bank?" gasped Suki, incredulously. "Really? Is that what you want to do?" She wrinkled her nose in mock horror. "I don't think I could cope with a job like that. Not that I'd stand a chance," she added, quickly. "I can't add up. Even when I try it with a calculator I seem to get it all wrong." She giggled her high-pitched giggle.

Maureen laughed too. "Have you got any qualifications?" she asked, hoping that the girl would say no. She couldn't have beauty *and* brains. Or could she?

"Well, certainly not in maths," Suki replied. "But I've got quite a few GCSEs. Not that I use them. You don't need a degree in computer studies to do this job."

Maureen glanced sideways at her, inspecting her eyes, her nose, her teeth. Her beauty. She knows how to use make-up, she thought. And she's got a great hairdresser.

"Do you do a *lot* of videos, then?" she asked.

"Not very many," replied Suki. "I'm mainly catalogues and holiday brochures."

Maureen's eyes widened. "Do you go abroad?"

Suki laughed. "Of course I do. Not as much as I used to, but I've been four times this year."

Maureen had never been on a plane … nor on a boat for that matter. Except on the Isle of Wight ferry, when Gran took her to Shanklin for a week.

"Where did you go?" she asked, enviously.

"Twice to Tenerife," she said, excitedly, "then to the South of France and then to Ibiza." She sighed, reminiscing. "Last year was even better. I used to do a lot of upmarket trips, but our agency took on some real top-class models – so the ordinary ones like me have been pushed to one side recently."

"I wouldn't consider Tenerife to be pushed to one side," grinned Maureen. "And I wouldn't consider you to be ordinary."

"Thanks," replied Suki, graciously.

"I'd love to go to Tenerife," mused Maureen.

"Oh, don't get me wrong," rushed on Suki. "It was a great trip." She sighed. "Oh, but you should see the Seychelles, Maureen. It's out of this world. I'd love to go back to the Seychelles, but I think Imogen's been booked to do that one this year."

Maureen gasped. "Imogen? Pete Shannon's wife?"

"That's her."

"I thought she'd given it all up," said Maureen.

"She's back again!" Suki raised her eyes to heaven. "What chance do the rest of us stand? She's absolutely stunning."

"But why would she want to work?" asked Maureen. "She's so rich. She could *pay* to go to the Seychelles."

"Quite!" replied Suki. "If *I* were married to Pete Shannon, *I* wouldn't work." She giggled. "Now there's a thought. Fancy being married to Pete Shannon. What a man!"

Maureen laughed. "You don't fancy him, do you?"

"Doesn't everybody?" asked Suki, genuinely surprised.

Maureen wrinkled her nose. "He's old."

"What's age got to do with it?" smiled Suki. "He's so handsome." She lowered her voice and whispered. "And so sexy."

Maureen began to blush. "He's not my type," she said, adding, "I met him once. Joe's his manager."

"I know," laughed Suki. "I've met him too! Joe introduced us. I'd been planning what I'd say to him if I ever I came across him at a party or something ... you know, like I'd be ultra-cool and charm the socks off him ... and then suddenly there he was! And Joe said, 'Suki, this is Pete Shannon,' and I just stood there with my mouth open, not knowing what to say. I think he must have thought, why is that demented-looking girl standing there, catching flies? Anyway, he just nodded at me and walked off." She shrieked with laughter. "Ooh, I felt such a fool."

"I suppose you get to meet lots of famous people, don't you?" asked Maureen.

"Well ... quite a few, yes," replied Suki.

"Trips abroad and all those famous people," sighed Maureen. "I do envy you."

Suki gave her a very warm smile. "Then be a model," she said. "You could do it, Maureen. You've got the looks."

Maureen gasped. "Do you think so?"

"No harm in trying, is there?" said Suki. She reached for her bag and took out a white card. She laughed, "Why spend your life in a bank?" She handed the card to her.

Maureen looked at it. *Zena's Models*, it read. There was a London address and a telephone number.

"Give them a ring," suggested Suki. "Tell them I told you to contact them. And tell them you want to see Zena, personally. Don't get put off by the woman on the switchboard. She hates models." She burst into high-pitched giggles once again. "God knows why she works there," she cackled. "Now *she'd* be better off in a bank!"

Maureen took the card and stared at it.

"You ring them," insisted Suki.

Maureen grinned, contentedly. "Thanks. I will," she said, knowing that she probably wouldn't.

The flames from the huge, log-filled fireplace in the dining-room cast a flickering shadow across Terry's face, highlighting first the flat cap, pulled down over his eyes, then the ragged shirt collar and finally the glint from the earring. Through the lens, Terry appeared as the stereotype gypsy boy, sitting at his camp fire.

"That's magic, Terry," said the director. "Magic!"

He had just the picture he wanted.

Chapter 47

"I'm here, honey!" called Ruby. She strode through to the back of the house, followed by Sherry Barbin's latest muscle-bound bodyguard.

Sherry, lying bikini-clad on a sun lounger beside the pool, peered over the top of her shades as her best friend scurried through the door to the patio.

"Ruby, baby!" she screeched. She leapt up from the lounger and flung her arms wide. "I've missed you like crazy."

"Missed you too, sugar!"

They hugged and theatrically air-kissed.

"Come and sit on the lounger with me and divulge all!" demanded Sherry. "I wanna hear about the dark skies of London … and the rain … and the Queen of England."

Ruby sat as Sherry dismissed her bodyguard with a flick of the wrist.

"He's new," purred Ruby. "Nice. What did you do with the last one?"

"This one's hunkier," laughed Sherry. "Did you see those muscles across his shoulders?"

Ruby grinned. "He's an employee. You're not supposed to fancy him."

Sherry sat beside her. "He's good at his job ... and on those rare, lonely nights, he's not a bad companion."

Ruby looked around the patio. "It's a bit sparse this place, isn't it? Where's all the bougainvillaea and the palms?"

"You wait till you see the rest of the house," giggled Sherry. "It's tiny. My little *casita*."

"I hope you're not trying to return to your roots, honey," tutted Ruby, mock-disapprovingly. "I like being in the company of the extravagant superstar, not the little snotty-nosed kid from the Bronx."

Sherry laughed. "We can fall out of the front of the house on to the beach. Malibu ain't the Bronx. No way! I got the apartment in New York and the condo downtown. I don't need such a big place here. This is just fine by me."

Ruby's eyes twinkled. "It's fine by me too, sugar."

Sherry changed the subject. "So tell me!" she said. "Did you take tea at the Palace?"

Ruby smiled. "No. But I had a good time. A really good time." She paused and gulped nervously. Then she went on, "There's something I gotta tell you, Sherry."

Sherry was bemused by Ruby's sudden seriousness. "Tell me."

"I wasn't on vacation, Sherry. I didn't go to London for a vacation."

"You didn't?"

"I went to work."

Sherry was taken aback. "Then why didn't you say? It ain't no big deal, honey. So you went to London to work. That's great. Better than dusty ol' Vegas. But why didn't you tell me?"

"It's the kind of work that you won't approve of, hon," she tried to explain.

"Don't tell me! You were a hooker!" joked Sherry.

"Worse!" She blurted it out: "I went to see Kendrick Simpson."

Sherry's smile dropped.

"My record company arranged it all," Ruby rushed on. "If I hadn't gone, they would've ditched me for sure!"

"But Kendrick Simpson!" sighed Sherry. "You hate his stuff. You're soul, honey. Or you *were*. Now you're *sold out*!"

"I need a hit single, Sherry," argued Ruby. "I wanna number one, just like the rest of us in this goddam business. And if Kendrick Simpson can't do it for me, who can?"

Sherry stood and looked down at her. "I can't believe you did that," she said. "I really can't. I've always admired you, Ruby. You've got real talent. *Real* talent. Not like me. I'm just a pop singer with attitude. But you're a class act, Ruby. You shoulda held on. You can have all the commercial success in the world with Kendrick Simpson. But what good's it gonna do you when people in the industry start dismissing you as another Patcha?"

Ruby began to seethe. She was sick of people telling her in one breath how talented she was while in the next they were asking why she wasn't successful. She stood and glared angrily at Sherry. "What *good*'s it gonna do me?" she snapped. "What *good*? How's about an apartment in New York, a condo downtown and a *casita* by the sea … for starters!"

Sherry turned her back on her, strolled to the poolside and sat with her feet in the water. Ruby followed her.

"How's about an entourage of bodyguards and accountants and PAs?" she went on. "How's about chauffeur-driven limos and cameras flashing as I arrive in Gaultier designs to Hollywood film premieres? How's about a little *comfort*, eh, hon!"

"I'm sorry," whispered Sherry as she stared down into the twinkling pool. "I'm sorry. You're right. That was selfish of me."

Ruby kicked off her shoes and sat beside Sherry, dipping her travel-weary toes into the water.

"It's a good song, Sherry," she said, softly. "It's a really good record. And I'm sure it'll be a hit. In Europe at least."

"I'm happy for you." Sherry tried to smile. "You deserve it."

"And there's something else," added Ruby.

Sherry couldn't think what other bombshell her best friend might drop on her.

"I'm in love," she said.

Sherry turned her head to stare at her. "You're *what*?" she said.

"Totally smitten."

"Not with Kendrick Simpson?" she gasped.

Ruby laughed. "Get outta here!"

"Then *who*?"

"Gary. Gary Brenn?"

Sherry's mouth dropped open. "Not that Hym kid?"

"Yeah."

"The one I took a fancy to?"

"The same."

Sherry, smiling, put her arm around Ruby's neck and kissed her on the cheek.

"Well, well, well!" she said. "And how does *he* feel about it?"

Ruby shrugged. "He didn't want me to leave, that's for sure."

"Then why did you?"

"I missed *you*."

"Bull!"

Ruby grinned. "OK. I had to work *and* I missed you."

The bodyguard appeared at the door and called out to Sherry, "Shall I mix some drinks?"

Sherry glanced across at him. "Bring us some champagne. We gotta little something here to celebrate."

Chapter 48

All three offices of Zodiac Promotions were of hi-tech design; black, white and silver with unidentifiable hanging mobiles and mirrored walls. Zodiac was one of the top promotion companies in London, handling every form of bankable face, from the top TV soap stars to Poogy Bear. Poogy Bear had, to everyone's surprise, pulled in more merchandising contracts in one year than Pete Shannon had in the whole of his career. Not that Pete Shannon had done badly for the company! The percentages that Zodiac had received from Pete Shannon T-shirts and calendars alone had forced them to listen to Joe Fisher when he'd told them about his new discovery.

Terry had come to the office knowing what to expect and, briefed beforehand by Joe, he knew what sort of questions he'd be asked. He'd arrived early and was placed in the smallest of the offices, serving as a waiting room, among piles of magazines and newspapers. He picked up a copy of *GO!* and, checking the date, he realized that it was today's copy and turned immediately, as he always did, to the charts. His eyes followed his finger as it slowly went down the page, indicating each of the top fifty albums. He noted each one. He knew most of them. He did the same with the singles, tutting disgustedly at the number one. The new entries in the top twenty rarely surprised him. He usually knew from the amount of needle-time they'd received from the BBC, and from his own musical taste, which records would enter the top twenty in any given week. He lowered his eyes. Number twenty-five; no surprise. Number twenty-six; that surely was destined for the top. Number twenty-seven. He stopped and stared. It couldn't be true. He read it again.

27 – *EASY* – *Bury The Rabbit (Sloop)*
And he was unable to hold the paper steady.

A woman appeared, mid-twenties, from the adjoining office.

"Terry Smith?"

"Yes," he croaked. He cleared his throat and tried again. "Yes."

She smiled. "Would you like to come through?"

He closed the paper and placed it back on the pile.

Then he saw it! The front cover! He hadn't noticed it before. Why hadn't he seen it before? Rosetti's face, grinning up at him, filling the whole page. The headline screamed at him, *"EASY, RAY, EASY!"* and in subtitles, "The Rosetti Interview."

Terry couldn't tear his eyes away from it. He kept staring … wanting to pick it up … wanting to read the article. And yet … *not* wanting to read it!

"Bury The Rabbit," said the woman, who'd noticed Terry's interest. "Have you heard them?"

"Yes," Terry almost stammered.

"Good record," she added, rubbing salt into gaping wounds.

"Yes."

"We're handling the merchandising," she said. "And we helped with the launch."

"Really?" was all Terry could muster.

"Got them moving pretty quickly too, I'm glad to say."

"Yes."

"It's because they had a good marketing line," she went on. "Schoolboy band and all that." She waited, expecting a reaction from Terry. "Did you know they were still at school?"

"Yes," replied Terry, knowing that they weren't.

Then came the bombshell.

"Their plugger's trying to get them on to *Chartbusters* for next week."

"*Chartbusters?*" Terry hoped he'd misheard.

"I hope he manages it. They're nice lads," she grinned. "Especially Rosetti. Absolutely charming."

Terry's head was swimming.

"Come on in," said the woman. "Let's see if we can find a good marketing angle for *you*."

Terry's promo-director had dicovered the perfect location for his second day's shoot: East London's Docklands. Among the rubble of a row of terraced houses, demolished to make way for a new upmarket development long since abandoned, his crew had built a huge bonfire. Old tyres and pieces of scrap metal were scattered across the site and water was poured everywhere before the ground was churned up by the wheels of the unit bus, to create piles of mud.

The film extras arrived by coach, brought from their Central London pick-up point. They were clothed to look like the director's idea of yesteryear gypsies. All the women wore headscarves and long, colourful skirts; the men, flat caps, torn shirts and baggy trousers. There was an abundance of beads, earrings and red and white spotted neckerchiefs. Their hands and faces were dirtied with mud and they sat around the fire eating stew and mashed potato from tin plates. In the background, hired at great expense, was an authentic Romany waggon, complete with its black and white horse.

Terry's stand-in was no older than thirteen; a handsome boy whose facial similarity to Terry was almost immaterial as only the back of his head and a glimpse of his profile would be filmed. Dressed in the costume which Terry had worn for the previous day's filming, he would sit, back to the camera, staring into the fire. It was at this point that the director had planned to superimpose Suki's face and Terry, on seeing her image in the flames, would begin to dream. The dream sequence was already in the can and the rushes had proved to be excellent.

As night fell, the director prepared his final shot: the Romany waggon disappearing from the site, watched by all the gypsies. From a distance, the stand-in, looking like Terry, peered back from the departing waggon at the beautiful girl who was trying to follow him but was being dragged back by his gypsy family.

"Cut!" called the director. Then, "Well done,

everyone. That's a wrap!"

"Well done, Suki," said Joe. "As beautiful as ever." He put his arm round her and she giggled. "You looked lovely on yesterday's rushes," he said. "I'm really pleased with them."

"Thanks for the work, Joe," she replied. She began to head for the bus.

"It should be good for you, you know," went on Joe. "If the record's a hit, it'll be shown quite a bit."

"Do you think it *will* be a hit?" she asked, genuinely interested.

"What do *you* think, Suki?" He grinned at her. "You've had a bit of experience in the pop world. You're the sort of audience we're aiming at."

Suki laughed. "Oh, no. Not me, Joe. It was Pete Shannon I liked. The man ... not his music. I hate pop. Give me Rachmaninov any day."

The director left the supervising of his crew and joined them.

"Well?" he asked.

"Very good," said Joe. "I think."

"You only *think*?" The director laughed.

"I'll reserve judgement till I've seen the fully-edited version."

"It's a pity Terry couldn't be here today," said Suki, innocently. "I'm sure he'll love the finished thing."

Joe looked at the director and smiled.

They both watched as Suki climbed on to the unit bus.

"I doubt it," said Joe.

Chapter 49

Stavros Vardakis warmly greeted Sherry Barbin before turning his attention to the beautiful singer lounging on the sofa.

"Sherry's told me all about you, Ruby," he said. "I'm afraid I've never gotten to see your act in Vegas but I've heard some good reports."

Ruby eyed him quizzically. Sherry had told her to expect an important visitor to the Malibu house, but she hadn't realized it would be the head of Sherry's record company. She wondered what Sherry had said about her.

"And I believe you're after a new recording contract?" went on the handsome Greek.

Ruby responded with a smile. "I've had a recording deal for the past six years," she replied. "It's only the hit record I've been waiting for."

Stavros sat beside her on the sofa. "Yeah, I know all about your deal," he said with a grin, "but I can get you released from that contract with just a phone call. No problem."

Ruby was taken aback. She looked across at Sherry, who threw back her head and laughed.

"Surprise, eh, hon?" said Sherry. "I decided it was time to act before you got all tied up in this Kendrick Simpson stuff."

Ruby was confused. "Hey! Just a minute, you guys. Hold back, eh? Who says I want to be released from my recording deal?"

Stavros looked puzzled. "Sherry told me you wanted out."

"Oh, *did* she?"

"I can get you a deal with my label," explained Sherry. "I've got the perfect song for you, Ruby. And with plenty of hype we can get you into the charts."

"But I've made a single in London," argued Ruby. "And it's a sure-fire hit."

Stavros sneered. "Yeah ... with Kendrick Simpson! With him you'll be a five-minute wonder, babe! After he's given you three hit singles, he'll suddenly take an interest in someone new – and you'll be dumped. You'll then get given sub-standard material to record and all his best stuff will go to his *new* discovery. He's always worked that way."

Sherry crossed the room, stooped and took Ruby's hand. "He's right, Ruby! Who needs Kendrick Simpson when you've got a song penned by yours truly and a recording deal with Stavros Vardakis?"

Ruby began to fume. "So, I don't get any say in this, is that right? You've both decided to take over my career, without even asking me what I want?"

Stavros looked at Sherry for some explanation. He hadn't expected there'd be any opposition to his offer.

"I thought you'd be delighted," said a surprised Sherry. "It's what you've always wanted, isn't it, Ruby?"

Ruby pulled her hand away from Sherry and stood, looking down on her friend.

"I don't believe this!" she exclaimed. "You could've offered me this three years ago, Sherry. You could've written me a hit song and got me a deal when I first started doing Vegas. Why now?"

"But you never asked me to," replied Sherry. "I would've done it for you any time, honey. You only had to ask."

Ruby looked at her, aghast. "Ask you? I was in no position to ask. The offer had to come from you. I couldn't suddenly jeopardize our friendship by asking such a favour. But can you imagine how many times I've lain awake at night wishing, praying that you'd give me the break I really longed for? You knew how much I needed it, Sherry. Why now?"

"I'm sorry, hon," Sherry replied. "I honestly had no idea. I thought you were so proud, that you'd want to do it on your own. I really did."

"So, what makes you think I'm willing to take up your offer now?" she asked, angrily. "Now that I've got a record that's going to give me a huge hit in Europe?"

"But it's with Kendrick Simpson!" snapped Sherry. "That's why. I don't want to see you selling yourself short."

Stavros stood. "I think I'd better be going," he mumbled. "I wasn't expecting all this, Sherry. I thought it was a simple deal."

Sherry grabbed his arm. "No, don't go, Stavros. I'm sure Ruby just needs a short while to think about it. She'll see it makes sense. She can't go with Kendrick Simpson. Not when I'm offering her a chance of success here at home."

"And who says I'm desperate for success here in the US?" asked Ruby. "Europe may just be enough for me."

"But you've always wanted success here, honey." Sherry spoke softly, trying to placate her. "From way back … the New York days … you've talked about being number one."

"Yeah, well I'm not number one, am I?" sneered Ruby. "You're number one. And you'll stay number one! You're not going to take a back seat and watch me climb, Sherry. No way! Maybe I can go back to London and be number one there! But here? Not a chance!"

"Perhaps she'd be better in London," said Stavros. "The way she's acting, she's just right for the Kendrick Simpson hit-machine."

Sherry was furious at Ruby's reluctance to even discuss the offer. "You don't want to return to London for your career, Ruby!" She spat the words. "You just wanna return to that bimbo you think you're in love with."

"Maybe!" shouted Ruby. "Maybe! So, what's it to you?"

"So, don't you come running back to me when your career bombs and dreamboy dumps you!"

"I won't! He won't dump me!"

"And just you be careful, Ruby," she warned her.

"You make sure that Gary Brenn isn't taking an interest in you just to get to me!"

Ruby was shocked at the comment.

"A boy like that, just starting out on a solo career? What could be better for US of A success than to get close to its female pop superstar?"

"I don't believe I'm hearing this," gasped Ruby.

"To Gary Brenn, I'm the American Dream, honey – and you just may be his passport to me!"

For a few seconds, Ruby was unable to move, stunned by Sherry's words. Finally, she swept to her room and began to pack her bags.

"Hi! It's me," said Ruby. "You sound sleepy."

"It's four o'clock in the morning," yawned Gary.

Ruby laughed. "Hey, sugar, I'm so sorry. No wonder you took forever to answer the phone."

"How are you?" he asked.

"OK. How's it going your end?"

"Good," he replied. "Apart from missing you, of course."

She sighed. "You say the sweetest things."

"How's Sherry?"

"Fine," lied Ruby.

"Give her my love."

"Sure."

"Is she there?"

"She's in Malibu," Ruby informed him.

He was surprised. "And you're not?"

"No. I'm at a friend's apartment in 'Frisco."

"A girl friend?" He sounded worried.

"No. But don't get jealous, honey. He'd be more

interested in you than in me."

"I see," grinned Gary. "So, when are you off to Vegas?"

"I'm not. I've cancelled the gig."

"Cancelled? But why?"

" 'Cause I'm coming back to London, that's why."

Gary was silent.

"That is OK, isn't it, Gary?"

"Of course it is," he said. "Hey, that's great. When will you be arriving?"

"Tuesday evening. Can you meet me at the airport?"

"Sure," he replied. "I'll be there, darling. I can't wait!"

Huw watched as his possible future replacement was put through his paces. Wayne Fielding would, until Huw left for his working-cruise, do just the weekend sessions. Then, if he came up to scratch, Wayne Fielding would be the Regent Tavern's resident singer for as long as he wished. Wayne hoped it wouldn't be for long. From the huge audience at Sherry Barbin's Hollywood Supergig to the two or three hundred drunken revellers in this Camberwell pub! It must have been the biggest come-down anyone in the history of pop music could have faced. Or so Wayne felt. He was wrong. It had happened to thousands of pop stars before him ... and *he* would certainly not be the last!

"The drummer's too loud," Wayne called to Huw, who sat at the back of the empty bar, directing the rehearsal. "And I can hardly hear the lead guitar."

"Sounds OK to me!" Huw called back.

"But the balance is all wrong."

"Not for this pub, boyo! You'll see the difference when it's full. They're not going to be sitting there quietly listening to you sing. This is a pub, not a theatre."

Wayne leapt down from the stage and approached the big Welshman. "I'm not exactly used to a quiet audience, you know! I've played to thousands of screaming fans, and I do know when the sound-balance isn't right."

Nick Cox leaned across the bar.

"Give him the sound he wants, Huw. I want him to feel happy with what he's doing."

"If I balance it to suit him, then it'll be wrong for *my* act," Huw argued.

"Not for long," grinned Nick. "You're going in September. Give the lad what he wants."

"OK, OK," Huw conceded. He walked towards the stage to have a word with the boys in the band.

"Thanks, Nick," said Wayne. "I'm sure I'm right."

"I was just wondering why you've chosen those two songs?" asked Nick. "They're good, standard ballads and you sing them very well…"

"Thanks."

"…but I was hoping for something a bit more up to date."

"Chart stuff, d'you mean?"

"Well, you've seen the punters," continued Nick. "They're not exactly into old time music hall."

"But…"

"Why don't you do some of your new numbers? The

band's very talented and Slim, on keyboards, could help you to arrange anything you want. He's brilliant."

Wayne liked the idea. If he were to be spotted by any record company scout who might wander into the Regent, he might as well show off his song-writing talent.

"And how about shoving in a couple of Hym numbers?" concluded Nick Cox. "That'll set their feet tapping."

"No, I don't want to do that," said Wayne, firmly. "Hym is finished. I don't want anything to do with all that stuff we used to dish out. It's got to be new material. I've got to move on!"

Nick Cox shrugged, resignedly.

Ruby snuggled up to Gary in the back of a cab which was carrying them towards the West End of London.

"You look tired," said Gary as he gently stroked her hair.

"It's been a long journey, honey."

"We'll have a bite to eat," he said, "then I'll leave you to sleep. Will you be OK in the flat on your own?"

"If you really *have* to leave me," she sighed, jokingly. "On my first night back, too."

"I'm sorry, Ruby. But you know I can't stay, don't you?" he explained. "There's nothing I'd like more but I've got to be in Birmingham for the *Breakfast Show* tomorrow."

"I know," smiled Ruby. "Don't worry about it. Will I see you tomorrow night?"

"Of course. I'd like you to come and meet my mother."

Ruby sat up and stared at him. "She'll hate me," she warned him.

Gary pulled her towards him. "Don't be silly. She'll love you. She wants to meet you. It was her idea."

"I bet she doesn't approve of us living together?"

He kissed her. "You can charm her round, I'm sure."

"What have you told her about me?"

"Nothing much." He laughed. "I've told her that you're in the same business as me and that you're very talented. And that you're very beautiful."

She grinned up at him. "Why, thank you, kind sir."

"And I've told her that you're older than me. She raised an eyebrow at that one, but she didn't make any comment."

"And you've told her I'm black, I hope?"

He was silent.

She pulled away from him. "Gary?"

There was a twinkle in his eye.

"You haven't told her, have you?" she said.

He laughed. "I thought it'd be a nice surprise."

The taxi trundled on.

"So, tell me all about Sherry," Gary said. "What's she up to?"

"Sherry? Why should we want to talk about her?" replied Ruby. She snuggled her head into his chest and pretended to sleep.

Chapter 50

Terry wasn't expected. He'd arrived on the off chance that there'd be a few moments to chat to Joe. He wanted to know if the record's release date had been finally scheduled and was also hoping to see the video, or at least the rushes.

"How about waiting in the office, Terry," suggested Joe. "I won't be long."

There'd been a few problems to iron out with the major record company which was distributing Joe's indie, but the meeting in the sitting-room was almost over.

Terry paced the office, pausing to gaze out of the window to the alleyway below. His mind was on Rosetti. If only Bury The Rabbit had released their record after his own. If only he'd entered the charts before them. Then he panicked. Supposing "Call On Me" didn't make the charts at all? He knew his record was better than Bury The Rabbit's! He could sing better than Rosetti and "Call On Me" was a better song than "Easy", but...

He ambled across to the desk and, without thinking, sat in Joe's chair. He looked around the room, noted Pete Shannon's gold discs, the limited edition cartoon prints, the designer wallpaper. His eyes flicked across the desk. Three telephones; a diary; a brown envelope marked *"TERRY SMITH"*. He was more than curious; couldn't think what it could contain. The envelope wasn't sealed. He lifted the flap, gently slid his hand inside and gripped its contents. At first he wasn't sure. He couldn't quite believe that these grainy photos, picturing the boy with the tear rolling down his cheek, were of himself. There was his mother and Billy, their faces contorted with the pain of grief. And the other mourners. The coffin. The flowers. Terry's eyes began to mist. His chest was tightening; his breathing shallow and fast. His fingers trembled. Then he knew! These were for the tabloid press; the gypsy boy pop singer at his father's funeral. He began to wonder about the video. The boy in rags. The dirty face. The earring. Terry left the photos where they fell and slipped quietly from the office. He could still hear voices from the sitting-room as he descended the stairs and staggered blindly into the mews.

Maureen wasn't at home. Gran had wheeled herself to the door and asked who was there. The knocking wasn't like Terry's usual knock, a gentle rat-a-tat-tat. This frantic banging had frightened her. She was always cautious about opening the door when she was alone; always called out to make sure she knew the caller. This time, when she'd heard Terry's voice, she was surprised.

"It's only me, Gran," he'd called back. "Terry. Is Mo there?"

"She's still at school, Terry," Gran had replied. She'd been about to open the door, knowing from the tone that there was something wrong. Terry would make her a cup of tea ... and she'd listen to him.

But he'd called out, "I'll go to the school, Gran. I'll see you later!" and he'd gone.

Jim was surprised to see Terry standing at the class-room door.

"Maureen left five minutes ago, Terry," he smiled. "She said she had to get some shopping for her gran."

From the way Terry looked at him, Jim immedi-ately knew that he wanted to talk.

"What's up?" he asked, seriously.

Terry sighed, plaintively, almost groaning, "Sir!"

"Is it Maureen?"

"No. Nothing like that." There was a slight tremble in the boy's voice. "It's Joe."

Jim saw that he was close to tears. "The record's all right, isn't it? It's still going to be released?"

"He's got photos of my dad's funeral. He's going to use them, I think – for the papers."

"For the papers?"

"You know, for publicity. He wants people to know I'm a gypsy."

"Oh!" said Jim. "Come and sit down."

Terry crossed the room and sat in a vacant chair, bowing his head. Jim sat beside him.

"What am I going to do, sir?" he mumbled.

There was a long pause. Jim didn't know the answer.

"Does he know how you feel about it?" he asked finally.

"Of course he does," said Terry. "Not about the photos. But about all that other crap." He looked up at Jim. His eyes filled with tears. "Why? Why does he have to do it? The record's good enough without all that."

"Perhaps he's thinking of *you*, Terry. He wants to make sure you're successful." The words were meaningless and Jim knew it. Joe's business depended on record sales and Terry was merely a commodity. The boy was too young to know anything about the early career of Pete Shannon, but Jim remembered only too well the blaze of publicity about Imogen ... and how she supposedly broke up Pete's first marriage. There'd been a lot of dirty linen washed in public and this was followed by the record release which had been Pete Shannon's biggest success to date.

"I'd rather pack it all in than let him do that to my father," said Terry.

"Then do it," replied Jim, sharply. "Pack it all in, if that's what you really want!"

"How *can* I?" Terry's voice rose. "The record's been made. So has the video. He can go ahead without me if he wants to."

Jim smiled. "You know he can't go ahead without you. What about the interviews and the PAs? Come on, Terry. You can't wait to be a star."

Terry glared at him. "I thought *you'd* understand!"

"I do understand," said Jim. "I understand you want to be a successful pop singer. It's all you've ever wanted and nothing is going to stand in your way. You told me. You want to leave poverty behind you. You want to be rich and famous."

"But I don't want—"

Jim didn't let him finish. "But there's a price, Terry. There's a price to pay for everything in this life and the sooner you realize that, the better."

Terry's temper began to flare. "I don't want my family background splashed all over the papers! I don't see why it should be. It's private. It's got nothing to do with my singing."

"It's got everything to do with show business!" snapped Jim. "Get real, Terry! You know you can't have the sort of fame you're after without the public wanting to know details of your private life: what you had for breakfast, what sort of house you live in, who you're sleeping with! The public are hungry for it. They want to know. And the tabloids supply it. It sells papers, son. It's big business."

Jim walked back to his desk. He wanted to help, but there was nothing he could do.

"Mr Buckley!" Terry followed him, pleading. "What do I do, sir? Tell me what to do."

Jim spoke the words kindly. "You'll have to weigh up the odds, Terry. Then decide if it's all worth it!"

Terry was grateful for the lack of moonlight. It would make his job easier. He'd arrived at the mews just before three o'clock in the morning, quietly pushing his bike past the sleeping cottages, up to the alleyway at the side of Joe's house. He leaned it against the wall and removed the old knapsack from the handle-bar.

As he slipped his arms through the straps, he looked up at the office window.

The house was in darkness and he hoped that Joe wasn't at home. If he were, he'd probably be in bed. And Terry, having seen the layout of the rooms, knew that the bedroom was on the floor above the office.

He'd done as Jim had suggested and concluded that the memory of his father meant far too much for him to allow it to be cheapened by Joe Fisher. He'd believed that success as a singer was the most important thing in his life. He now knew differently. He couldn't sacrifice his family for fame and fortune. He wouldn't sell his soul for pop.

He used the wisteria to climb the wall, finding enough twisted branches for foot-holds, putting hand over hand as he pulled himself upwards, just as he'd been taught in the gym when rope-climbing. Good old Jamieson! He laughed at the thought, almost out loud. The man had had a purpose in Terry's life after all.

He rested half-way, and listened. There was silence; not even the distant hum of a passing car or a dog barking to be let in. The only sound came from his own heavy breathing and the thump, thump, thump of his heart.

He'd never done anything like this before. Others had. Others of his age who lived on the campsite had done it. But only for lead and not that often nowadays. Terry had always declined to join them, even when Billy had done it. This was the first time he'd ever stolen anything. And this wasn't really stealing. Or was it? No, it wasn't! He was only taking back what was rightly his!

As he climbed further, he wondered how he'd cope without Billy and his mother. There was no way he could go with them. It wasn't for the sake of his career ... which was now finished before it had begun. But he couldn't leave Maureen. Not now. She was the only person in the world who really understood him. There were no secrets with *her*.

He pictured the trailer setting off, Belcher driving, taking Mum and Billy to the Promised Land, which Terry was sure they'd never find. Jane at Berryfield was sad when she'd heard they were leaving. Mother had been there for years, since Billy was born. That's when they'd stopped travelling. Jane had watched the boys grow up. She'd seen Mother go through the good times and the bad. Mostly bad, culminating in the death of poor Josh. Now their trailer would be replaced by somebody else's.

Terry tried the window, just in case. But it was locked as he'd expected though why, he wondered, would anyone want to lock a window this far out of reach? He then began to worry that despite its inaccessibility the window might be alarmed. He used the stone that he'd wrapped in his handkerchief to break the glass. One short, sharp smash. Then he waited and listened. On the first screech of an alarm or any slight sound which meant that Joe had been woken, he was ready to scuttle down the wall a lot faster than he'd climbed it. He waited and waited, but he heard nothing, so he slipped his sweating hand through the broken pane and released the catch. It was a tight squeeze, but he pulled himself through and tumbled, head first, on to the office carpet.

Then a thought struck him – that perhaps the tape wasn't there. Perhaps Joe had already passed it on to Del Stuart for the re-mix. His heart beat even faster. He groped around the darkened room until he touched the desk. He grappled for the switch and put on the lamp. Then he crossed to the filing cabinet and opened the drawer. It was all there! The cassettes. The master tape. Even the envelope containing his photos. He slid the cassettes into his coat pockets and the master tape into his knapsack. He knew he should leave. Immediately. But there was one more job he wanted to do. He removed the photos from the envelope, tore each one in half and spread them across Joe's desk.

With his body now heavy with the master tape which had once been destined to raise him to a bright new future, Terry began to worry that the climb down would prove difficult. But knowing that he had, with one defiant gesture, honoured the memory of the man he'd so loved, the descent to obscurity was easy.

Chapter 51

The Porsche excited her almost as much as the man who drove it and she'd slid, seductively, into the seat beside him, allowing her skirt to rise just a little too high.

He took his eyes off the road from time to time to glimpse her thighs … and smiled. How often this had happened. How easy it was to pull when you were riding high in the charts.

"Are you sure you're not expected home?" he asked.

"No." She flicked, nonchalantly, through the rack of CDs fixed below the dashboard. "I live with my flat mate. Near my old drama school."

"A student, eh?" He sounded thrilled.

"*Was* a student." She thought she'd already explained that. Hadn't she told him she was an actress? She repeated it.

He laughed. "What did you need drama school for?" he said. "With looks like yours?"

They sped on through the winding, unlit lanes of the Kent countryside, saying little, listening to the CD she'd chosen. His latest album. Naturally. They always did that.

"My parents live down this way," she said. "Near Tunbridge Wells."

"Tunbridge Wells, eh?" He grinned. "That's where we're going."

"We're not?" She sat up and tugged at the skirt, suddenly aware that she was, maybe, being a bit *too* provocative.

"Perhaps we should call on them," he said. "Get them to make us a cup of tea."

"You are joking?" She wasn't sure.

"Of course I'm joking. I've got a little cottage in Ashton."

Ashton Village. It wasn't far from Tunbridge Wells. She hoped that nobody would see her arrive. She wondered if her parents knew anyone from that village. She leaned forward and turned up the volume.

"I like this track."

He knew she would. They all did. This was his previous hit single which had reached the top five and had sent *Alone On The Freeway* to the top of the album charts for the second time in his career.

"I like the heavy bass-line," she sighed. "It's so sexy."

The party had been a glittering affair: a three-storey town house off Barnes Common filled with soap stars, models and a very high-profile weatherman from breakfast television. The young, raven-haired actress had wandered from room to room, hoping that someone would introduce her to a producer or casting director who would set her on the road to stardom.

Her search stopped on the top floor, as soon as she'd seen the famous pop star talking to the leggy, blonde model.

He looked exactly like his publicity shots; the tall, lean body, dressed immaculately from the collar of his Armani suit to the toes of his Gucci shoes. And as the model tried to tease him, sipping at the champagne through her sensuously parted lips, Pete Shannon threw back his mane of sun-bleached hair and laughed in that world-famous irresistibly foggy voice which had set everyone from pubescent girls to middle-aged housewives squirming for more than a decade.

The actress stared at him, trying desperately to catch his eye. She was prettier than the model. And younger. And if only *half* those stories in the tabloid press about his preferences were true, then this young and seemingly innocent girl was the sort that Pete Shannon really desired.

He glanced across at her and smiled; a smile which, despite the ad for his over-priced LA dentist, made her shiver with anticipation of what might come her way … if she were to play the game properly. He was no spring chicken, that was for sure. But he was good-looking. And rich. And famous. And he knew all the right people. And she wanted him!

"That's who'll be taking me home," she'd determined as she'd returned to the kitchen to pour herself another glass of Dutch courage.

Chapter 52

"What do you think I am? Some sort of monster?"
Joe was furious.

"The boy felt that the privacy of his family was being threatened," replied Jim. "What did you expect?"

Joe had woken early the following morning and was deeply shocked to find what Terry had done. He'd picked up the phone, intending to call the police, but had changed his mind and had rung Jim instead.

"It's Joe. I've got to see you."

"What's up?"

"Can we meet? It's about Terry."

"I'm teaching till four."

"Couldn't you get the morning off? It's urgent."

Jim wasn't sure what Terry had been up to. Perhaps he'd told Joe that he'd had enough. That he wanted out. But it was none of Jim's business. And he had no intention of being a mediator.

"Please," said Joe. "I don't know where he is. I've rung that number at Berryfield, but the woman wouldn't tell me anything."

"I've got a job to do, Joe," said Jim.

"I don't want to call the police," went on Joe, "but if I don't find him, then I'll have to."

Jim couldn't imagine that Terry would do anything to warrant calling the police.

"The police? What for?"

"Can we meet?" Joe asked again.

Jim knew he had a couple of free periods after registration and so offered to meet the man in the local greasy spoon.

"There's a big florist's shop opposite," he said. "You can't miss it."

They ordered two teas and sat among the workmen who were eating their egg and bacon breakfasts.

"Where's this campsite then?" asked Joe. "I'll strangle him if I get hold of him."

"Hold on a minute," replied Jim. "I'm not telling you anything until you explain what he's done."

"He's broken into my office and stolen the master tape. That's what he's done."

"He told me about the photos," said Jim. "How could you even think of doing something like that?"

"Look!" said Joe. "I've invested a lot of money in that kid. I knew I could get it back, because he's good. Probably better than Pete Shannon, if I'm honest."

"Then why didn't you talk to Terry about the publicity? Come to some sort of arrangement?" argued Jim.

"I was going to," lied Joe. "He didn't give me a chance.

"You didn't tell him about the photos, did you?" Jim started to yell.

Heads turned and stared.

He lowered his voice and continued. "Why didn't you tell him about the photos, Joe?"

"I had the photos taken before Terry had said he didn't want his gypsy background mentioned. When he was so adamant about it, I decided to destroy them. I just hadn't got round to it, that's all."

Jim couldn't tell if Joe was telling the truth.

"If he hadn't gone poking around, he'd never have known about it."

"So what do you intend to do now?" asked Jim.

"Talk to him, of course. Explain that he got it all wrong. That he's got *me* all wrong." There was a pathetic look in his eyes as he spoke softly to Jim. "I'm not like that. Really I'm not. That stuff you hear about unscrupulous pop managers exploiting their artists just to earn a fast buck is all cock and bull. Storybook time!"

Jim was being convinced.

"I care about that kid, just as I care for Pete Shannon. I wouldn't hurt him. Not for the world. I want success for that lad, Jim. I've had my share. Ten years at the top in this business and I've grossed a fortune. I don't need Terry Smith. He needs me! I could make him into something, Jim. I could make that boy a rock 'n' roll star!"

Jim swigged back the last of his tea and stood.

"Come on," he said. "I'll show you where the campsite is."

Sylvie saw them first. Her eyes were sharp and although the figures were still far away on the path which led to

298

the campsite, she could tell by their gait that these were strangers approaching.

She called to Abi, who was throwing more branches on to his fire. "Gorgios, I think!"

Abi confronted them before they'd reached the camp. "Yeah?"

"We're looking for the Smiths," said Joe.

"Who wants them?" Abi's tone was threatening.

"We'd like a word with Terry," said Jim. "I used to be his teacher. I've been here before."

He hoped that that would make a difference. It didn't.

"He's not here," said Abi.

"Do you know where we could find him?" asked Jim.

"No idea." Abi was giving nothing away.

"Then could I have a word with his mother? She knows me."

"She's not here, neither."

Joe decided to take up the conversation. He was getting impatient.

"What time will she be back?"

"She won't," said Abi. He turned and started to walk away. "They've gone.

"Gone?" asked Jim. "Gone where?"

"No idea. Took the trailer off this morning." He walked slowly back along the path.

Joe whispered, "He's lying."

"I don't think so," replied Jim.

"Do you know there their caravan is?"

Jim led the way along the path. Abi looked back but said nothing; only shrugged and walked over to his fire.

"It was just here." Jim wasn't surprised.

Where the Smiths' caravan had once stood, the grass was longer, greener.

Levi opened the door to his trailer and called out, gruffly, "If you're looking for them, you've had it! They've gone up north!"

Abi poked at his fire with a long stick as he watched the two men disappearing into the distance. The fire crackled louder than usual.

"What you got on there?" asked Sylvie as she approached with a pot of potatoes.

"Just rubbish," replied Abi. He picked up the master tape which Terry had asked him to burn, and threw it into the flames alongside Belcher's discarded belongings.

"I'd better get back," said Jim. "Double English this afternoon."

"Well, thanks for trying to help, anyway." Joe shook his hand. "If you get any indication as to where I can find him…"

"I'll let you know," interrupted Jim.

Jim had no intention of ever contacting Joe again. Terry had made his decision. He'd obviously gone north with his family and had given up the idea of becoming a pop singer. As far as Jim was concerned, the book was closed. And he felt a sense of admiration for young Terry Smith. He could have had it all. He could have been rich and famous, but he'd stuck to what he believed in. And that boded well for a kid just starting out in life.

"What about that Maureen?" asked Joe. "She goes

to your school, doesn't she? Perhaps she'll know where he's gone."

"Maureen?" asked Jim. "Maureen who?"

"Doesn't matter," replied Joe. "See you around."

Maureen turned down the radio a little. Radio Viscount. She hardly listened to anything else nowadays.

"You should be at school, my girl," said Gran.

Terry opened the local paper. The back pages. "I'll have to get a job pretty quick," he said. "I'm skint."

"You could always come back to school," suggested Maureen. "They'll let you."

"No way," replied Terry. "I'm not going back there. I hated it."

"It's not that easy to get a job, Terry," warned Gran. "They keep telling you on the telly. There's loads want them."

Terry laughed. "I'll be all right. If the worst comes to the worst, Levi says I can help him with the scrap. It's good money if you work hard."

Gran smiled. "I'm sure you'll be all right," she said as she wheeled herself towards the parlour.

"I'm off," said Maureen. "Double English this afternoon." She slipped on her coat.

"You won't say nothing, will you?" It was silly to ask. Terry knew that she wouldn't.

" 'Course I won't. As far as anyone's concerned, I don't know where you are."

"Thanks."

"I'll see you later then." She began to leave.

"Maureen?"

She crossed to him and knelt by his chair.

"Are you all right?" she asked.

"Have I done the right thing?" He gently placed his hand on the back of her neck.

"Of course you have," she assured him.

"Not that it really matters," he said. "I don't give a monkeys about anything as long as *you're* here."

"*I'm* here," she said. She ruffled his hair and smiled at him. "But I *shouldn't* be here. I should be at school." She stood and crossed to the door.

"Terry?"

"Yeah?"

"Love you."

"Denson Sound Studios," said the voice.

"Could I speak to Andy Davis, please."

"Speaking."

"Oh, Andy. It's Joe Fisher."

"Hello, Joe," said Andy. "What can I do for you?"

"Got a little problem, Andy," said Joe.

"What is it? Pete's new single?"

"No. It's nothing to do with Pete. It's that song we did with Terry Smith."

" 'Call On Me'?"

"That's the one. You know I took the master…?"

"That's right. My mix not good enough for you, eh?" He laughed.

"You know what it's like," said Joe. "An outside ear and all that."

"I do, mate. Don't worry about it."

"I've had a bit of a disaster with it, I'm afraid," went on Joe.

"Disaster?"

"I'll explain when I see you," added Joe. "I just want to check. You've still got the sub-master haven't you?"

Andy laughed. "You're living with the dinosaurs, Joe. It's all computer linked. When do you want it?"

"What are you doing this afternoon?" asked Joe. "Del Stuart's doing the remix tonight!"

Chapter 53

It was a live edition of *Chartbusters*, worrying enough for those DJs and pop groups used to television, but for newcomers, knowing there could be no retakes, it was terrifying.

Rosetti and the rest of Bury The Rabbit were called for eleven o'clock and Franco drove them there in his van, parking at the top of the multi-storey car park and entering Horizon TV through a side entrance, as advised.

A small group of girls, as always on *Chartbusters* day, had gathered at the main gates, awaiting the arrival of their idols. Rosetti already had a small following, mainly because of the handsome photos of him in the pop weeklies, but today he was overshadowed by Gary Brenn, who had entered the charts with "Only Me And You".

Bury The Rabbit's dressing-rooms, near to studio four, weren't spacious, but each member of the band had his own, with a wash basin and a couch. They all gathered, however, in Ray Rosetti's room, none of them wanting to be alone, each wanting reassurance from the others.

A dresser from the costume department came to check that everything was all right and a girl from make-up made herself known to them, advising that perhaps they should see her just before transmission so that she could look them over. She'd already noted the Leroys' pimples, but thought that Rosetti and Scotty were fine.

A floor assistant, wired for sound and carrying a clipboard, asked them not to leave their dressing-rooms until he'd given them a "clear" for lunch and informed them that although they'd been at Horizon since eleven o'clock, they weren't called to the studio until twelve, as there'd been two acts to rehearse first. Both were much higher in the charts than Bury The Rabbit and both had appeared on *Chartbusters* before.

A flashing light warned of the rehearsal in progress as the floor assistant finally led them past the security guard and into the studio. Rosetti was shocked. He'd watched *Chartbusters* regularly since he was a child. It had always seemed to be on an epic scale; an enormous dance floor, crowded with people and backed by huge, flashing lights. Now it seemed so small, the dance floor filled with cameramen, boom operators and milling crew. Four metal stages had been erected on each side of the floor and on stage B, Wooden Decoy were rehearsing their latest hit, their lead singer, Damien, gyrating and winking at the camera.

Rosetti was very frightened. He wasn't sure if he could perform like that. Not with all these technicians staring at him. He was suddenly aware that later that evening, millions of viewers would be watching Bury The Rabbit for the first time. They had to be good. He had to impress. But could he do it? How could *he* look into the camera and wink, when he didn't know *which* camera to look into?

"You're in area C," said the Assistant Floor Manager. He pointed. "That stage there."

Bury The Rabbit headed for area C, where their instruments were already set up. They climbed on to the stage and positioned themselves ready for a rehearsal. Franco Rosetti looked on with pride.

There'd been great excitement at the school when friends of the ex-pupils, now pop stars, had spread the news that Bury The Rabbit would be appearing live on *Chartbusters*. Maureen hardly knew how to tell Terry who, to her surprise, took it quite calmly. He'd been expecting it since his meeting at Zodiac and had simply shrugged when she'd told him, forcing a smile and saying, "Let's watch it together."

Gran was very excited about watching Rosetti and Scotty on the telly and had got Maureen to buy some cream cakes, so that they could make a special occasion of it. She'd even pulled the curtains, although there was still daylight outside, so that they could get a good picture.

The theme music for *Chartbusters* set Maureen's feet tapping. And Terry's heart thumping. Maureen looked firstly at Terry's sullen face and then at Gran's non-stop grin as they both stared, wide-eyed, at the box in the corner. She couldn't help but smile.

*   *   *

If Terry's heart was thumping, Rosetti's was breaking through his chest and screaming, "Let me out!"

The dress-run in the afternoon had gone well, Rosetti learning very quickly that the camera with the little red light on it was the one to seduce with his smile. In contrast to Damien from Wooden Decoy, he kept his act very still. Dressed in denim, he played at being Mr Cool, occasionally giving a smouldering look at the camera. The producer had liked what he'd seen on the monitor and had no notes for him.

"Just do it like that tonight, and you'll be fine," he'd said.

Supper break had been long enough for a meal in the canteen or a drink and a chat in Horizon's bar, but Rosetti and the rest of Bury The Rabbit were too nervous to eat or drink.

The floor assistant came to warn them, "Five minutes please," and this was soon followed by the sound of the *Chartbusters* theme on the dressing-room speaker.

"I'm going to be sick," said Rosetti.

"You dare!" warned his father. "It'll be the last thing you do!"

The smoke-machine had pumped "atmosphere" into studio four, taking away the cold look that it had had all day and giving it the appearance of a dance hall. The milling crew had been replaced by effervescing pop fans: ordinary young members of the public who'd applied for tickets to the show and, on arriving, could hardly believe their luck to find that Gary Brenn was appearing live! Bury The Rabbit was the last thing on their minds.

The AFM led Rosetti and his group across the floor to area C. Most of the audience was gathered around area B watching Gary Brenn, who was coming to the end of "Only Me And You".

Rosetti knew that from here there would be a shot of the DJ. There'd be a bit of chat, then a run-down of the chart from forty to eleven. Back to the DJ ... and then they were on.

"Oh, God!" he said out loud.

"Good luck, mate," said Scotty as he climbed behind his drums.

The Leroys smiled at each other, reassuringly.

From the floor, Franco gave them all the thumbs-up.

Rosetti gulped and tried to stop the muscles in his cheek from twitching as he heard the run-down of the chart. The cameras were speeding away from area B, where Gary had finished his song. They were now being directed at Bury The Rabbit.

"Oh, God, oh God," said Rosetti again.

Then the DJ was talking to another camera on the far side of the studio.

"A group of schoolboys climbed to twenty-two this week with their debut single, 'Easy'."

"Oh, God, oh God, oh God," panted Rosetti.

"A warm *Chartbusters* welcome for ... Bury The Rabbit!"

The audience applauded. The AFM dropped his raised arm as the light on Rosetti's camera burned red.

But there was panic in the gallery, where for the first time ever on a live broadcast of *Chartbusters*, a smoke-detector had gone off. Throughout the whole of Gary's number, messages had been flashed backwards and forwards from security to studio four.

The show's producer was just saying, "Cue Bury The Rabbit!" as the technical co-ordinator arrived.

"I'm sorry," he said. "You'll have to stop. We're evacuating the studio."

When the DJ announced Bury The Rabbit, Maureen and Gran both leaned forward in their chairs. Terry sank down in his. He wished he hadn't watched the programme. He wondered if there was still time to excuse himself. To go for a walk. He didn't think he could face it.

The DJ announced, "A warm *Chartbusters* welcome for … Bury The Rabbit!"

Then the screen went blank.

"Oh, no!" said Maureen.

"Oh, for rice cake!" added Gran, who was furious. "Why does it always do that when there's something you want to watch?"

Terry's mouth dropped open. He couldn't believe what had happened.

An announcer said, "We're sorry about the loss of *Chartbusters*. We seem to have a technical problem." He paused, then went on light-heartedly, "We'll return to it as soon as possible. In the meantime … here's one we made earlier."

A video of Wooden Decoy's previous hit lit up the blank screen.

Gran flicked off the sound with her remote control. "We don't want this rubbish," she grumbled. "We'll wait till they go back to Ray and Scotty."

Maureen looked at her watch. "There's not time, Gran. If they went back now, they'd only show the number one."

Terry was surprised at his own feelings. He knew what this would mean to Bury The Rabbit and he tried to imagine himself in their position.

"What a shame," he said. "Poor Rosetti."

"You know what this means to us, don't you?" snapped Rosetti.

"I'm sorry," replied the AFM. "It's nothing to do with me."

Bury The Rabbit had been given the clear. They could go home. The studio had been evacuated and the programme was cancelled, though no reason could be found for the smoke-alarm having reacted.

"Never mind, son," said Franco. "Perhaps we'll get another shot."

"I'm all right, Dad," replied Rosetti. "Go and see if Scotty's OK, will you?"

Franco left the room and walked along the corridor.

Ray called after him, "I'll be with you in a minute! I just want to wash my face!"

He closed the door and slumped into the chair where he gazed at his reflection in the mirror. Then he laid his head on the dressing-room table and burst into tears.

Chapter 54

"Oh, no! Someone's having a party," the woman sighed.

The incessant THUD! THUD! THUD! pounded in the distance as, staring into the dressing-table mirror, she removed the last of her make-up with a tissue. She was tired and she'd been looking forward to a good night's sleep.

"That's *all* I need," she added. "A party."

Her husband entered from the bathroom in his pyjamas and pulled back the sheet on their king-size bed.

"I remember when you used to party all night long," he smiled.

She sighed.

This new house was all that she'd dreamed of; a large, rambling, nineteenth century vicarage, walls covered with ivy, set back from the road in a beautiful Kent village. She needed peace and she was sure that this was where she would find it.

The thud of the bass grew louder.

"It's not a party," he said. "It's a car radio."

He crossed to the window and peered out, squinting, trying to make out the approaching car headlamps. The large oak in the middle of the lawn obscured most of the view, but yes, he was sure. It *was* a car.

Del Stuart started the tape of Terry Smith's single. The voice which boomed from the speakers made the hairs on the back of Joe's plump neck tingle; a rarity for the man who'd been in the business since the discovery of the Beatles.

Terry Smith sang:

> *"You call on me*
> *When you are lonely*
> *And I know*
> *I can only*
> *Be a friend."*

"Yeah. It sounds good, Del," said Joe. "Certainly better than the original mix."

"I think I can better it," Del replied. "I'd like to have the string section re-written. Can you give me till Monday night?"

Joe Fisher puffed on his large cigar while pretending to give the matter some thought. Del Stuart knew the fat man was only playing games. Del was greatly respected in the music business and everyone knew that if it wasn't for his expert production, neither Shout! nor Max'n'Stuff would ever have charted.

"You do what you think best, Del," Joe said, finally. "I can't argue with a genius."

"It's a sure-fire hit," Del assured him. "This Terry Smith's certainly got an ace voice."

Joe snarled. "Yeah. I was going to use him to launch my new indie, but he's disappeared."

"Disappeared?"

"He didn't like the publicity we were going to use for his launch."

Del ran the tape back to the beginning. "So what publicity was this, then?"

Joe grinned. "He's a gypsy kid and we thought that that would be a tasty little morsel to dish to the tabloids. The silly little idiot didn't agree, did he? He didn't want his gypsy background mentioned. So he just went."

"He'll be back," said Del, confidently. "As soon as he hears his record's in the charts."

"I hope so," replied Joe. "I really do. I think I've got a good 'un there."

"In the meantime you've still got Pete Shannon selling vinyl by the truck load, and now his contract with Sloop Records is about up, you're laughing."

Joe looked serious. "Pete Shannon can't go on *much* longer, Del. He's had ten years at the top."

The phone rang and Del Stuart picked it up.

"Just a minute," he said.

He handed the receiver to Joe.

Nobody was quite sure how it happened. The car wasn't travelling particularly fast, though perhaps its driver had forgotten how sharp the bend was.

The woman's eyes widened and froze, staring in disbelief as the Porsche careered across the lawn towards the house. Her husband threw open the bedroom window just as the car hit the oak. He watched as it rebounded across the flower-bed, turned over several times, and finally came to rest on its splintered roof, inside the newly built conservatory. The sound of breaking glass was drowned by the THUD! THUD! THUD! from the car's speakers.

The man grabbed his slippers and dressing-gown and leapt down the staircase, two steps at a time, calling back to his wife, "Dial 999! Tell 'em we need the lot! Ambulance, police and fire brigade!"

"What's taking them so long?" the girl moaned, softly. "My leg hurts."

She lay on the lawn, covered in blankets, surrounded by neighbours who'd rushed to help as soon as they'd heard the crash.

"They won't be long," the man replied. He squeezed her hand. He *hoped* they wouldn't be long. It wasn't *her* he was worried about. She didn't seem too bad at all, considering the state the car was in. She must have been thrown clear as the door was ripped off, though he wondered momentarily why she hadn't been wearing her seat-belt. Thank God she wasn't.

She began to cry and somebody wiped a tear from her cheek with a crumpled Kleenex.

The woman arrived and whispered to her husband, "Can I have a word?"

He left the girl in the care of the baby-faced curate, new to the village.

314

"Are you all right, darling?" The man put an arm around his wife's shoulder. She was trembling. "You're cold."

"No. No, I'm not," she replied. "It's just…"

"I know," he said. "It's the shock. I can't believe it myself."

She shivered violently, from head to toe. How could she tell him that it was neither cold nor shock that was making her feel like this? How could she explain that despite the horror of the evening, she'd felt strangely excited as she'd taken a closer look inside the car…

"Did you recognize him?" she asked, quietly.

"The driver?"

"Yes."

"No. Should I have done?" He began to panic. "It's nobody we know, is it?"

"No. Nobody we know."

"Thank God," he sighed.

"I think we'd better prepare ourselves for the world's press, though," she explained. "They're going to be hammering on our door over the next few days."

"Joe Fisher?"

"Yes."

"Steve Hawkes, Joe," said the voice. "*Daily Mirror*."

"Hi, Steve. How yer doin'?"

"Fine, mate. Thought you'd like to give us a few words on Pete Shannon."

"On *Pete*?"

Joe had, long ago, ceased to be surprised by the antics of the press. They'd call at the oddest hours if they'd thought they'd got wind of a story.

"It's nearly midnight, Steve," he grumbled. "Couldn't you wait till tomorrow and call Sheena in the office? I'm in the studio, working on another of my artists. Sheena's got the full itinerary for Pete's American tour."

Steve Hawkes was silent.

"You still there, Steve?" asked Joe.

"You don't know, do you, Joe?" replied Steve. "You haven't heard."

"Heard what?" And at that moment, the fat man realized that something awful had happened.

"Heard *what*, Steve?" he asked again. "Where's Pete?"

"He's had an accident, Joe. Crashed his car."

"Is it bad?" Beads of sweat began to form above Joe's top lip.

"Yes, I'm afraid it is, Joe. It's very bad."

The young actress was discharged after a thorough check-up. There was nothing seriously wrong; just a few minor scratches and a badly bruised right leg. As she left the hospital with her parents, who'd come to pick her up, she was blinded by dozens of flashing cameras belonging to the press, who'd gathered in force, waiting for news of Pete Shannon. Immediately there was a barrage of questions:

"What's your name, love?"

"How old are you?"

"Have you known him long?"

"Have you been allowed to see him?"

And

"Did you meet his wife?"

She kept her head down, saying nothing, as she walked towards her father's waiting car.

Her mother turned on the reporters, angrily. "Mr Shannon was just giving my daughter a lift home, that's all! She's never even met him before!"

Chapter 55

Gary was annoyed that Phil Lemont hadn't vetoed the questions being fired at him by the *Breakfast Show*'s glamorous hostess. He didn't want to talk about Hym yet again. Whatever had to be said on this subject had been said. It was over. And anyway, every time the touring question was raised, Gary remembered Tokyo. And that was one subject he wished to forget. He didn't mind talking about Kendrick Simpson and he certainly didn't mind being asked about "Only Me And You" and the shooting of the video. But the question he *wasn't* expecting was the next one to be fired at him.

"Are you and Ruby Gold talking of marriage plans?"

"No," answered Gary, nervously.

"But you are an item?"

"We're going out together, if that's what you mean."

"And it's serious?"

He tried to joke. "No, it's not serious. We have quite a lot of fun together, actually. No, I wouldn't say we were the serious kind."

"And what does your mother think about this relationship?"

He was shocked at the way in which the questions were being asked. "My mother?"

"She's the author, Felicity Glenn, is she not?"

"Yes."

"Is she happy about your relationship with Ruby Gold?"

Gary's smile dropped. "I thought this was an interview about my latest single? I didn't realize we'd be discussing my relatives."

"But your mother's second novel, *North Of Alabama*...?"

"Yes?"

"Correct me if I'm wrong ... but wasn't it criticized by some as having racist overtones?"

Gary's mind was racing. How to handle this? With charm and dignity. Don't let her get to you, Gary, he thought. Raise the smile.

"It was a long time ago," he said. "I wasn't even born."

"No."

"And if my mother *ever* thought in that way, which I honestly doubt, then she's certainly a very changed woman now."

"Have you ever read the book?"

"No." The smile grew tighter. "Look, I really am not here to discuss a novel which my mother wrote way back in the sixties."

"She gets on well with Ruby then, does she?" continued the interviewer.

"Why shouldn't she?" replied Gary. "Ruby's a

very beautiful, intelligent woman." He laughed, embarrassed. "I'm sorry," he said, "but this is ludicrous. I honestly can't see that this has anything to do with my life as a pop singer." He felt his hands begin to shake and he wondered how, on live television, Wayne would have treated this smug interviewer.

"Forgive me," replied the hostess of the show. "I didn't mean to offend. Perhaps I'll just let you get on with performing your latest single."

"I don't think so," replied Gary and, still trying to smile, he left the set and walked out of the studio to his waiting car.

"That was really stupid of you!" snapped Phil Lemont. "It had echoes of a Wayne Fielding interview right through it."

"Oh, did it?" hissed Gary furiously as he hammered on BJ's desk.

The recording company executive jumped, never having seen Gary react in such a violent way. He stared across at Phil Lemont, who was trying to calm the situation.

"Now, come on, Gary," said Phil. "BJ and I are only trying to help."

Gary raised his voice. "Oh, really? I'm beginning to wonder if Wayne was right about the way he treated some of those berks out there. That wasn't an interview. That was a cross-examination of my private life."

BJ grinned. "You *have* no private life, sunshine. Get that into your head *now*."

"I hate to think how the press'll deal with that little outburst tomorrow," tutted Phil.

"They'll probably back me," argued Gary. "She's an idiot, that woman. I don't know how she got her job."

"You should've performed the single!" snapped BJ. "You shouldn't have walked out!"

"The single's doing all right as it is," said Gary. "We didn't need the *Breakfast Show* anyway. I told you that, when you booked it."

"You said you weren't at your best in the mornings," contradicted Phil Lemont. "That's a different thing altogether."

"Well, now you see what I'm like before eight a.m., don't you?" sneered Gary. "So perhaps you'll listen to me in future!"

Kendrick Simpson met Ruby for lunch near to his studio.

"I hope this is to give me the release date for the single, Kendrick?" she asked. "I'm busting to get out there and do the promos. I'm so bored with hangin' around, sugar!"

"Not quite as simple as that, Ruby," he stated. "There's a small domestic problem we have to sort out first."

"A domestic problem?"

"Gary Brenn," he said.

"Gary? What's my single got to do with Gary?"

"I've written and produced 'Only Me And You' and I'd like to see it get to number one, Ruby, as I'm sure you understand."

"Yes, but—"

"I've been talking to BJ at Gary's record company and we've decided that perhaps … while Gary's doing his promotion, you and he should … you know…"

Ruby feared the worst. "No, I don't know, Kendrick. What are you trying to say?"

"We think you should cool it. That's all. Give Gary a break."

"End our relationship? Is that what you're saying?"

"Gary's hawking his stuff for the girls, Ruby. He's the typical pin-up pop star with the two-, maybe three-year life span. He's got to appear available, if you know what I mean."

"And I'm in the way?" She was shocked and angry.

"Did you see the *Breakfast Show* this morning?" he asked.

"No!" She glared at him. "I wasn't up. Why?"

"Let's just say that your relationship with him is becoming a little too … high-profile? The fans won't like it, Ruby. It wouldn't take much for them to turn their attentions elsewhere."

"And what does Gary think about all this?" asked Ruby, who had visibly begun to tremble.

"His manager is putting some ideas to him this very minute," explained Kendrick. "I'm sure he'll see the sense in it."

"And what about me?" She hardly dare ask. "What about the release of my single?"

Kendrick took a sip of his wine. "Let's just say, we're putting that on hold for a few months."

"Until I fully comply with your demands!"

"Not demands, Ruby," he smiled. "Suggestions.

322

Surely you can see it's for the best."

Ruby glared at him. "It's blackmail!" she said.

"Don't be ridiculous!"

"Gary and I are in love!" she informed him. "He'd never agree to this."

Kendrick laughed. "I don't think you know Gary as well as you *think* you know him," he said. "Unless he's told you about the young model he was dating when you were in America?"

"Is Gary there, Mrs Brenn?" asked Ruby.

"No, Ruby. I'm sorry," she replied. "Isn't he at home?"

"No. I've been waiting here for hours, but he hasn't showed. I've tried his mobile, but it's switched off."

"He should be there soon, Ruby," continued Gary's mother. "He's probably with his manager. Have you tried there?"

"Yes. Phil Lemont's secretary said that Phil hadn't been in the office today."

"Really?" She was surprised. "I thought Gary said he had a meeting there this afternoon."

"That's what *I* thought." She hadn't believed a word the secretary had told her. "If Gary calls you, would you ask him to ring me as soon as possible?" asked Ruby. "I shall be at the Savoy."

"The Savoy?" Gary's mother was shocked. "Why? What's happened? Have you two had a tiff?"

"I'm sure Gary will tell you all about it, Mrs Brenn," she said. "If he calls you, will you tell him I've moved out of the apartment? I've dropped the key into the mail-box."

"Of course I will, Ruby," she said, kindly. "I'll get him to call you straight away."

Ruby curled up on her hotel bed, shivering between bouts of crying. It was nearly nine o'clock. Why hadn't Gary called? She could only suspect the worst.

The phone rang and she grabbed for it.

"Yes."

"We've put through your international call, Miss Gold," said the operator.

"Thank you."

She waited.

"Ruby?"

"Sherry!" she blurted. "Oh, Sherry. It's me!"

Sherry took a deep breath. "Oh, honey! Am I glad you called. What did I *do* to you? I can't believe it. I've been in torment ever since you left."

Through sobs, Ruby tried to explain what Kendrick Simpson was doing to her.

"Oh, Ruby. Baby. I can't bear it. Come home," she said. "Get the next plane out of that damp, foggy country and come back to Malibu. I've missed you, honey. I need you here with me."

"But I can't leave without seeing Gary," she argued. "I can't understand why he hasn't called me."

"Come home," repeated Sherry. "Give yourself time to think and then, if you really want to, you can call him from here."

"I've got to talk to him, Sherry," Ruby tried to explain. "He loves me. He won't do as the record company tells him. He just isn't like that."

"Think about it, Ruby," Sherry said. "The deal still

holds here. Stavros will do exactly as I say. We'll get you a hit single in the States within months and you can tell Kendrick Simpson what he can do with his pap!"

The call came at nine-thirty.

"Ruby?"

"I thought you'd never call," she sobbed. "What are they trying to do to us? Where are you?"

"I'm in the lobby downstairs," replied Gary. "Can I come up?"

"Of course!" she said. The tears began to dry. "As long as you're not coming to tell me it's all over."

There was an ominous silence.

"Oh!" she whispered. "I see."

"Not over, Ruby," he said softly. "It could never be over."

She helped him along. "Just put on hold."

"Ruby...?" He was about to plead for her understanding, and from the tone of his voice, she *knew*!

"OK, Gary," she sighed deeply. "Message understood."

"No. No, you don't understand, Ruby," he rushed on. "Listen to me!"

She hung up, waited for a few seconds and then dialled for a taxi.

"I want to get to Gatwick Airport," she said. "Like *now*!"

Chapter 56

Trembling, the beautiful young actress put down the phone. The guy with the thin, tight voice was calling from the offices of the newspaper which she had always ridiculed. And how much had the man offered her? She could hardly believe that she could earn that sort of money, simply by talking about her last few hours with Pete Shannon.

"There's nothing to tell you," she'd said. "I only met him last night. He was giving me a lift home to my parents' house."

"Oh, come on!" the journalist had laughed. "We know that Pete Shannon owns a little cottage in Ashton Village. That's where you were going, weren't you?"

"No!" She wondered what else they knew.

"You're an actress, aren't you?" the man had said, his voice sounding much calmer, much friendlier.

"That's right."

"Of course, the publicity would be a great help to you."

The raven-haired girl knew that publicity for a young, pretty actress fresh from drama school could be worth its weight in gold. She'd probably get an agent; be seen and then cast by TV directors.

"I'll have to think about it," she'd said.

She'd have to think about it *very carefully*. About the publicity. And about the money, of course.

Joe Fisher was saying nothing to the press. Not yet. He arrived at the hospital within a couple of hours of receiving the news and met Pete's wife, as arranged, in the waiting room outside the ward.

She rushed towards him and flung herself into the fat man's arms, weeping uncontrollably.

"Oh, Joe! Isn't it awful?"

"Terrible, Imogen. Terrible."

He looked around for Pete's young children.

"The kids not here?"

"No." She tried to stop the flow of tears. "I've left them with the nanny. They don't know. I didn't know how to tell them, Joe."

"There's no point, Imogen. Save it till he's on the mend. You can explain everything to them then."

She pulled away from him and looked up through puffy eyes.

"Joe, I don't think he's going to mend," she said, pathetically. "I've seen him. I don't think he'll last the night."

Later, having seen his protégé for himself, broken and scarred almost beyond recognition, Joe had to agree with Imogen. If, by some miracle, Pete did begin to breathe again without the aid of the machine to which he was now attached, he'd never be the same as before. He'd never again set the hearts of a million women fluttering as he strutted about the stage, growling sexily into his microphone.

Pete Shannon's days as one of the world's greatest live rock performers were over. That was for sure. The planned American tour, only days away, would have to be cancelled and, even with the insurance payments, Joe Fisher would be truly out of pocket. And Joe knew that the launch of his new independent record label was now in doubt, as Sloop records had the rights to all the *old* Pete Shannon material. He'd been depending on Pete to record a new album for the newly launched indie, but now...

As he left the hospital and passed, without speaking, through the flashing cameras and questioning reporters, Joe Fisher's mind was working overtime. For the moment he'd forget his indie. Terry Smith's single would have to be put on hold. Just for a while. There were more urgent matters to attend to and the launch of his little gypsy boy would have to wait. There was still a large percentage of the royalties to be collected from the *old* Pete Shannon material. A lot of bread, especially if all his albums were re-issued on CD.

Especially if there was over-kill publicity.

Especially if Pete Shannon died!

Now, that would really send record sales soaring.

Chapter 57

Despite the horrifying news she'd received in the early hours of the morning and apart from the slightly puffed eyes, Imogen Faith Dubedat looked, as ever, immaculate. On receiving the call she'd automatically brushed her long, blonde hair and reached for the grey and fairly sober Giorgio di Sant'Angelo skirt and blouse. She took the dark blue Mercedes, rather than one of the fun cars. The Merc was useful for delivering the children to playschool (when Piru was too busy preparing dinner for house-guests) and of course, for serious occasions such as funerals and visiting her parents' house for Sunday lunch.

The drive to the Kent and Sussex hospital in Tunbridge Wells had seemed interminable. The roads were packed with late Friday nighters … and her mind was in turmoil. Why was he driving to Ashton when he said he was staying at Joe's? They had business to discuss over dinner and then he'd stay the night. He could have a few brandies without having to worry about the police, who were always watching him, ready to pounce, just because of who he was. That's what he'd told her.

The way home was quieter. It was a very warm Saturday morning, clear blue skies promising a scorching summer's day. And at five a.m. the roads were clear, until she hit Peckham where the clubs were turning out.

She'd reached Camberwell Green by the time the tears had started to flow again and, deciding not to overtake the milk-float ahead, she pulled into the kerb and slumped across the wheel.

Remembering.

It hadn't been six years of pure joy. They'd certainly had their problems; more problems than she could have imagined on that day when they'd met at the Farm. But then he *was* one of the world's most sought-after pop stars ... and not only by concert promoters, his reputation for dating young, leggy models being almost legendary. His sexual conquests had become, much to his annoyance, more important to America's *National Enquirer* and Britain's *Sun* newspaper than his talent, which, after three Grammy Awards, went unchallenged.

Imogen had been on a modelling assignment: a three-day booking for an enormous fee, on Lake Geneva. She was just nineteen and still an innocent. Her convent education had given her a string of qualifications, with which, one day, she intended to surprise the world. A book about her life with Pete Shannon would show those hacks who constantly referred to her as a bimbo that she had more talent in her little typing finger than they had in the whole of Fleet Street.

Her parents had not, at first, approved of her modelling career, but now that she was world-famous, they'd conveniently forgotten the family rows. They were proud of her; were prouder still in those early days, before she'd met Pete Shannon. She'd made it to the top in the world of high-fashion modelling long before she'd met him. Just a dozen catwalks in Paris and she was commanding huge fees from the best photographers in the business. Then, after the stills, came the commercials, as more and more advertising agencies realized that Imogen was no dumb beauty. Imogen could talk. Imogen had class. She was more Princess Di than Princess Di. And America loved her.

The shoot had been easy. It always seemed easy to Imogen and she couldn't understand why so many models complained. About the cold. About the heat. About the hanging around as the photographer lined up his next shot. She had no time for whingers, especially whingers being paid hundreds of thousands of dollars a month.

"How's about a visit to the Farm tonight?" the photographer had asked her.

She wasn't sure. Of course she'd love to go. She'd heard so much about it. But Verbier was some two hours' drive around the lake.

"You'll love it," he said. "You can't come to Switzerland and not see the Farm."

"We've got an early shoot tomorrow," she argued. "It's all right for *you*. It takes me two hours to do my make-up."

"Supposing I promise you a noon start?"

"No funny business?" she asked.

"You're beautiful, darling," he grinned. "But I prefer the Italian Navy."

"Great! You're on!" she laughed.

And she was glad she went. The Farm changed her life. As they entered the club, Princess Stephanie left. Imogen was impressed. "A good start to the night!" she whispered to her companion.

The Farm was packed with the aprés-ski crowd, some dancing wildly, some sitting on rustic stools, knocking back the house speciality, Russian vodka.

There were film stars, politicians, designers and ... Pete Shannon. Imogen's heart skipped a beat. And she knew, from that very moment, as soon as he'd returned her stare, that this was going to be the night she would always remember.

She returned to the modelling location in Pete's Porsche ... and married him three weeks later.

Having crossed Chelsea Bridge, she headed for their London residence in Cheyne Walk, wondering if Piru had got the children out of bed yet. They were usually up by six. She hoped they'd been washed and breakfasted and were ready to be told that Daddy was quite ill and might not be home to see them for some time. Or should she tell them what she knew to be the truth?

Chapter 58

Levi carefully manoeuvred his beaten-up lorry along the narrow, potholed road which led to the back entrance of a row of shops.

"There!" Terry noticed two old fridges and a rusty cooker pushed against a large, red skip.

Levi leapt from the cab and made his way across the rubbish to the door marked Goods Entrance, where he rang the bell. Terry switched on the radio. It might be a long wait.

Levi earned a good living from his scrap metal business, though the wage he gave to Terry for helping him was only just enough for the lad to survive. Still, it was cash in hand. Tax free. And it stopped Terry from going on the dole.

The fitted-kitchen shops were the best. When new kitchens were put in, someone had to take away the old used stoves and fridges, most of them in poor condition. Levi would offer to clear them away for nothing.

Terry had only been doing the work for a few

weeks, since Belcher had taken the trailer North and Gran, to Maureen's delight, hadn't hesitated to give the lad a roof over his head.

"Just so long as you behave yourself with Maureen," she'd said. "I don't want any of this creeping from room to room in the middle of the night. Understand?"

Terry understood. And surely Gran knew that Maureen wasn't a bit like that. More's the pity! he sometimes thought.

Today had been a very successful one for Levi and therefore an exhausting one for Terry. He wasn't exactly powerfully built and moving heavy pieces of metal all day and every day was beginning to take its toll, especially on his back. He knew he couldn't stay in this job for ever, but he had no idea what else he could do. He'd only ever had one ambition. To sing. To write songs. To make records. And now that was gone! For the time being, anyway.

"Why don't you come back to school?" Maureen has asked him. "Take your exams?"

But Terry couldn't face that. Everyone knew that he'd left to become a pop star, so how could he return to face the jeers from those who were only too happy to see him fail?

Especially as Ray Rosetti *hadn't* failed!

Levi emerged from the back of the shop and nodded at Terry. He'd had permission to take the scrap.

"And this is the number four single!" said the DJ on Radio One. " 'Easy' ... from Bury The Rabbit."

Ray Rosetti sang:

"Got no intention o' waitin' for the giro
Or windin' up servin' in a burger bar.
I'd bust a gut before I'd give up losin'
My faith in me, to make it as a star!
And it's easy.
You know what I mean?
Easy!"

Easy for some! thought Terry. He switched off the radio, climbed down from the cab and went to help Levi with the rust-covered cooker.

Chapter 59

Pete Shannon died at seven p.m. the following Tuesday, conveniently early enough for the tabloids to fill Wednesday's front pages with the news.

The young actress's phone didn't stop ringing, and taking advice from her father's solicitor, she finally went for the *biggest* offer. More money than she would ever have dreamed of … for just one little story. She was aware, of course, that she would have to embellish it a little. After all, there was nothing much to say. Still, a few white lies couldn't harm anyone, could they? They certainly couldn't harm Pete Shannon.

"How can people do this?" sighed Maureen as she held up the Sunday paper for Gran to see. "What must his wife and kids be feeling?"

Gran tucked into her usual weekend breakfast of bacon and egg, peering over the top of her glasses at the headlines.

MY LAST HOURS WITH PETE

"It's a wicked old world," was all she said.

Gran's favourite line. No matter what catastrophes were being referred to in the newspapers or on the TV it was always the same: "It's a wicked old world."

Terry arrived late for breakfast, having promised Levi he'd go to the campsite to help him unload yesterday's haul.

"It's in the oven, Terry," said Maureen. "Probably all shrivelled up by now."

"I'm not hungry," he replied. He took out a fifty-pound note and pushed it across the table to Gran.

" 'Ere! What's all this?" she asked.

"Redundancy money I suppose you'd call it," grinned Terry.

"Redundancy? You ain't got the sack have you?" She seemed very concerned.

"Would it upset you, Gran?" he asked, genuinely worried that it would.

She smiled at him, dribbling egg yolk on to her chin.

"Don't bother me, Terry, love. It's you I'm worried about."

"Have you packed it in then?" asked Maureen. He'd told her that he probably would.

"Yes."

"You'll find something else," she said, comfortingly.

"Hope so."

" 'Course you will," added Gran.

"I'm not afraid of hard work," mumbled Terry. "I know it was doing my back in, but I could've coped with that. It wasn't that that was bothering me. It was the filthy looks I couldn't take. 'Look out! Here come the pikies!' All that. And they watch you like hawks every minute, just in case you nick something."

"You're better off out of it, Terry," advised Gran. "You don't need all that."

"I'll go to the job centre tomorrow morning," he said. "They must have something I can do."

Gran pushed the money back across the table.

"I don't want this," she said. "You don't eat more than a mouse. And anyway, you'll need it."

He pushed it back towards her.

"Take it!" he laughed. "Even if you just use it as a napkin to wipe that egg off your chin."

She grinned, wiping her chin with the back of one hand while reaching out with the other to give him a mock clip round the ear.

Imogen Shannon should have expected it. She'd been living with the publicity machine since she'd met Pete. At first she'd loved the media's attention, always answering their questions, posing for the photographers. And although a top model in her own right, she couldn't possibly have expected, when she first set out on her career, that one day her name would be known all over the world.

"Imogen," said Joe, "no one will believe that rubbish. Everyone knows that that newspaper's a joke."

Imogen sobbed into the phone. "As if it isn't bad enough already, Joe. How can anyone be so cruel?"

Joe promised to arrive early at the funeral, to give Imogen the support she'd need. As if he hadn't enough to do!

"I'll be with you at ten tomorrow," he said. "I have to go now, Imogen. I've got a meeting." He hung up

the receiver and switched on the radio. The Top
Forty. He wondered if Pete's death had sent his new
single into the 20s. The mid-week sales had certainly
looked promising.

Maureen had two free periods on Monday morning so
she accompanied Terry to the job centre, where they
scoured the boards hoping there would be something
worthwhile for him to do. Most of the jobs were for
skilled workers and those that weren't didn't appeal to
Terry in the least.

"Woolworth's?" asked Maureen as she eyed the
cards.

"No thanks!"

"That bakery at Orpington's looking for people to
work on the night shift."

"Let 'em look."

"How about bar work?"

Terry was mildly interested. It would do as a fill-in.

"The Three Stars," she added.

He grinned. "Forget it!"

"Now, this one's perfect!" said Maureen.

"What's it say?"

"Pop singer required. No experience necessary.
Must be good-looking, under eighteen years of age
and prepared to travel the world in search of fame and
fortune."

Terry laughed. "I see! Mickey-take time, is it?"

He held up his fingers, claw-like, wiggling them
about.

"Oh, no, Terry. Please!" She began to giggle. "Not
in here."

"You know you have to be punished for taking the Michael!" he said. "It's tickle time!"

"Oh, no. Don't!" she pleaded.

Terry rushed towards her, wriggling his clawed fingers. There was no need even to touch her. Maureen screamed and fell to the floor in anticipation of what was to follow, curling up into a little ball and laughing convulsively.

The woman behind the desk called out to them: "Do you mind?" adding, "Do you know where you are?"

"Dole office, innit?" replied Terry as he pulled the still giggling Maureen to her feet. He whispered in her ear, "She thinks it's a church."

"It's not a playground!" snapped the woman, noting Maureen's clothes.

Maureen began to worry. "Let's go, Terry," she said. "She's bound to recognize the uniform."

"But what about the pop singing job?" he asked, trying to look serious.

Maureen took his hand and pulled him towards the door.

"Got any money for McDonald's?" she asked.

"I've got enough for a bag of chips," he replied. "One between two. How does that grab you?"

Chapter 60

As Pete Shannon's coffin was carried into the church, Joe wished he were anywhere but supporting the distraught Imogen. The press had gathered in force outside the cemetery and the fat man hoped he was playing his part well. What irony to think that he'd intended to use a graveyard scene to launch young Terry Smith's recording career while now the same scene was being used to boost his other property: a property he'd believed had almost run its course. With a bit of luck, "Don't Tell Me", the third single taken from *Alone On The Freeway*, would climb higher than the nineteenth position it now occupied. Then, with careful handling, perhaps they could, yet again, get the album back to number one.

Chapter 61

Sherry glided shark-like beneath her friend, as she was gently treading water above her. She suddenly wrapped her arms around Ruby's legs and dragged her to the bottom of the pool.

Both girls spluttered to the surface, giggling like infants.

"I knew you were gonna do that!" laughed Ruby between snatched breaths.

Sherry gently laid her hands on Ruby's glistening shoulders.

"So happy you're back," she said.

"Me too."

"How you feelin' this mornin'?" she asked.

"Better than last night," sighed Ruby. "It seemed like a dream. That long flight and then me blurting out all that stuff that's been fillin' this tired ol' head."

"It'll take time, Ruby," Sherry gently warned her. "You ain't gonna forget about him over night. But I sure am pleased you got outta there before he broke your heart."

342

Ruby tried to smile. "I think he already did," she replied.

Both women swam to the side of the pool and pulled themselves out, sitting on the edge with their feet in the water.

"Hey!" enthused Sherry. "How's about we take off to La Paloma tonight? Gloria E's struttin' her stuff down there."

"I don't think I could face the faces, Sherry," Ruby replied. "There'll be all that tugging at you and the witty remarks and the autograph books shoved under your chin. I'm not ready for all that yet, hon."

"You'd better done *git* yourself ready, girl," grinned Sherry. "When Stavros pushes out your single, then the autograph hunters'll be after *you*!"

"If the record hits!"

"It'll hit! Believe me! 'Beggin'' is one o' the best songs I ever wrote. Come and listen to it again, eh? And then we'll shower and hit town."

The phone rang and Sherry reached behind her to pick up the mobile.

"Yeah?"

"It's Gary Brenn," said the voice.

"Hold!" replied Sherry. She turned to Ruby. "It's Stavros," she lied. "I'll take it inside."

As Sherry hurried through the patio doors, Ruby dived into the water and began to swim the length of the pool.

"This is Sherry Barbin talking, Gary. What can I do for you?"

"I thought Ruby might be there," he said.

"She might be."

"*Is* she?"

"Nope."

"But she has been there?"

"Yep."

"Are you expecting her back?"

"Are *you?*"

"Sorry?"

"Are *you* expecting her back? 'Cause if you are, forget it, honey. She ain't comin' back to you, that's for sure."

"What has she told you?" he asked.

"All."

"She didn't give me a chance to explain," he sighed, plaintively. "I had to make it look as though I was taking my manager's advice, didn't I? And *he's* in a difficult position ... being pulled this way and that by Kendrick Simpson and everyone at the record company."

"Oh, yeah?" she sneered.

"Couldn't you explain that to Ruby for me?" he pleaded.

"I ain't explainin' nothin'," replied Sherry, harshly. "As far as I can see, you ain't right for Ruby anyway, honey. She don't want some wimp who can't stand up for himself."

"But you know this business better than anyone, Sherry," said Gary. "You know how you have to play along with the big boys – the money men."

"Bull...! *I* don't. And I never have!"

He sighed. "Then perhaps you're tougher than me."

She laughed. "Get a life, honey! This is the

nineties. You don't go gettin' manipulated, unless you want it that way. And you don't go dumpin' those who really care for you … not for *nothing*!"

"I just thought Ruby and I could lay low for a while," he tried to explain. "I still want to see her…"

"But not in public!"

"Please understand, Sherry. I was just…"

"Just following orders?"

"I love Ruby, Sherry. You've got to believe me. I love her very much."

"So much that you had to go playin' around as soon as she was outta sight."

"What?" He was shocked.

"That's what she heard."

"Who from?"

"Does it matter?"

"Of course it matters. It's not true."

"Go tell it on the mountain!"

"It's not. Honest. Please Sherry … tell her to call me. I must talk to her. Tell her that I miss her."

"I'll tell her. But don't sit up waitin' for her call."

"Tell her that I love her. And I want her here with me in London."

"And?"

"Tell her it's all going great guns here … but without her here to share it with me…"

"Yeah, yeah, yeah…"

"Tell her that 'Only Me And You' has gone in at thirty-two, and –"

"Congratulations," she replied, mechanically.

His voice cracked. "– And I wish she was here to celebrate with me." Tears welled up in his eyes. "And will you tell her that we've both been invited to the official opening of KANSIT."

"KANSIT?"

"It's this new recording studio complex in Earls Court. Owned by one of the top record producers here. Chas Atkins."

"Yeah?" She sounded uninterested.

"It's going to be a really big do. Everyone in the business over here'll be going ... and she should be there."

"Really?"

"And we've been invited ... as a twosome."

"Ironic, eh?"

"Yeah."

"Be sure to tell her, eh?"

"Sure."

He sighed. "Suppose I'd better go."

"Take care, honey," she replied flatly. "And I hope the single gets to number one."

"Thanks."

They both hung up.

Sherry pondered on what to tell Ruby. As yet, it was too early to tell her anything. She aimed to get Ruby Gold into the studio first. Make a hit single out of "Beggin'" ... and *then* she'd let Ruby know about the call ... and the invitation to this KANSIT place. *Maybe!*

Chapter 62

As soon as Franco Rosetti heard the news about Pete Shannon, he made an urgent appointment to meet with Sloop Records' managing director.

With Bury The Rabbit at number four in the charts, the managing director was keen to see Franco.

"I suppose you want a release date on their follow-up single, Franco?" he asked.

He moved across to his cocktail cabinet and took out a decanter of scotch and two cut-glass tumblers.

"How's it going?" he added. "Are they getting on all right with Chas Atkins? Good producer, is Chas. It's a wonder he was free."

He brought the whisky and the glasses to the desk.

"Actually," said Franco, "I've come to see you on another matter."

"Another matter?" He raised his eyebrows. "Not another group, I hope?" He laughed. "Let's get this one properly established first, eh?"

"It's not another group," replied Franco. He wasn't sure where to begin. "Actually, in a roundabout way, it's to do with Pete Shannon."

Sloop's managing director shook his head, sadly. "Terrible! Terrible thing to happen!"

"Terrible!" agreed Franco. "Shocking for his family."

"Awful!"

"And for Sloop Records, naturally."

"Yes. Most unfortunate for Sloop Records," he replied, suspiciously. "OK. Let's have it. What are you after?"

Franco spat out the words. "Bury The Rabbit are an album band, I'm sure of it. I know that the single's a bit lightweight, but…"

"Lightweight?" He laughed. "Hold on. Hold on. What d'you mean, lightweight? It's top five, isn't it? That's all that matters to me. I'm delighted with it. *I* don't consider it lightweight."

"What I'm trying to say," explained Franco, "is that the boys can do much more than that sort of stuff. 'Easy' is good, but, well … Ray's writing some great material at the moment. Much better."

"And you want to do an album, now!"

"I know when we made the deal you said you'd want two hit singles first," said Franco. "But, well … now that Pete Shannon's gone, there's a gap for a good album band, isn't there? I know that my boys could fill that gap. They just need the break."

The managing director was silent. He crossed to the window and gazed out into the busy shopping centre below.

"Well?" asked Franco. "What do you say? We won't let you down."

His reply stunned Franco. "Have you thought

about Ray doing it on his own?"

"How do you mean?" stammered Franco. "On his own? Solo d'you mean?"

"That's exactly what I mean, Franco," he laughed.

"But…"

"We need a solo act to replace Pete Shannon. Not a group."

Franco grinned from ear to ear. "I don't believe I'm hearing this."

The managing director poured two large whiskies from the decanter. "Let's suppose we give Bury The Rabbit the album they want," he went on.

"Yes?"

"And then we remove Ray and replace him with another lead singer?"

Franco gasped.

"So we get our album band *and* our solo singer."

"Are you serious?" asked Franco, amazed at the suggestion.

"Very. I'm *very* serious, Franco. Look," he explained, "everyone here at Sloop thinks Ray Rosetti has a great future, *if* he's handled with care! With his looks, he's almost tailor-made for pop stardom. He stands out a mile from all those other young kids aiming for the charts at the moment. And if 'Easy' is anything to go by, he writes good songs."

"The others'll never go for it," said Franco. "Scotty'll go crazy."

"Why? He'll have his album deal. What's he got to worry about?"

"But without *Ray*?" said Franco. "They'll never last without Ray as their front man. *You* know that."

The managing director smiled. "That's not my problem, Franco. You're their manager. I'm sure you can sort that one out."

"I'm gonna *have* to, aren't I?" Franco mumbled into his whisky tumbler.

"But I suggest you don't let any of them know at the moment. Right?"

"If you say so. Right."

"Get me half a dozen Ray Rosetti tracks as soon as possible … just to reassure me, eh? Then we'll talk further." He raised his glass. "Cheers!"

"Cheers!"

"Now, Franco … the boys' new single…"

Ray Rosetti flared, "Unless we get it right, you idiot, there won't *be* an album! You know the deal!"

Scotty leapt from behind the drums and grabbed the front of Rosetti's shirt. Although tempers had been rising all day, it was the first time in his life that Scotty had reacted in such a violent way towards his old school mate.

"*I* want it to be as right as *you* do, Ray!" he screamed. "It's not just *your* future that's at stake, remember?"

The Leroy twins stood in front of their shared microphone, saying nothing, looking helplessly through the studio's glass panel towards their producer, Chas Atkins.

Chas had handled many temperamental artistes in his time and was determined not to get worked up over two hot-headed teenagers.

Bury The Rabbit was recording "Gimmee!", their

second single for Sloop, and they'd personally chosen Chas Atkins as their producer. He'd had a list of hit singles to his credit, including three number ones. Chas was expensive, but the boys were aware that having had a top five single with their first release, they couldn't afford not to chart with the second one. As far as they were concerned, the album deal depended on it.

The boys were tired, having been up early for a photographic session for a German magazine. ("Easy!" was due for release there before the end of the month.) They'd then spent the day at KANSIT, Chas Atkins' new rehearsal and recording studio in Earls Court.

Chas had opened the rehearsal studio three months previously with his proceeds from "Jam-On-Jam" which he'd co-written with Soul Sparks. The record had gone to number one and stayed there for six glorious weeks. Most of the European charts had followed. Then, with a super-hype campaign from Soul Sparks' record company, they had, against all odds, topped the American charts.

As the money flowed in, Chas began to look for premises to build his dream: rehearsal studios to be hired out at reasonable rates to top pop groups so that they could work in comfort and privacy. At the moment, it was small time, just one studio; but the huge Victorian building had the potential for at least six more units and Chas had great plans for the place: a rest-room, canteen, offices etc.

The word had begun to spread and in the past few weeks the studio had been booked solidly by some of the top names in the industry.

351

Chas liked "Easy!" and was in no doubt about the future success of "Gimmee!" but he was surprised at just how good Bury The Rabbit's material was. Very commercial. Even the flip-sides were potential hit songs. He was also very surprised at Ray Rosetti's input, which was practically nil. It was, he suddenly realized, Scotty who was the real talent behind the group. It was Scotty who came up with most of the ideas, the lyrics and the catchy guitar riffs allowing Rosetti to change just the odd line here and there. In public, Bury The Rabbit was Ray Rosetti's group. In private, it was definitely controlled by Scotty.

Chas laughed to himself. He'd seldom come across any young pop singer who was as arrogant and up front as Rosetti and yet, apart from his incredibly dark and handsome looks, the boy had very little talent.

"OK, lads. That's enough," said Chas, through the talkback system. "Time's money! We'll do just the drum break again, Scotty. The rest of you can come in here."

Scotty glared at Ray Rosetti and climbed back behind his drums. Ray and the Leroy twins went into the control room and sat on either side of the loudspeakers.

Franco entered the control room and, noting that the boys had broken, asked Chas if he could talk to them for a few minutes.

Scotty joined them.

"What d'you want first, boys?" grinned Franco. "The good news or the brilliant news?"

"Let's have the brilliant news first eh, Dad?" laughed Ray.

"I think I may have convinced Sloop Records that you're ready to make your first album!" he explained.

"Fantastic!" yelled Scotty.

He smiled at Ray Rosetti who smiled back at him. For a moment their quarrel was forgotten.

The Leroy twins said nothing, as usual. They simply nodded their approval.

"And now…!" Franco announced, dramatically. "Here's the *good* news! How about … you've just been booked for your second *Chartbusters*!"

"Great!" said the young Rosetti. "Brilliant! Number one, here we come!"

Chapter 63

Franco had booked the Friday night gig three weeks previously, before anyone could have dreamed that "Easy!" would have made the top five. *Hot Hits* had just featured the boys on their front cover and *CD Plus* had done an in-depth interview with Scotty and Ray. But it was their *Chartbusters* appearance, the night before the gig, that had brought out even more fans than expected on to the streets of Scarborough.

Franco had taken the van containing their instruments through the narrow side streets while the boys, in a hired black Rolls, arrived intentionally at the front of the club, to screams of delight from the frenzied fans. The police tried to protect the group by holding back the crowds, while ushering Rosetti and Co. quickly through the glass doors.

"Silly little idiots," said one police officer to his female colleague. "Look at 'em, wetting their knickers over four spotty youths! If this isn't a waste of manpower, I don't know what is!"

The WPC laughed. "Leave 'em alone," she said. "While they're here, they're not causing trouble anywhere else." She grinned, remembering the time she'd been a "silly little idiot" over the Bay City Rollers.

"Why can't we just cancel?" Ray Rosetti had earlier asked about the Scarborough gig. "I'm knackered! We've been doing photo-shoots all week. Tell them we've been working on our new single. They'll understand. Tell them we'll send them an advance copy of it!"

"Oh, sure!" snapped his father. "And can you imagine the papers tomorrow? *TOP POP GROUP LETS DOWN THEIR FANS!*"

"They wouldn't do that," replied young Rosetti. "The press love us."

Scotty smirked at Ray Rosetti's naïveté. "Give over, Ray," he said. "They're just waiting for something like that. One false move and they'll be at us."

The screams from the excited fans could be heard from outside the club as Bury The Rabbit set up their instruments on the small stage at the end of the dance floor. There was no need for a sound check as they wouldn't actually be playing their instruments. They'd simply mime to "Easy!" and its B side.

"What a waste of time this is," sighed Mark Leroy.

John Leroy agreed with his twin. "I'll be glad when we start playing live," he said. "This is dead boring."

Franco came to inspect the stage.

"Fifteen minutes before they open the doors, lads," he said. "So if you want to go and tidy yourselves up…"

Scotty and the Leroy twins headed for the room

which the club's management had designated as their dressing-room for the evening.

Ray Rosetti lingered behind, pretending to fiddle with the strap on his guitar as he watched the others leave.

"You said you wanted a word, Dad."

Franco leaned against one of the huge speakers set up at the side of the stage and removed a pack of cigarettes from his pocket. He took out one for himself, handed one to his son and then lit them both with a solid gold lighter.

"I've been at Sloop Records again today," he began. "There's been some business to discuss."

"Oh, no!" grimaced Rosetti junior. "Don't tell me! They've changed their mind about the album."

"Not exactly. No," said Franco. "But – and this is a *very big* but, Ray – I've been wanting to tell you all week. Holding it back's been killing me."

"Go on. Go on!" He gulped, fearing it was bad news.

"They want to replace you with a new lead singer. They want you out of the group!"

Ray Rosetti's face whitened.

"What?" he gasped. "Why the—?"

"Don't panic!" interrupted his father. "It's better than you think. They've decided to drop the album deal for Bury The Rabbit. For the moment."

"But they can't!"

"Listen, son," he went on, "they don't want an album, just yet, from Bury The Rabbit. But they *do* want one from Ray Rosetti. You're going solo!"

Ray Rosetti gazed, open-mouthed at his father. He-wasn't sure if he'd heard correctly.

"Are you kiddin' me?" he said.

"Now, why would I do that?" laughed Franco. "They want to hear some demo tracks from you before they sign the deal, but that's no problem. Everyone at Sloop thinks you can do it on your own. To tell you the truth, none of them believe that Bury The Rabbit will survive the year. Sloop's managing director was saying he doesn't like the group's image; he thinks they all pale into insignificance when you're on stage."

"I'm glad he thinks that," sneered Ray Rosetti. "I've always thought so. As far as I'm concerned Bury The Rabbit is Ray Rosetti's backing band!"

"Not any longer," smiled Franco. "Sloop aims to build you into another Pete Shannon. Everyone there thinks you can do it, son. And so do I."

"I know I can do it," said Ray Rosetti. "I'm better than Pete Shannon, any day."

The screams from the fans outside began to drown their conversation.

"When are you going to tell Scotty and the Leroys?" he added.

"Certainly not tonight," replied Franco. "We've got a gig to get through."

He drew deeply on his cigarette.

"Monday. I'll break it to them on Monday!"

Chapter 64

It was a wet Monday morning and Terry was soaked to the skin by the time he'd arrived at Camberwell. He'd had to take a train and two buses from Gran's house to the Regent Tavern, and the A–Z she'd lent him to find his way was sopping wet.

Maureen had seen the advert for bar work in the *Evening Standard* and Terry had rung the pub immediately. It was the "Live Entertainment" bit he liked. He imagined spending his time with struggling pop groups, all gigging for practically nothing in the hope of being discovered by some record company talent scout. He missed the music business like crazy. His brush with it had excited him beyond imagination and he wished – oh, how he wished it hadn't all gone wrong.

He looked up at the red brick building that faced him, then took off his glasses and wiped them on a damp tissue. He should have worn his lenses as he did almost every day now, but he'd had to get up very early and couldn't face putting them in. Through the smeared spectacles he read, "Regent Tavern". He rang the bell.

"You're too young for a barman. I'm sorry!" said Nick Cox. He smiled kindly at the boy.

Terry was disappointed. The thought hadn't entered his head.

"Oh!" was all he could say.

"You can't go home like that," added the manager. "Come through to the kitchen and dry off. I'll make you some coffee."

They walked through to the back of the pub and into the vast kitchen where two young women in white overalls were making sandwiches. A man of about the same age, also in overalls, was stirring a large pot on one of two stoves. The room was very warm and Terry's glasses immediately began to steam up.

"Take your coat off," said Nick. "Hang it over the back of the chair."

"Coffee's hot, Mr Cox!" called one of the girls. "Do you want some?"

"Yes. Thanks, Helen," replied the manager. "And one for the drowned rat, here."

He gestured for Terry to sit at the well-scrubbed, wooden table then pulled up another chair to sit beside him.

"I'm sorry about the wasted journey," he said. "You sounded older on the phone."

Terry shrugged.

"Just left school, have you?"

"Yes," replied Terry.

"And no work round your way?"

"Not a lot, no. Nothing I'm interested in."

Helen called across to him, "D'you take sugar?"

"Yes, please." Terry smiled at her. She was very pretty and couldn't have been much older than himself.

"So what *are* you interested in?" asked Nick Cox.

Terry laughed. "Music, mainly."

He wondered if he should tell Mr Cox the story of how he'd left school before taking his exams, because he'd got a recording contract with the famous Joe Fisher, Pete Shannon's manager, and how he'd been promised the world – only to discover that Joe Fisher was a snake who'd done the dirty on him.

Helen brought two cups of coffee to the table.

"One with and one without," she said. She put them down and returned to her sandwich making.

"It was the 'live entertainment' that grabbed me," explained Terry. "I thought I'd enjoy that."

"Oh, I'm sure you would," Nick replied. "We've got a great reputation here. It's taken years to build up, of course, but now people come from all over the place. It's the freebies, you see. I think that's half the trick. No entrance fees. And normal drinks prices."

Terry sipped on his coffee.

"How desperate are you for a job, then?" Nick asked him.

"Well, I need to get some work pretty soon," replied Terry. "I'm skint."

Nick smiled. "I'll scratch your back if…"

Terry didn't know what he was talking about.

"Helen's leaving," explained Nick. "Going off to college. You can take her place if you like."

Terry wasn't that desperate. He knew that he could get a job making sandwiches near his home. Why travel all the way to Camberwell to do it?

"Helen's been very happy here," Nick added. He called out to her, "Haven't you, love?"

"Very," she called back. She smiled at Terry. "This bit's not much fun, but the evenings are great."

"It's a long day, mind you," added Nick, "making the lunchtime sarnies from about nine o'clock. Your afternoons are free, but then you'll have to help backstage in the evenings."

He knew, with that line, that he had Terry's attention. He could tell by the look in the boy's eyes.

"Interested?"

"Yes," replied Terry.

"And suppose we keep it all hush hush?" suggested Nick.

Terry knew what he meant: no National Insurance; no tax.

"No forms to fill in," said Nick. "You scratch my back…"

"And I'll scratch yours," grinned Terry.

"It's a long way to travel every day," said Gran. "You'll spend half your wages in fares."

Terry wasn't sure how they were going to react, especially Maureen.

"I won't be able to travel," he explained. "The last train leaves before I finish work."

"You're not going to live there, are you?" asked Maureen.

"Well…"

"I see," she said.

Gran looked even more disappointed than Maureen. She'd got used to having a man round the house. Not that Terry was good at the practical things that men were supposed to be good at. He could only just about change a plug. And that took him hours! Maureen was much better at doing things like that. No, that certainly wasn't the reason she liked having him around. It was because she felt safer. At night, when she couldn't sleep.

Before Terry lived with them she would often be woken in the night, by a passing car or late party-stragglers. That was the trouble with having to sleep downstairs. And, once awake, she would start to worry. With every creak and bump she would imagine that somebody was in the house, looking around for something worth stealing. Or worse! She'd seen it on the TV: how youngsters had no respect for old people nowadays and had done the most awful things to them. Terrible. But now ... now that Terry was in the house, she felt safer. Nowadays, if she woke, she'd think about him, up there in the bedroom just above hers, and she'd go straight back to sleep again. With Terry in the house, she felt secure.

"They've got a nice room there," said Terry. "And they'll give me all my meals for nothing. I might even be able to save a few bob."

"Will you be home weekends?" asked Maureen.

"Don't be daft, Mo," said Gran. "It's a pub. Week-ends are their busiest times."

"I've got Mondays and Tuesdays off," explained Terry. "I'll come home on Monday mornings and stay till as late as I can on Tuesday."

Maureen felt really sad. There was a strange tightening in her throat.

"I'll have to take Mondays and Tuesdays off school then, I suppose. If I'm going to see you at all."

Gran looked at her disapprovingly, over the top of her glasses. But she didn't say anything. Not yet. Now wasn't the time.

Chapter 65

Chas Atkins knew nothing about the impending split of Bury The Rabbit and found Rosetti's mood strange, to say the least. Rosetti was the self-elected spokesman for the group, and would usually spend much of the recording session telling the producer how to do his job. Today he was quiet. Chas put it down to the fact that the boy was satisfied with the two tracks for the new single which were almost finished. There were just a few backing vocals to record and then, of course, the long, painful process of the mix.

Franco sat silently at the back of the control room, sipping coffee as he flicked, aimlessly, through a copy of *Music Forum*.

"Right, boys. That's it!" said Chas. "Come in and listen."

As the group entered the control room to listen to a rough-mix playback of "Gimmee!", Ray Rosetti looked across at his father and gave a half smile. He was dreading what was about to happen. He wasn't looking forward to Scotty's reaction at all!

Chas started the tape and Rosetti's voice, sounding more powerful than it had ever done, screamed from the speakers:

> *"I took the warnin'*
> *Like a storm in a teacup.*
> *What d'you want me to do*
> *If yer world is warmin' up?*
> *We're goin' out soon*
> *So I'll live it up while*
> *I'm still in credit.*
> *Yeah I'm goin' in style!"*

Scotty thumped Rosetti on the back.

"You sound fantastic, mate!" he said.

Rosetti stared straight ahead, saying nothing.

John and Mark Leroy grinned contentedly.

Chas Atkins faded the tape as he turned to face the group. "Well?" he asked.

"Great, Chas!" said Franco. "Even better than 'Easy!'. It can't fail."

Scotty opened his mouth to speak and Franco held up a hand to silence him.

"I'd like a word with you, Scotty," he said, seriously. "And with John and Mark."

They could tell by the tone of Franco's voice that all was not well.

Ray Rosetti started to tremble. "I, um … I'll just go and get us some coffee," he said.

Scotty exploded. "You can't do that! We've been working for six months solid on this group. We've just gone to number two in the charts, for God's sake! You just can't do it!"

"I'm sorry, Scotty," replied Franco. "But we can. You look carefully at the management contract. And at the contract with Sloop Records. We can do it, son."

"He doesn't mean legally!" added a fuming John Leroy. "We know you can do it legally. But morally? How can you, after all this time, just tear everything apart? We've worked hard for this success…"

"And how do you think Ray'll cope on his own?" interrupted Scotty. "I wrote seventy-five per cent of 'Easy!' And nearly all of 'Gimmee!' Ray's not a song writer and you know it!"

Ray Rosetti appeared at the door with a tray of coffee.

"That's all you know!" he said.

Scotty glared across at him. "You creep!"

"Now, come on, lads," Franco said, quickly. "Let's not get into a slanging match."

Chas Atkins took a coffee from Rosetti's tray and left the control room without speaking.

"I suppose he knew all about this, too, did he?" snapped Mark Leroy.

"No," replied Franco. "This is the first he's heard of it."

"So…!" said Scotty. "What happens to 'Gimmee!'?"

Franco kept his voice low, trying to calm the boys.

"It'll be released as soon as 'Easy!' is out of the top forty."

"As Bury The Rabbit or under the name of Ray

Rosetti?" sneered John Leroy.

Ray Rosetti looked at his father, nervously. What would be the reaction to this bombshell?

"As Bury The Rabbit featuring ROSETTI," he said.

"No!" screamed Scotty. "No! No! No!"

There was a brief silence, broken calmly by Mark Leroy.

"No way. You can count me out."

"Me too," added his twin. "I'm having nothing to do with it."

Franco's face reddened with anger. "You'll all do exactly as I say!" he said. "I own this group and I'll manage it in whatever way I see fit."

Scotty approached him and looked closely into Franco's eyes. "You don't own me, Mr Rosetti! Nobody owns me! You go ahead and release the new single in any way you like. But I won't be there to promote it. As from now, I quit!"

"Me too," added Mark Leroy.

John Leroy nodded his agreement.

"I'll sue," threatened Franco.

"So, sue!" replied Scotty.

He left the control room, followed by the Leroys.

Franco grinned across at his son. "That wasn't 'Easy', Ray."

Ray Rosetti smiled, encouragingly. "Had to be done, Dad."

"And I suppose it's even better than I'd hoped for," added Franco. "At least we don't have to worry about Bury The Rabbit. They no longer exist."

"One-hit-wonders!" laughed Rosetti.

Chapter 66

Ray Rosetti's mother knocked on the bathroom door.

"Ray?"

"I'm in the shower, Mum," he called. "Did you get it?"

Mrs Rosetti opened the *Sun* and folded back the appropriate page.

"Yes," she said.

"And?"

"It's all right."

"Front page?" he asked.

He opened the bathroom door, still dripping wet, with a towel wrapped around his waist.

"No. Not quite."

He made a grab for the paper but she pulled it away from him.

"You dry yourself first," she said. "You're dripping water all over the carpet."

She turned her back on him and began to head up the next flight of stairs to his bedroom. "I'll put it on your bed."

He tore past her, snatched the paper, leapt up the stairs and hurried into his room, closing the door behind him.

"Raymond!" she shouted. "Don't you sit on your bed in that wet towel."

He sat on the bed and read the article, headlined:

BURY THE RABBIT BREAK UP...
EXCLUSIVE

and he liked what he read. There were no misquotes; Rica Stubbs, bless her, had written exactly what she'd said she would. She'd promised to show him in a good light ... and she'd kept her word. Scotty and the Leroys came across as just untalented hangers-on, although she'd been very careful not to use those exact words.

He'd met up again with Rica at the Brit Awards, two days after his band had split and, having discovered that apart from her work for *GO!* magazine she was now also working as a freelance journalist, he immediately, as before, set out to seduce her with his dark brown eyes; fluttering his long eyelashes as he smiled at her with straight, white, perfect teeth. And instead of circulating and talking to fellow-musicians, Rosetti insured his future with the press. It had paid off. He wondered if he should ring to thank her and ask if he could take her for dinner. She'd enjoyed his company last time! She obviously really fancied him. But then, didn't most women?

He stood and looked at his still wet body in the full-length mirror. He wasn't surprised that he'd got all those girls screaming for him. The body was perfect. No gym. No weight training. All natural. He ran his hands over his firm, smooth-skinned chest; nicely tanned with regular use of his mother's sun bed, and smiled, checking the teeth as he did so. He squeezed a little gel on to his fingers and ran them through his already shiny, jet-black hair. He removed the damp towel and lay on his bed, arms behind his head, looking up at the ceiling. And he thought about the attractive Rica Stubbs. And pretty little Lynette, who followed the group wherever they went, pushing love notes into his hand, and ... Maureen. He thought of Maureen. Again. He was always thinking about her. Why couldn't he get her out of his head? Hadn't she dumped him for that gypsy? Smith! Terry Smith! How Rosetti hated him. Nobody had ever dumped Rosetti. Nobody except Maureen. His heart began to beat faster. Maureen, the only girl he'd ever really wanted. She could have had it all if she'd stayed with him: money, reflected glory through his success as a pop singer and ... he ran his hands once again over his body...

And he wondered ... what if he called on her? Perhaps if he just turned up one day, one day when Smithy the Gyppo wasn't around... He wondered ... he wondered if she...?

Chapter 67

Scotty arrived at Joe Allen's just before one o'clock to find Chas Atkins waiting for him at the bar.

"Drink?" Chas asked.

"Just some orange juice or something," replied Scotty. He looked around in search of the well-known television faces who were supposed to frequent this famous restaurant. There was no one he recognized.

"Lunch-time isn't much cop for star-gazing, I'm afraid," laughed Chas, knowing exactly what the lad was doing. Didn't *he* always do it too? "It's better late at night, after the theatres close."

"So, what's this all about then?" asked Scotty.

The maitre d' approached them.

"Your table's ready when you are, gentlemen."

He led them to a small table tucked into a dimly-lit corner.

"I've got a proposition to put to you, Scotty," said Chas, "which you may or may not be interested in."

He picked up the menu and studied the wine list.

"We can't order just yet," he said. "I'm expecting someone else."

"I'm here!" said a voice from behind Scotty's chair.

"Sam!" smiled Chas Atkins. He stood and shook the newcomer's hand.

Scotty stared at the tall, good-looking man who pulled up a chair and sat between them. He'd seen him before, but he couldn't place where. He was in his forties, at least, with strikingly handsome features; very long, blond, almost white hair and brilliant blue eyes.

"Scotty, this is Bif," said Chas. "Bif ... this is Phillip Scott. Scotty from Bury The Rabbit."

Both men shook hands.

Bif from the Thunderdomes. He looked so different in a suit.

Scotty laughed. "I didn't recognize you at first," he said. "Sorry." Then he added, "I think you're great. One of the best drummers around."

"*Was* one of the best drummers around," corrected Bif with a grin. "We haven't done anything for two years."

Scotty couldn't believe it was that long. He was sure they'd been in the charts recently.

"What about, 'Coming On Cold'?" he asked.

"Re-mix," explained Bif. "Probably recorded before you were born."

"Bif's looking to invest some of his millions in KANSIT," explained Chas.

"Well, a few thousand anyway," Bif interjected, winking at Scotty.

"We're aiming to expand in a big way."

A waiter arrived at the table, pad and pencil in hand.

"Are you ready to order, gentlemen?"

"Not quite," replied Chas. Then he added, "Just bring us a bottle of the Beaujolais."

"We've been talking for ages about getting together on a business venture," continued Bif. "Ever since the Thunderdomes stopped going out on the road."

"But now it's serious," added Chas.

"I've got to do something pronto or I'll go crazy, man," Bif went on. "George Harrison and the Who can keep their film companies, or whatever it is they're into. But it's still rock 'n' roll for me!"

"You've seen the premises, Scotty," said Chas. "It's gonna be fantastic."

"The builders are working on it right now. KANSIT will be the best studio complex in London before we're finished," Bif enthused. "There isn't an artist in the business – solo performer or pop group – that won't be using it by the end of the year. We're determined it's gonna be mega successful!"

"And from there, as a side-line, we're also going to run our own production company," explained Chas Atkins. "Our own small indie label."

Scotty looked from Bif to Chas Atkins and back again.

"Hold on!" he said. "Why am I here? What's it got to do with me?"

Bif grabbed his arm. "I've heard your stuff, Scotty," he said. " 'Easy' is a great song. Really commercial. And I happen to think that 'Gimmee!' is even better."

Chas looked across at Scotty, guiltily.

"Sorry, Scotty," he said. "I ran off a rough mix so he could hear it."

"And the two flips," added Bif. "Great stuff. You can definitely write hit songs, man."

"Thanks," said Scotty. "But you're forgetting something. I wrote those numbers with Ray Rosetti."

"Bull!" laughed Chas Atkins. "I know how much Rosetti put into those numbers. I've watched you working, don't forget." He paused. "Why on earth did you let him take all that credit?" he said. "He's a parasite."

"His father held the purse strings, didn't he?" said Scotty. "Without Rosetti there wouldn't have been a group."

Chas looked at Bif. "Told you!"

The waiter arrived with the wine, uncorked it and poured a little into Chas Atkins' glass.

"I'm sure that'll be fine," said Chas.

The waiter poured all three glasses, placed the bottle on the table and left.

Silently, each of the three drank.

"Well?" asked Chas.

"How about joining us, Scotty?" added Bif. "You and Chas can write and produce the numbers and I'll see to the business side."

Scotty almost choked on his wine.

"Could make you a very rich man," said Chas.

Scotty put down his drink and toyed with the stem of the glass.

"I … I don't know," he replied. "I don't know if I'm *that* good a song-writer."

Bif squeezed his arm again. "Of course you are, man. And if you're not, Chas *is*!"

Scotty was surprised. "I didn't know…"

" 'Jam-On-Jam' … 'A Little Too Old' … 'Write Me'…"

"I had no idea," said Scotty. "I knew you produced them, but–"

"How else d'you think I got the mansion in Surrey and enough bread to fulfil my dreams of building a studio complex like KANSIT?" laughed Chas. "By producing groups like Bury The Rabbit?"

"I'd have to think about it," said Scotty. "I … I'm not sure."

"Don't take too long, man," smiled Bif. "You're at the top of a very long list."

"When do I have to decide?" he asked, knowing that he was very interested in the idea, but not sure if he wanted to give up his performing career for a life in the studio.

"How about giving us a call tomorrow?" said Bif.

The waiter arrived, once again, to take the order.

"We're still not ready," said Chas. "But bring us some champagne while we decide."

"Yes, sir," replied the waiter.

"Champagne?" Bif grinned. "Bit early to celebrate, isn't it? Mr Scott here hasn't agreed to anything yet."

Chas was confident. "Oh, but I'm sure he will."

He lifted his glass.

"A bit premature, perhaps," he said, "but let's drink to chart success, eh? And possibly the number one indie in Europe!"

Maureen was on prefect-duty from eight forty-five. She looked at her watch and wondered how Terry would be feeling, knowing that he would be starting his new job within the next fifteen minutes.

She'd woken, this dark and wet Wednesday morning, feeling empty, and … a little afraid. She couldn't understand why she'd felt like that. He'd left late the previous evening, seemingly quite happy, telling her he'd see her next Monday. She, on the other hand, was not happy; far, far from it. She was so miserable that she could hardly speak, though she didn't let him see just how bad she felt. She didn't cry. Not until he'd turned the corner. Then, when Gran had asked her if she was all right, she'd just nodded and gone to her room where, lying face down on the bed to stifle the sobs, she'd thought her heart would break.

"Do you want a crisp, Mo?" asked Tracey. Maureen jumped. She hadn't realized there was anyone else in the cloakroom. The red-headed girl from 4M was sitting on one of the wooden benches below a row of pegs from which hung dozens of wet coats.

"You shouldn't be in here, Trace," said Maureen. She sat beside the girl and helped herself to a crisp.

"It's raining," said Tracey. "I ain't standing out there in the pouring rain."

"You should be in your classroom," Maureen corrected her. "Not sitting here in the cloakroom."

Tracey didn't attempt to leave. She offered Maureen another crisp and both girls sat, crunching and staring into space.

"Terry starts his new job this morning," volunteered Maureen. "In Camberwell."

"Camberwell?" replied Tracey, sounding surprised. "That's a long way to go."

376

"Yes," said Maureen, trying to make it sound as though it hadn't affected her at all. "He's going to live there."

"Really?" said Tracey. "Do you mean he's left your gran's?"

"Yes. He moved out last night."

"Won't you miss him?" asked Tracey. "I thought you two were in love."

"We are," said Maureen. She felt her bottom lip tremble slightly and bit on it. She didn't want Tracey to know. Not Tracey. Anyone but Tracey.

"Like me and Scotty," went on Tracey. "We felt like you two. But then he had to leave for his job, didn't he? And now look at him. They've gone up to number two, you know."

"I know," replied Maureen.

Tracey sighed. "He'll be rich, I expect. Him and Rosetti."

"Yes. I expect so."

"You should have stayed with Ray Rosetti, you know." She started her lecture. Maureen had heard it so many times before. "You'd have been rich too."

"I didn't love Rosetti, Tracey," said Maureen. "I love Terry."

"But now he's left you," said Tracey, insensitively.

"He's coming back," Maureen replied harshly. "He's only gone away to do some work."

"Yeah," said Tracey. "Scotty said he was coming back. But he never did. The pig!"

Maureen could feel the tears welling up. She looked through the window that ran the full length of the cloakroom. She couldn't bear for Tracey to see her cry.

"It's pouring down now," she said.

The playground was full of puddles and two Year Seven boys, laughing their heads off, were jumping in and out of them, soaking their shoes and trouser bottoms.

Maureen sighed, deeply. "Kids." She'd never felt so alien from them.

"Yeah. You should have stayed with Rosetti," Tracey said again, adding, "D'you want another crisp, before I finish 'em?"

Bob Jamieson peered over the top of the pegs and glared at Tracey and Maureen.

"Tracey!" he bellowed. "Get to your classroom!"

Tracey rushed away, without saying a word.

"And what do you think you're doing?" he bawled at Maureen. "You're supposed to be on duty, Madam! Not sitting here discussing boyfriend trouble."

He couldn't have known. He hadn't heard any of the conversation. But he wasn't terribly surprised when Maureen suddenly burst into tears and rushed into the girls' toilets. He often got that reaction from the girls, especially the older ones. He always put it down to "time of the month"! Hyper-sensitivity. Part of growing up.

"Kids!"

Helen had been right. Making sandwiches for the Regent Tavern's lunch-time trade hadn't been much fun and Terry hadn't got on at all well with the young chef who was in charge of hot snacks. He was extremely bad-tempered and seemed to be snapping at everyone all morning.

"Don't take any notice of him," whispered Helen. "He's always like that."

Terry had liked her immediately. She was staying on for another week, basically to show him the ropes, but Terry noted that she worked extremely hard and he wondered how he'd manage to cope with her work load as well as his own, once she'd left. There seemed to be so much to do.

Apart from being extremely pretty, Helen was also a cut above most of the girls that Terry had met. She was very well spoken, never dropping her aitches as he did, and he wondered how she'd react if she knew that he was a gypsy. She'd probably never come across a gypsy in her life, except for the ones that sold lucky heather at the tube stations.

"This evening'll be fun," she'd said. "You'll enjoy it." And she was right. He did.

Terry's job was to work the lighting, tape-deck and curtains for the acts who were to appear on the tiny stage at the end of the saloon bar. Helen showed him how it all worked and Terry picked it up in no time at all. It was nowhere near as difficult as it had first seemed.

The resident three-piece band, with their Welsh singer, Huw, made Terry feel immediately at home.

"It's a good pub to work in, TelBoy," smiled Huw. "Great clientele. You'll have a great time."

Chapter 68

It had been one of the worst Sundays Maureen had had in ages. She'd done the usual chores: getting Gran's papers, doing her French homework, cooking the roast, etc., but all this without Terry by her side to make light of it. She missed him so much. Saturdays and Sundays were always the days she looked forward to. But not this week. And for how many more weeks? She couldn't bear it if it was always going to be like this.

As Gran dozed in her chair, half-listening to the hymn singing on the telly, Maureen took the radio through into the back room. She and Terry always did this on Sunday afternoons. They never missed the Top Forty. And today, after that splurge of publicity about the split between Rosetti and Scotty, she was sure that Bury The Rabbit would climb that one place to the coveted number one slot. With that thought, perhaps it was best Terry wasn't here. She hated seeing that look on his face whenever Rosetti made new ground in the charts. Number two was bad enough, but...

Maureen had been unusually irritated by Gran, who'd woken just as the countdown had reached the top five, calling out, "Mo, love! Make us a nice cup o' tea. There's a good girl."

So she'd carried the radio with her into the kitchen to wait for the kettle to boil, just in case the group had dropped to number four or three. Though she very much doubted it.

She'd managed to deliver the tea and return to the back room just in time to hear the number two record. A non-mover! "Easy!" From Bury The Rabbit. So they hadn't made it! Not this week, at least! And what irony! The number one record was by someone else she knew. Well, someone she'd met – albeit briefly.

"And that means there's a new number one," the DJ said. "Climbing eighteen places it's 'Don't Tell Me', from Pete Shannon."

There was a knock on the street door and Maureen's heart suddenly skipped a beat. For a fleeting moment she wondered if Terry had been given the day off but then, remembering he had his own key, she switched off the radio and made her way along the hall.

"Someone at the door, Mo!" called Gran.

"S'alright, Gran," she called back. "I'm here."

The visitor knocked again. Louder this time.

"I'm coming!" said Maureen.

She opened the door.

And stared.

"Well, well, well," she smiled. "Hello, stranger."

"Who is it, Mo?" shouted Gran.

"Can I come in?" he asked.

"Of course." She stepped back, allowing him to pass into the hall.

"Mo?" Gran shouted again. "Who is it?"

Sunday was the Regent Tavern's busiest evening of the week and the saloon was packed to capacity with people coming for miles to watch the cabaret, which as Nick Cox had said, was a "freebie". Terry had noted that it was free for the audience all right, but apart from the resident band and its lead singer, it wasn't free for the performers. Each of the acts had to pay five pounds for what Nick called "a licence" and this allowed them to do a spot lasting no more than five minutes. If they over-ran, they got "the gong", which meant a five pounds penalty fee on top of what they'd already paid.

"Clever," Terry had thought. "Everyone wants to be in 'show-biz' and here they are, paying for it."

"Most of them are hoping to be discovered," Helen had explained. "We do get quite a few talent scouts in here, actually; variety agents and that. People from record companies: that sort of thing."

Terry was excited by the prospect. "And has anyone been discovered?"

"A few," she'd grinned. "Mickie Teazle started here."

"He didn't, did he?" Terry had asked, amazed.

Mickie Teazle was, some thought, the best magician in the country and now had his own television show.

"Before my time, of course," Helen had added.

Nick Cox popped his head through the curtains.

"OK, boys," he said to Wayne and co. "I'll give 'em

five more minutes to get their drinks in, then we'll start."

Huw's ex-musicians – now Wayne Fielding's band – began to tune up.

Nick turned his head towards the "prompt corner". "Five minutes, Terry! Then dim the house lights."

Terry climbed into bed without even cleaning his teeth. It had been a long, exhausting day … though one he'd enjoyed immensely. He'd watched Helen at work all week and tonight, the busiest night of all, the responsibility for the stage management had been entirely his. Helen, of course, was by his side throughout the whole show, should anything go wrong, but fortunately he hadn't needed her advice.

Tonight was Helen's last night and from Wednesday Terry would have to run the whole show by himself; something he was quite looking forward to. He was also looking forward to tomorrow morning when he could go home to see Maureen. Two full days with her. Well, two full evenings and a couple of snatched lunch-times, anyway. He didn't want her to take time off from school. He didn't want her to fail her exams, just because of him.

He wondered if she'd want to hear how much he was enjoying his job. Perhaps he should play it down a bit, in case she thought he wasn't missing her. But he'd have to tell her about Wayne Fielding who used to be in Hym. What a great voice he had. It had made Terry feel really jealous when he realized that as a solo performer Wayne Fielding, if he were to be rediscovered, would knock spots off his successful ex-partner Gary Brenn. And Maureen would want to hear about Maurice, who told the naffest of jokes and then stripped to his Union Jack underwear whilst singing "Land Of Hope And Glory". And he'd tell her all about the talented people who paid their fivers in the hope of being discovered; the juggler who rode a unicycle and the ventriloquist with the red-headed schoolgirl dummy who looked a bit like Tracey.

And then there was Terry's favourite, of course. He'd have to tell Maureen about the Dancing Skinhead. Have to! The twenty-year-old guy with a skinhead hair cut, tight jeans (held up with red braces) and DMs who'd got the loudest applause of the evening by doing the can-can! "A speciality act," he called himself. And he didn't need a tape because, "The boys in the band play it great!"

Terry laughed and then yawned, turning on to his side to sleep, hoping that he'd remembered to set the alarm but knowing that there was no way he could get out of bed now, to check it. He was drifting away. And he wondered if Maureen had missed him as much as he'd missed her and he decided to avoid even mentioning Helen: pretty, sophisticated Helen, who, as they were operating the lighting board, allowed her hand to brush against his too often for there not to be anything meant by it. Helen, who said she'd pop in to see him one evening next week, just to see how he was getting on without her!

Chapter 69

Having spent two weeks at number two in the charts, "Easy!" dropped like a stone; nine, fourteen, twenty-six, thirty-nine … and out! Franco and Ray Rosetti had hoped that it wouldn't disappear quite so quickly. It wouldn't have been so bad had there been a follow-up single ready for release, but both father and son agreed that "Gimmee!" should be forgotten.

The upper floors of KANSIT were still under construction, although the basement and ground floors were ready: one recording studio, two rehearsal rooms and a half-functioning canteen. Franco, having no idea that Scotty had joined forces with Chas Atkins, hired the smallest of the rehearsal rooms so that his son could work with a group of session musicians. Most of the album had been written, but expert musicianship was needed to hone and polish the songs before taking them into the recording studio.

All of the musicians loathed the supercilious young

pop singer (who would scream abuse at them if he felt that they were slacking in any way) but every one of them had to agree that the songs were good and with the right producer, Ray Rosetti had a hit album on his hands.

"He's gonna be a big star, that's for sure," said the drummer.

"Without doubt," agreed the keyboard player. "More's the pity. The arrogant little yob!"

"How about SCAB records?" Scotty said, in all seriousness. "The SC from Scotty, A from Atkins and B from Bif."

"Do us a favour, Scotty," laughed Bif. "Sounds like a refugee from the punk era."

"SAB would be better," said Chas Atkins.

Scotty, Chas Atkins and Bif were working from Chas' home, aware that the office suite at the top of KANSIT would take at least another six weeks to complete.

"Why don't we turn it round?" suggested Bif. "BAS records."

"BASS."

"DOUBLE-BASS."

"BASS-BEAT."

"BASIC BEAT." This from Scotty.

"Good one, Scotty," said Bif. "BASIC BEAT."

And BASIC BEAT records was born!

Chapter 70

Terry took the coach to Leicester. It was cheaper than the train. Maureen had wanted to take a couple of days off school to go with him, but they couldn't afford the two fares. He gazed out of the window at the passing scenery and cursed at the thought that his treasured two days off work, always spent with Maureen, had to be wasted in travelling North.

Billy, his younger brother, had come down to their old campsite, Berryfield, a few weeks previously and paid Maureen a surprise visit. It was just to inform everyone that Mother was getting married again. And would Terry be able to make it to the wedding? Terry wouldn't! Even if he wasn't working on that Saturday!

"You mustn't be like that, Terry," Gran had said. "She needs a bit of happiness, does your mother. Look what she's been through. Don't begrudge her a bit of happiness, love."

But he did. He couldn't help it. He begrudged her *that* sort of happiness! It was too early. Disrespectful and far, far too early.

Belcher met him at the coach station. The huge bear of a man flung open the door to the van and yelled out, "So you've made it then!"

Terry hauled himself up into the cab, and the two drove along in silence until they reached Grange Farm. Belcher had obviously wanted to speak. Terry didn't.

"See?" said Belcher, as they bounced down the dirt track towards the dozen or so trailers. "Better than Berryfield, innit?"

It wasn't better. It was much worse. More mud. More scrap metal. More dogs running around than Berryfield had ever had. And two tethered ponies looking, Terry thought, rather undernourished. He wondered if he was being unfair. Perhaps his mind had been clouded by the thought of his mother actually marrying this man whom he'd never liked: Belcher.

Mother was waiting, nervously, on the trailer steps, aware of what Terry would be thinking. She hoped he wouldn't react as aggressively as young Billy had. At least he'd come all the way to Leicester to see her – she hoped to wish her well. The wedding was to take place the following Saturday and it was a pity he wouldn't be able to come to the ceremony. All the family and many of their friends said they'd make it; even Uncle Render, who was right up in Scotland now. It was a pity Terry wouldn't be there. But, she understood that he couldn't take time off from his new job. It was silly to think that he might. And at least he'd taken the trouble to write and say he would come up this Monday. She hoped he was going to be kind. She didn't want any more aggression.

She wrapped her arms around him.

"Oh, Terry," she said. "Thank you for coming, boy."

On the journey he'd planned what he was going to say. "My father's lying six foot under – hardly cold yet, in a grave which you've conveniently deserted to come and live up here, with your boyfriend – and now that you've decided to marry him, supposing you tell us the truth, eh? That you've been at it with him for ages, even while my father lay dying in hospital!"

But he didn't say any of these things. He squeezed her tightly to himself and sighed, "Mum. Oh, Mum!"

Terry and Billy walked across the field towards the Grange Farm campsite. Terry had needed this time alone with his brother, to find out what he truly felt. The night before, after tea, they'd all sat and talked about old times, just like they were a real family; except of course they weren't a real family … and could never be. Not without Dad.

Terry had to set off for the coach station within the next hour or so and he felt no sadness at leaving; although, curiously, the thought of feeling no sadness in leaving his family did sadden him. A little. This place had never been his home. Even Berryfield was no longer his home. His home was now with Maureen and Gran. That's where he felt he really belonged.

"How's the new school?" he asked Billy.

"Same as the old one," replied Billy. "I hate it!"

"No friends?"

"Only me mates from here. From the campsite." He paused. "I hate gorgios," he said, finally.

Terry put an arm around his brother's neck,

affectionately, as he always used to. "You don't, Billy," he said. "Don't be daft. Not all of them."

"Gorgios hate us," said Billy, "so why can't we hate them back?"

"You don't hate Maureen, or her gran, do you?" asked Terry. "They're gorgios. You don't hate them!"

"I wouldn't rob them," replied Billy.

Terry waited for him to qualify this strange statement. He didn't.

"I ain't stayin', you know?" Billy suddenly burst out. "I ain't stayin' here, with 'im and 'er."

"You have to, Billy," sighed Terry. "Where else are you going to go?"

"Dunno, yet."

"Mum would be ever so upset if you ran away," he added. "She really cares, you know."

Billy sneered at the comment. "Oh yeah? Then why's she marryin' 'im when she knows I hate 'im?"

"Billy..." he pleaded. He remembered Gran's words. "She needs a bit of happiness. Look what she's had to put up with. Don't begrudge her that, Billy. Please."

They walked on in silence for a while.

"You shouldn't have given up that record thing, you know," said Billy, suddenly.

"You know why I did it." Terry had thought that he'd explained all this once.

"Yeah. You did it for the family. You told me. Because you didn't want to hurt 'em."

"That's right."

"They don't mind about hurting people though, do they?"

"Don't be daft."

390

"It's true!" Billy's voice was getting louder. "You cared about her and she's gonna marry Belcher, no matter what we think about it. And you cared about Dad … and he's bloody dead, Terry. And you cared about me! And I wanted you to be a pop star. So why'd you do it, eh? Why'd you do it, Terry? It was the only thing I was looking forward to. My brother doing something. And now you're doing nuffink! Just like I'll do nuffink!" He burst into tears. "Just like Dad did nuffink." He covered his eyes with his sleeve. "Why'd you do it, Terry? Why'd you do it?"

Chapter 71

The Leroys were over the moon. They'd thought that their careers had ended before they'd really begun and had even discussed with their parents the possibility of returning to school. Now, with a song-writing/management/production team like this behind them, it was all systems go! Make or break! They'd decided to put themselves into the hands of BASIC BEAT. Totally! Allow themselves to be controlled, manipulated, whatever! They had nothing to lose and, from what Chas Atkins had said, they had everything to gain.

A stylist was immediately employed to handle the image of the good-looking, if somewhat pimply, twins. The outfits would have to be "street" if they were to grab the audience they were seeking: affordable clothes for young fans. Suntans, even if from a bottle, were essential to cover the pimples. And the hair? Cropped short, just like the defunct group, Hym.

Bif called the publicist who'd successfully handled the Thunderdomes' career and arranged a meeting.

* * *

A tall, dapper, Spaniard greeted the twins with a firm handshake.

"This is Santiago Gomez, boys," said Bif.

"And you are John and Mark Leroy," smiled Santiago. "Or should I say *were* John and Mark Leroy."

"*Were?*" asked Mark, surprised. He hadn't thought that they'd be changing their names.

Santiago shook his head and tutted.

"I don't like this name. No." He looked closely at Mark. "You don't look like a Mark. Marcus, I think. That's much better. No?"

Before Mark had time to speak, Santiago turned his attention to John.

"John is all right. For sure."

"Thank you," laughed John.

"John and Marcus," he went on. "And the name of your group is...?"

"The Leroys," interrupted Bif. "As simple as that."

"No!" argued Santiago. "Le Roi, I think. No? Le Roi!"

Bif thought about it.

"Le Roi."

Mark – now Marcus – looked at his brother and grinned. He wasn't sure about the new name and wondered how John felt about it.

John shrugged, resignedly. He didn't care. Let them do what they wanted. They knew best. He hoped!

Within two days, a very worried Santiago Gomez asked to meet again with Bif. In private.

"I think you have a problem on your hands here," warned the publicist. "I have tried to have some decent talks with your boys, but it is almost impossible."

Bif smiled. "They're not the best conversationalists, are they?"

"How can I sell a group for interviews when they have nothing to say?"

Bif sighed. "They're great musicians, you know."

Santiago shrugged. "That means nothing unless they can sell it to the public."

"But that's your job." Bif winked at him. "Come on, Santi! That's what you're paid for."

"If I can get them on to the TV shows ... fine. They look very good. Just so long as they stick to performing their music. But the radio? Impossible. It'll even be difficult selling them to the magazines. They have no story to tell."

"Then *give* them a story," suggested Bif. "Give them a new background. Nobody really got to know anything about them anyway, when they were with Bury The Rabbit. Make something up. They'll go along with it. They're very intelligent kids."

Santiago shook his head. "I'll try, but..."

"That's all I'm asking you to do, Santiago. Give it all you've got. I'm sure that once they've had their first hit record, they'll grow more confident. We won't be able to stop them talking then."

Santiago grinned. "Such high hopes for two very insignificant boys."

"Two extremely good-looking boys."

"Thin and pimply," argued Santiago.

"With a great musical talent and street appeal. I'm sure of it."

Santiago raised his eyes heavenwards. "If you say so."

"I *do*," said Bif, firmly. "Besides, at the moment we've only offered them a contract for one single. That's all. If it doesn't work…"

"You'll bring me someone new?"

"Maybe."

The publicist laughed. "Someone who can *talk*, eh?"

Chapter 72

Terry had changed his clothes three times. He couldn't decide what to wear. Both pairs of jeans were grubby and his trousers and best shirt were in need of ironing. He settled, finally, on the trousers. Better to look crumpled than dirty.

Helen tapped lightly on his bedroom door before entering. "Are you ready?"

"Nearly," he said. "I've just got to put my lenses in."

It'd been nearly two months since she'd left the Regent Tavern, but she'd popped in to see him at least twice a week. Her college wasn't far from the pub, though she never came to visit him before the evening shift, remembering how she'd treasured her afternoon naps when she'd worked there.

She'd return to her parents' house in Chelsea, eat, shower, change, watch a bit of TV and then borrow the Mini to drive herself to Camberwell. This meant that she could drink "afters" in the lounge bar with Terry and "the boys in the band".

She tried, regularly, to persuade Terry to invite her to his room, but he would always feign tiredness. This became a standing joke between Terry and Nick, the landlord.

"Get in there, Terry," Nick would say. "She's beautiful. I wish she'd invite herself up to my room."

It wasn't that Terry didn't like Helen. That was the trouble. He liked her a lot! And he didn't want to be left alone with her, just in case...! He couldn't do that to Maureen. He loved Maureen too much to hurt her. And it *would* hurt her, if ever she found out that he'd...

"I thought we were going to meet down in the kitchen?" he said. "At half eleven."

"I was early, so I came up. You don't mind, do you?"

"Er ... no," he replied, though he did.

He began to wish he'd never accepted her invitation. A party in Brixton. All her college friends would be there, celebrating somebody's twenty-first. He wouldn't know anyone and was sure he wouldn't fit in with those posh college types; so at first he'd refused. He liked to get to bed early on Sundays, anyway. As soon as the pub closed. Then he could get up very early and get back to Gran's, before Maureen went off to school. She had two free periods on a Monday morning.

"Don't be such a spoil-sport," Helen had said. "It won't be a late night. The party starts at eight, so by the time we get there it'll be almost over. I promise you I'll get you back to the pub before two o'clock."

So he'd agreed.

"Have you got any booze to take?" he asked her. He

never drank alcohol, and she wouldn't be able to drink as she was driving, but he knew they daren't turn up to a party empty-handed.

"Two bottles of wine in the car."

"Is this shirt all right?" he asked her. "It's not too creased is it?"

She approached him and gently ran her fingertips across his chest.

"It's a bit creased, yes," she said.

Her hand continued moving ... slowly ... down his sleeve. She leaned forward and put her lips against his. He tried, gently, to pull away.

"What's the matter?" she whispered.

"Nothing." He could feel his body start to tremble.

"Kiss me, Terry," she said, pathetically. "Please."

"I can't," he replied. He gulped, nervously. "I'm sorry, Helen. But I can't."

She kissed him again.

He weakened under the softness of her lips as he felt his passion uncontrollably rising. He put his arms around her and pulled her closer.

And this time, *he* kissed *her*.

Helen parked the car on the main road, under a street lamp.

"It's down there," she said to Terry, pointing to a narrow side street. "But I'd better not take the car down there."

He knew what she meant. At this time of night, in this area, they were likely to find all four wheels had disappeared by the time the party was over.

He picked up the bottles of wine from the back seat.

"How much do I owe you?" he asked.

She smiled. "Nothing. You've already given me more than I could've dreamed of." She laughed. He didn't. "Sorry," she said. "That was unnecessary." She pecked him on the cheek.

Terry knew within the first five minutes that this sort of party wasn't his sort of party. It wasn't at all what he'd imagined. He'd expected to find either a group of "la-dee-dahs" sipping their wine as they discussed "green" issues, or a group of head-bangers, leaping around to some weird heavy metal group that he'd not heard of. That was his idea of students. He was wrong on both counts.

"Of course they're a bit strange, Terry," Helen had replied, somewhat defensively. "They're art students."

They'd entered the tiny, terraced house and climbed a rickety, unlit staircase to the top landing, where they'd climbed over piles of coats to get to the kitchen.

Terry placed the wine on the formica-topped table which held two dozen or so empty bottles, a few polystyrene cups (most of them used), several paper plates with congealed curry and rice and a mountain of cigarette butts in a chipped saucer. The stove, covered in grease and dripping with the earlier-cooked curry, was in a worse condition than any that he and Levi had taken away for scrap. The floor was filthy; likewise the walls. Dirty clothing was piled up on the draining board and two very well spoken young women were standing either side of the brown-stained sink, flicking their cigarette ash on to the lino.

"This is disgusting," Terry mouthed at Helen.

She laughed and put her arm around him, affectionately. "Don't be such a snob."

Snob? Him? If only she knew.

The host of the party staggered into the kitchen, clutching a can of lager. He was tall and good-looking though his expensive, designer T-shirt was covered in stains: wine, ash and curry.

"Helen!" he slurred as soon as he saw her. "You've come!"

She flung her arms round him. "Happy twenty-first, Tim."

"Brilliant party," he drawled. "I've never been so squiffed in my life."

"Where is everyone?" she asked. "I can't hear any music."

He put his finger to his lip. "Sshhh. They're in there." He pointed towards a closed door. "They're watching a movie."

She laughed. "A movie?"

"*The Rocky Horror Show*. It's so camp, darling."

She cuddled him and kissed him on the cheek. "You're outrageous, Tim."

He looked over Helen's shoulder and saw Terry.

"Hello," he said, with a smile.

"This is Terry, Tim," said Helen.

The two young women at the sink decided to join Rocky Horror, taking their cups of wine with them.

"Aah! So this is Terry, is it?" grinned Tim. "Hello, Terry. Nice to meet you at last. I've heard so much about you."

Helen noted the surprised look on Terry's face.

"I've mentioned you once or twice to Tim," she giggled with embarrassment.

"Come and watch the movie, you two," said Tim. "They're all in there. Everyone." He took Helen's hand.

"In a minute, darling," replied Helen. "I'll just get myself a drink."

Tim waved a finger at the table. "Plenty there," he said. "There's some … er…" he noticed the bottles that Terry had just put down "…some wine and stuff. Just help yourselves." He left them and went into the movie room.

Helen turned to Terry. "Do you want a drink?"

"I hope you've said nice things to him about me," he smiled.

"What do you think?" she laughed.

She noted the haunted look, behind the smile, in Terry's eyes. "Don't worry," she said, sadly. "I know what you're thinking, Terry. I only told him there was someone I fancied. That's all. I said I used to work with you and that I was bringing you to the party. I also told him I didn't really stand a chance with you, because of Maureen." She gripped his hand. "I'm not stupid, Terry. You've made it quite clear about the love of your life. I've known from the beginning."

"I'm sorry, Helen," he whispered.

She bit hard on her lip, fearing that she might cry. "It didn't stop the way I was feeling about you," she continued, quickly. "But that's *my* problem. You've got nothing to be sorry about."

"But I shouldn't have…"

"Let's have a drink," she rushed on, interrupting

him, not wanting to hear what he was about to say. She looked around for a corkscrew. "What do you want? Wine or beer?"

"Nothing," he said, softly. "I don't drink."

She put an arm around his waist. "You're such a…" She struggled for the words, not wanting to sound patronizing. "I don't know – you're…" she reflected, "…such a nice person, Terry."

"Nice?" He laughed. "Wet, do you mean?"

"No." She looked serious. "Far from wet. Just old-fashioned plain old nice."

She saw the corkscrew on the draining board, picked it up and silently began opening one of the bottles of wine. Before he could see the solitary tear which trickled down her cheek, she quickly turned her back on him and then deftly flicked away the tear with her fingertips.

He approached and put his arms around her waist, resting a cheek gently on to her back, whispering, "I think I'd better go, don't you, Helen?"

He felt the involuntary sob vibrate through her body.

She turned and looked at him, gulping rapidly, not wanting him to be distressed by *her* distress. "Perhaps you should. Yes." She sighed, heavily. "I don't think you really belong here, do you?"

He smiled at the tragic irony of her words; the unintentional double entendre – and he looked around the kitchen, and he thought about the spotlessly clean trailer in which he used to live, with its scrubbed and polished surfaces and the shiny, brass ornaments and the freshly washed net curtains blowing in the breeze … and he realized she was right. He didn't belong here at all. He felt dirty. And he realized that it wasn't just the squalor around him that made him feel this way.

Del Stuart used Triumphant Studios to finish the remix of Terry Smith's single. He worked late into the night until he and Joe were pleased with the result:

> *"Call on me*
> *You'll find a stranger.*
> *Yeah, I gotta change.*
> *It's not the same, any more.*
> *I … I've been down;*
> *I've been a loner.*
> *I don't intend staying one, any more."*

"That's it, Joe," beamed Del. "A smash!"

Joe sighed. "I could've made that boy a star. I wonder what the silly little idiot's doing for a living now?"

"Tarmacking, probably," replied Del. "That's what they all do, don't they, gypsies?"

The late Pete Shannon had, Joe was sure, run his course. The number one single had succeeded in putting *Alone On The Freeway* back at the top of the album chart and now there was really nothing else to achieve in that camp. Now it had to be the launch of the indie.

Fat Tracks was ready to go, with one of the top "majors" handling its distribution; and "Call On Me", whether Terry Smith liked it or not, was to be the first release.

"I'd like you to take another look at the video, Del," said Joe. "Tell me if you think it needs editing."

They left the studio by the main entrance and the receptionist locked the door behind them.

"Mr Fisher?"

A youth was standing in the shop doorway, opposite.

At first, Joe thought that his wish had come true and that Terry Smith had returned to ask for a second chance.

"Are you Mr Fisher?"

"Yes?" Joe was curious. So was Del Stuart.

The youth approached and handed Joe an envelope.

"It's a cassette," he said. "Please listen to it, Mr Fisher."

The lad was handsome. His voice sounded tired. As he stepped from the shadows, Joe recognized him.

"I write all my own songs," he went on. "And if you want to see me perform live, I do a regular gig in South London."

"What's your name?" asked Joe.

"Wayne Fielding," said the youth. "I worked for you on Pete Shannon's album."

Joe smiled at him, kindly. "I'll listen to it."

"Where's this regular gig, Wayne?" asked Del Stuart.

"The Regent Tavern," he replied. "Do you know it?"

"Of course," said Joe.

"I do Saturdays and Sundays," Wayne said, quickly.

"I'll listen to the cassette," Joe assured him. "If I like it, I'll come along and see you, OK?"

"The Regent Tavern," Wayne repeated.

"Right!" grinned Joe. "The Regent Tavern."

As Wayne hurried away, Joe raised an eyebrow. "Funny old business," he whispered to Del. "A top pop star one minute and then begging on street corners the next."

"I *thought* that's who it was," said Del. "The lad from Hym, no?"

Terry intended to get a cab back to the Regent Tavern. It wasn't too far from the party and he could have walked, but there were several groups of youths aimlessly strolling the streets and he thought that this would only be asking for trouble.

As he approached the mini-cab office he saw a night bus approaching and, noting that it was going to New Cross, he leapt aboard. From New Cross he thought he might be able to get another bus to Gran's. If not, he'd get a cab. It would be expensive, but at least he'd be there in the morning, when Maureen woke and they could have a few extra hours together before she started school. Maureen would like that, he was sure. Maureen. He needed her more than ever. Without *her*, what else was there?

Gran's house was, as he'd expected, in total darkness. He slipped his key into the lock, and opened the door very quietly. He knew he mustn't wake Gran, as she would panic, thinking that someone had broken in. He heard her snoring loudly and knew that she hadn't stirred.

He tiptoed along the hall, groping for the stair rail, and as he did so, he crashed his ankle against the pedal of his bicycle. He cursed. How many times had Gran told him not to leave his bike there? Nowadays he always wheeled it through to the back yard. But obviously Maureen had been using it and had left it at the bottom of the stairs. He rubbed his ankle. He'd have an enormous bruise there in the morning which he'd show to Maureen at breakfast time and say, "Look what you did to me last night!"

He smiled to himself as he crept up the stairs, past Maureen's closed door and into his bedroom. He undressed without turning on the light and climbed into bed, feeling ... content. Feeling at home.

He was just dropping off to sleep, when he decided he needed to use the toilet. He climbed out of bed and, with his eyes now accustomed to the dark, made his way to the bathroom. Suddenly, the whole landing was lit by the headlamps from a car. He crossed to the window and looked down into the street. It was a taxi. Two people got out. A young man and a girl.

The man paid the taxi driver. The taxi pulled away. The man gently pushed the girl against the lamppost and kissed her. She responded by running her hand through his gelled, black hair.

"Oh, no!" said Terry. "Oh no! Oh no!" He turned away from the window, feeling sick. It couldn't be true. It couldn't! Not Maureen. Not Maureen and him. Not him! Not Rosetti!

Chapter 73

Santiago Gomez had proved to be worth every penny to BASIC BEAT. Within two months of the formation of Le Roi, everyone in Britain knew who they were. Their first single hadn't as yet been released, although various discos throughout the country had been issued with a special club mix of "Get Up", penned by Chas Atkins and Scotty. The number was, it seemed, destined to be a top ten hit.

Apart from the usual, "What do Marcus and John have for breakfast?" articles in the pop weeklies, Santiago had managed to interest all the tabloids with the *"ROSETTI SACKED US"* story. Rosetti was furious and foolishly responded, which in turn gave the boys even more publicity. Thus, having been fed both sides of the story, the public (those who were interested in such matters) had to decide for themselves which was the truth. Were the Leroy twins just hangers-on who couldn't even play their instruments? Or were they the real talent behind the now defunct Bury The Rabbit?

Santiago Gomez quickly followed this story with an exclusive to the *Daily Star*:

JOHN LEROY HURT BY FANS

Handsome John Leroy from the pop group Le Roi has been injured by over-enthusiastic fans. John, seventeen, was taken to hospital last night after several hundred fans swooped on the teen idols as they entered the new KANSIT recording studios complex in the Earls Court area of London.

Twin brother Marcus, who suffered a few minor scratches, said: "It was terrifying. The fans tried to grab the Le Roi medallions from round our necks. John was almost strangled."

Both brothers were released after hospital treatment, but, on doctors' advice, they intend to cancel their engagements for the next few days.

A spokesman for the group said that the boys would not be wearing their medallions in future.

"Are you all right?" asked Mrs Leroy. "Was it as bad as they said in the paper?"

"I'm fine, Mum," replied John. He covered the receiver with one hand and called out to his brother, "Mark! It's Mum. I told you she'd panic."

The Leroys had moved into Bif's London flat so as to be nearer the photographic and recording studios. Their diary was packed with appointments, and they'd decided that travelling to and from Kent every day had just been wasting time.

"You're not going to be scarred, are you?" she went

on. "I told you those things round your neck were dangerous."

"It's not true, Mum," explained John. "They made it all up."

She was silent.

Mark picked up the extension.

"It was just a publicity stunt," added John.

"There must have been some truth in it," she argued, naïvely. "What about all those girls mobbing you?"

Mark interrupted their conversation.

"No girls, Mum. No mobbing. No grabbing for medallions. We weren't even at the studio."

"Then why did they say…?"

"Listen, Mum," said John. "You've got to get used to this. Don't take any notice of anything you read, until you speak to us first. Right?"

The following day, the *Daily Star* held a competition, exclusive to their readers:

WIN! WIN! WIN – A LE ROI MEDALLION!

Chapter 74

New Year's Eve

Gary had spent Christmas sweltering in the sun: a Christmas Day picnic on the beach. With "Only Me And You" just entering the top twenty in Britain, he felt safe to fly off to Sydney for a TV special. His first solo single, "Take It All" had reached number five in the Australian charts and, following on the heels of the enormous success that Hym had had there, Gary was greeted as a star. Still there were questions about the split of the duo and the rumours of his fights with Wayne, but all in all, he'd enjoyed every minute of his time there. For a while, he'd even been able to push Ruby to the back of his mind, though now, on New Year's Eve, he began to wonder if he'd ever see her again. As he ate from the barbie on the patio of the spacious home of one of Australia's top concert promoters, he wondered if he should call Sherry's number. But if she told him that Ruby was out, dating another man, he knew he wouldn't be able to bear it. He hoped that Ruby would be coming to London for the official opening of KANSIT studios. He'd sent on a copy of their invitation to Sherry's Malibu home. Perhaps she'd just turn up; and they could continue, discreetly of course, with their relationship.

Sherry Barbin, dressed in outrageously skimpy underwear, bumped and ground her way to the final notes of "Paraíso". The audience went wild. The TV executives were delighted; their advertisers, ecstatic. A New Year Sherry Barbin Special, live from the Hollywood Bowl. There was no doubt that America's Queen Of Pop was Sherry Barbin. Patcha was now simply a courtier.

"Hey, gee – thanks," she wheezed. "D'you like the outfit?"

The audience screamed its approval.

"For a long time, there's been a lady out there in the showbiz world of late night cabaret who, I know, has the ability to be one of America's big, big stars. Those who've seen her perform, know what I'm talking about. Those who haven't, are in for a treat! Ladies and gentlemen … Ruby Gold!"

Ruby, dressed in a tight golden cat-suit, slunk moodily on to the stage and belted out Sherry's dramatic ballad, "Beggin'".

And Sherry was right. There was no doubt about it. Ruby was set to hit the heights.

Wayne had turned down Nick Cox's offer to work on New Year's Eve, with the excuse that he had a long-standing invitation to a party. He thought back to the previous Christmas period, when invitations to "star" parties had been piled high on his kitchen table. He and Gary had dashed by taxi from one to another, trying to cram in as many as possible and had ended up at the Pepperazzi bash, where the hostesses were missing, but their guests had extravagantly seen in the New Year with Dom Perignon, caviare and fireworks.

Tonight he sat alone, watching the television. Firstly there was that dreadfully tacky pop show which featured appearances by new bands playing their debut singles. Most of them were destined to extinction before they'd even started and the only bright spark in the middle of this dirge was a duo calling themselves Le Roi. Nowhere near as good as Hym, of course. But the boys looked good. And their record, "Get Up", was well produced. It would probably be a minor hit.

Then came *Chartbusters' New Year Show* which featured some of last year's hits. And there was Hym. Looking great. Sounding superb. And Wayne swallowed yet another gin and tonic, knowing that by the time the clock struck midnight, he'd be able to block out the pain.

Ray Rosetti had spent the day in school uniform. The video shoot of "Down On Me Gently" was controlled by Franco, who wanted to make sure that the very best was coaxed from his son, in the gentlest way possible. During the last verse of the song, Rosetti left his school desk and, watched by admiring fellow-pupils, tore off his blazer, tie and shirt, revealing his tanned, lean body. He removed his shoes, socks and trousers and, in just his white Calvin Kleins, he approached the young, beautiful teacher, mouthing the words of the chorus. She helped him into denim jeans, jacket and T-shirt and he threw the discarded uniform from the classroom window.

"Shall I open the champagne?" asked Mrs Rosetti. "It's nearly twelve."

The Rosettis sat together on their sofa, watching *Chartbusters' New Year Show*, surprised that Bury The Rabbit wasn't featured.

"I'm quite pleased in a way," Ray Rosetti shrugged. "I don't want to be remembered as part of that group."

"You were brilliant today," said his father, proudly. "I can't see as it can fail."

"It's a very good song, Ray," added his mother.

"The song's nothing," grinned Franco. "You wait until you see the video. The girls'll go crazy. If my son isn't the new year's pop idol, then I'll eat my own family-sized frozen lasagne verde."

They all laughed.

"Then you *must* be confident!" concluded his wife.

As the countdown began, Terry stood in the wings, watching Maurice waving his Union Jack, as shouts of "Four … five … six…" topped the sound of Big Ben booming from the radio.

There was another hour before the punters would be turned out on to the streets and then there was all the clearing up to do. It would be at least three o'clock before he got to his bed. And he wondered how Maureen would be seeing in her New Year. She'll probably be at some party with Ray Rosetti, he thought ... and on the stroke of midnight, they'd kiss passionately. He felt his stomach lurch and he wondered if he would ever be able to forget her.

Gran had gone to bed at her usual time of ten-thirty.

"I can't be doin' with all that noise," she said, adding, "You can keep the telly up loud though, Mo. I won't hear anything once my head's hit the pillow."

Maureen put on the paper hat, which she'd kept from her Christmas cracker, and as the clock struck twelve, she blew a squeaker at the TV screen, and watched all those happy people jumping up and down and hugging each other and laughing and cheering.

And she surprised herself by saying out loud, "Happy New Year, Terry. God ... I miss you!"

Book Three

Something's wrong. The image, maybe. I
dunno. *Something*. Let's talk tomorrow.

BIF

He had dreams, just like you had. His never
came true, poor old sod. Yours nearly did. But
you chucked it.

LEVI

And after all that hype! Well, you can only fool
some of the people, some of the time!

FRANCO ROSETTI

Didn't take to schoolin'. Got no int'rest
Couldn't take to doin' what I had to do.
I'm rebellin' to prove I'm somethin'
I aim to get me somewhere, tellin' you!
And it's easy!
You know what I mean?
Easy!

ROSETTI/SCOTT

Chapter 75

She wrote,
Dear Terry,

I've picked up the phone several times, intending to ring the Regent, but at the last minute, I just couldn't do it. I didn't know what to say. I thought if I put it all down in a letter, then perhaps you'll understand exactly what happened. Firstly, I'm so, so sorry. I wouldn't have hurt you for the world and to do what I did was really unforgivable. Having said that, I hope you can find it in your heart to forgive me.

Ray just turned up out of the blue, when I was feeling really low. I was missing you like mad 'cos what with the job and everything, I hardly ever see you any more. Anyway, he asked me to go out for a drink with him and I had nothing else to do, so I went. I knew at the time it was stupid, but I was really fed up, just sitting in night after night with Gran.

Well, one thing led to another, and he asked me out again. He's not like he used to be, Terry. He's not at all big-headed, and you'd think he would be, wouldn't you,

*now that he's famous? I suppose that was the thrill, really.
Going out with a famous pop star. But I haven't fallen for
him or anything like that, Terry. Honest. I wouldn't even
let him kiss me until that night when you saw us. It's
something I really regret, Terry. And when I saw you
standing in the hall, I nearly died. I think Ray did too. If
only we could have talked then, I'm sure we would have
sorted it all out. I've been worried about you riding off
like that. I hope you got back safely. Sorry I hadn't
replaced the battery in the lamp. I hope you weren't
stopped by the police. Anyway, Ray realizes how upset I
am. And he understands that I won't be seeing him any
more. I won't. Terry. Honest. Please, please, call me. Or
even better, come on Monday. Please. Gran misses you too
and she's furious with me. She said I was stupid. She's
right. Please come home, Terry. I love you and miss you.*

Yours for ever,
Maureen.

Terry read the letter over and over again. Then
he tore it up and put it into the Regent's kitchen waste
bin, along with the rest of the garbage.

Chapter 76

John and Marcus Leroy arrived at KANSIT just before four o'clock. They took the lift to the top floor where Scotty, Chas and Bif were waiting for them in the newly furnished offices of BASIC BEAT.

"You managed to get through all those screaming fans outside, then?" laughed Chas.

"There were only about six," grumbled a very disappointed Marcus. "We signed autographs for them and they left."

"Probably 'cause it's Sunday," said Bif, trying to keep a straight face. "Everyone's at church."

Scotty laughed.

The brothers Le Roi didn't find it funny.

The hype preceding the launch of "Get Up" had been extravagant, to say the least. "The Big Sell", as one of the up-market Sundays had called it. The twins had appeared in every single pop weekly, in every single tabloid newspaper, on twenty-two television programmes and on almost every radio station throughout Britain. They were exhausted and more than relieved when "Get Up" entered the charts at number thirty-eight.

"Top forty!" Bif had exclaimed, adding, confidently, "Now we can get you on to *Chartbusters*."

His confidence waned a little however when his initial talks with the *Chartbusters* producer proved to be unsuccessful. The Thunderdomes had been on the programme so many times in the past and Bif knew the whole Horizon TV team so he couldn't understand the producer's reticence about Le Roi.

"I'm not promising anything," he said, "but let's see how far it rises on Sunday. If they're anywhere near the twenties, I'll think about having them on next week's show."

Bif hadn't been in the least surprised when "Get Up" had entered the Top Forty. Indeed, after all the money that had been spent on the promo, not least the purchasing of records from the stores and small record shops on which Gallup based their chart, he was shocked to find that they were only at thirty-eight.

Chas switched on the radio and they listened intently to the countdown, noting, as they'd expected, that "Get Up" was at neither forty nor thirty-nine, both of these numbers being new entries.

The DJ was about to play the number thirty-eight sound when a usually quiet Mark Leroy yelled, "Please don't let it be us. Don't let it be a non-mover!"

It wasn't. And it wasn't anywhere in the countdown from forty to thirty.

Scotty gave a sigh of relief. "You don't think it could have gone right into the twenties, do you?" he asked.

"That's what I'm hoping," replied Bif. "I don't see why not."

The Leroy twins grinned, nervously. John Leroy's forehead was running with sweat.

The countdown had reached as high as number eighteen and still "Get Up" hadn't been mentioned.

"Any minute now. It's got to be," said Chas Atkins.

"Perhaps it's gone straight to number one!" laughed Scotty.

No one spoke.

"Well, it's been known to happen, hasn't it?" he added.

"I can't stand this," said Bif, seriously. He crossed the room, picked up a phone and dialled.

"Who are you calling?" asked Chas.

Bif mumbled, "An informant."

They all continued listening to the countdown, while Bif received inside information. "You sure?" he said into the receiver. "Absolutely sure?" He paused. "OK. Thanks."

He put down the phone and turned, gazing into space.

"I don't believe it." His voice was hushed.

It *is* number one, thought John Leroy.

"It's dropped!" said Bif. "Number forty-six."

Scotty gasped.

"But how?" asked Chas Atkins.

Bif shrugged. "No idea."

John Leroy looked down at his feet. Mark buried his face in his hands.

"I'm going home," said Bif, sharply. "I think we'd all better meet here tomorrow morning. Nine o'clock.

Something's wrong. The image, maybe. I dunno. *Something*. Let's talk tomorrow."

"It's dropped right out!" screeched a delighted Rosetti.

Franco looked surprised. "And after all that hype!" He laughed. "Well, you can only fool some of the people, some of the time!"

Franco had decided to hold back the release of the Rosetti single until Le Roi had peaked in the charts. He hadn't favoured a contest between the ex-members of Bury The Rabbit, just in case Rosetti had lost. That would never have done! It hadn't occurred to him that they would peak as low as thirty-eight. He was ecstatic!

"Right! I'll work out a release date with Sloop Records tomorrow," he said. "We'll have 'Down On Me Gently' in the top twenty before you can say ... Bury The Rabbit."

Chapter 77

Jim Buckley gave out the marked English books. He'd been pleased with most of the essays and felt sure that many in his class would eventually achieve good results, though he still regretted that his best pupil, Terry Smith, had left school in order to pursue a career in pop music. Terry wasn't the only one he'd lost — though he was only too pleased when Ray Rosetti had left for exactly the same reason. Unfortunately, but not surprisingly, Rosetti had achieved his goal. Terry Smith hadn't.

"Maureen," he called, as the lunch-time pips sounded, sending his pupils rushing from the classroom. "Can I have a word?"

She approached his desk, a little shamefaced.

"I know what you're going to say, sir," she said. "I know it was awful. I'm sorry."

"It was the worst piece of work you've ever given me, Maureen," he affirmed. "What's up? You've always been one of the best in the class."

She didn't hesitate: she was grateful she could talk to someone she trusted. "It's Terry."

"Terry? What's the problem? He's all right, isn't he?" Jim sounded concerned.

"I don't know, sir," replied Maureen. "I haven't seen him for nearly two weeks."

Jim was surprised. "I thought he came home to see you every Monday?" He smiled. "You told me how much he loved you, remember?"

That was all that Maureen needed. She began to pour out her heart. She told Jim Buckley everything.

Joe Fisher invited Del Stuart to his luxury office-cum-home, so they could watch the video on, as Joe put it, "the big screen".

The video, depicting Terry Smith as a gypsy being rejected by a beautiful aristocractic young girl had, Del thought, "great style".

"To be honest, Joe," he said, "I thought 'Call On Me' was a top five hit. I'm now convinced it's a number one. That video is superb!"

"*I* thought so too," replied Joe. "Can you now see why I'm desperate to get that kid back? He's got the makings of a great star. Even bigger than Pete Shannon, I'm sure of it."

"You don't have an address or anything, then?" asked Del.

"No." He sighed. "Just the address of a gypsy camp-site in Kent. I went there, but the whole family has moved on. Taken their caravan up north, somewhere."

"And no one could tell you where, exactly?"

"Oh, I'm sure they could. If they'd wanted."

He laughed.

"Bloody gyppos," he went on. "They're such a

tight-knit lot, you know. Won't let anyone into their circle unless they're absolutely sure about them."

"I'm sure they can be bought," sneered Del. "You know what pikies are. Give 'em enough bread and they'll soon forget all that 'loyalty' bit."

Joe was all ears. "D'you think so?"

"Sure so!" replied Del. "They'd sell their own grandmothers for a tenner."

Joe switched off the video and crossed to his tape deck.

"Perhaps I should pay Berryfield another visit," he said. "And this time take a few tenners in my pocket."

"I should," said Del. "What can you lose?" He grinned. "Apart from your front teeth?"

Both men laughed.

"Here. Listen to this," said Joe. "Tell me what you think."

And he played the cassette of Wayne Fielding's demo.

Chapter 78

"**D**own On Me Gently" had a low-key launch. After the super-hype campaign from BASIC BEAT in their attempt to make Le Roi the next teen-idols, Rosetti and his father decided to go for a calmer approach. It had already begun to work. Rosetti was clever at interviews; was always humble, forever talking about his working-class origins and how his parents had sacrificed everything to give him a chance in life. The record was selling in modest quantities by the time it appeared on the BBC playlist and from then on the sales figures shot up.

The video was simple; no exotic locations as Bury The Rabbit had appeared to use for the video of "Easy!". Rosetti, dressed as a schoolboy, his tie loosened and his shirt collar undone, sat at a desk, gazing lovingly across a mist-filled classroom towards a beautiful model.

He sang, romantically:

"All I need is the opportunity
To tell you what you really mean to me
But if you feel the need to
Put me down…
Then put me down, gently.

If, when you're within my arms you find
You don't relax within these arms o' mine
And you feel you have to
Put me down…
Come down on me, gently."

And as the video was shown on Saturday morning TV, thousands of girls throughout Britain began to fantasize about the schoolboy Rosetti. Somehow, dressed like this – dressed as one of their own – he became more attainable. And they thought about the Peters and the Matthews and the Davids in their own classrooms and they wondered why they didn't have a handsome, half-Italian, tight-trousered hunk like Rosetti to get them through double maths.

Yes, the girls loved him. And the boys hated him. And as they watched, a flood of memories came back for others … those who'd actually shared a classroom with him: Scotty … and Terry … and Maureen!

Chapter 79

Bif left the twins sleeping and set off earlier than planned, having first pinned a note to the cork board in the kitchen:

John and Mark,
Had to go out on other business, so today's meeting cancelled. We'll talk tonight. Have a good day.

Bif

Scotty and Chas arrived punctually at the offices of KANSIT, where Bif was waiting for them.

"The boys not here yet?" asked Scotty.

"They're not coming," replied Bif.

Chas Atkins nodded. "I didn't think they would be."

Bif opened his briefcase and took out several printed sheets of paper, stapled together.

"I've been checking around," he said. "And there doesn't appear to be anything sinister. The chart position genuinely reflects sales in these record outlets. And these are the ones that Gallup used last week."

Chas shrugged. "Unbelievable. I truly thought it was a great song."

"It is," replied Bif. "It's a good song and it's well produced. It's just that Le Roi haven't caught the record-buying public's attention. And for what reason, I've no idea. We couldn't have done any more. We hyped them till even I was sick of them."

"Perhaps that's what's wrong," suggested Scotty. "Perhaps we over-hyped the product and the public saw through it."

Bif laughed. "You can't over-hype in this business, Scotty."

"You know what I think?" said Chas. "I think it's because the boys can't talk. As simple as that. We do this great build-up and then as soon as they get in front of a microphone, they're monosyllabic. Anyone would think they were a couple of morons."

"That's what Santiago's been worried about from the very beginning," stated Bif. "They're lacking in personality and they can't string two words together. I thought they'd improve, but…" He shrugged. "No one would believe they're so intelligent."

"That's why we wouldn't let them do any interviews when they were with Bury The Rabbit," added Scotty. "Franco never let them near a radio station."

"Right!" said Bif. "We now think we know why they've failed. So what are we gonna do about it?"

"*Talk* to them, I suppose," suggested Chas. "Explain what we think is lacking. And get them to do something about it."

"What about you, Scotty?" asked Bif. "What d'you think?"

"Dunno. I agree with Chas, I suppose," he replied. "Nothing else we can do, is there?"

"Wrong!" said Bif. "There *is* something else we can do. And I think we should do it."

Chas and Scotty knew what he was going to say.

"There's a whole lot of talent out there, just waiting to be tapped. Young kids who'd give their eye-teeth for the opportunity that Le Roi have been given. So, what d'you say, we start looking around, eh?"

Chas and Scotty silently nodded their agreement.

"OK," said Bif. He packed his papers into his briefcase. "I'd better go and tell John and Mark it's all over."

Chapter 80

Joe had been curious. He and Del had liked the demo handed to them by Wayne Fielding and they'd both decided to watch the boy performing "live". The Regent Tavern was packed with its Sunday night clientele and both men stood at the bar watching the fire-eater.

During the regular acts from Maurice and the Dancing Skinhead, Terry always looked through the prompt-corner peephole to watch the audience reaction, as this had begun to amuse him more than watching the "turns". When he saw Joe, whisky in hand, puffing on the habitual cigar, he began to panic. If he ended up before a judge on a case of house-breaking – of stealing the master tape of "Call On Me", then he wouldn't stand a chance! He had no previous criminal record; had never done anything wrong before. But he was a gypsy. Of no fixed abode. There'd be no fine. No community service, like they gave to the gorgios. He'd be slammed straight into the starry, just like his parents before him. He had no doubt about that.

Terry left the prompt corner, telling Huw that he had to go to the toilet. He rushed up to his room, threw his belongings into his holdall and left by the back door, where he kept his bike.

Joe and Del liked Wayne's act and, as he came off stage, they approached him. Joe handed him his card.

"Give me a call in the morning," he said. "Let's arrange a meeting."

When Terry arrived at Berryfield, it was gone midnight. The dirt-path to the campsite was unlit and, as there was no moon that night, Terry had to grope his way around trying to find Levi's trailer. He hoped, as he stumbled across one of the many washing-line supports, that he hadn't woken Abi's dog. It would be no good trying to explain to that ferocious mongrel that he wasn't a gavver looking for stolen lead; that he was in fact, one of their own. The beast would have his neck in its jaws before he had a chance to cry out.

The journey by pushbike to Camberwell, carrying his holdall of meagre possessions, had been arduous, but when Terry had seen Joe enter the saloon bar, he knew that he had to get out. Immediately. Maybe the fat man was just there looking for new talent (hadn't Helen said that record company scouts often popped in?) but Terry felt there was something more afoot; that somehow Joe Fisher knew he was there!

He found the trailer he was looking for, tapped lightly on the door and waited. The two plots on either side of Levi's, which once housed his parents' and Belcher's respective trailers, had already been re-occupied.

"Who is it?" a voice called.

"It's me, Levi," Terry replied. "I need somewhere to stay."

Levi turned on the lights and opened the door.

"You'd better come in then, hadn't you?" he growled. "But don't bring that bike in with you."

"Hi, Gary. It's Phil," announced the voice on the end of the phone. "Bit of good news."

Gary stared down into the street watching the fans, who were already gathering although it was still only eight a.m. He drew the curtains. Most days now seemed to be spent in darkness.

"Don't tell me … 'Only Me And You' has shot to number one?" He laughed.

Phil sighed. "I'd love to be able to tell you that. Maybe I *will* be able to next week."

"So it's still on its way up, then?"

"Sure is. Kendrick Simpson's very confident it'll make it."

"So BJ'll be pleased?"

"He's in seventh heaven. He wants to talk about an album, as soon as possible."

"Brilliant!" said Gary.

"Now," said Phil, "are you going to this official opening of KANSIT studios?"

"I thought I ought to," said Gary. "It seems everyone in the business'll be there. Why?"

"It's just that you've been booked for *Chartbusters* on that night."

"Hey! Great! That'll help boost sales, eh?"

Phil grinned. "Thought you'd like that bit of news."

"Too right, I do."

"So, if I come to the studio to watch the recording, we can both head off for KANSIT afterwards. Yeah?"

"OK. Yeah, that'll be good."

Immediately, Gary's thoughts turned to Ruby. There hadn't been a word from her since she'd left, and he was now sure that it was all over between them. But he was hoping, against all hopes, that the official opening of KANSIT would bring her back to London for a brief visit. He had to see her. If only to say goodbye to her ... and to wish her all the luck in the world.

Terry couldn't sleep. Levi had only one bed so he'd spread a few coats across the settee in "the room".

"It'll have to do," said Levi. "I ain't a guest house."

The thin, wooden slats beneath the cushions dug deeply into Terry's back and he knew he wouldn't be able to stand this for more than a couple of nights, though he had no idea where he'd move to. There was no way he'd go back to Gran's. He wouldn't crawl back to Maureen; not after what she'd done to him. He missed her like mad but he had his pride. Had it been any other bloke in the world that she'd gone out with, then it might have been different. They could have talked about it. After all, hadn't he gone out with Helen? His mind began to wander. Helen. He wondered if she ever thought about him. She'd never been back to the pub to see him.

Yes, had it been any other man. Anyone but Rosetti!

"Whatcha gonna do then?" The voice made Terry jump. It was almost three in the morning and Levi had got out of bed to come and talk to him.

"D'you want a cuppa tea?" asked Levi. "I can't sleep."

"Me neither," said Terry.

Levi crossed to the tiny kitchen and lit the gas under the kettle.

"Whatcha gonna do?" he asked again. "I ain't got a job for yer. Sylvie's lad's helping me now."

"I don't know," Terry replied. "I don't want to go on the social. I've got to find something."

"I suppose you've finished mucking around with this singing lark, 'ave yer?" asked Levi as he took out two mugs from the cupboard above his head.

"Yes," said Terry.

"You was a fool there," added Levi. "The only traveller I know to be given the chance of getting out and you go and balls it all up."

Terry snapped, "I didn't balls it all up. I weighed it up, carefully. I decided what was the right thing to do. And I did it!"

Levi sneered. "Oh, the right thing, was it? You're given the chance of getting on the telly and making records and earning the sort of dough like none of us have ever seen before, and you chuck it all in and end up moving scrap metal for a living instead. And it was the right thing, was it? Right for who? Not for you, surely?"

"It was for my dad." Terry's voice was hushed. "It was for him. I told you. They were going to print pictures of his funeral. Just to publicize a pop record."

"He'd have loved it," said Levi.

Terry was shocked at the comment.

"Loved it!" Levi repeated. "You didn't know him, did yer? You didn't know him like I did. You can't have done. He was one of the best, was your dad. The best. We grew up together, we did. Did the horse fairs. Epsom. All of 'em. I think I knew him better than you did. I knew him when he was well. When you and Billy was just chavvies. When his arms were brown and his face was pink. Before the ticker went. We did the hop fields and the fruit picking together ... before it was all done in."

He spooned some tea into the pot and took a bottle of milk from the fridge.

"It was hard work. But he never stopped dreaming, did your dad. Was always gonna buy horses and show 'em at the fairs and that. That's what he wanted. Don't know where he thought the money was coming from." He laughed. "Yeah. Always dreaming, he was. Just like you. Chip off the old block, you are. He had dreams, just like you had. His never came true, poor old sod. Yours nearly did. But you chucked it."

The kettle began to bellow steam. Levi didn't notice.

"Yeah, I bet he's up there now ... in his white gown and wings ... and his new boots ... looking down on you and saying, 'Don't be a prat all yer life, Terry.'"

Terry shivered.

Levi smiled at him, kindly. "Yeah, getting cold, innit?"

Terry smiled back. "Kettle's boiling. You gonna make that tea, or not?"

Chapter 81

Jim pulled up in one of the side turnings near the Regent Tavern.

"I shouldn't be doing this, you know, Maureen," he said.

"I know, Mr Buckley," she replied. "But I'm ever so grateful."

He smiled at her. "You wait here."

Maureen had told Gran that she was going over to Suzanne's for the evening. She only lived over the road, on the sixth floor of Toronto House, and Suzanne had hired a video and she wouldn't be home late; would Gran be all right? It was an extravagant lie, but Maureen, who went out so seldom, was sure that Gran would take a lot of convincing. She couldn't tell her the truth, could she? She'd think that Maureen was really demeaning herself by chasing after a boy who'd dropped her; even if that boy was Terry Smith. Anyway, Maureen was sure that Gran had believed the lies.

Gran hadn't. She had a good idea what Maureen was up to. And she didn't blame her. If she were her granddaughter, she'd have done exactly the same thing.

Jim Buckley found the pub to be quiet. But then it was mid-week, and it was still only eight-thirty. There were only about a dozen or so people at the bar and the curtains on the tiny stage were drawn.

"Pint of bitter, please," he said to the girl behind the bar, and as she reached for a glass he asked, "No cabaret tonight, then?"

"About nine-thirty," she replied with a smile. "We don't get busy till then."

She began to pull the pint.

"Terry Smith around?" he asked.

She stiffened. "Er…? Who…?"

"Terry. He works here, I believe."

She placed his drink on the counter.

"I'm not sure," she said. "Hold on. I'll ask the manager."

She left.

Within a couple of minutes, Nick Cox appeared.

"Yes, sir?"

"Terry Smith," said Jim. "Could I have a word with him?"

"Sorry," replied Nick. "Never heard of him."

Jim smiled. "I'm not the taxman, if that's what you're worried about." He explained who he was and why he was there.

"I believe you … thousands wouldn't," laughed Nick. "But I still can't help you, I'm afraid. Terry Smith left on Sunday night during the cabaret, without even saying goodbye. He must've been in a terrible hurry. He didn't even stop to collect his wages."

Chapter 82

"Maureen!" she screamed.

Other heads turned. Maureen's didn't. She walked on, across the playground, pretending that she hadn't heard. Ridiculous. She would have had to have been stone-deaf not to have heard Tracey's piercing voice.

"Mo!"

Tracey rushed across the netball court, leapt the flower bed and hurtled up the stairs to the school's main entrance where she caught up with her "friend".

"I've been calling you for ages!" panted Tracey.

Maureen feigned surprise.

"Sorry, Trace. I didn't hear you. Must've been miles away."

"I was wondering if you wanted to go to Flicks tonight," she said. "I've got no one to go with. I was gonna go with Naomi, but she's going with that rat-faced boy from your class. That Benjamin."

Maureen hadn't been to Flicks for weeks – not since Terry left; but she couldn't face the thought of spending a whole evening with Tracey.

"I can't, Trace," she said. "I'm sorry."

They went into the cloakroom and Maureen hung her coat on her labelled peg. Tracey sat on the bench below the pegs and sighed.

"Oh! Why not? It's not Terry's night, is it? He works on a Friday."

Maureen knew she had to tell her. She'd kept it from Tracey for too long already and she was bound to find out sooner or later.

"Terry and I are finished, Tracey," she said.

Tracey's mouth dropped open.

"What d'you mean, finished?"

"He's left. Left his job and left me."

"Since when?" gasped Tracey.

Maureen had the feeling that Tracey was really enjoying this.

"Since a few weeks ago," she explained. "He just … disappeared." She shrugged, trying to pretend it was just one of those things. "I don't even know where he is."

"I do," said Tracey.

"*What?*" Maureen wasn't sure she'd heard properly.

"I saw him a couple of days ago, from the top of the bus," Tracey went on. "I wondered what he was doing there. I thought perhaps he'd gone to get some of his belongings, or something."

"Where?" Maureen tried to hide the excitement in her voice. "Where did you see him?"

"Just coming out of that gypsy campsite," Tracey replied. "Berryfield, innit?"

* * *

442

It was just an idea and Terry was sure that nothing would come of it, but he couldn't lose anything by asking, could he?

He'd been thinking about it all day. Sitting on Levi's settee and staring out at the churned-up mud and thinking. There was no way he could go back to collecting scrap metal, even if Levi had had a job for him. And tarmacking was certainly not his scene. It had to be something in the business that he loved. The music business. Maybe not as a singer. But if someone gave him the chance to work in a recording studio, he could learn the trade from the bottom. And work his way up. In time. Become an engineer. A producer, maybe. If someone would give him a chance. He'd run errands. Make tea. Anything, just so long as he was where it was all at. He thought about doing the round of all the studios in London. Just knocking on doors and asking.

Then he got to thinking about Scotty. He knew he had something to do with the production side of records now that Bury The Rabbit had split. He'd read it somewhere; how he was with a production team whose first signing was Le Roi. They'd even had a hit. A minor one ... but a hit, at least. And he racked his brain trying to think of the name of Scotty's company. If he could find out where they were, he could apply for a job. Anything.

He knew that Scotty hadn't been friendly when they were at school together, but he was sure it was only because of Rosetti. Scotty did everything that Rosetti did. But then, didn't everyone do what Rosetti did? Even when it came to making fun of the pikies?

443

Yes, Terry was sure that it was only Rosetti's influence that had made Scotty behave like that. But what was the name of his company? He just couldn't remember. But he remembered something. He remembered where Scotty used to live. His parents had the large white house on the other side of the Belling Estate. Not very far from Maureen's.

And he made up his mind. He'd go there. This evening. And he'd ask Scotty's parents for Scotty's new address. And then he'd call on him and ask him for a job!

Levi returned from work at six o'clock expecting to find Terry still moping around in his trailer. He wasn't. He'd gone to Berryfield's main house to take a shower and he would've left a note saying where he was, had he thought that Levi would be able to read it.

The water felt good: warm and invigorating, his head tingling under the needle-sharp jets as he altered the pressure-control. He wondered if Scotty's parents would be at home. And he tried to work out what he'd say to them.

"Hello, I'm a friend of your son's. Well, not a friend, exactly. We knew each other at school. Terry. Perhaps he mentioned me? He didn't? Well, I'm the one that he used to bully. Along with his accomplice, Ray Rosetti. I'm the one who was put through hell, nearly every day of my school life, by Rosetti and your son. Terry Smith. Smithy the Gyppo. The thievin' pikie? Aah! Now you know who I am. Well, I was wondering if your son could give me a job…"

Terry laughed out loud as he rinsed away the last of

the lather and turned off the shower. He began drying his hair on Levi's large green towel. Even if Scotty couldn't give him a job, he didn't regret leaving the Regent Tavern. He had to move on sometime. He couldn't spend the rest of his life cueing up tapes for novelty acts and two-bit singers. Not that Wayne Fielding was a two-bit singer. He was talented and was sure to go places as a solo act. Terry wondered if that's why Joe was there. Perhaps he'd heard about the young singer and had come to see him perform. But then, supposing he took Wayne on and they got talking about Joe's client who'd run away and Joe showed Wayne a picture? Wayne would be bound to say, "That's Terry, who works backstage at the Regent." And then Joe would know that Terry was still around. That he hadn't gone up north at all. And he'd be bound to come looking for him.

"Whatever you do, don't tell anyone I'm here, will you, Levi?" Terry asked. "As far as anyone's concerned, you've no idea where I am. Right?"

Levi smiled. "Haven't clapped eyes on yer for weeks."

"Thanks." Terry ran the comb through his hair and put on his coat.

"I'm off then," he said. "I won't be late back. I'm going to see a man about a job."

There was no need to pass through Maureen's street. He could have taken the road parallel, to reach the other side of the Belling Estate. But it drew him like a magnet. He hoped in his heart of hearts that Maureen

445

would be looking out of the window as he passed. She'd rush from the house and call after him and beg him to come back and … of course, he'd say yes.

Life without her was so painful; there wasn't a day when he didn't think about her, but he couldn't go to her. She would have to come to him. But as she didn't know where he was living, there was little chance of a reconciliation. Unless they bumped into each other. Or unless she heard from someone that he was back at Berryfield. If she came to him there … if she knocked at Levi's trailer and said, "I'm sorry, Terry. Can we get back together again?" he'd be so happy!

Levi opened his door and stared at her.

"Yes?"

"Hello, Levi," she said. "It's Maureen."

"I know who you are," he said, coldly. "What do you want?"

"I've heard that Terry's back." She gulped, nervously.

"Who told you that?"

"A friend. Can I see him?"

"No," replied Levi, remembering Terry's instructions. "You've been told wrong," he added. "I ain't seen Terry for weeks. And I've no idea where he is."

He shut the door in her face.

Mrs Scott opened the door.

"I'm an old friend of your son…" he began.

She immediately called along the hall. "Phillip! It's someone for you!"

Terry was surprised. He wasn't expecting Scotty still

446

to be living there. He imagined he'd now be living in some smart apartment in London. He was even more surprised when Scotty greeted him like a long lost friend.

"Hello, Smithy!" he said, sounding really pleased to see him. "What are *you* doing here? Come in."

He led Terry through to the kitchen.

"We're better in here," he explained. "Mum and Dad are watching the telly in the lounge."

He switched on the kettle. "Coffee?"

"Please," replied Terry. He felt nervous. He was already taken aback at such a friendly welcome. Now ... how did he ask for a job?

"Terry Smith?" the fat man asked.

People rarely called on Levi, yet this evening he'd had two callers, both asking for the whereabouts of young Terry.

"Nope!" said Levi.

"Have you any idea where I could contact him?" Joe enquired.

"Nope!"

Joe looked at Del, questioningly.

Del nodded.

Joe took out his wallet, opened it and slowly peeled off five ten-pound notes.

Levi shook his head.

Joe peeled off another five notes.

Levi put out his hand.

"Memory coming back, is it?" grinned Joe. He placed the money into Levi's palm.

"Wait there," said Levi.

He left the two men at the foot of the trailer steps and crossed the campsite to another trailer, which he entered without knocking.

A few minutes later he re-emerged, flanked by two tall, well-built gypsies. All three of them strode aggressively towards Joe and Del.

"Oh!" gasped Del. "I think we've done it wrong, Joe."

Levi came right up to Joe and placed his hand, heavily, on the fat man's shoulder. "These are my two friends," he smiled. "Abi and his son Jimmy. They've come to say thank you for the drink, gents."

"Very good of you," grinned Big Jimmy as he waved the wad of ten-pound notes in Joe's face.

"Good 'ealth to you," added Abi.

Levi whispered, menacingly, "Now, vanish! Before I set the dogs on you."

Joe and Del left.

"I'd like to help, Smithy. Honest," said Scotty, "but it's not really up to me. It's Bif who takes care of the business side of things."

Terry's face showed his disappointment.

"Look, I'll have a word with him," added Scotty, kindly. "Where can I contact you?"

"You can't," said Terry. "I haven't got a phone."

Scotty handed him a card.

"Give me a ring at KANSIT tomorrow," he said. "I should be there all day."

And as he saw Terry to the door, Scotty was already making plans. He remembered when Terry Smith had sung at school. Hadn't he astounded everyone?

Everyone including Rosetti! That voice! Terry the Gyppo could sing. Really sing! And how Ray Rosetti hated him for it!

If Scotty could get Chas Atkins and Bif to listen to Smith the Gyppo, singing, he was sure they'd take him on. No doubt about it. And think of the hype. "Gypsy Boy Makes Good!" The old Rags to Riches story. It never failed. Yes, Scotty was sure they could do great things for Terry Smith. And Terry Smith could do great things for BASIC BEAT. And if they got him into the charts ... if they got him to number one ... well!

What would Rosetti do then, poor thing?

Chapter 83

Terry had persuaded Levi to lend him some cash to get through the week. He'd promised that as soon as he had a job, he'd repay it, though the prospect of a job in the immediate future looked doubtful. He'd rung Scotty as arranged, but the meeting with the rest of the BASIC BEAT management team had to be delayed for a few days, as Bif had some radio interviews lined up to promote a compilation CD which featured the best of the Thunderdomes.

"Come to KANSIT studios on Friday about three o'clock," Scotty had told him on the phone. "It's a big day for KANSIT, so we'll all be there."

"I'm impressed, Wayne," said Joe. "Very impressed. There are four or five tracks that I like, but Del Stuart reckons the up-tempo one's the winner. What do you say?"

Wayne Fielding sat trembling in Joe's office-cum-flat, looking around at Pete Shannon's wall-mounted gold discs and framed photos. He couldn't tell if Joe was offering him a contract, or just giving him a bit of career advice.

"Yes. I quite like the up-tempo one too, Mr Fisher," replied Wayne.

"Joe!" corrected the fat man. "If I'm going to be your manager, we'd better drop all this Mr Fisher lark, eh?"

"Are you saying you're taking me on?" asked Wayne, nervously.

Joe laughed. "Why else do you think you're here?"

"Oh!" gasped Wayne. "Oh!" His mouth felt dry. He was still trembling, but now it was with excitement.

"We'll sort out the contract as quickly as possible and then get you into the studio with Del," explained Joe. "I'd like a single out within the next couple of months."

Wayne could hardly catch his breath.

"It'll go out as the second single on my new indie, Fat Tracks," went on Joe. "I've got another single to put out first." He crossed to the tape deck. "A ballad. Here. Tell me what you think," he said.

He switched on Terry Smith's, "Call On Me".

And as the wailing saxophone gave way to Terry's haunting voice:

> *"You call on me*
> *When you are lonely…"*

Wayne Fielding sighed gratefully that Joe had chosen the up-tempo track for *him*. He could never in a million years compete with a singer like that!

"What a great voice," he said. "I'm so jealous."

Joe laughed.

"What's his name?" asked Wayne.

Joe's phone rang, interrupting their conversation.

Terry arrived at Earls Court Underground and walked to KANSIT, following Scotty's instructions. A crowd of girls lined the street outside, sitting on the low stone wall and on the bonnets of parked cars. All knew that today was the official opening of KANSIT Studios and that the guest list featured all the luminaries of the pop world. Most of them wore T-shirts and badges bearing the name of their latest pop idol, Gary Brenn.

As Terry climbed the steps to KANSIT's reception, two of the waiting fans, both very young, rushed up to him.

"Are you going inside?" one of them asked.

"Yes," replied Terry.

"Can you get *me* in?" she asked.

Terry smiled. "Of course I can't," he replied.

Scotty had already told him about KANSIT's security: to give his name through the intercom at the main door and then wait until his identity had been thoroughly checked. KANSIT was taking no chances today.

"Well, will you give him this letter?" asked the girl, pushing a crumpled piece of paper into Terry's hand. "Tell him I love him."

"Tell him we both love him," the other girl giggled.

"I might not see him," said Terry, kindly.

"Please!" the first girl pleaded.

Terry laughed. Had he not given up the chance of

his own stab at becoming a pop idol, they might have been sending notes of undying love to *him* instead of to Gary Brenn. And he wondered, once inside the building, if he should introduce himself to Gary Brenn and to tell him that he'd been working at the Regent Tavern with his old partner: Wayne Fielding.

"I'll try," he said to the two excited fans.

He pressed the bell, gave his name through the intercom and waited for a security guard to open the door. As he entered the studio complex, he looked at the grubby fan letter in his hand.

It was addressed to *Ray Rosetti*.

Chapter 84

Joe Fisher arrived at Cheyne Walk with an armful of flowers for Imogen and toys for the children. Piru showed him through to the drawing-room, where Imogen, looking more radiant than ever in a simple white blouse and green skirt, idly plumped up the already well-plumped scatter-cushions on the sofa.

"Joe," she said, softly. "How lovely to see you again."

He handed her the flowers which she admired, sniffed and then passed over to Piru. "How lovely. Thank you."

"And I've got these for the kids," he said, holding up a bag of wrapped gifts. "I suppose they're in bed?"

She smiled. "They are indeed. And I won't wake them, if that's all right. If they know Uncle Joe's here, I'll never get them back to sleep."

"I understand," he replied. He handed the bag to Piru who, now laden, left for the kitchen.

"Don't tell me I'm the first guest to arrive this evening?" said Joe.

"You are. But you're not too early. Drink?" She crossed to the dresser.

"Scotch on the rocks, please."

She poured as he looked around the room. "You've decorated."

She laughed. "*I* haven't."

"No." He laughed too. "I mean, you've had decorators in."

"Yes. Do you like it?"

"Very tasteful."

"I know what you're thinking," she said.

"Pete's gold discs."

"Yes," she smiled. "They're upstairs, adorning the walls of his studio. Where they should always have been."

His eyes twinkled. "But no one sees them up there."

"Quite!" she said. She handed him his whisky. "Oh, don't get me wrong," she added quickly. "I'm very proud of Pete's achievements, but I think that displaying them on the drawing-room wall is a little … ostentatious, don't you?"

"Well…" Joe's own sitting-room was covered in gold discs. "Yes. I suppose it is."

"So. How's Fat Tracks?" she enquired.

"All set and ready to be launched on to the record-buying public." He raised his glass. "Cheers."

"When's the first single being released?"

"I'm not sure. Soon, I hope. Though I might go straight for an album. Singles are only really being used as promos for albums nowadays."

She nodded in agreement. "How things have changed."

"I've had a bit of a delay, anyway," he informed her, "what with the disappearance of one of my artists." He shrugged. "Still, at least that's given me time to reassess my strategy."

"Disappeared?"

"Too long a story," he said. He sipped on his scotch. "I'm now thinking of taking on some kid who used to be in a hit pop duo."

"Oh?"

"Hym."

"Oh, yes."

"Wayne Fielding."

"Good idea," she enthused. "I'd wondered what'd happened to him. His partner's done all right, hasn't he?"

"Yeah. Gary Brenn." Joe laughed. "I wish I'd taken that one on."

The doorbell rang and immediately Piru scurried from the kitchen and along the hall.

"Pity Pete wasn't around long enough to see the launch of your indie, Joe," she said sincerely. "He'd have liked that."

"Yes." For a moment, Joe seemed to be lost in thought. "I was hoping to take him away from Sloop and get him to record for Fat Tracks." He smiled at her, affectionately. "Selfish of him to die, wasn't it? Just as his contract was up for renewal."

He wondered how she'd react to his attempt at a very black joke. She laughed.

"Is it getting any better?" he asked.

She shrugged. "I miss him. Every day I miss him. But I keep myself busy."

"Modelling?"

"Yes. I can't believe I'm still in demand."

He scrutinized the face before him. "*I* can. You grow more beautiful by the day."

"Flatterer," she beamed.

Piru entered with a slim woman in her sixties, immaculately dressed and coiffured.

"Zena!" said Imogen. "How nice." She hugged the woman. "This is Joe Fisher ... who used to manage Pete's illustrious career."

"How do you do?" drawled the woman in a dark brown voice. She shook Joe's hand. "Nice to meet you at last. We've spoken on the phone a few times."

"Have you?" Imogen was surprised.

Joe nodded. "Models for video shoots."

"You've never booked *me*," laughed Imogen.

"You're too expensive," replied Joe. "And deservedly so."

At midnight the dozen dinner-guests were still seated at the grand dining-table, sipping coffee and liqueurs, all lost in animated conversation.

Zena, seated next to Joe, had taken to the fat man. And he to her.

"So ... just as *you're* starting to expand your business, *I'm* beginning to pull back a little," Zena confided in him.

"But why?" he asked. "I thought your agency was firing on all cylinders."

"No. Not really. I shall keep on the models I'm already taking care of," explained Zena, "but I can't take any of these new, pretty young things straight from school. There just isn't the amount of work around that there was a few years back. It's a shame. I've had some beautiful young women knocking on the office door, portfolio in hand ... but it's impossible." She sighed. "Still, I haven't done badly in the past."

"So Imogen is safe in your hands?"

"She's one I'll fight tooth and nail to keep," stated Zena, firmly. "She'll never grow old ... just more elegant. It's the breeding. You can't mistake the quality."

"I suppose managing models is quite similar to managing pop stars," said Joe. "It's a young persons' business and we both have to make as much as we can for our clients before they grow too old to be necessary."

"Necessary?" Zena laughed, her deep, husky voice bouncing off the dining-room walls.

"You know what I mean," said Joe. "Pete Shannon was one of the rare exceptions in the business. Pop singers aren't known for their longevity."

"Ironic, isn't it..." grinned Zena, "...that the exception for Zena's Models is Pete's wife. I can still sell Imogen for enormous fees."

Joe looked the length of the table to eye Imogen, now in hushed conversation with a handsome, silver-haired man in his late forties.

"I'm not surprised," he replied. "Look at her. She's a stunner." He grinned at Zena. "What a pity she's not a pop singer."

"This is my favourite of all Pete's songs," said Imogen. She took her seat at the grand piano in the drawing-room as the guests gathered around, drinks in hands, listening intently as their beautiful hostess tinkled casually on the keyboard.

"Was this planned by *you*?" Joe whispered to Zena, with a smile.

"No. Cross my heart," Zena whispered back. "I know no more about this than you do."

Imogen began to sing. Softly. Breathlessly. Beautifully.

> *"I passed the slipway tho' I didn't see it*
> *Only saw you smilin' through my tears.*
> *I kept recallin' how it was,*
> *And I lit another cigarette*
> *Though I haven't smoked in years.*
>
> *All alone on the freeway...*
> *Yeah, alone on the freeway..."*

Imogen stopped singing as the door was opened by Piru, who stepped aside, allowing the handsome, silver-haired man to enter, carrying a large cake.

"Happy birthday, Imogen," he said.

The guests immediately began to chant, "Happy birthday to you..."

Imogen, beaming, waited until they'd finished their song. Then she crossed to the cake and blew out the solitary candle.

Everyone cheered.

"I had no idea it was your birthday," said Joe, shame-faced. "If I'd known..."

"I didn't tell *anyone*, Joe," replied Imogen. "Except

for Peter here." She slipped a hand through his curled arm and laughed mischievously. "And before anyone says it," she announced, "yes ... perhaps I *do* have a penchant for Petes."

Zena quickly changed the subject. "And if anyone dares to ask how old she is today..."

"I'm twenty-one ... again!" laughed Imogen.

She took the cake from silver-haired Peter and headed for the kitchen. "I'll go and help poor over-worked Piru to cut this," she called back to her guests. "If you'll excuse me..."

Joe followed her to the kitchen.

"That was a wonderful meal, Imogen."

"Thanks," she replied. "I'll let the caterers know."

"And there was I, thinking it was all done by your own fair hand," he smiled.

She looked at him with raised eyebrows. "Are you crazy?" She laughed. "Me? Cook? As long as Pete's money holds out, I'll pay someone else to do all those menial tasks!"

"He certainly left you well provided for," replied Joe, knowledgeably.

"He did. God bless him." She took a knife from the drawer and placed the blade on the cake, while Piru fetched small plates and napkins. "And of course, I'm still earning really well in my own right."

He knew that now was the time. "You could earn more. Much more!"

"I doubt it." She cut through the cake. "Zena's brilliant. A wonderful agent."

"But with her as your modelling agent and with me managing you as a pop singer."

She stopped what she was doing and turned.

"Pardon?"

"You could make it, Imogen. I'm sure of that."

She sighed. "Look … thank you, Joe. But I don't want to ride to success in that field … on the back of my late husband."

He took her hand. "You'd ride to success on the back of your own fame … as a model."

"*And* my late husband's fame."

"Well…"

"No, Joe."

"Think about it, Imogen," he said. "Take your time. *Think* about it. And then let me know."

Chapter 85

Terry took the lift to the top floor as instructed, hoping that he wouldn't bump into Rosetti. He wasn't sure how he'd react. He hadn't seen his arch enemy since that night at Gran's, when Rosetti had brought Maureen home in a taxi: the night that Terry felt he was capable of murder.

Bif and Chas Atkins couldn't have been nicer as Scotty introduced Terry to them. Immediately, Terry felt that this would be a good outfit to work for. He hoped they had something definite to offer him: tea-boy ... general dogsbody ... anything.

"So, what do you think of KANSIT?" asked Chas Atkins.

"I don't know," replied Terry. "I haven't seen much yet."

"We'll show you around later," Chas continued. "Party starts at five in the conference room and goes on all evening. So, if everyone turns up, it should be pretty star-studded."

"Is Gary Brenn here?" asked Terry. "I'd like to see *him*."

Bif grimaced. "You don't like all that Kendrick Simpson stuff, surely?"

"Er ... well..." Terry wasn't sure how he should reply.

Scotty hushed Bif. "Careful. Don't forget Kendrick Simpson's been invited too. He might be lurking in the corridor outside."

They all laughed.

"Not that we need to impress *him*," added Scotty. "He's hardly likely to use KANSIT when he's got his own studio."

"I don't want to impress him," smirked Chas Atkins. "I wanna make him jealous. There's not a studio complex in London that can top this one now. Not even his."

Scotty winked at Terry. "And when BASIC BEAT really gets going, we're gonna knock all that Kendrick Simpson stuff straight out of the charts."

Terry smiled, nervously. He liked the Kendrick Simpson stuff and he couldn't imagine that BASIC BEAT would ever do any better than the maestro of pop.

"Gary Brenn won't be here until late," added Scotty. "Apparently he's doing *Chartbusters* tonight. But there's someone else here who you might be pleased to see!"

"I know," grunted Terry. "Ray Rosetti."

Chas Atkins was surprised. "Oh, so you know Rosetti, do you? Lovely lad, isn't he?" He grimaced.

Scotty laughed. "Yeah. *Smithy* knows him quite well."

"Shall we get down to business," interrupted Bif. "We're a working studio, don't forget ... even on our big party day."

"I notice you haven't got your guitar with you, Smithy," said Scotty, with a grin.

"Guitar?" asked Terry. "What for?"

"Scotty's been raving about your talent," explained Chas. "So before we offer you a job as BASIC BEAT's errand-boy, we thought we'd give you a chance to audition."

"Audition?" Terry gasped.

"We'd like to see if Scotty's right," smiled Bif. "I'll go and get my guitar from my office," he added. "Why don't you two take the lad to the showcase studio."

Terry couldn't believe what he was hearing.

Rosetti was working with his producer, remixing a few of the tracks for his first album, simply entitled, ROSETTI. If "Down On Me Gently" were to reach number one as expected, this album had to be ready for immediate distribution.

Franco had booked KANSIT's only available studio for that week, fully aware that Scotty now had a finger somewhere in Chas Atkins' lucrative pie, but also figuring that to be within the complex on the day of its official opening, when anyone who was anyone in the recording industry would be attending, could only bode well for young Rosetti.

"High profile, son," Franco had said. "We gotta use it. But if it really bothers you, I can go for Denson Sound Studios."

"No. KANSIT's just fine, Dad," he replied.

"Couldn't be better in fact."

Rosetti was revelling in the fact that his solo single stood in the top forty and he hoped that he'd come face to face with Scotty. He couldn't wait! The whole record industry was aware that BASIC BEAT had failed disastrously with the over-hyped Le Roi and Rosetti knew that he wouldn't even have to mention it. He'd just pass Scotty by with a cursory, "Hi!" That would be enough.

Terry sang:

> *"Gotta get myself in line.*
> *Find the words to say to you.*
> *Tell you how I feel, 'cause I'm*
> *Hung up, waitin' on you.*
>
> *Call ... call on me,*
> *You'll find a stranger..."*

Bif looked at Chas Atkins and grinned. Scotty was right. This boy did have talent. An extraordinary talent.

"Why don't you go and get yourself some tea, Terry?" suggested Bif. "Canteen's down in the basement. I want to have a chat with Chas and Scotty."

He took his guitar from Terry and slipped a fiver into the boy's hand. "Order us *all* some tea and we'll join you in five minutes."

Terry left the showcase studio, almost in a trance. He hadn't been expecting this at all. He had no idea that he'd be asked to sing. And he was thrilled with the result. His voice had never sounded better. Maybe it was the adrenalin that had given it such power or maybe it was because, for the first time since he'd written the song, the lyrics had had some relevance in his life. He could have been singing them for Maureen.

He pushed the button for the lift and waited, the song still going through his head. Bif had seemed delighted with his performance. And Chas Atkins had said, "So – a star is born!" Terry wondered if he were joking. Or did that mean that they were going to take him on? Were they going to give him a break? Was Terry Smith at last on the verge of becoming a pop singer? He tried not to get too excited. After all, he'd been here before, only to lose the lot. He wouldn't lose it this time, if it were offered! This time he'd grab the opportunity with both hands. This time it had to happen for him. There was so much at stake. He remembered young Billy's disappointment when he threw it all away the last time. And he thought of Maureen, who talked of the thrill she felt about going out with Rosetti, just because he was a pop star. And most importantly, he thought about his father and Levi's words, "He'd have loved it!"

The lift arrived. The doors opened. Terry stepped inside. The doors closed behind him. And there … standing beside him … was Ray Rosetti.

Rosetti was shocked. Terry wasn't. He'd been aware that this might happen as soon as he'd discovered Rosetti was in the building.

"What the hell are you doing here?" snarled Rosetti.

"An interview," replied Terry. He began to shake; a mixture of anger and fear. "An interview for a job."

"Not with Scotty?"

"Yeah." He knew he should tell Rosetti to keep his nose out of it. It had nothing to do with him.

"What sort of job? You gonna be Scotty's Yesman?"

Terry didn't reply. He looked up at the floor-indicator lights. Had he pressed *BASEMENT*? He couldn't remember.

"You'll do anything for a few pence, won't you, you pikies?"

Terry told himself, Don't rise to it. Don't let him spoil this day.

"How's Maureen?" asked Rosetti, grinning widely. "Still seeing her, are you? Or did she dump you after she'd been out with me?"

Terry silently fumed. His heart began to race. He felt the tightening in his stomach, the sickly feeling rising in his throat.

"Did she tell you how much fun we had, eh, Pikie?"

Terry turned on him. It was stupid. He knew he shouldn't have done it.

"You shut your mouth, Rosetti! Maureen's OK. *We're* OK. So you shut your mouth before I put my fist in it!"

"Ooooh!" laughed Rosetti. "Temper! Temper!"

Terry clenched his fists. He could feel his fingertips digging into the palms of his hands.

"I only asked about her because I care about her, Smithy. That's all," Rosetti went on. "But then I've always cared about Maureen. You know that."

"Shut it, Rosetti! I'm warning you!"

"She only went out with you because she felt sorry for you. That's all. She told me. She was always one for the underdog, was Maureen. And you can't get more underdog than you, can you, Smithy? Lowest of the low, aren't they, pikies? Scum!"

Terry suddenly leapt at Rosetti and both boys tumbled to the floor, rolling over, punching and kicking.

The lift arrived at the basement and as the doors opened, they spilled out into the corridor, still thumping each other.

A group of musicians, just leaving the canteen, rushed along the corridor and tore the two boys apart.

"Come on! Cut it out, you two!" one yelled.

Terry stood, panting and glaring at Rosetti; his arms held behind his back by one of the musicians, a burly six-footer.

Terry looked none the worse for his battle.

Rosetti, still lying on the floor, mopped his split lip with a handkerchief. "I'll get you for this, Pikie!" he said.

A security guard raced from the canteen. "What's all this about?" he asked.

"Dunno," smiled the six-footer as he let go of Terry's arms. "Think he must've heard Rosetti's new single."

Everyone laughed. Everyone but the two people concerned.

Rosetti got to his feet and silently made his way back to the lift.

Terry called after him. "Here. I've got something for you!"

He followed Rosetti, took out the crumpled note from his pocket and handed it to him.

"Love letter, I think. From two ten-year-olds!"

Rosetti snatched the letter.

"And by the way," said Terry. "I'm not here to be Scotty's lackey!"

He lowered his voice. He didn't want anyone else to hear what he was saying.

"I'm here to record a single."

The look of disbelief on Rosetti's face was something that Terry would never forget. Never! Even if he wasn't to be given the chance to make a record, it had still been worth saying, just to see that look!

Chapter 86

Imogen looked around Joe's sitting-room. She smiled, noting the gold discs covering every wall.

"I haven't been here for ages," she said.

Joe poured her a glass of white wine. "Should be champagne, I suppose."

She tutted, playfully. "Not yet, Joe. I haven't signed anything. And I *won't* until I'm sure it's just as I want it."

"One single only."

"That's right."

He laughed. "For starters!"

"Let's take it slowly, eh, Joe? One step at a time."

"I promise."

"And I have approval on the song?"

"Of course."

"I'm too old to stand in front of a camera jigging about to some up-tempo number."

"Too old? You'll never be too old, Imogen."

"Too classy, then." Her eyes twinkled, mischievously.

He smiled at her. "Far too classy."

He poured himself a large scotch and joined her on the sofa. "Seriously. We've got to choose the song very carefully. A ballad. Wistful. Haunting. Like your voice. A big orchestra with you almost whispering the melody on top."

"Sounds good."

"A modern, folksy kind of song."

"Folksy?"

"You know, something like…" He stopped. He'd remembered. Yes. Yes, of course. *Of course!* It was perfect.

As soon as he'd seen Imogen into a taxi, Joe went into his office and opened his directory. He picked up the phone and dialled.

"Jim Buckley, please."

"Speaking."

"Jim, it's Joe here. Joe Fisher."

Jim was immediately suspicious. "I can't help you, Joe. I haven't seen him and I'm not likely to."

"It's not Terry I'm after," replied Joe.

"No?"

"No. It's *you*."

"Sorry?"

"That song," he said. "*Sparrow*."

Jim felt his heart skip a beat. "Yes?"

"Still available, is it?"

"Yes."

"Great!" he said. "Let's meet!"

Chapter 87

Kendrick Simpson saw Ruby as soon as she entered KANSIT's lobby.

"Ruby Gold!" he announced, dramatically. "How are you, babe?"

"Beat it!" she hissed. She walked by him, pinning on her security badge, and headed towards the lift.

He caught up with her. "I only wanted to say how pleased I am. I see your single's doing OK Stateside."

"No thanks to you, sugar!" she sneered. "You had me blown out, don't forget, just because I wouldn't play along with your little power game."

"Aw c'mon!" he said. "I know what I'm doing, Ruby. I was only trying to protect Gary's career. You *do* know that 'Only Me And You' is at number ten, by the way?"

"I couldn't give *that*..." she said, clicking her fingers in Kendrick Simpson's face, "...for 'Only Me And You'. Not for Gary. Nor for you. Now beat it!"

The lift arrived and Ruby stepped inside.

"I hope you'll be nicer to Gary than you were to

me," he said with a sickly grin. "He'll be arriving later. He's doin' *Chartbusters*."

"*Is* he indeed?" she snapped.

The lift doors began to close.

"And don't be too hard on his latest little girlfriend, will you, Ruby?" he said. "She's a terribly sweet little thing … sugar!"

It was a lie. Gary had no girlfriend. He hadn't dated anyone since Ruby had returned to the US.

As the lift rose, Ruby's heart began to thud. She knew that if Gary arrived on the arm of another woman, she just couldn't bear it. She'd only accepted KANSIT's invitation in the hope of seeing him again. The TV appearances in Britain, arranged by her manager to promote her single on this side of the Atlantic, were of secondary importance to her. She hadn't been able to get Gary out of her mind. She wanted him desperately. But now it was too late. He had someone new.

Rosetti moved, glass of champagne in hand, from group to group, as advised by Franco, who did the same thing. If there was anyone at KANSIT's official opening party who didn't know, before the evening began, who Ray Rosetti was … then they certainly knew it now. He looked around the room for Terry Smith and on seeing Scotty and his cronies huddled up with a group of pop journalists, he decided that Smithy the Gyppo must have gone home. Then he saw the beautiful black girl in the red leather skirt … and he began to drool. He knew all about Ruby Gold. He knew that, for a short while, she'd dated heartthrob Gary Brenn. Everyone in the business knew that. He knew that her best friend was the American superstar, Sherry Barbin. Everyone in the business knew that. He knew that Sherry Barbin had written Ruby's new single and that it was going to make Ruby Gold a big, big, name in the States. Everyone in the business knew that. And he was determined that everyone in the business would know, before the end of the week ... this side and Stateside ... that Ray Rosetti had dated Sherry Barbin's best friend.

He crossed the room and approached her.

"Hi! I'm Ray Rosetti!"

Ruby was relieved to be able to leave the party on the arm of a handsome young man like Ray Rosetti, even though his split lip had already got her wondering as to what sort of brawl he'd got into. What type of company did this guy keep? Neither of them minded being photographed together as they left KANSIT and climbed into a taxi. Ruby, who had already drunk far too much champagne, could think only of Gary and his new girlfriend ... who didn't exist ... and wondered if, when this photo appeared in tomorrow's tabloids, it would have any effect on her ex-lover.

Rosetti could think only of the publicity he'd receive ... and what it would do to the immediate sales of "Down On Me Gently". He couldn't depend totally on Rica Stubbs for his tabloid headlines. He couldn't rely on her for ever. And he knew that just by dating Sherry Barbin's best friend, he'd re-oiled the cogs of the publicity machine. He was aware of course that Ruby Gold had to be dumped pretty quickly. One

... maybe *two* nights would be enough for his needs. But he had to make himself free for his adoring fans as soon as possible. They'd forgive him a quick fling, especially with Sherry Barbin's best friend. But they'd never allow him to get hooked. He belonged to *them*!

At Groucho's they dined undisturbed, though Rosetti was aware that Franco would be lining up more photographers for their departure from the restaurant. And they talked, on and on ... and Ruby drank and drank, until it was very late.

Ruby admired the boy, his obsessive ambition reminding her of Sherry's early days, when she'd do practically anything to get to the top.

As the wine loosened her tongue, she asked him, "What do you think of Gary Brenn, Ray?"

"How d'you mean?"

"Do you think he's talented?"

"Yes. But not as talented as me," Rosetti smiled.

"Do you think he'll be around for long?"

Rosetti laughed. "Hope not. There isn't room in the charts for two solo pop idols. And I aim to be the number one."

"So does he," she grinned.

"I know. But he's gonna be disappointed."

She reached out for her wine and knocked the glass over. The waiter raced across and mopped the table before bringing her a new glass.

"Sorry," she said. "Too much champagne at that party."

And two bottles of wine here, thought Rosetti.

"I went out with him, you know. With Gary Brenn."

"Did you?" Rosetti feigned surprise.

She became dreamy-eyed. "Yeah. Sure did."

"And?"

"He's great," she was slurring her words. "A really nice guy. Or he was, until his record company started dictating how he should run his private life."

Rosetti sneered. "Private life? Gary Brenn couldn't have had *much* of a private life. I shouldn't have thought he had any *life* at all to speak of."

Ruby became defensive. "What do you mean?"

"Well, he's a bit wet, isn't he? All muscles and no brain. There can't be much private about sweet Gary Brenn."

Ruby laughed loudly, drunkenly. "You don't know him. That definitely isn't true."

"You're not trying to tell me that inside that cropped head there's something going on?"

"Lots going on," she slurred. "Lots and lots."

Rosetti watched her sway slightly as she gripped the edge of the table. He wasn't surprised. He'd filled her glass to the brim every time, while he'd drunk very little. His original idea, badly miscalculated, was to *mellow* the black girl, who he'd heard could be quite fiery. He didn't want her rejecting him.

"There's a lot inside that cropped head if you must know. More than you'd ever dream possible."

She was still coherent. But only just.

Rosetti leaned forward to listen. "Such as?" He was only mildly curious.

"He has to be very careful about what he does, of course, because of his fans."

"We all have to be careful about that," replied Rosetti.

"Aah, yes," she went on, "but Gary has to be very, very, very careful." She began to sway again. "He has to be very … very careful after what he's done."

"*Done?*"

Rosetti wondered, *hoped*, that she was going to dish the dirt. He wasn't expecting this. It was almost too good to be true.

"Shall I order another bottle?" he asked.

Ruby drained her glass. "Why not?"

He did.

"He was very cruel to me, you know."

"Was he?"

"He dumped me, you know," she slurred. "He was very, very cruel to me."

Rosetti reached across the table and squeezed her hand.

"I don't know how anyone could be cruel to you," he said, sounding sympathetic.

"*He* was."

"That was very bad of him," tutted Rosetti.

"You don't know the half of it," she said. "If you knew what he did in Tokyo. Him and his friend."

"His friend?"

"Wayne."

"Wayne Fielding?"

"Yes."

"Hym?"

"Yes. Him and Gary in Tokyo."

What? What? What? thought Rosetti. "Tokyo?" he asked nonchalantly.

The waiter arrived with a fresh bottle and poured more wine into Ruby's glass. Rosetti covered his glass with his hand and shook his head at the waiter.

"No. He's definitely not wet," she slurred. "Not Gary. And it wasn't a very…" She sought for the jumbled words in her befuddled brain. "It wasn't a very *kind* thing to do, was it?"

"What?" asked Rosetti, still trying to sound cool. "What did Gary do in Tokyo, Ruby?"

And she told him.

Chapter 88

Tokyo: One year earlier

Hym had been booked to play just two gigs at the Tokyo Dome, as a support band to the Japanese cult group, Chuo-ku. Phil Lemont had insisted that his boys arrive two days before the show, having heard from the concert promoter that the cultural shock for these young, unseasoned travellers to the East could result in a lack-lustre performance. It'd killed off many pop groups before them and Phil was determined not to let it happen to Hym. According to their record and video sales, they were doing very nicely in Japan. But BJ at Blunt Edge had said they could be much bigger. Huge. There was a great deal of yen to be earned here and, played right, Hym could clean up.

From Narita airport, Phil accompanied his charges to the prestigious Hotel Okura, where all three settled into their luxurious rooms overlooking the Japanese landscaped garden.

"This place is brill," said Wayne when they met up

as arranged at one of the hotel's many bars. "Can we afford it?"

Phil shrugged. "Blunt Edge is picking up the tab. It's BJ's idea."

"So that's why you haven't brought your tent, you ol' Scrooge," laughed Gary.

"So, what are we doing tonight?" asked Wayne. "What adventures have you arranged for us, Phil?"

Phil Lemont gave an inane grin.

"He's staying here at the bar all night, obviously," Gary guessed correctly.

"Well, *we're* not," said Wayne. "I want to see a bit of this Tokyo nightlife."

"Too right," added Gary.

Phil handed them both a wad of yen.

"Here. Expenses," he said.

"Also from BJ?" asked Wayne.

"Yeah. It's not cheap here, so watch it. The cab prices are sky high."

"You don't expect us to take the underground, I hope?" smiled Gary.

"No," replied Phil. "All I'm saying is, be careful. Right?"

"Right!" This from both of them.

They headed straight for the Kabukicho area and having paid a sullen cab driver his astronomical fare, they strolled through the oppressively humid streets, the sound of cicadas almost drowning out the passing traffic. They hurried by the karaoke bars, peepshow clubs and McDonald's restaurants ... until Gary found what he'd been searching for.

007's was mainly for Westerners, most of its customers being Americans, now living and working in Tokyo. The air-conditioned bar was small and plush, with a central podium on which danced a small troupe of young and beautiful skimpily dressed Japanese girls. American and British chart music accompanied their bumping and grinding: the sounds of Patcha and Sherry Barbin … plus the odd Madonna classic.

"We might as well be in Soho," groaned Wayne. "I thought you said this place was supposed to be really special?"

Gary agreed. "Sorry. That's what I heard."

"Shall we go?"

"We could have one drink first," replied Gary. "At least it's cool in here."

They ignored the *sake*, ordering two small beers instead from the Australian barman.

"Hi!" said a soft voice from behind them. They turned to face a pretty, slim girl in her late teens. Her blonde hair stood in small, uneven tufts, some of which were strung with rainbow-coloured ribbons. "Mine's a beer too," she said with a smile. The accent was cut-glass. Very upmarket.

Gary ordered another.

"Hym, isn't it?" she said.

"That's right." Wayne found it strange, being recognized so far away from home.

"You're Wayne … and you're Gary."

"Well done," laughed Gary. "And you're…?"

"Perdita," she replied, adding, "I like your music."

Wayne was curious. "Are they playing our stuff a lot out here then?"

She picked up her drink and sipped at it.

"I wouldn't know," she replied. "I've only been here a few weeks."

"So you know our music from England?" asked Gary.

"Yes," she said. "I liked your stuff from the beginning."

"Thanks," grinned Gary. "We aim to please."

"Are you on holiday?" she asked, turning to face Wayne. "Or is it business?"

"We're playing at the Tokyo Dome," Wayne informed her. "On Monday and Tuesday."

"Oh, really?" she enthused. "I've read about the Dome." She giggled. "I've been to the Dome in London, of course – but I think the Tokyo one's a bit bigger."

"Just a bit," laughed Wayne.

"So I take it you're on holiday ... er...?" Gary struggled for her name.

"Perdita," she repeated.

"So I take it you're on holiday, Perdita?"

"Sort of," she said. "I'm over with my mother." She smiled. "If she knew I was here, she'd kill me. She thinks I'm back at the apartment."

"So, you don't know this city any better than we do?" asked Wayne.

"Well ... I've got to know it quite well over the past week or so," she replied.

"So you could show us what's what?" said Gary.

She whispered, "You really should see the Shinjuku area. It's terribly decadent."

Gary quickly drained the last of his beer. "Take us to it," he said.

Shinjuku had the tallest buildings in the city.

"More like New York," said Wayne. "If it wasn't for all these Japs walking around, you'd swear you were in the States."

Perdita led them to Nichome, where they sat in the park and watched the passers-by, the young in the latest of fashions, taking the last of the sun's rays before heading for the Nichome clubs and bars.

They strolled to Snoopy's Disco which, by eleven o'clock, was pounding with dance music from all over the globe. The lightshow topped even London's Dome and the sound system was the best that Gary and Wayne had ever heard.

"Clever, these Japanese, aren't they?" laughed Wayne to Gary, above the sounds played by the American DJ.

Gary smiled. "Japanese? Look around you. There's no Japanese to be seen!"

Perdita swigged back the remains of a glass of wine. "I'm just going to the loo," she informed the boys. "Won't be long."

Wayne watched her go. "I know her," he said. "I don't know where from, but I definitely know her."

"I thought so too," agreed Gary. "I think it's from the TV. I've seen her in some soap opera, or something. *EastEnders*, I think."

Wayne laughed. "You sure? *EastEnders*, with an accent like that? Give over. She's far too grand."

"Well, perhaps it's *The Avenue*."

"No. It's not *The Avenue*."

Wayne looked across at the staircase which led to

the toilets. Perdita was talking to a short but well-built Japanese man, in shades.

"A genuine native at last!" said Wayne.

Gary followed Wayne's eye-line. "Looks like the Japanese Mafia to me," he said.

The man took a small packet from his shirt pocket and handed it to Perdita. She in turn handed him an envelope.

"You don't think it's a drug deal, do you?" asked Gary. "Surely not. Not someone of her class."

Wayne raised an eyebrow. "Well, that's what it looks like. Perhaps we ought not to get involved, Gary. We don't want to end up in some Japanese hell-hole prison for the rest of our lives."

Gary laughed. "This is Tokyo. Not Bangkok."

"It's still a long way from home," argued Wayne. "I don't want anything to do with it."

Gary suddenly grabbed Wayne's arm. "Hey!" he shouted. "It's just hit me. I know who she is."

"Who?"

"Well it's not a soap opera, for starters," grinned Gary.

"Tell me!"

"The Royal Rebel!"

"What?"

"The daughter of Princess Catherine. *Lady* Perdita."

Wayne gasped. "You're joking!"

"Think about it. She's the one who was splashed all over the tabloids last year when she was busted for drugs."

"Of course," said Wayne. "Of course it is. I knew I knew her." He began to panic.

"Do you think we ought to go?" he asked. "Before she gets back. We don't want to be involved in all that, do we?"

"You are joking, of course," tutted Gary. "She's British Royalty! Somewhere in line to the throne. The Americans'll love all that. It won't do us any harm out *there* … and let's face it, America's where we've got to break. Japan's great – but America, Wayne."

"Don't be ridiculous!" protested Wayne. "It'll do us no favours at all, getting mixed up with some junkie … no matter what sort of family she comes from!"

Gary eyed Lady Perdita, who was approaching from the toilets and hurrying down the staircase towards them.

"Don't let on that we know," hissed Gary. "And when she introduces us to her mother, we'll just act surprised." He laughed.

Perdita walked straight past them, grabbing Gary's hand and leading him towards a darkened alcove, where she sat at the small, round bar table. Gary and Wayne sat opposite her.

"I've got some stuff," she whispered.

"What sort of stuff?" Gary whispered back.

Wayne stood. "Not for me."

Perdita looked at him, amazed. "But you're a pop star."

"A pop star who prefers a nice cup of tea and the occasional drink!" he said, bluntly. He looked at Gary and shook his head in dismay. "I'm going to look around the club," he sighed. "I'll be back in *ten* minutes!"

He left.

Perdita appeared concerned. "He's *all right*, isn't he?"

Gary grinned, nervously. "He doesn't approve. But he won't say anything."

She looked around to make sure no one was watching. "So ... are you on for it?"

"Not tonight," replied Gary. "We've got a photo-call tomorrow. I don't want to be floating till the early hours."

She smiled at him. "Shame."

"Yeah."

"How about tomorrow?"

He thought about it. "How about after our last gig?"

"When's that?"

"Tuesday night. All I've got to do on Wednesday morning is to sit on a plane to the States."

"Great!" She reached over and took his hand.

"So where shall we meet?" asked Gary.

She took out a card and handed it to him. "That's the address of the apartment where we're staying. The Tatemi Tower. Just a block away from here. We're on the top floor."

"I can't get there before midnight," explained Gary. "The concert doesn't finish until ten-thirty."

"That's fine," she replied. "My mother's away until the end of the week, so it'll be safe."

She saw that Wayne was approaching them and hurriedly completed the arrangements.

"Get a cab ... *to here*," she said. "And then walk. And if there's anyone hanging around outside the Tatemi Tower, wait until they've gone. If you use the restaurant door around the back of the building, beneath the TAGHeuer ad, you'll avoid the concierge. I don't want anyone knowing that I've been visited by a pop singer! My mother would go ape."

"You can trust me," he smiled.

She stood as Wayne sat to join them.

"I've got to get back," she said looking at her watch. It was two o'clock.

Wayne faked a yawn. "Yeah. It is a bit late. We should be going too, Gary."

"Give me five minutes, eh?" said Perdita, hurriedly. "Before *you* leave, I mean! I wouldn't want anyone to see us leave here together."

Both shows proved to be enormously successful for Hym, though Gary and Wayne were at first disconcerted at the polite reception they'd received from the packed Tokyo Dome audience.

"It's just their way," Phil informed them after the final concert. "They react differently from British audiences, that's all. They loved you, all the same."

"Are you going to the airport straight from here, Phil?" asked Wayne. "Or do you want to go for a meal first?"

Phil eyed his watch. "I'd better go now. Back to dear old Blighty."

"So we won't see you again till we do that LA gig?" said Gary.

"No. But I'll call daily ... just to make sure you're behavin' yourselves." He picked up his bag and began to leave the dressing-room. "All the best, lads. Sock it to them in the US of A. I want you to have a number

487

one single out there before the end of the year."

"We'll do our best," grinned Wayne.

"And say hi to Sherry for me," he added.

"Will do."

He left.

"Right!" said Gary, excitedly. "Ready?"

Wayne looked at him, quizzically.

"For our little party with Lady Perdita."

Wayne sighed. "I've told you. I'm not going."

"Please."

"I'm not getting involved."

Gary began to sulk. "If *you're* not going … *I'm* not going. I'm not going without you." He wrapped his arm around Wayne's neck. "Please, please, please, please…"

Wayne sighed. "We're not staying there all night," he said.

They arrived at the Tatemi Tower and, making sure there was no one around, they entered through the rear entrance, walked up two floors and then took the elevator to the fifty-seventh.

"I hope her mother hasn't suddenly decided to return," grinned Wayne. "She's probably in bed."

"No. I wouldn't have thought so," said Gary. "Shame, though," he added, feigning disappointment. "I'd quite like to meet Princess Catherine in her dressing-gown and curlers." He grinned wildly at the thought.

Perdita greeted them in whispers, until they were safely behind closed and very heavy doors. She was obviously disturbed by Wayne's presence and was quick to say so.

"I wasn't expecting both of you."

Gary grinned at her. "We're inseparable."

She looked at Wayne, accusingly. "Well," she informed him. "It's all hush-hush. OK?"

Wayne stared blankly at her.

"There's a little bar by the pool," she went on. "My mother hates it. 'It's so vulgar,' she says. But I quite like it. We can have a drink ... and whatever ... and a swim at the same time."

The pool bar was locked.

"Damn!" exploded Lady Perdita, in a fit of pique. "I'm sorry. I don't know where she keeps the key."

"We don't need booze," said Gary. He smiled at her. "I'm sure you must have something else that'll keep us happy."

"I'm sure I have," giggled Perdita.

"Where's the toilet?" Wayne said, quickly. He wished they were back at the hotel. He didn't want anything to do with this. He'd never taken anything in London and he certainly wasn't going to start here.

Perdita pointed in the direction of the palatial patio. "Along there and down the corridor. You can hardly miss it. It's huge."

Wayne returned five minutes later to find Gary's and Lady Perdita's clothes lying on the side of the pool. The two of them were in the water, frolicking around and laughing like small children.

"Gary!" he hissed. "Oh, come on. Please. If anyone

should come in…"

Lady Perdita swam to the side and pulled herself out of the pool. She sat on the edge, totally ignoring the remonstrances from Wayne, as she grappled in her jacket for a small packet.

She opened up the packet and removed some tiny capsules, calling to Gary, "Do you want one of these?"

Gary swam towards her.

She swallowed one and handed him another.

Wayne glared at him. "Gary! Please! You don't need it."

Lady Perdita laughed. "Nobody *needs* it. Nobody *needs* caviare or champagne, but everyone enjoys it!"

Gary took the capsule from her and swallowed it.

"How long?" he asked. "How long before it works?"

She shrugged. "Fifteen minutes." She placed the remaining capsules back into her pocket and dived, giggling, into the pool.

Wayne decided to leave them. Lost in their romp, they didn't see him go.

He wandered aimlessly through the grand apartment, wondering if he should either get a cab back to the hotel or wait until Gary came racing after him. He was shaking with rage. And he was scared. Hym had everything on tap. It was going to be mega-successful, he was sure of that. But if Gary was caught now, drugged up to his eyes, swimming with the daughter of a British Princess, then…

He allowed thirty minutes to pass and when Gary still hadn't appeared, he went back to the pool. He had to get him out of there. For both their sakes. If Gary wasn't careful, he'd ruin everything.

He stood at the pool entrance and saw Gary, white-faced and shivering, staring down open-mouthed at the water.

Perdita was floating face down.

"What the hell...?" yelled Wayne.

Gary looked at him, pathetically, child-like.

"Gary?"

"She had some sort of fit," he mumbled. "One minute she was all right ... and then she had this sort of fit. And she just went under."

Wayne whisked off his shoes, jeans and shirt and dived into the pool. He struggled to turn the girl over on her back, before dragging her to the edge.

"Help me!" he screamed to Gary, whose right arm was going into an involuntary spasm. "Help me, you idiot!"

Gary managed to pull the dead weight from the water and Wayne leapt out and knelt beside the ashen-faced Lady Perdita. He tried as best as he could to help, but she refused to breathe.

"Go and get some help, Gary, for God's sake!" yelled Wayne. "Go and get some bloody help!"

"You've got to be joking!" replied Gary. He hurriedly began to dress. "We can't be found here like this. We'll be crucified for this!"

Wayne could hardly believe what he was hearing. "If you don't get her some help, she'll die, Gary! She'll die!"

Gary threw Wayne's clothes to him. "She's dead anyway! There's nothing we can do!"

"If they get her to hospital..." Wayne tried to argue.

Gary flared. "She's dead, Wayne! Get dressed. Come on. Let's go!"

Wayne began to throw on his clothes, pleading, "Gary! We can't just leave her here. Not like this."

He picked up Perdita's jacket and laid it across her naked body.

"Don't be stupid!" said Gary. He picked up the jacket and searched in the pocket for the packet of drugs. "If you cover her up, they'll know someone was here with her." He threw the jacket to the side, having confirmed that the pills were still there. "They'll think she got high and went for a swim. No one will know we were here."

Gary grabbed Wayne's sleeve and began dragging him towards the pool-exit. "Come on! Come on!"

Wayne pulled his arm from Gary's grip. "We can't just leave her, Gary. We could be signing her death certificate. We've got to get some help."

"Well, *I'm* going!" shrieked Gary. He began to run. "*You* take the rap if you want to. But I'm going!"

Wayne took one last look at the dead – or dying – Lady Perdita, and then raced after him.

Chapter 89

Ruby Gold woke with a pounding head. She staggered to the bathroom and splashed her face with cold water. It had been months and months since she'd drunk like that. She'd only ever done it when she was feeling really low. And yesterday, on hearing that Gary had found a new girlfriend, she'd felt the need to cloud her mind. But she wished she hadn't. And she wished that she'd not accepted Ray Rosetti's invitation to supper. She could hardly remember arriving back at the hotel. There was a vague recollection of a short taxi ride and Rosetti leading her to the hotel's foyer, before kissing her on the cheek and disappearing. And there was that awful feeling that she'd said too much. She didn't even know this Ray Rosetti and yet she remembered telling him about Gary and Wayne in Tokyo. What a stupid thing to do. She hated Gary for dumping her like that. But she'd never wish him any harm. And if a story like that got out, it would totally destroy his career. She hoped she could trust Ray Rosetti not to say anything.

* * *

Rosetti wondered how best he could use the information for his own ends. The story certainly wouldn't do much for Gary Brenn's career – and *that* would certainly be one less rival in the charts. But surely the story was worth more than that? Deliberating all morning he finally put a call through to *GO!* magazine.

"Rica Stubb's office please."

She was delighted to hear from him.

"Hi! How did you know I was here?" she asked.

"I didn't. I thought I'd try *GO!* before I rang your mobile. It's cheaper."

She laughed.

"But just to show I'm not mean … I thought it was time I took you to lunch," he added.

"Great. When?"

"Today."

"Oh. I'm not sure, Ray," she said. "I've got a deadline to meet for the pop page here. At the moment the Big Chief is encouraging me all the way, but if I miss my deadline on *GO!*, I think he might change his mind about all the freelancing I'm doing. I don't want to lose my input here."

"You won't need *GO!* after today," Rosetti informed her. "One hour," he insisted. "It's in both our interests that we meet."

She was curious. "Why the urgency?"

"I've got a story for you that'll blow your mind. A story any freelancer would die for."

"If this is a wind-up, Ray…" she warned him. "I'm honestly very busy."

"No wind-up. If you don't meet me today, I'm gonna call one of the tabloids. They'll leap at the story."

She was silent.

"Well?" he asked.

"I'll see you in the Duke of Wellington just around the corner from the office. One o'clock."

"Right!"

"On the dot, Ray. I've no time to waste."

She hung up.

They carried their ploughmans and lagers through to the chilly garden, "To avoid," Rosetti suggested, "being recognized."

Rica laughed. "Or is it just to hide the fact that you lost in a fight?" she said, eyeing his boxer's wounds.

He licked the sore lip. "I don't want to be disturbed."

"No one here's gonna disturb you," she smirked. "These are all City gents. I shouldn't think any of them have ever heard of Ray Rosetti."

They sat at the splinter-dangerous wooden bench and tried to get comfortable.

" 'Down On Me Gently' is shooting up the charts," argued the offended Rosetti. "Of course they've heard of me!"

She couldn't argue with the *first* part of that statement. "Looks as though it could be heading for the top five," she conceded.

He gulped down most of his lager. "Got to be number one."

She shrugged. "Who knows?"

"*Got* to be," he said. "I've got to get this single to number one, Rica. It's everything to me."

"It's everything to every pop singer, Ray. Although

495

many of them would deny that."

"You could help," he said, softly.

She was irritated. "I hope you haven't brought me here simply to discuss 'Down On Me Gently', Ray? I've done a hell of a lot for that single already. And for *you* in general. You saw the article in last week's *GO!*?"

"Thanks." He grinned at her.

"I thought you had some major story for me? That's why we're here."

"It's all tied together," he informed her. "Stories like the one I have for you *cost*, Rica."

She frowned. "I see."

He reached out and took her hand. "Come on," he said. "You won't be sorry, I promise you."

She hardened. "What do you want, Ray?"

"The front cover of *GO!* within the next two weeks."

She shook her head. "Impossible. Covers are all tied up for the next three weeks."

"Never!" he laughed. "I'm not that green, Rica. You can't decide who's going on the front cover of a pop music magazine that far ahead."

Her silence proved his point.

"You can persuade your editor, Rica," he said. "Tell him that you're sure Rosetti's gonna be at number one by the end of the month. With your success rate at picking the top discs, he'll go for it, without a doubt."

"What have you got for me, Ray?" she asked coolly.

"Can you get me on the cover of *GO!*?"

"I could. I suppose. It depends."

"And at least one big article in each of the major tabloids?"

"I could try." She paused and smiled at him. "OK. Now what have you got for me?"

"Finish that drink," he said. "I'll order us another." He smiled back at her. "Then get out your notebook, honey chile. This is gonna freak you out."

Rica gasped. "That's the most incredible story I've ever heard."

"Isn't it just?" said Rosetti.

"If it's true!"

"I can't see why she'd lie."

"To get her own back on Gary Brenn?"

"No. She was too drunk to have worked all that out. It was the truth all right."

"It seems very unlikely to me," she said.

"Nonsense!" He excitedly took both of Rica's hands in his. "Listen. The whole world knew about Lady Perdita's death. It's common knowledge that she OD'd and drowned."

"But…"

"But it was assumed that she was alone when she died."

"Not by everyone," Rica contradicted. "There was quite a bit of doubt at the time, if you remember. All those articles about whether she was helped out of the pool … or did she pull *herself* out."

"Stories soon dismissed, though," argued Ray. "The coroner decided it was an accidental death, didn't he?"

"Yes." Rica grinned. "Looks as though it was the *wrong* decision! If Gary Brenn and Wayne Fielding left her to die … surely that's manslaughter?"

They both paused as they sipped their drinks.

Rica's hands suddenly began to tremble. "I don't believe I've just heard this," she said. "This is an investigative journalist's dream."

"Told you!"

"Or nightmare."

"You've got a lot of careful digging to do," suggested Rosetti.

"You're not kiddin'." She thought about it. "First things first. I'll put in a call to Blunt Edge. Ask them for the exact dates of Hym's Tokyo gig."

Rosetti grinned. "You've got a story here involving Royalty, drugs and a top British pop star. Couldn't want for much more, could you? You may even be able to bring in the Ruby Gold connection. Her relationship with Gary Brenn. And Ruby Gold leads you straight to America's Queen of Pop, Sherry Barbin!"

"Ray," said Rica, still trembling, "if this comes off … I'm made!"

"The number one freelance journalist, eh?" he replied.

"Could be."

"And you won't forget my cover-shot will you?"

She laughed. "You've got it!"

Chapter 90

Rica Stubbs with the aid of Ray Rosetti had hit the big one. That was for sure. At first there were just hints in the press, harking back to the mysterious death of Lady Perdita ... and of persons unknown being present at the time. Soon the popular British tabloids began to use the unsubstantiated story of the involvement of an unnamed pop group, whilst the "quality" press skirted around the subject, more fearful of the possible libel involved.

The foreign press was bolder. Italy's papers had spoken outright about the pop star lover of the daughter of Princess Catherine, and the French and the Spanish immediately picked up the story, revelling in the scandal. America's *National Enquirer* went even further, printing pictures of Hym: Wayne Fielding and Gary Brenn who were, apparently, in Tokyo at the time of Lady Perdita's death. The pictures used, however, were of Hym on the Sherry Barbin Roadshow.

"We'll sue!" said Gary's mother. "They've no right to

go dragging you into all this nonsense. You must sue, Gary!"

Gary was silent; staring into space. He hadn't stopped shaking all morning. As soon as he saw the headline, he knew. This was the beginning of the end.

His father immediately returned from Ireland, tailed all the way by reporters.

"We can't sue," replied his father. "Not yet, we can't. They're not actually saying Gary's involved. They can't!"

The evening papers told a different tale.

Gary's father took his weeping wife into his arms, trying his best to comfort her. "All they're saying *now* is that Gary and Wayne had been with the girl – Lady Perdita – earlier, on the night she died."

"Why didn't you tell us, Gary?" sobbed his mother. "Why on earth didn't you say you knew her?"

He didn't reply. There was nothing he could say.

"Let's all just calm down," suggested Gary's father. "They can't say Gary's involved. They won't say it. Because he wasn't!"

Gary broke his silence. "They *can* say it and they *will* say it … eventually."

His parents stared at him, open-mouthed.

"I *was* involved. I'm sorry."

"It doesn't look good though, does it, Wayne?" said Joe Fisher.

Wayne gripped the phone with trembling fingers.

"It's got nothing to do with me, Joe. It was Gary. I tried to help. It wasn't my fault."

That wasn't what Joe wanted to hear. He'd hoped

Wayne would tell him that he was amazed by the stories; that it was all totally untrue.

"So you *were* there, then? Are you telling me that you were actually with her when she OD'd?"

"I tried to help, Joe. Honest. It was all Gary's fault," he argued.

"Look, Wayne, I can't get involved in any of this," said Joe. "I've got a good reputation in this business."

"Don't dump me, Joe," pleaded Wayne. "Please, don't dump me. I just couldn't bear it. Not now!"

"I'm sorry, Wayne," hissed Joe, unsympathetically. "I don't need all this."

He put down the receiver.

Phil Lemont wasn't expecting the visit. He'd paced the office all morning, feeling sick, trying to get Gary on the phone. His home number was engaged; the mobile switched off. He read the articles again. Over and over. Why didn't he know anything about this? He was with them the whole time. *Most* of the time.

Kendrick Simpson burst into the office, white-faced.

He eyed the newspapers on Phil's desk.

"So you've read it all, then?"

"Of course. Sit down, Kendrick."

He sat. "And?"

"What can I say? I'm as appalled as you."

"Are you telling me you knew nothing about it?"

Phil looked at him, amazed. "Are you kidding? I'd have dumped them, straight off." He sighed. "I wish I'd never taken them on in the first place. They've brought me more grief than money."

501

"You wish *you'd* never taken them on? What about me?"

"It can't harm *you*!" snapped Phil. "But it'll finish Gary Brenn ... and *me* in this business ... if it's true."

"Oh, it's true all right," stated Kendrick. "BJ's been on from the record company. He drove round to Gary's this morning. Just ahead of the Special Branch!"

"*What?*"

"Gary's confessed all. And he and Wayne are being questioned as we speak."

Phil collapsed into his chair. "I don't believe it! Why me?"

"Why any of us? It's the death-knell, you do realize that, Phil? We'll all be dragged into this story whether we're innocent or not. BJ, me and you. Gary's just hit number six in the charts. I wrote and produced it. BJ put it out here on Blunt Edge, and..."

"And I manage him."

"*Managed* him, Phil! Past tense, son. Past tense for all of us! It's time to cut and run!"

Ruby Gold, horrified at what she'd done, fled back to the States and into the arms of a bewildered Sherry Barbin.

"So what?" boomed Sherry, defiantly. "You had a short relationship with an English kid who's been implicated in some sort of scandal. Forget it. We ain't involved."

"I think *I* am, sugar," explained Ruby. "Gary told me the story when we first met and I went and told the whole thing to some English pop punk."

Sherry stroked the tearful girl's hair, comfortingly.

"Hey, honey," she said. "That story could've come from anywheres. It ain't nothing to do with you. Forget it!"

"But they've dragged your tour into it!" said Ruby. "The *Enquirer*'s on to something. I just know it."

Sherry laughed. "Hey, chill out, will you? The only picture they had of Hym was from the Roadshow. That's why my name was mentioned. I ain't got nothing to do with some drug-crazed British royal. There *are* things in my past that would upset the record-buying public, I admit, honey, but this is definitely not one of them!"

The record-buying public *was* upset. They were used to indiscretions and scandals in the world of show-business, but none seemed as bad as this. The name of Gary Brenn was deleted from all radio playlists world-wide and "Only Me And You" plummeted from the charts. Number six to obscurity.

Sherry and Ruby had remained cool about the situation until a call from Stavros Vardakis sent them both into a panic. Sherry's latest single, ready for release, had been put on hold. There had been rumours, Stavros informed her, about Hym at Buck West's Hollywood party. There was talk of Gary Brenn and Sherry and Ruby involved, allegedly, in some kind of drug-taking. The very same Gary Brenn who had now been charged with manslaughter! Stavros was, of course, aware that it was all nonsense. He was sure that the story had no foundation. That as soon as the rumours had died down, both Sherry and Ruby's futures in the business would continue as before. No problem.

503

If, on the other hand … but that was too ridiculous to even contemplate … wasn't it?

Chapter 91

Rosetti sat in the rear of a limousine which had been hired to take him to Horizon TV. "Down On Me Gently" had climbed to number eighteen in the charts and today he was recording for *Chartbusters*. He flicked through last week's edition of *GO!* and occasionally glanced through the blackened windows at the build-up of traffic on the M25. He hoped he wasn't going to be late.

The swelling on his lip had almost disappeared. It was hardly noticeable now and, with a bit of help from the make-up artist, it would be difficult to tell he'd ever been in a brawl. He fumed: a brawl with Terry Smith! That pikie had got under his skin yet again! But this time Rosetti had *really* got his own back! He thought about his schooldays and he remembered how Terry Smith had always made his flesh creep. Gyppos! Scroungers, all of them. Living off Social Security, paid for by the likes of his father. Hardworking businessmen like Franco, paying huge sums of money in tax, to support scum like Terry Smith and his family. And then of course Terry Smith had to go and top it all by stealing his Maureen. She'd belonged to him and the pikie had stolen her – just like they steal *everything*. He'd taken Maureen away from him. And he'd never forgive him for that.

He'd enjoyed his recent nights out with Maureen. They'd talked over old times and they'd laughed a lot. And things seemed to be going really well ... until that time when they'd got back to Maureen's gran's and found Terry Smith standing in the passage, white-faced and shaking with rage. And when he'd gone, Maureen was so upset. That's what really surprised him. She had the handsome pop star standing by her side and all she could think about was Terry the Gyppo riding off into the night. And she'd said that she loved him! She still loved the pikie! He couldn't understand for the life of him, why. How could she prefer that little nobody to him?

And now he was at KANSIT, recording a single! For Scotty's record label. For BASIC BEAT. Or so he thought! Rosetti was sure he'd put a stop to that! Just by one, short phone call. What that smug little pikie didn't know, was that during his last little tête-à-tête with Maureen, Rosetti had learned something about Terry's previous venture into the music business: how he'd made a record for Joe Fisher. And how he'd stolen the master tape and disappeared. And Rosetti realized that Terry Smith must still be legally bound to Joe Fisher and that he had no right to go signing recording contracts with anyone else. He was still Joe Fisher's property. And Joe Fisher *had* to know! It was only fair. So Rosetti had looked up Joe's number and had made an appointment to see him.

BASIC BEAT had put aside one of its own studios at KANSIT so that Terry could make his first single and Scotty and Chas had worked half-way through the night, finishing the song, which had turned out to be far better than Le Roi's number. Although it was still a little rough at the edges, a day in the studio would, they were sure, get them the big hit that BASIC BEAT needed.

Terry was expected at noon. At ten o'clock there was a phone call from Joe Fisher. And all hell broke loose.

Terry took the tube to KANSIT, lost in dreams that perhaps this would be the last time he'd have to use public transport. Soon he'd have a hit record. Appear on *Chartbusters*. Sign autographs. The record company would get him a chauffeured car.

There were no young fans outside the studio today so obviously there was no one of importance inside. He pressed the bell and waited for the security guard to open the door. Bif was standing at the reception desk, waiting for him. And Terry knew, immediately, that something was wrong.

"We've had a call from Joe Fisher!" said Bif, sharply.

"Oh!" Terry responded.

Bif sat on one of the reception sofas and opened his briefcase. Terry slumped beside him.

"Why the hell didn't you tell us?" asked Bif, not looking at the boy. "Why didn't you say?"

Terry shrugged. "I thought it was all over."

Bif took out several sheets of paper. "This is a copy of the contract you signed with Joe. Faxed to us this morning from Joe's solicitor. We asked to see it because we just didn't believe it was true."

Terry looked down at his feet.

"We didn't *want* to believe it was true."

He handed the copy to Terry, who folded it in two and slid it into his jeans pocket.

"Aren't you going to read it?" snapped Bif.

Terry shook his head. "What's the point? I know what it says."

Bif tried to remain calm. "How could you do this, Terry? You must've know it would come out sooner or later."

"I didn't think he could do anything about it," replied Terry. "I thought he'd just drop me after I destroyed the master. He's got nothing on me. No material. Nothing. And he can't force me to make another record if I don't want to."

"Don't be so naïve!" Bif's voice rose. "Of course he can! He can force you to fulfil your contractual obligations."

"He can't make me *sing*!" argued Terry.

"No. He can't make you sing," conceded Bif. "But then you can't sing for anyone else, either. Not for us. Not for anyone! Not even in a live performance. Ever! You signed a management contract, too. Joe Fisher owns you ... lock, stock and barrel!" Bif sighed. "What in God's name was your solicitor thinking about ... allowing you to sign a contract like that?"

"I didn't have a solicitor," mumbled Terry. "I just

signed it. I wanted to make a record."

Bif shook his head in disbelief. He'd seen it happen to so many youngsters. Desperate to become pop stars, they'd sign away half their lives. Even *with* solicitors helping them, they'd managed to give away great chunks of their merchandising rights to unscrupulous record company executives; the fat cats of the business. He also realized that there was often no other choice. Either sign on the dotted line, or be dropped for another bright young talent who *would* sign.

"So, what happens now?" asked Terry.

"Nothing," replied Bif. "Naturally we don't have any hold over you. So I suggest you go along with Joe Fisher's contract. You haven't any choice, have you?"

The phone rang and the receptionist picked it up.

"Good morning. KANSIT. Can I help you?" She paused. "Just a minute please." She called across to Bif, "There's a Mr Fisher to see you. Shall I pass him through security?"

Terry leapt to his feet.

"Joe Fisher? Here?"

"You'd better talk to him, hadn't you, Terry," Bif stated.

"No!" replied Terry. "No! No!"

Bif noted the fear in Terry's eyes. "All right, all right!" he said. "Calm down. I'm not going to make you. Your future's got nothing to do with me, son. Not any longer."

The receptionist repeated, "Shall I pass Mr Fisher through security?"

"Yes," replied Bif. He turned to Terry. "Perhaps you'd better disappear to the Gents' for five minutes.

I'll get Joe Fisher upstairs to the office. Then you can leave without seeing him."

"Thanks," said Terry. "And I'm … I'm really sorry about all the fuss I've caused. Honest."

He headed for the toilets.

"Terry!" Bif called after him.

Terry turned.

"It's a shame, son," he said. "A real shame!"

Chapter 92

Levi pulled up outside the trailer, just as Terry was leaving.

"Where you goin'?" he asked.

"Nowhere. Just out for a walk."

"I wanna word," said Levi. He climbed down from his lorry, carrying a newspaper-parcel under his arm. "Had your tea?"

"I'm not hungry."

"Got a nice bit o' steak," he said. "Fell off the back of a butcher's van. There's enough for two."

"I'm not hungry," Terry repeated.

" 'Course you are," he argued. "Get that frying pan goin'."

As Terry cooked the steak … burnt … just as his dad used to eat it … he began to worry about "the word" Levi wanted with him. It was two weeks since the episode at KANSIT. He'd been to the Job Centre every single day, but there was nothing he felt that he could do for a living and he just wished that Scotty hadn't mentioned his singing to the others at BASIC

BEAT. If he hadn't got into all that, he might be working as a back-room boy for the record company. Now he was back to square one. He still owed money to Levi and he didn't have a penny in his pocket. Not even to buy food. And every time Levi offered to share his tea with him, he felt guilty. Levi's work was back-breaking. He knew. He'd done it. So why should Levi give him anything out of his hard-earned cash? That was why Levi wanted a word with him. He was sure of it.

Levi shoved a large forkful of the shrivelled-up steak into his mouth, chewed, swallowed and then spoke.

"Now then, let's be having it," he said. "I don't mind supporting you, but I hate having the wool pulled over my eyes."

"I don't know what you're talking about," said Terry. "I'm trying to get a job, Levi. I look every day."

"And what about this singing lark, then?" he asked. "What about this record?"

"There isn't a record," replied Terry. "I told you. I've given it all up."

Levi suddenly banged his knife on the table, angrily. Terry jumped.

"You bloody little liar!" he shouted. He glared across the table at Terry. "I don't mind thieves! You know where you are with thieves! But I can't stand liars!"

Terry was shocked at the outburst.

"I'm not lying. There isn't any record."

"You liar!" Levi shouted again. "I heard it! This afternoon on the radio! Terry Smith, they said. 'Call On Me'. Terry Smith. That's *you*, innit?"

* * *

"Gran!" called Maureen. "Gran!" She rushed into the parlour with the radio. She was shaking. "Listen!" She turned up the volume. "Listen!"

Gran tapped her fingers on her jigsaw tray, hoping she was keeping in time with the music. She wasn't. But she wanted to display to Maureen that she wasn't completely past it.

"Quite nice, isn't it?" said Gran.

"Don't you recognize it?" Maureen asked. "Don't you recognize the song?"

Gran's face was blank.

"It's Terry, Gran."

"Terry?"

"My Terry! That's his song. 'Call On Me'. And that's him singing it!"

"Never!" said Gran. "Turn it up a bit, Mo."

Maureen adjusted the volume.

"It is! Definitely," Maureen said. "I was there when he recorded it the first time, don't forget. He must've gone back to Joe Fisher and recorded it again!"

"Well!" exclaimed Gran. "For rice cake! Why didn't he tell us?"

Sylvie hammered on Levi's door at six o'clock the following morning.

"Thought I'd better come early and tell you," she explained. "Jimmy's been sick and bad all night. And he's got spots. Looks like chicken pox or something. Anyway, he can't work. So I thought I'd better let you know early."

Levi sighed. "All right, Sylvie. Ta!"

513

From his makeshift bed, Terry heard the conversation. He leapt up and started to dress.

"I suppose you'll want me to help you then?" he asked through sleep-stuck eyelashes.

Levi ruffled his hair. "Good lad."

Terry had managed to convince him that he'd known nothing about the release of "Call On Me"; that it was as much of a surprise to him as it was to Levi; that he'd thought the master tape had been destroyed.

Then they'd talked on and on into the early hours about Terry's career and what he should do about it. Levi's answer was simple.

"You go straight up to Joe Fisher's office and say, 'Right! I'm here! So give me my share of the royalties, you thievin' Gorgio ... or I'll do yer!' "

Terry had laughed at Levi's directness. But he wasn't sure if that was the way to handle the situation.

He laughed even more as he climbed up into Levi's lorry, wearing his ripped jeans and the working shirt with the buttons hanging off it.

"I'm a pop star," he said to Levi. "And here I am, shifting scrap metal."

Levi grinned. "Yeah. And I'm John Wayne. So let's get this waggon rollin'!"

They called, as usual, at the fitted-kitchen shop and as Levi negotiated payment for a couple of well-worn cookers, Terry picked up Levi's copy of the *Sun*. He never understood why he bought this paper every morning. Save for a few, very simple words, Levi couldn't read. Terry opened it. Page three. A very well-endowed girl. *That's* why he bought it! Terry turned the page. And he saw the picture. Of himself! Smiling at the camera and looking extremely handsome. And the headline:

WHERE'S TERRY?

"Levi!" he called. He jumped down from the lorry. "Levi! Look at this!"

Handsome young Terry Smith may be bounding up the charts with his haunting ballad, "Call On Me", but his manager, Joe Fisher, is hoping TERRY will call on HIM.

Schoolboy Terry made the record earlier this year and then ... he DISAPPEARED.

Fisher, who also managed the late, great PETE SHANNON said: "Terry is very shy. When he realized the record was going to be a smash, he didn't think he could face the publicity."

So, where are you, Terry? Have any of you SUN readers seen him recently? If you have, we'd sure like to hear from you.

Terry read the article over and over again. There was no mention of his background. No mention of him being a gypsy.

"Bounding up the charts?" said Levi. "What do they mean? It's in the hit parade?"

"I've no idea," replied Terry. "But there's one way to find out."

Levi was as excited as Terry and could hardly wait to drive him to the nearest newsagent's where they hurriedly flicked through copies of all the music weeklies, looking for a chart.

"This'll do," said Terry. "The Network Chart. It'll give us some idea."

Levi had never before felt quite so frustrated at his inability to read. He looked over Terry's shoulders as the boy ran his finger up the list of hit records.

"What's it say? What's it say?" he asked, impatiently.

Terry found what he was looking for, closed the magazine and grinned up at Levi.

"Number thirty-seven!"

"Thirty-seven? Is that good?"

"Good? It's brilliant!" laughed Terry. "Number thirty-seven? That's high enough to get me on to *Chartbusters!*"

Chapter 93

"Down On Me Gently" had climbed to number six and Rosetti had been booked for his second solo *Chartbusters*.

"Dead important, this one, son," said Franco. "This is the one that could send it right to the top."

Rosetti climbed into the modified school uniform that he'd used on the video. It'd caused such a fuss among his thousands of fans that he had no intention of changing the image while he was on to a winner! Some of the letters he'd received (explaining what they'd like to do with him if they ever managed to get him alone) had been so explicit that they'd even made him get a little hot under the collar.

The assistant floor manager knocked on Rosetti's door, just as the *Chartbusters* theme-tune sounded on the dressing-room speaker.

"Stand by in the studio, please, Mr Rosetti," he said.

Rosetti headed for studio four, feeling much more confident than he'd ever felt on a *Chartbusters* appearance. At least it wasn't "live" as it had been when Bury The Rabbit had done their first show here. So he felt a little more secure in the knowledge that if anything should go disastrously wrong, they could go for a second take.

Rosetti knew from the day's rehearsal which of the metal stages he should head for. He was third on the running order; just after the new release section and just before the video sequence.

The new release was considered, by many, to be a future number one: the beautiful Imogen singing a haunting ballad called, "Who Let The Sparrow Die?" Rosetti watched the performance. He hated the song and he hated Imogen Shannon's voice. He was sure that she was only here because of her late, great husband … but he had to concede that her undisputed beauty would help to push the song right to the top of the chart. He wondered – and he feared – that it might be the stunning Imogen who would keep "Down On Me Gently" from attaining its rightful number one position.

She brought the song to its close:

> *"Didn't think he mattered*
> *Until he took the sky and climbed higher.*
> *Now the crowds below had gathered*
> *To see him die."*

The *Chartbusters'* audience applauded and cheered and stamped.

"Now…" the DJ announced "…if you've got a thing about school uniforms … this one's for *you*. Rosetti. 'Down On Me Gently'."

518

There were loud screams from the audience.

And Rosetti smouldered as he mimed the words to his song,

> *"All I need is the opportunity*
> *To tell you what you really mean to me…"*

The girls in the studio continued to scream. Rosetti peered, through hooded eyelids, straight into camera.

> *"And if you feel you have to*
> *Put me down…*
> *Come down on me, gently."*

Girls, viewing at home, squirmed with delight. The *Chartbusters'* cheerleader whispered to a Horizon TV dresser, "Subtle, ain't he?"

"Well done, son," said Franco as Rosetti left the stage and headed towards the studio exit.

Rosetti stopped as soon as he heard the song. He knew it from somewhere. He knew that voice. He looked up at the huge screen suspended at the side of stage three, the screen that was showing the video. A gypsy boy. Dressed in rags. Sitting at a camp fire. Singing.

> *"You call on me*
> *When you are lonely*
> *And I know I can only*
> *Be a friend…"*

And he realized that by contacting Joe Fisher, he'd started the ball rolling for Terry Smith.

"Oh, no!" he said. "Oh, no! Oh, no! Please! What have I done?"

Chapter 94

"Cheers!" Joe clinked his glass of scotch against Terry's glass of Coke.

"Cheers!" said Terry.

"I knew you'd come back."

"Did you? *I* didn't."

"Are you happy you did?" asked Joe.

"We'll see," Terry replied. "Depends what happens from here on in, doesn't it?"

"Can only get better."

Terry smiled. "Or worse!"

Joe turned up the radio. Sunday afternoon – and the all important Top Forty. It was somewhere in the top five. They knew that much.

It wasn't at five.

It wasn't at four…

"If we're not at number one this week…" said Franco Rosetti.

"Got to be!" interrupted his son. "Got to be! If it's not mine … it's *his*!"

He paced the room, like a caged animal. "I couldn't

bear it if it were *his*!" His hands were running with sweat. He wiped them down his jeans. "Please … let me be number one. I'll do anything!"

It wasn't at number three.

"And climbing to number two … it's 'Down On Me Gently', from Rosetti."

"No!" screamed Rosetti. "No! No! No!"

Chapter 95

The police had had to cordon off two of the main streets leading to the shopping mall as, after seven weeks at number one, Terry Smith had been booked to open the new MegaSounds store in the City Centre. The girls had flocked in their thousands. Just to get a glimpse. Some had been queueing since dawn to get a closer look, knowing that if they bought a copy of the remixed CD, Terry Smith would autograph it. For some, that was almost too much to bear. To be that close.

"Just a few at a time!" called the manager as members of his staff opened the glass doors, allowing the first group of screaming fans to tumble inside. As each of them came face to face with their idol, most were reluctant to speak. None screamed once they were inside the building.

"Would you sign *two* copies for me, please?" she said. "One's for my gran."

Terry felt his heart race. He looked up at her, and smiled.

She returned his smile. She looked beautiful.

"You didn't queue, did you?" he asked. "Not with all these others?"

"How else d'you think I got in?" she laughed.

The fans surrounding him, all eagerly thrusting forward their CDs to be autographed, now seemed an intrusion in his life.

"Terry ... Terry ... Terry..." They wanted his attention.

"I'll call you," he said. "If you want me to."

"*Call on me...*" she sang, "*...when you are lonely.*"

He smiled. "I *am* lonely."

"Then you know where I am," she said.

She kissed him on the cheek, then turned her back on him, and walked away.

The glass doors were opened for her.

"Terry!" they screamed.

"Terry!

"Terry!

"Terry!"

Point

Pointing the way forward

More compelling reading from top authors.

Flight 116 is Down
Forbidden
Unforgettable
Caroline B. Cooney

Someone Else's Baby
Geraldine Kaye

Hostilities
Caroline Macdonald

I Carried You On Eagles' Wings
Sue Mayfield

Seventeenth Summer
K.M. Peyton

The Highest Form of Killing
Son of Pete Flude
Malcolm Rose

Secret Lives
William Taylor

Point Romance

If you like Point Horror, you'll love Point Romance!

Are you burning with passion and aching with desire? Then these are the books for you! Point Romance brings you passion, romance, heartache, . . . and *love*.

P●INT CRiME

If you like Point Horror, you'll love Point Crime!

A murder has been committed . . . Whodunnit?
Was it the teacher, the schoolgirl, or the best friend? An exciting series of crime novels, with tortuous plots and lots of suspects, designed to keep the reader guessing till the very last page.

Encounter worlds where men and women make hazardous voyages
through space; where time travel is a reality and the fifth dimension a
possibility; where the ultimate horror has already happened and
mankind breaks through the barrier of technology...

The Obernewtyn Chronicles:
Book 1: Obernewtyn
Book 2: The Farseekers
Isobelle Carmody
A new breed of humans are born into a hostile world struggling back from the
brink of apocalypse...

Random Factor
Jessica Palmer
Battle rages in space. War has been erased from earth and is now controlled by
an all-powerful computer – until a random factor enters the system...

First Contact
Nigel Robinson
In 1992 mankind launched the search for extra-terrestial intelligence. Two
hundred years later, someone responded...

Virus
Molly Brown
A mysterious virus is attacking the staff of an engineering plant ... Who, or
what is responsible?

Strange Orbit
Margaret Simpson
Jessica Barron is going to the moon. She has been specially trained ... and
nothing can go wrong...

Scatterlings
Isobelle Carmody
Merlin awakes from a terrifying accident, and finds herself in another world...

Look out for:

Strange Invaders
Stan Nicholls

The Year of the Phial
Joe Boyle

Siren Song
Sue Welford

Read Point SF and enter a new dimension...